JACKASS
BRANDY

BY BRUNO BUTI

JACKASS BRANDY

Illustrations and Dust Jacket Design: Dug Waggoner
Word processing/Co-Editor: Marisa Murphy

For information regarding this publication, please write to the publisher:
Buti Publications, P. O. Box 304, Cloverdale, CA 95425.

ISBN 0-9648960-1-X

A Simple Definition of
"JACKASS BRANDY"

An alcoholic product made in a similar fashion as grape brandy, however using grains instead of grape products and with added ingredients.

The grains are treated with malt, sugar and water (to facilitate fermentation). The "maltose" and "dextrin" so formed (a starchy gooey mass) ferments by the addition of yeast.

Allowed to ferment, the sugary mass converts to an alcohol-laced liquid mixture. Since alcohol evaporates at a lower temperature than water, this liquid, when properly distilled, produces alcohol at various strengths (170 proof preferred) up to 100% pure neutral spirit (200 proof).

The high-proof is then cut to suit with plain water (pure spring water preferred), colored and flavored with caramel (also referred to as burnt sugar), in many cases made on the spot by heating sugar to 338% - 356%F.

The product is then aged and purified by suspending charcoal in charred oak barrels with an added occasional rocking motion. Also, heat may be applied to speed up the aging process.

Once aged, the end result is a potable, intoxicating beverage, with the kick of a "Jackass."

Dedication

In memory of my father, Michele (Mike) and my mother, Livia Buti, and to Frank Jacklich, Ercole (Al) Giovanetti, legendary heroes of the Prohibition Era, and to their countrymen, friends and colleagues, some whose names crop up in my writings or were in some way associated with them during this colorful but chaotic era I write about, the Roaring Twenties.

And to Honorable Chief Justice Earl Warren, then District Attorney of Alameda County for his relentless pursuit of justice, and to the law enforcement agencies and their personnel, regardless of the role they play in this saga, for they, too, were good people but, as with many others, were caught up in the circumstances of the times and therefore must be forgiven and remembered.

Acknowledgement

The input from the descendants of my father's associates and colleagues is credited with stimulating my memory and enhancing my imagination, thus lending authenticity if not actual fact to this story. Therefore, various names of relatives, family friends, businesses, and ranches, along with their owners and families, do crop up in this story. To them, and their descendents, whether they be alive or dead, I share my cherished memories, for the intent is to glorify them along with my parents. My respectful thoughts and pleasant memories of them have contributed to inspiring me in writing this book. I am extremely grateful to those that I was able to contact and talk to. Their encouragement, rather than objection to the use of their family names was most gratifying.

A special thanks to Georgina Tognotti Seals for coming to my rescue by applying her professional expertise in the fields of English and computers; and to Raymond Burdette for volunteering to apply his 35 years' experience in the field of Education to the final proofreading. Since it was at the urging of my immediate family that this story be put in book form, I can hardly avoid expressing my gratitude for their encouragement to put pen to paper. Hopefully they, such as I expect the reader to, understand that creative imagination has been applied to better depict the people I write about.

Although parts of this story can be documented by court transcripts, newspaper articles, and verified by reliable hearsay, I, the author, cannot vouch for the accuracy or authenticity of any of the above.

Since hearsay, my own childhood memories and creative imagination have been applied, this book, having been dramatized and put into novel form, must therefore be deemed a work of fiction, yet is factually based. The names, characters, places, dates and incidents are, to some extent, either the product of my imagination or are used fictitiously, and resemblance to actual persons, living or dead, or to events or locales are coincidental.

The use of the word fact, regardless in what text or term used, is to be construed as fact only in my opinion, and therefore not meant or intended to be implied or inferred as actual fact.

Preface

Having had a taste of what Prohibition had to offer, Mike and his fellow paesano countrymen abandoned their San Francisco wine hijacking endeavor in favor of the more profitable but riskier business of bootlegging; namely, cranking out high-proof alcohol and converting it into what was then referred to as "Jackass Brandy." Pucci and Primo chose to bow out. Pucci especially felt that dealing in high-proof alcohol or its related products spelled trouble. They preferred to stay with what they understood best: raiding warehouses, even if it wasn't wine. So a new team was formed:

Michele (Mike) Buti, assumed the position of "Capo" (the leader) of this group of enterprising Italians. He eventually was to become a tough, domineering boss.

Julio Matteoli, ramroding production at the stills, was second in command. His ever-pleasant disposition gradually hardened.

Al Giovanetti, in addition to being the driver, enforcer and henchman of sorts, set out to thwart interference by federal prohibition agents. No easy task, but once he got behind the wheel of a 1925 Buick touring sedan that was more of a match for the federal agents' cars, Hudsons and Essexes, it became a different ballgame. Not only did he constantly harass them, but whenever the opportunity presented itself, he would set out to destroy them as well. Hell-bent on destruction, their car dueling encounters escalated to where doing each other in became an obsession with them.

Julio's cousin (Matteoli) managed the chicken ranch, the front and headquarters for the operation. He was also called upon as a counselor of sorts. His Italian military training taught him strategy and discipline.

Guido Bronzini, the truck driver, along with his brother, Lepo, Al's brother-in-law, kept up the supply of sugar to the stills. Since they were not fighters, they looked to Al to ward off would-be hijackers.

Al's childhood buddy, Raymond "Fats" Meehan, an Italian-speaking Irishman, along with a handful of paesano drifters made up the rest of this gang of rascals hell-bent on exploiting the Prohibition era for all it was worth.

Others soon appeared on the scene, each with different objectives:

Federal agents stalked the operation using their position of authority to solicit bribery; shake the operation down for a piece of the action. They were not at all bashful about continually demanding more and more money as well as kegs of aged "Jackass" for their own consumption. At least the senior agent referred to in the story was an outright alcoholic. Once his activities became known to his superiors, rather than take him out of the picture, they set out to use him to their advantage. But his mentality being what it was, they soon learned, as did the bootleggers he was shaking down, that, among other things, he was a double crosser; therefore, untrustworthy.

The newly elected Sheriff of Alameda County, Burton F. Becker, immediately upon taking office, with the aid of several select deputies, set out to extort money from the alcohol-related industry, gambling, prostitution and bootleggers. He did in fact perform a worthwhile service to those that were able and willing to meet his demands, but came down hard on those who, for whatever reason, did not cooperate.

Joseph P. Lacey, Mike's legal counsel, a crook in his own right, an extortionist of unbelievable proportions who preyed on average citizens as well as professional bootleggers, in order to save his own hide attempts to sell Mike out to the D.A.

Honorable Earl Warren, the then District Attorney of Alameda County, with political ambitions stoking his fires, embarked on a campaign to throw the lot of them in jail: bootleggers (Mike's gang especially), hijackers, tainted Federal agents, Sheriff Becker and his deputies, extortionists of their own making, crooked fellow lawyers (Lacey especially), and any and all that had anything to do with the illegal alcohol and gambling trades. He was to give no quarter, not even to his own.

Introduction

The Prohibition Era

The beginning of World War I saw Congress pass the Act of August 10, 1917, which prohibited the manufacture of distilled spirits for beverage purposes. This was followed by passage of the act of November 21, 1918, which now included beer and wine. This same Act now prohibited the sale of these alcohol products for beverage purposes after June 30, 1919. All of these acts were later consolidated in Title I of the National Prohibition Act, which became effective October 28, 1919. This was the start of the Prohibition Era in the United States, which was to remain in effect until 1933.

The Eighteenth Amendment to the Constitution now also prohibited the sale, transportation, importation, and exportation of alcohol into or from the United States as well. The Amendment was to be effective one year from the date of ratification in order to allow the distillers to dispose of their products on hand, which amounted to between 58 and 60 million gallons.

The Volstead Prohibition Enforcement Act that followed set forth which Federal agencies would investigate and enforce as well as prosecute offenders and license for nonbeverage purposes. However, the passage of these acts did not dampen America's thirst for liquor or alcohol-related beverages of whatever sort. What had once been the legal liquor industry now became the illegal liquor industry.

By the mid-twenties, criminals of all types entered the illegal liquor traffic in order to supply the ever-increasing demand. Large criminally controlled syndicates were formed, especially in areas such as Chicago, New York, and many other large Midwestern and East Coast cities. Territories were allocated by the block. Gang slayings became frequent. The words "mafia" and "mafioso" were spoken in hushed whispers for they gave no quarter. The knife, gun and garrote were the tools of their trade. These syndicates made such huge profits in their alcohol-related endeavors that enforcement officers, prosecutors, politicians and judges alike were corrupted and elections influenced.

Licensed legitimate industrial alcohol manufacturing firms producing nondrinkable denatured alcohol joined with the syndicate in diverting their product to beverage purposes. Elaborate cleaning and rectifying (redistilling) plants managed by imported expert foreign technicians were erected and operated by the syndicate, sparing no expense in putting up distilling plants that were equal in quality to anything in use by the legitimate industry. Internal revenue stamps were counterfeited in order that the product could be sold as if manufactured under Government authority.

Bankers (criminals of sorts themselves), eager to rake in higher than usual interest rates, were soliciting the syndicates as well as independents for their business. Flaunting the Usury laws was commonplace.

Lawyers not only applied their expertise in defending their clients, the criminals, but also connived to bilk their clients out of their huge profits through devious methods, therefore becoming criminals themselves.

Professional hijackers soon established themselves hijacking the finished product, as well as supplies such as sugar, the basic ingredient for making high-proof alcohol, and gasoline to fire the stills, thus adding to the criminal activities.

Smugglers, such as rum runners, operating under foreign flags, teamed up with the syndicates, adding to the flood of liquor. The product transported from foreign countries was transferred from ship to shore by high speed launches to waiting souped-up trucks and transport vehicles driven by steady nerved young drivers in it for the excitement as well as high pay.

Prostitutes, both experienced and inexperienced, charged into the fray with real gusto. Some operating as independents, and some joining the many brothels set up by the cash-burdened criminal element.

Profits from bootlegging, as the industry was called, were tremendous, especially since no taxes were ever paid. All transactions were done in hard cash. Books and records were kept by accountants and bookkeepers bonded by the threat of a .45 caliber lead slug in the brain if they didn't keep their mouth shut.

Fiscal year 1925 saw 3,700 federal employees engaged in the work of narcotics and prohibition enforcement alone. Despite the many corrupt Federal and state agents that were on the take, more than 77,000 arrests for violations of the probation laws were made in that year alone, with $11,200,000 in property value seized. Also in that year 7 agents were killed and 39 injured in the performance of their duties.

On July 1, 1930, enforcement responsibility was shifted from the Internal Revenue Bureau to the Federal Prohibition Bureau in the Department of Justice. Many officers, clean and tainted alike, shifted from one agency to the other accordingly. However, by this time the criminal element had virtually taken over the liquor industry throughout the country. Local authorities were largely out of sympathy with enforcement activities and often had corrupt connections with the bootleg element. In many instances, federal agents themselves were shaking down the bootleggers instead of arresting them.

Smaller independent distillers, referred to as "moonshiners" because of their nighttime activities, operating outside the areas dominated by the syndicates, also placed their alcohol product on the market in the absence of legal whiskey. Their product took on identifying names such as "jackass brandy," "jackass whiskey," "moonshine," "white lightning," "rotgut," "brain embalmer," and others, depending on its method of manufacture and the reaction to its consumption, which at times included death.

At least for a while, in the absence of large criminally controlled syndicates, the West Coast independents were able to gain a foothold without resorting to the extreme violence being experienced in the Midwest and East Coast. But that soon changed, especially when seasoned, tainted federal agents were shifted around the country to break their ties with the criminal element. The West Coast independents such as Mike soon found themselves confronted with extortion coupled with violence, a deadly brew.

This story deals with just such a melting pot overflowing its brim with a concoction of bootleggers, hijackers, extortionists, tainted lawmen, crooked lawyers, and supposedly respectable businessmen and citizens also eager to cash in on this alcohol related feeding frenzy.

The place: Across the Bay from San Francisco, in Alameda County, on the outskirts of Hayward, in Crow Canyon. The time: During the Roaring Twenties, at the height of Prohibition.

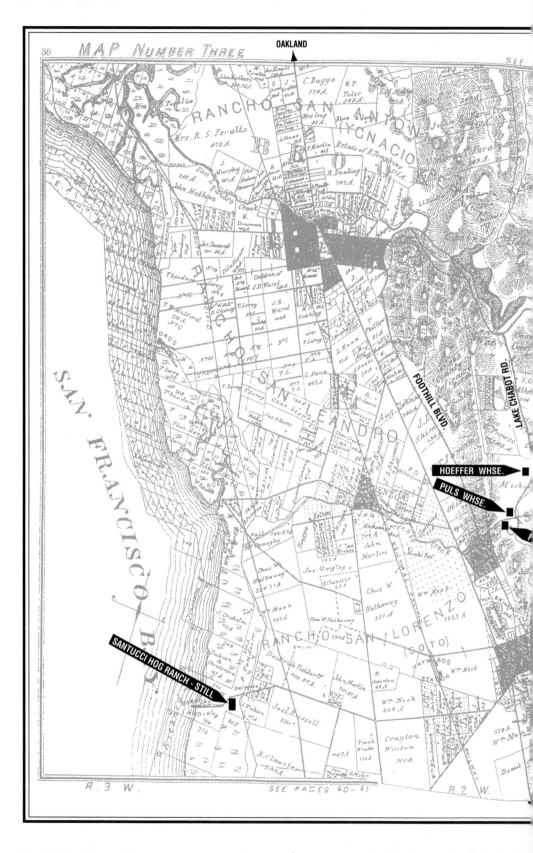

OAKLAND

SAN FRANCISCO BAY

FOOTHILL BLVD.

LAKE CHABOT RD.

HOEFFER WHSE.

PULS WHSE.

SANTUCCI HOG RANCH - STILL

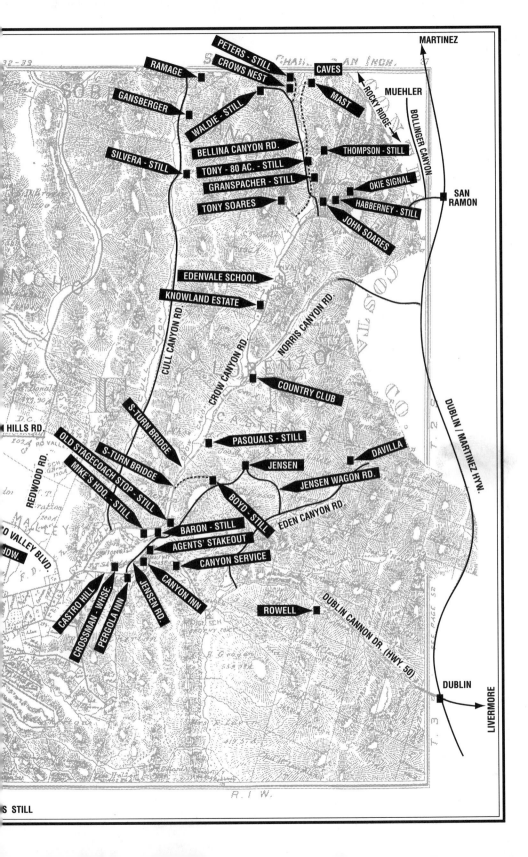

CHAPTER 1

Sheriff Kelly pulled into Mike's ranch yard at San Bruno and parked his black Dodge Brothers touring sedan in the usual spot, off to one side under the protective cover of an elm tree. The car's sheriff's emblem painted on the side of its door stood out brilliantly as if purposely trying to convey a message of significant authority. Beneath the elm tree, the first frost of the 1923 fall season had turned its fallen leaves into a dry, brown mat that crunched under the weight of the Sheriff's heavy boots.

As the Sheriff walked across the yard, Mike stepped out from the basement of the farmhouse extending a greeting while, in the same gesture, inviting him in for the customary glass of wine.

"It's good to see you—come in, while the boys put a crate of cauliflower in your car, we can enjoy a glass of wine," he said, then added: "The winter cauliflower is now at its peak; I'm sure your wife will enjoy having some."

"Thank you, Mike, I'm sure she will," answered Sheriff Kelly as he extended his right arm for a handshake. "How's the wife and family?" he asked, in a somewhat concerned and serious manner.

"Fine, just fine," answered Mike, wondering about the seriousness being expressed.

The two men exchanged pleasantries as they walked into the basement. As usual, Mike opened a fresh bottle of wine, set two glasses on the table and proceeded to pour as the Sheriff sat down, hooking his wide, stiff-brimmed hat on the back rest of the empty chair alongside.

Sheriff Kelly was a husky big Irishman in his late forties, well respected and always fair in dealing with the Italian immigrants who settled in his county. He expected them to know the difference between right and wrong, whether morally or by the written law. But he also understood their difficulty in interpreting the fine letter of the law. Besides, he believed in taking into consideration their customs and way of life when dealing with them. The immigrants respected and looked up to him rather than fearing him.

The two men raised their glasses slightly in a gesture of cheer and good health before taking a long draw. As the glasses were set back down on the

1

table, Sheriff Kelly repositioned himself in his chair with his arms resting on the table. He then leaned forward in a manner so as to seriously address his friend seated across the table.

"Mike," he said, "you have a nice family, a good paying ranch operation, and a nice wine peddling business on the side. You're making money."

"Well, yes, of course, and thanks to y——." The Sheriff cut him off short, an intentional interruption.

"Mike, please listen to what I have to say!" The manner in which the statement was made was an indication that there was more to the visit than the usual customary social calls of the past.

Mike was now attentive, sitting straight in his chair, searching the Sheriff's concerned expression, asking himself the question: "Why is he so concerned about me and my family's well-being?" Before he could come up with a reasonable answer, the Sheriff continued in a no-nonsense manner and right to the point:

"Mike, take my advice; don't screw around with alcohol! It's bad stuff!"

"Holy Christ!" thought Mike. "He must know something about the still we raided over at Bayshore." The worrisome expression on his face was a dead giveaway; the Sheriff knew he had hit pay dirt.

Convinced that he was on the right track, Sheriff Kelly proceeded to press the issue and express his dislike of having a bootlegging operation centered in the area of his jurisdiction. It was comforting to Mike as it became apparent that the Sheriff was not there to search the premises or make an arrest. Nevertheless, the thought of just how much he did know, and how he found out, was causing a nervous anxiety within him. He refilled the glasses; another glass of wine was needed to calm his nerves. As for the Sheriff, his nerves were made of steel; he accepted and drank the second glass because he enjoyed it, not because he was nervous. He continued to press his point:

"Every law enforcement agency on the peninsula knows you and your friends have control of the one single, largest concentration of sugar around these parts. Certainly you're not going to deny that, are you?"

The salvaged shipload of sugar moored at Central Basin was common knowledge; it could hardly be denied. But, did he also know they were hauling it across the Bay to Alameda with tug boats, selling the sugar to bootleggers? Looking away momentarily, Mike raised his wine glass to his lips and proceeded to drain it. Sheriff Kelly did likewise, but kept his gaze fixed on his friend, hoping for a truthful response.

"No," said Mike meekly, "I guess that by now it's pretty well-known, but we're not making any alcohol," he quickly added.

For the first time during the discussion, the Sheriff cracked a smile: "I know you're not, but knowing you, you soon will be! You and your friends have done a pretty good job of cleaning out that rat's nest over at Bayshore a while back. Now I don't want that mess brought over here in my county! Do I make myself clear?" The question was firmly put with an expected answer.

Mike swallowed hard. He felt like he was shrinking in his chair, cowering like a misbehaved hunting dog at the feet of his master. His somewhat boyish facial features had now taken on a hollow-eyed worried look. Although taller and more slender than most immigrant Italians, he saw his friend, the Sheriff, as a giant compared to himself. Now this big Irish lawman was sitting across the table from him and bringing up the subject of the Halloween night raid on the still at Bayshore; a subject he'd rather not talk about. There was no question in his mind that his lawman friend, in his calm thoughtful manner, had put two and two together when the news of the Bayshore incident reached him. Maybe the Sheriff wasn't sure exactly what had taken place that night, but he was on the right track as far as the whereabouts of the missing still components. It was logical that he, and his paesani, would be prime suspects. Who else would go through so much trouble to acquire a ready-made, ready-to-go alcohol distillery other than someone with a large supply of sugar on hand? Mike preferred to not argue the point. Without answering in too many words, he nodded in agreement: "Yes, I understand." Sheriff Kelly expressed satisfaction with the answer; the message had gotten across, his friend's word was good enough for him.

The paesani's on-going wine peddling operation was of no concern, but an alcohol bootlegging operation would not be tolerated. The problems it would create wouldn't be worth the benefits, if any. Besides to the Sheriff's dislike, it would attract a horde of greedy Federal agents shaking down everyone in every phase of the operation, and that alone was something he couldn't stomach. As for poking his nose into the barns, he never had the need to do it before, so why do it now. Besides he didn't have to; he knew what he would find. To uncover the remnants of the still amongst all those contraband barrels of wine would surely result in the whole lot of the paesani ending up in jail for sure. An unthinkable thought.

The sound of Mike's wife, Livia's, footsteps coming down the back steps ended their conversation abruptly. The Sheriff rose from his chair and greeted her with a pleasant smile, giving no indication of the sinister business matter that had just transpired. Her light brown, blondish hair was braided and tied back into a pug. A single long needlelike hairpin stuck through the pug held everything in place. She was carrying her baby boy in her arms while her other two children bashfully tagged along hanging onto her apron. She greeted the Sheriff with a smile and a heavily accented "hello." He in turn made comment about the appearance of such good health amongst the children, especially how good the baby was, peacefully sleeping in her arms. In her best English, she explained to him that such was not necessarily the case:

"He's a year and a half old and wants to be held all the time. He sleeps all day and cries all night."

To her comment, Mike added: "Yes, that's true, and if he doesn't shut up, one of these nights I'll throw him out the window."

This comment brought about a round of laughter. For the moment it eased the tension between the two men. The presence of Livia and her young family was convincing proof that these immigrant Italians were fine people. A good man-to-man talk with the head of the family was all that was needed to keep them in line and strengthen their respect for authority. Without further comment in reference to their business matter, Sheriff Kelly bid them all good day. Stepping into his car, he glanced back at the crate full of cauliflower cradling a gallon of fine wine in its midst. With a wave of hand and a smile of satisfaction, he thanked his host for his generosity. By the Sheriff's standards, today's endeavor was a job well-done.

A real friend, thought Mike as he stood in the middle of the yard watching the Sheriff's car pull out onto the highway. He stood there for a moment pondering the question of bootlegging and its related problems. Pucci's past comments were already weighing heavily on his mind; now Sheriff Kelly's to-the-point warning and advice added weight to the burden. His thoughts were disrupted by the sight of Julio with the Graham truck pulling into the ranch next door. He watched the truck loaded with empty vegetable crates and disguised wine barrels swing out around the hen house and disappear around back of the barn. "For all the good it does to disguise the wine barrels," he thought. The Sheriff is well aware of the on-going wine operation, and so is almost everyone else. Nevertheless, since it was hijacked wine, it was best to be cautious. A thought crossed his mind; he'd best have a talk with Julio.

By the time he walked across the cabbage patch and approached the truck, Julio and his helper had already untied the load and were stacking crates off to one side, exposing a half dozen returned, empty wine barrels.

"Well, how did it go?" asked Mike as he walked up.

"Fine," answered Julio. "I have orders for another load; I'll take it out first thing in the morning—before daylight."

"No trouble? Nobody watching you?"

"No, there's been no problem. Why do you ask?"

"Oh, I just thought—you know—one can never tell, it's always best to be careful." The answer appeared to be worrisome.

"The local boys (referring to the cops on the beat) are no problem; they don't give us a bad time. I wouldn't worry about it."

"No, I guess not. With all the wine you give them, they should help you unload it," commented Mike.

"They don't help us unload it, but they do block off the street for us whenever we need it," answered Julio laughingly. No matter what he said or how he said it, the smile was always present. Mike liked that, it relieved the stress and put him at ease.

"Julio, tomorrow morning I want you to stop by the garage and tell Al I'd like to see him. Tell him to come in early Friday morning and meet me at the produce market before he goes to work. And tell him to have Primo meet us there with Pucci. We have something to talk about. I'll want you there too." There was a sense of urgency to the order.

"Fine, I'll do that," answered Julio, as Mike walked away. Julio watched him make his way back across the cabbage patch, but couldn't help noticing a feeling of anxiety within him. "Something heavy was on his mind, no doubt about it," he thought. "Oh well, he'll share the matter with me when he's ready to do so," he said to himself.

Livia waited until Mike reached the edge of the yard before calling down to him from the back porch: "Michele," she called out, "bring me up a head of cauliflower for supper."

He glanced up at her for an instant, but said nothing. Changing his course in the direction of the opposite field across the yard, he called out to Sal to cut him an extra head of cauliflower for supper. A couple of quick slashes with the machete produced a fine, clean-trimmed head ready for the pot. The two men walked towards each other until they were in range for it to be tossed into Mike's outstretched hands. Sal turned away and headed back to the spot where a couple of other paesani were busy packing cauliflower as he cut and trimmed it.

Mike remained standing there for a moment watching Sal slash and trim heads of cauliflower like a Mongolian warrior working his way through a contingency of enemy soldiers, swinging his sword, grabbing heads full of hair and tossing them aside without ever breaking stride. Like Pucci, he wondered just how this determined Sicilian settled the score with the man called Occhio, his hated, but fellow Sicilian. The fact that the long-standing vendetta had been resolved was certain. Sal had told him nothing and neither had Julio, his closest and most trusted friend. It was the fact that Sal had informed him of his leaving for the old country right after the harvest that convinced Mike of his successful endeavor. Had he not caught up to Occhio,

5

he would not be leaving. No way would he be returning to Sicily without having first settled the matter. No doubt the machete was not the weapon used, but nevertheless, a knife of some sort was. The knife was this particular clan's stock and trade.

"Thank God Sheriff Kelly doesn't know anything about that affair," mumbled Mike. What he didn't know was that it would hardly be possible to determine the cause of death to Occhio after the high-speed passenger train devastated his body beyond all possible recognition. Whatever parts of his body that may have been found would probably not be associated with the still raid anyway, since the two incidents were the better part of a mile apart and on the opposite ends of the train tunnel. Nevertheless, the gruesome thought weighed on his mind.

Livia, waiting for him at the head of the stairs, posed a question as he handed her the cauliflower: "What's the matter with you? You don't look well; something bothering you, are you sick?"

"No," answered Mike, "I'm all right, just a little tired. I'll fetch some wine and be right up."

CHAPTER 2

Mike's nephew, Primo, took comfort in being Pucci's buddy and was therefore easily swayed by him. Both he, and his fireman friend, were single, young and adventuresome; however not so adventuresome as wanting to get into the risky bootlegging business. Even though it was he who master-minded their lucrative wine hijacking endeavor, Pucci was cool towards alcohol. The two buddies were sitting in Primo's car talking it over.

"So, your uncle wants to talk to us in the morning; about bootlegging, no doubt. I'm not so sure I'm going to like that. We could be getting into something we don't understand. Cranking out alcohol is a rough business. It will invite tough characters to say nothing of those damned federal agents. We sure as hell don't need them." Pucci had more to say: "Al's doing a good job selling the sugar across the Bay to Terzo. Your uncle ought to let him get rid of all of it. And as for that God-damned still, he ought to get rid of that too. The sooner he gets it out of San Bruno, the better. I sure as hell don't want any part of it."

"Pucci, you know damned well he'll do neither. Uncle Mike wants to keep most of the sugar as well as the still. He'll eventually set it up somewhere and get started. Ya wanna bet?"

"No, I won't take that bet, but I'll bet you his so-called friend, Sheriff Kelly, eventually will give your uncle a boot in the ass. You wanna bet on that?" Primo said nothing as Pucci continued: "And Julio, Al, and the rest of that bunch of nuts will be right in the thick of it. By the way, just how are you related to Terzo over in Alameda?"

"Well, he's my mother's cousin, the same as he is to my uncle," answered Primo. "Why do you ask?"

"Oh, I just think he's a hell of a lot smarter than the rest of you, your uncle included."

"Uncle Mike can handle him," responded Primo, while sporting a broad grin accompanied by a chuckle.

"You're pretty proud of your uncle, aren't you? Well, I wouldn't get to cozy with this bootlegging idea. We had a pretty good taste of it the other night." It was obvious, Pucci was still being bothered by the events that took

7

place on the night of the Bayshore still raid.

"Hey buddy, are you still bothered by the Halloween raid?" asked Primo.

"You better believe I am. We may not be out of the woods on that one yet," warned Pucci. "We better hope to Christ the mafia was not connected with that still or we'll sure as hell hear from them one of these days, and that won't be pleasant, to say the least. And, if they tie that in with the warehouse and the ship, we're dead; like the dead bird they'll leave at our doorstep."

Primo listened attentively for he knew there was more to come, there was also the gruesome matter of the Sicilian "Occhio," the notorious operator of the raided still. Pucci was convinced that Sal, their Sicilian friend, had killed the man during the raid in order to settle his family's long-standing vendetta. "And another thing, that Occhio affair, I'd like to know what happened that night on the south end of the train tunnel," Pucci asked while shaking his head in disbelief, then added: "Al knows something, but he ain't talking and neither is Sal. The handcar sitting in the path of that high-speed passenger train must have had something to do with the disposing of Occhio."

"For Christ's sake, get off the subject; what's done is done, and besides, you can't be sure of anything, so forget it!"

"What I'm trying to tell you is that we're already involved in some pretty rough doings without setting up a still. Imagine what it will be like once we're underway."

"OK, so what the hell, you've warned Uncle Mike of the pitfalls and expressed your feelings; next time we see him we'll both tell him again. As for the mafia, I believe Sal; Occhio was a Mafioso outcast with a price on his head. If anything, they're looking for who done him in so they can reward him. Sal saved them the trouble of doing it themselves. Ya wanna bet?"

"No, I won't take that bet either, so get this bucket of bolts in gear and let's go home, it's getting late."

"Don't call my Hudson a bucket of bolts!" snorted Primo as he worked the gearshift lever, trying unsuccessfully to avoid the usual stripping and grinding of gears.

"OK, so it's a rock crusher," grunted Pucci in response to the sounds emitting from the car's transmission.

CHAPTER 3

Friday morning at the produce commission market proved to be one of Mike's most frustrating days. Apparently word was out amongst the brokers that cauliflower was in short supply, but they were not passing this information on to the growers. since the demand was high, this now behooved the brokers to buy the cauliflower outright rather than work on the usual 15% commission, thus increasing their margin of profit at the expense of the growers. But Mike was wise to this sort of thing, and it so happened that his load was made up of nothing but cauliflower and, of course, some of the crates contained jugs of wine, which he'd sell himself. As he worked his truck past the various brokerage stalls heading for the one brokerage firm he preferred to deal with, he was constantly approached and propositioned to sell his cauliflower, but at last week's low prices. Realizing that something was afoot, and since in his opinion the brokers were all prone to cheating even under the best of conditions, he shunned their advances. As the Model T truck moved along, brokers were now jumping up on its running boards, riding along while trying to negotiate a deal. But the more they pressed him, the more he resisted, until finally he was cursing them mercilessly.

"Get the hell off my truck!" he commanded. "You're all a bunch of crooks, and not very good ones at that!"

"Mike, how can you say that? We're doing you a favor," they pleaded.

"A favor . . . ? Since when do you buggers do anyone a favor? Look at you, you're like a pack of wolves moving in for the kill—bah! You're crooks—it's a wonder you're not in jail!"

Irritated with Mike's indifference, they cursed him back, and as they stepped off the running board they added the traditional "up your ass" Italian gesture (clenched fist jerked sharply upwards). Mike retaliated with the insulting inference "you're wife is cheating on you" by jabbing at them with the pair of horns hand gesture.

Finally, after much hassle, Mike reached his destination and backed his truck up against the curb in preparation of unloading his cargo. The proprietor of the brokerage house, a fellow Italian hungry for cauliflower, sporting a big smile, rushed out to greet him. However, in the course of the hand-

9

shakes and hugs, no mention was made of a shortage of cauliflower. The overwhelming greeting reminded Mike of the symbolic approach of the pick-pockets of Italy. The sudden feeling that he was about to get screwed rushed to mind, but regardless, he proceeded to unload the crates of cauliflower while the broker now made his pitch.

"Mike, is that all you have this morning—'cauliflower'...? he said in a disinterested manner. To make matters even worse, in a sly manner the broker added: "Don't you know the market is loaded with the stuff?"

The broker was obviously trying to play down the fact that 'cauliflower' was indeed in high demand in hopes of conning Mike into selling the load outright. But he wasn't aware that he had just run the gauntlet of thieves just minutes before down the street.

"Oh, so the market is loaded? Well, what do you know about that . . . " responded Mike.

"Yes, I'm afraid that's right. But since we are friends, and as a favor to you, I'll buy the load outright so you can be on your way," offered the broker.

"And, I suppose you'll pay me last week's price—also as a favor to me," said Mike as he shook the ashes off his Toscanello cigar.

"Of course! Why, of course! That is the best I can do for a friend."

While the statement was being made, Mike, cigar clenched between his teeth, tossed a crate of cauliflower back on the truck, then fuming mad, followed up with a to-the-point inference:

"Crooks! You're all in cahoots, aren't you? Well, let me tell you something 'friend'—you are not going to screw me like you screw the others!" stated Mike firmly. "Because I'm going to stay right here and watch you sell it. And, at top dollar!!" To punctuate the statement, he slammed his cigar to the pavement and stomped it like crushing a venomous snake.

Set back on his heels at the inference that his integrity was questionable, the broker elevated his body by standing up on his toes— arm outstretched with index finger pointing directly towards his opponent —snapped back with raised eyebrows in an indignant to-the-point manner:

"You, of all people' a Toscano, inferring that I, a Genovese, am of questionable character! When here you are, selling contraband wine disguised in vegetable crates!! And, on my sidewalk!!"

Mike, with his fuse now burning even shorter, responding in a like manner, took up the challenge:

"How dare you make such an insinuation! Are you not buying my wine? Does that not also make you afoul of the law . . . ? And now, because you have insulted me, I'll reload my cauliflower and leave you nothing!! How do you like that?" With that firm response, he picked up a crate of cauliflower with the intention of tossing it back on the truck. But the broker was not about to let the cauliflower get away from him.

"You'll do nothing of the kind—put it back!" he snorted. "You have placed it on my sidewalk so it now belongs to me!!"

With that comment firmly planted, the broker grabbed at the crate Mike was holding, and in the ensuing tug-of-war, caused the crate to pull apart thus scattering cauliflower every which way. This now catapulted the whole affair into the damnedest hullabaloo imaginable.

While all this was going on, Al was working his way through the crowds, looking for Mike, when he came across Julio doing the same thing.

"How come you're looking for Mike?" asked Al. "Didn't you come in with him in the Model T?"

"No, I came in with the Graham. It's parked down the street with a load of wine," answered Julio.

"A load of wine . . . ? Parked down the street . . . ?"

"Don't worry about it. Sal's down there with it—if that's what you're thinking. By the way, what's all the ruckus about up ahead?" asked Julio as the two men approached the scene of battle.

"I'm not sure . . . what the hell . . . that's Mike! Holy Christ, look at that!"

Mike, by now in a fit of rage, was reloading the crates back on the truck while the broker, in desperation, was grabbing at them, spilling the contents in the process. The insults and profanity rising above the din of chuckles and laughter emitting from the gathering circle of spectators, added to this hilarious spectacle.

"For God's sake, they'll have cauliflower scattered all over hell's creation. We've got to stop that!" said Al in seriousness as he pushed his way through the spectators.

"Heck, that's nothing," put in Julio in his pleasant calm manner. "At least the cauliflower is easy to pick up. You should see the incredible mess when it involves radishes."

To the crowd's disappointment, the two men's intervention broke up the scuffle. Upon so doing, merchants immediately moved in to bid for the cauliflower. It was obvious; Mike had won out, the broker had no choice but to adhere to his demand—sell to the highest bidder and satisfy himself with the 15% commission only.

Primo and Pucci were standing outside the Chinese restaurant, as Mike, followed by Al and Julio, approached from the direction of the confrontation that had just taken place. They had already been apprised of the hilarious spectacle that took place and were therefore chuckling as a question was posed by Primo:

"Uncle Mike, are you going to leave the truck there, blocking the front of the brokerage house?"

"Exactly!" came the sharp answer. "The hell with these damned crooks! They touch that truck and I'll send Sal over there with his machete and give them a lesson or two in cutting cauliflower. Come on, let's go inside before I send him over there anyway." The threat was intended to include all the brokers in general.

They took a table in a remote corner of this establishment with a saw-dust-covered floor called a restaurant. The Chinese proprietor knew Mike well. He therefore prepared himself for the worst as he approached the table to take their breakfast order. In a still somewhat grumpy manner, Mike said to the others in their native tongue:

"No matter what we order, it will come out tasting the same: oily and indigestible, with plenty of fried rice whether you like it or not. That's the Chinaman's specialty. He'll shove it up your ass if he has to."

The proprietor couldn't speak many words in Italian, but since he was constantly subjected to their language, he could understand it quite well. Having understood the somewhat slanderous remark, and being aware of Mike's delicate stomach, he responded accordingly in his best English.

"Gentlemen, we have an Italian specialty we are offering for breakfast this morning. I'm sure you'll enjoy it."

"Well, what do you know. And what might that be?" inquired Mike, in an amused and skeptical manner, his English being no better than the proprietor's.

"Rice with chicken gut gravy, Dagos like it!" With that comment, the proprietor turned away disgruntled and made his way back towards the kitchen shuffling his feet through the sawdust unintentionally piling it up ahead of him and into the kitchen area.

Although a common dish among poor Italian families, Mike would rather starve to death before eating chicken gut gravy. It tastes just like it sounds. Pucci, having witnessed these scenes before, joined in on the laughter, but not until he was to remind him that, this time, he really had asked for it:

"The Chinaman got the best of you this time. I hope you like sawdust sprinkled over your eggs."

It took a while for Mike to shed the joke and get his paesani to calm down. Once the laughter settled down to grins and chuckles, he seriously announced: "The San Mateo County Sheriff, in some manner, has determined that we were responsible for the Halloween raid at Bayshore. Also that the still, along with its related equipment, is being stored there at my ranch in San Bruno."

The grins and chuckles now changed to frowns and mumblings as the statement of fact sunk in. Each one of these men had taken a lead part in the raid, to say nothing of the part that Sal, down the street guarding the Graham truck, had played in disposing of his family's arch enemy, the man called "Occhio." Julio, with a question, was the first to break the silence that followed. First clearing his throat, Julio asked, "Did he mention anything about— Occhio?" He said this in a worried manner through gritted teeth and tight lips, his ever-present smile fading.

The others, while concentrating on the posed question and eagerly waiting for Mike's answer, didn't notice Al leaning back in his chair as if trying to distance himself from the question altogether. Neither did they notice his eyes shifting from side to side as if trying to avoid looking at the scene still embedded in his mind of the violent struggle between Sal and Occhio that took place at the south end of the train tunnel that night. The stench of gut gases and human excrement was not to be easily forgotten.

Pucci leaned forward: "Mike, did you hear the question Julio asked?"

"Yes, I heard him. The Sheriff mentioned nothing about that, thank God," came the answer in low tones.

Julio leaned back expressing a sigh of relief. Unlike Al, he had not witnessed the scene, but Sal had indicated to him that the family vendetta had been fulfilled, and he was therefore making preparation to return to his beloved Sicily. He had no further reason to remain here in America.

Primo's eyes shifted from his Uncle Mike to Pucci, remembering well what his buddy had warned about the pitfalls of bootlegging: "Alcohol is rough stuff." Also coming to mind was, "How would the Church view dealing in alcohol? In the course of doing penance for such a sin, how many 'Hail Mary's' would it take to clear the slate?"

"Did the Sheriff give any indication as to what he intends to do about it?" asked Pucci.

"All he said, was not to set the still up in San Mateo County." Mike then proceeded to brief the others, in detail, on what transpired between him and Sheriff Kelly.

The serving of breakfast was to some extent a welcome interruption. Even to the unconcerned Chinese proprietor, it was obvious that these men's minds were being burdened with a heavy matter. He politely commented that the "Italian Special" he had mentioned was merely a joke, and no offense intended. Knowing of his fondness for Italian cigars, Mike reached into his vest pocket and handed him a fresh-cut half cigar. This time, the proprietor didn't have to wait to pick up a discarded stogie off the sawdust floor. There was no time wasted for him to get over to the gas burner and fire it up. A fresh-cut half Toscanello cigar was a rarity for him.

As they concentrated on eating their breakfast, comments were being made in reference to the serious matter at hand.

"Mike, you better take Sheriff Kelly's advice, don't set the still up there at San Bruno. Move it out of the county as soon as you can. He's giving you a break, you may never get another," advised Pucci. "Since there is the sugar at stake also, maybe you should move it out of the city as well. You can have my share," he added, coming right to the point.

"Mine too, Uncle Mike," put in Primo.

"No, if we do that, both of you will eventually be paid your share. What's fair is fair."

"You really do intend to get into the moonshine business, come hell or high water, don't you?" Before the question could be answered, Pucci turned to Al and asked, needlessly, "How about you, Al . . . are you staying in?"

"He'll never make it by sticking to farming. It's his best shot, why not push it? Yes, I'm staying in."

Al's favorable comment was no surprise, neither was Julio's grin, indicating concurrence with Al. Pucci's glance went from face to face, then nodding his head slowly in an up and down motion, he commented:

"Just as I thought, you're all crazy, but I suppose what must be, must be; nevertheless, count me out."

"Uncle Mike, I think it would be best for me to also bow out. Whenever you're ready, let me know and we'll give you a hand to move the stuff out. We can use the Mack to move the rest of the sugar," said Primo with a satisfied grin. He couldn't very well hide his pride for his Uncle.

CHAPTER 4

Al was not surprised to see Mike step off the lead tug, but Terzo was. He wasn't fully aware of his cousin's purpose for being there—to advise him of the curtailment of further sugar deliveries. Al had hinted as much, but Terzo hadn't put much stock in his statement. The dim glare of lights that reflected from the industrial buildings along the Oakland-Alameda estuary penetrating the darkness were enough to distinguish his outline, and his all-too-familiar duck-like walk. There was no problem distinguishing him from the tug crew, or its captain.

As crew members hurriedly handed sacks of sugar to the several men that had been waiting for the loaded tugs to tie up to the dock on the Alameda side of the estuary, Mike made his way up the steps leading to the truck loading area above as Terzo posed a question to Al:

"What's he doing here—riding the tugs across the Bay at this late hour?"

"It's about the sugar—this is it, your last load."

"No—it can't be . . . "

"The hell it ain't—I tried to tell ya."

Once within hand-shaking range, a solemn greeting took place between the three men. They stepped off to one side out of the way of the loading operation, and out of hearing range of the hired help. Terzo, in his laryngitis-sounding voice, made the opening statement:

"Mike," he said, "Al here tells me we'll soon be cut off of our sugar supply. For what reason? The price is good, isn't it?"

"Yes, the price is good. But you see, we can't spare any more sugar."

"What do you mean? What are you talking about? You have the better part of a shipload left."

"That's right, and we'll need it all for ourselves. We can't spare any more —that's it."

"Need it for yourself!" exclaimed Terzo. "What do you intend to use it for? You don't have a still, and it would take you months to get one made up," he insisted. "These bootleggers I'm selling to are paying top dollar; why cut them off now?"

"For your information and for your ears only, we do have a still, made up

15

and ready to set up," responded Mike with the confidence of a poker player holding a winning hand. "If you don't believe me, ask Al here; he'll tell you what we have."

"Al, is that true? Does he have a still?"

"You better believe he has a still, along with everything else that he needs to go with it," came the positive answer.

"Well, I'll be damned! You son of a gun! Why didn't you tell me this before? I wouldn't be peddling this sugar to others."

"I wasn't ready to, besides I didn't think it was much of your concern."

"Not my concern! The hell it isn't! I've been waiting for just this kind of opportunity to get into the bootlegging business for real. Those buggers out there are making money like you can't believe. We should set it up immediately and get started right away, 'partner.' "

"What do you mean, 'partner'? I already have two partners in the deal. What's with this partner thing?"

"I don't care how many partners you have, you still need me, damn it! Now don't argue with your elders. I'll see you at the ranch in San Bruno next Sunday morning. Have your partners there so we can talk." Terzo wasn't mincing words. It was obvious he wanted in, in the worst way. For the moment, there was little point in pursuing the discussion much further.

Mike turned to Al: "What do you think, shall we get together with him?"

"It might be a good idea. No harm in talking."

"Is Al, here, one of the partners?" inquired Terzo.

"That's right."

"Good, I like it even better. Who's the other one?"

"Julio" came the sharp, to the point answer.

"Ah, good, a calm, sensible man, just what we need." It would have made no difference who the partners were, for he was not about to let this opportunity get away from him, regardless.

"All right then, we'll all meet at the ranch on Sunday, bring your wives and families. Livia will enjoy having them visit for the day." Mike's parting words as he boarded the tug were: "Terzo, don't forget to tell your friends, the next load is the last one, and if the cash isn't there, they don't get that one either."

"All right, all right, don't worry about it, we'll get paid," said Terzo.

"He has no doubts about you getting paid. He just wants to be sure he gets paid, and I'll see to that," said Al in a no-nonsense manner.

"Why do you talk like that, Al? Are we not partners now?"

"Not yet we're not."

"For Christ's sake, you're just as bad as my cousin. Don't you trust anyone . . . not even me?"

"Not in this business. Come on, pay up before the tugs pull out or we reload the sugar."

Terzo had gone through this before, he therefore knew that Al meant exactly what he said, so both loads were paid for, in cash, right then and there, but not without comment:

"Maybe after we're partners, your attitude will change."

"Don't count on it," came the blunt response.

Terzo momentarily stood there in the semi-darkness, wondering how he'd have to deal with Al as a partner. The way he was shuffling through the handful of bills as he walked away was a sure indication that he'd be tough to handle if ever short-changed.

Satisfied with the count, Al stuffed the bills in his pocket, climbed into his red racing roadster, and took off in a burst of speed. In addition to being street worthy, the car was also designed as a two-man dirt-track racer. The car's manufacturer, the Chevrolet Motor Company, offered it as an 'assemble yourself' kit. Its design, a rather short wheelbase, open cockpit, wedge-shaped body supporting bicycle-like fenders over narrow tires, gave the impression the fenders were detached from the body itself. The absence of running boards gave it an even more bullet-like appearance. As for performance, it could be said that it was fast and snappy, with incredible maneuverability, ideal for reversing direction of travel and cutting across empty lots and between buildings. Well-suited for Al's purpose—outrunning highway robbers and over-eager lawmen alike. Nevertheless, he did exercise caution by making it a point never to follow the same route two nights in a row. And, he drove the streets as if they were a racetrack. The cash he carried added little to his enthusiasm for speed.

CHAPTER 5

Sunday morning at the ranch turned out to be a dismal, drizzly winter day. Nevertheless, the usual festive gathering of families always seemed to be enjoyed regardless of weather. The women all pitched in with the cooking and other kitchen chores in preparation of a midday feast. Babies were allowed to crawl around the floor, under the watchful eyes of the older children, primarily the girls. As for the men, unbeknownst to their wives, this gathering was intended for a specific purpose: to put together a bootlegging organization. In this endeavor, the men wasted no time whatsoever in getting down to business.

Mike, followed by Al and Terzo, made his way across the cabbage patch following the path that connected the two ranch barns. At the paesani's ranch, Julio was already at the barn waiting for them. They entered the somewhat distorted huge barn that had partially collapsed during the first rain of the season. The pyramid stack of wine barrels that had caused the catastrophe, had for the most part been removed and sold. Empty barrels stacked on end had been used to further support the structure from the inside. All-in-all, considering its appearance, it was quite stable. The four men stepped inside under the protection of its patched-up roof. At least once inside they were secluded, out of earshot and in out of the drizzle. Their audience was the draft horses housed in the makeshift lean-to where they could be seen over the row of mangers that separated it from the main barn.

"All right," said Mike, as he sat down on a bale of hay, "let's talk."

"Where's the still you were talking about?" inquired his cousin, somewhat curious.

"It's behind those bales of hay," answered Mike. He then addressed Al and Julio: "Let's move a few of those bales and show it to him, or he won't believe we have it."

With that a stack of hay bales was pulled down exposing the still and all the rest of its related equipment. Terzo's eyes lit up; his face took on an expression of complete satisfaction as he exclaimed:

"By God, you weren't kidding! That's a pretty good size unit, certainly enough for a pretty good start. How in God's name did you get that thing?"

18

he asked, but the question went unanswered.

Bales of hay were restacked in place as the matter of an alliance of sorts now got under way in earnest.

Julio, having been briefed beforehand, and knowing of Terzo's tough, self-serving business reputation, well-established back in their hometown, the city of Buti, Italy, was not all that keen on the idea of having him as a partner. He listened carefully to the two cousins' argumentative discussion.

Al, having been the one assigned to the matter of overseeing the sugar deliveries and collecting payments, didn't have to have known Terzo back in Italy. He had come to his own conclusion as to why, and how, he had justifiably earned the nickname "Veleno", meaning "Poison". But in his case, that didn't bother him much. He knew what to do to get his attention and adjust his attitude if the need were to arise.

Mike, as a baby, having been anointed with olive oil squeezed from the olives harvested on the slopes of the mountains of Buti, where nestled the city of Buti, well-saturated with the clan bearing the same name, certainly was aware of the pitfalls of entering into an alliance with another of his kind. So, the discussion now centered on the aspects of cooperation, trust, and above all, to define the traits of their argumentative ways, the one thing that many, if not most Italians are either cursed or blessed with, depending on how you look at it.

"Mike, for Christ's sake, all clans argue for some reason or another; that's what it means to be an Italian. That doesn't mean we're not going to get along; be reasonable. Besides, it's not only the Buti clan that's cursed with this trait. How about the Lucca clan? Don't tell me they don't argue." Terzo was now making reference to Al and his ancestral clan, which therefore opened the door for him to inject his families' argumentative traits:

"The Giovanetti's don't argue," he responded. "It may appear that way, but such is not the case. Since they all talk at once and no one is listening to each other, you could hardly call that arguing. Besides, no matter how many are present, they're all talking about a different subject at the same time. There again, you see, it's not an argument. When the shouting and yelling finally subsides, no one really understood or remembered the discussions that took place or the reasons behind them, because no one was listening. Therefore, they always part on the best of terms, looking forward to their next gathering so they can rehash the same issues all over again, in the same manner and with the same end results. How can you call that arguing? Besides we don't come from Buti, we come from Lucca. There is a substantial difference, even if it is located just on the other side of the mountain. Ask Livia; she's from Lucca, she'll tell you the difference between the two clans."

Terzo was not about to ask Livia anything of the sort. To do so would not only result in a lambasting of the Buti clan from her, but most certainly would embroil his own wife, of the Piemontese clan of Northern Italy, into the same long-standing issue between their two clans. He then turned and looked at Julio in a pleading manner, but since the Buti and Matteoli families back in the old country only lived a stone's throw away from each other, all he got from Julio was a pleasant smile. No words need be spoken to express his feelings: A good friend, yes; but a business partner, that was another matter entirely. His expression reflected it.

"All right," conceded Terzo. "What can I expect? Certainly there's room for me somewhere in the deal. Don't forget, I have a lot of connections that can be helpful."

"Yes, cousin, I understand that, and for that reason you do fit in, but not as a full partner. You see, you're too smart to let yourself be exposed to the risk of arrest such as we will be. So, therefore, knowing this, I can hardly see how we can share and share alike. So, this is what I propose."

Mike outlined a plan whereas Terzo would in fact be independent of the operation, but supplied with high-proof alcohol. This way he would be paying wholesale price and taking advantage of the markup after cutting, coloring and aging. The extent of risk would be to his own choosing. In exchange for the arrangement, he would offer his expertise, experience, and other assistance and help when needed. It was also agreed that Mike would not solicit business in the city of Alameda proper. This would be Terzo's exclusive territory.

All parties agreed to the arrangement, a round of handshakes sealed the alliance. They were now ready to move on to the matter of locating the still somewhere in Alameda County and getting underway. They would spend the next few weeks divesting themselves of the rest of the wine, and moving the still out of San Mateo County as soon as possible in order to appease Sheriff Kelly.

Approximately three miles somewhat northeast of the city of Hayward, in the community of Castro Valley, in a rented chicken ranch approximately one mile up Crow Canyon from Dublin Canyon Road (Highway 50), the still was finally set up. In addition to the old yellow farm house that Mike's family moved into, the ranch buildings consisted of a huge hay barn, one long chicken house, a garage and smaller outbuildings. This was an ideal situation for a bootleg operation since the buildings were nestled close together, therefore movement from one to the other could not be easily detected.

A chicken and egg-producing ranch was indeed a perfect setup for the bootlegging enterprise. The truckloads of sacked sugar, cracked corn, barley, and whatever else needed to make up the mash under fermentation to feed the still did not raise suspicion while being hauled into the on-going chicken ranch. Neither did crates of eggs with containers of "alcohol" disguised among them look suspicious being hauled back out again. Telltale distillery waste material odors were easily disguised by mixing the waste in with the perpetual and ever-present piles of putrid-smelling chicken manure. San Lorenzo vegetable growers were then hauling it off to fertilize their lettuce fields. Once worked into the ground, all traces of the stuff was gone.

Crow Canyon Road wound its way along the creek and over the top of the ridge to where it crossed the Alameda-Contra Costa County line terminating at San Ramon, thus a little community on the highway, midway between the town of Dublin and the city of Martinez. By means of the Martinez-Benicia ferry, the Sacramento River could be crossed, thereby adding Solano County to their distribution territory.

Terzo's expertise in the cutting, coloring, purifying, and aging process was passed on to Mike with unbelievable success. The finest, smoothest "Jackass Brandy," as some preferred to call it, was now available in the East Bay to anyone who had the cash to pay for it. There were any number of reasons offered as to why the labeling of this alcohol product came to be known as "Jackass Brandy," the most logical being that the Italians were using a similar technique in making it as they did in making brandy from grape products, and using mules to transport supplies to the remote still sites.

As the demand grew, so did the operation. Before long, there were several stills set up in various locations. When one was down, the others came on line, thus keeping up production of high-proof alcohol, the basic ingredient for making "Jackass Brandy."

Old houses and barns owned by cattle ranchers located along the length of Crow Canyon and its spur canyons, housing Mike's stills, were now producing good rental income for their owners. Opportunity had knocked on their doors as well.

So far, this paesano gang of Italian immigrants was not being interfered with. Julio was maintaining alcohol production while Mike was processing it into the finished product, "Jackass" as Al was forever expanding the sales territory. They were getting their share in spite of the fact they were pushing their way into established competitive territories. But Al's aggressiveness soon brought on problems. Confrontations in the form of push and shove incidents began to surface.

CHAPTER 6

The quality of Mike's "Jackass" was tough to beat. For one thing, he used the best of grains—fortified with brown sugar—in his fermentation process, therefore giving the finished product a smoother texture and better flavor. Thus the term "Brandy," rather than "Whiskey," was used to identify it, although either term used was proper. Regardless of what some chose to call it, the consumers, women especially, liked it, and preferred it over the harsher products being offered by less finicky distillers.

One such distiller, an established bootlegger from West Oakland, with connections, became disgruntled with the introduction of a better product than his own into his territory, the city of Oakland. And since his competition's stills were located out of the city, the intruder, Mike, wasn't being assessed the protection fees that he was obligated to pay. The bootlegger, a "snitch," no less, therefore put the pressure on his pet, paid law enforcement authorities to shut out this intruder, or at least put the "bite" on him as well.

The lawmen, already knowing who the intruder was, exercised the option that served them best: collect protection fees, or as they put it, a contribution for some cause or other. In soliciting the contribution, they didn't bother with details or offer any explanation as to the cause. Their demands were brief and to the point: "Pay up here and now or stay the hell out of Oakland!" Not being given much of an option, Mike made the first of a series of contributions to the cause: "extortion."

Al was infuriated. As much of a ruffian as he was, there was hardly anything he hated more than a "snitch," or a cop, with his hand out. His idea of returning a favor to a cop was to drop off an occasional keg of "Jackass," and/or setting the cops up with a first class prostitute, enlisted from one of his "Speakeasy" customers, but not hard cash. Through his own cop friends at the Oakland Police Department's Eastern Station at Melrose, namely Captain Brown, a tough, no-nonsense cop, but partial to Italians, bootleggers especially, Al soon learned who the "snitch" was, and the identity of his driver, a party to the conspiracy, and so advised Mike:

"I know who that snitching bugger is that put the finger on us, and believe me, he'll get his just due!" announced Al angrily.

"What do you mean, his due? There isn't much we can do about it if we want to stay in Oakland."

"Oh, we'll have to keep paying alright, but we sure as hell can even the score with the bugger that snitched on us. He's not the only one who has friends in the law business, and besides, his man's out on the streets at night delivering his stuff the same as I am. I also know that he, too, has been shooting his mouth off. That son-of-a-bitch is in for an attitude adjustment, that's for damned sure!"

Having experienced Al's methods of handling such matters in the past, during their wine hijacking escapades, sent chills up and down Mike's spine. He'd just as soon pay blackmail than go through that again, Either way was bad, but with Al's method, you would have to live with it the rest of your life.

"No! Damn it!" he swore in anticipation of what Al might have in mind.

"Calm down—hold your horses, I'm not going to kill anybody. Take my word for it."

"That's what you said the last time," said Mike nervously, "but look what happened in Benicia. And that 'Occhio' affair, how ab. . . . ''

"Now wait a minute," interrupted Al. "The Benicia affair backfired, that I'll admit, but those two guys in the Essex hit the Mack on their own . . . . And it wasn't me that gutted Occhio," he countered in a steady voice.

"Alright! Alright! Let's not talk about it. I'm sorry I brought it up. What do you have in mind?"

"Wreck their car! And if they don't get the message, I'll wreck their whole damned still!"

"There, you see, just as I thought. No!"

"O.K. I'll just wreck the car then."

"Wreck their car? I don't know about that; have you seen it? Can you be sure that will do the trick?"

"Yes," answered Al to the questions. "It's an Overland sedan, and I've seen the driver up close."

"Where did you see it?"

"At the Villa Francais, up on Foothill Boulevard."

"What the hell were you doing up there? That's a French whorehouse. They don't buy their booze from us."

"No, but they soon will be."

"Don't tell me you've been screwing around with those 'French' whores?"

"The whores, no; the Madam, yes."

"Damn it, Al! She's a whore just like the rest of those women. Besides, she's old enough to be your mother."

"Mike, don't knock experience."

Disgusted with Al's intentions, and the discussion drifting off course as it was, Mike pursued the issue no further. Not having scored any points, he walked away from the discussion thus leaving the option open for Al to act on his own. In parting, Al wondered: "How come Mike knows so much about that place, or the Madam, for that matter?"

That same evening he stopped off at the Eastern Station, up the street from the auto repair shop at Melrose where he once worked full time as a mechanic. Although still considered as an employee, lately he'd spent little time at the job. He approached his whiskey drinking policeman friend, Captain Brown:

"I need a favor," said Al.

"Name it," came the response.

"You guys are familiar with the Villa up on Foothill Boulevard aren't ya; the whorehouse?"

"Yeah, what about it?"

"Well, there's a guy that hangs around that place who needs an attitude adjustment. When I pass the message on to him, I'd like a couple of you fellows standing by, just in case he happens to have a gun."

"I hope you're not planning to have a gun."

"No, I don't carry a gun."

"O.K. What do you want us to do?"

Al laid out the details. Satisfied that he could depend on the Captain to back him up, he sought out his unemployed Irish buddy, "Fats" Meehan. He found him in his usual haunt — the pool hall. Fats had backed him up on many a street fight before, so it was no surprise that he'd be called upon once again, only now they were adults and not kids. Fats' wide belt hooked over his hips, cradling his fat belly, gave the impression that his chest had dropped and his ass disappeared somewhere in the mass of his body. He pushed his weight around like a bully. In a fight, he could hold his ground against any two average size men. And being a typical burly Irishman, he loved to fight. Al propositioned him; he responded to the request favorably:

"Hey, you know me. If you've got a problem, I'll help ya. But what's the beef with this guy?"

"The bastard fingered us. He's a lousy snitch. I just want to even the score. That's all."

"Any guns?"

"No guns. All I really need is for you to drive the Chevy; follow me out and drive me back after we dump the Overland. It's that simple."

"Dump it where?"

"Redwood Canyon."

"How about the cops?"

"They'll be on our side."

"What's in it for me?"

"Ten bucks."

"O.K., you've got a deal providing I don't soil my hands. If it develops into a fight, the price doubles."

"Fine," said Al. "I'll pick you up here in front of the pool hall tomorrow night at about 11:30."

Fats watched his buddy pull away from the curb in the 1924 Chevy touring sedan. When loaded down with "Jackass," it was sluggish, but when empty such as it was, quite snappy. He commented as he re-entered the pool hall: "One of these days that little fart's apt to get his ass kicked. This town's getting tough." Those that heard the statement placed little significance on the comment.

The following night, Al picked up Fats and headed for the Villa Francais where he expected to encounter the driver of the Overland. The whorehouse featuring supposedly "French" prostitutes was located on Foothill Boulevard just off 35th Avenue behind, and upstairs of, the restaurant bearing the same name. It could be entered from either the restaurant fronting on the Boulevard or the alley to the rear. How many of these enterprising women were actually "French" was of little concern to the Johns. In the frame of mind they were in, once viewing this array of peddlers of passionate sex, they cared less of their ethnic origin. As they drove along, the two buddies went over the details of the night's endeavor. Fats asked a logical question:

"Do ya think the guy'll be there tonight?"

"He'll be there. It's his last drop off."

"Ya gonna lay for him and jump him the minute he shows?"

"No," answered Al thoughtfully. "I'll get him on the way out. Let the whores work on him awhile, then I'll nail him."

"Now that's real thoughtful of ya. Only a Dago would be so considerate," commented Fats with a chuckle.

"I ain't being considerate; I want to catch him while he's still panting."

Fats' chuckling expanded to outright laughter. Once regaining his composure, he added a sobering thought: "Suppose he has a gun?"

"That's where you come in; come down the alley wide open with horn blowing. There'll be a cop's car up the other end of the alley. If it comes to that, they'll move in quick."

Upon reaching their destination, Al swung around the block. The cop's car was there, close enough to view the alley. He continued on past, then over to within sight of the other end of the alley where he expected the Overland to come cruising in. They parked and waited.

"Have ya got a smoke?" asked Fats.

"Yeah, good idea. I can use one too," said Al appearing a little nervous. They lit up, then Fats asked:"

"How big is this guy?"

"Big enough. He won't be no pushover, even after the whores work him over, he'll still be a handful."

"In that case—let me tell ya something. Give him a left and a right in the midsection first thing. That'll finish what the whores started. He'll be pumping too hard for air to put up much of a fight after that. If he doesn't buckle, plant your foot in his crotch; that'll bring him down to your size . . . "

"That's him!" announced Al as they viewed the Overland sedan swinging into the alley at a fast clip.

"Damn, he's in a hurry. Those French whores must be something else again," responded Fats.

"Better than you think," answered Al before giving last minute instructions: "O.K., he'll be tied up in there for a good half hour . . . maybe more. I'll walk over and wait'll he comes out. You plug this end of the alley. The cops'll have the other end blocked off. If any shooting starts—duck!"

"Ya sure ya don't want me along?"

"No! You stay with the car. We'll have to pull out fast once he's down. The minute you switch on the headlights, the cops'll pull away. Now remember, for Christ's sake, don't run over the bastard."

"Suppose someone else shows up, a John or . . . whatever; then what?"

Al thought for a second, then answered:

"Tell them the place is quarantined; you know—syphilis, that'll back 'em off." The last words Al heard as he closed the car door were: "You jerk." Apparently, Fats had his own opinion.

It turned out to be a longer wait than expected. But finally, the driver's footsteps could be heard coming down the inside stairwell. He was stepping quite lively for a man just having gone through a series of variegated sex sessions. He pulled the door shut behind him as he stepped into the darkened alley. Before his eyes could adjust to the darkness, Al buried his right fist deep into the man's midsection. As he bent forward from the battering ram punch, he took a smashing left to the face, thus rocking him back against the door. Al was not about to wait to assess the effects of his punches. His right boot came up sharply, smashing into the stunned man's testicles. Emitting a gasp and hefty grunt, he grabbed at his crotch. What reproductive fluids the whores hadn't drained out of him, that blow sure as hell did. As the man rocked forward, Al, in a broad stance, planted a stiff hard right straight into the man's face crushing his nose flat against his face, thus producing a gusher of blood. Amidst moans and groans, the man fell flat on his face, out cold. He had succumbed to the element of surprise.

Despite the victory, Al wasn't all that steady. He was nervous about the outcome of his attack on the driver; if not a bigger man than himself, at least just as tough. He didn't care to stick around until he came to. It wouldn't be the first time a fighter picked himself up off the ground and proceeded to beat the living daylights out of his opponent. He was eager to split the scene. Not wasting any time, he jumped behind the wheel of the Overland, felt around with numbed hands for the ignition switch, then hit the starter as he nervously put the car in gear. The instant the headlights came on, the cops pulled away from the alley, not caring to investigate the scuffle that had taken place in the alley or the ensuing consequences. As far as they were concerned, nothing out of the ordinary had taken place. They'd been patient. But, the anticipated dropping of a 5 gallon barrel of "Jackass Brandy" into their patrol car the following night was certainly worth the effort.

The Overland roared out the alley with Fats following close behind in the Chevy. In a somewhat still shaky condition, Al put the car through the gears. He was impressed with its maneuverability and ease of shifting. This was understandable since the car was practically new. In an unsteady voice, he uttered a respectful comment directed at the car: "You're a dandy—sorry to do this to ya."

They traveled up 35th Avenue to where it transformed into Redwood Road, a graveled, narrow mountainous road that wound its way through the forested area leading to the grove of redwoods and canyon that bore their name, "Redwood Canyon," to finally terminate in Castro Valley. The scattering of gravel as the sharp turns were negotiated was a sure indication that Al was anxious to get this affair over with. The Chevy, although lagging behind, was able to keep the Overland in sight. Through lingering dust, the occasional glimpse of its taillights up ahead assured Fats that he was keeping up. Talking out loud to himself as the wind whistled through the open touring car, he addressed Al as if he could be heard.

"Ya damned little Dago . . . " he cursed. "Back off! What the hell do ya think I've got here, a Pierce Arrow? What's the goddamned hurry? Ya didn't kill the guy . . . I hope."

At a point where the road wound its way high above the steep side of the canyon, Al backed off, swung the Overland in a tight turn and stopped just short of going over the edge. The light beams from the car's headlights pierced the darkness high above the canyon floor. Fats pulled up, disembarked from the Chevy, swaggered towards Al, cursing every step of the way:

"Ya damned Dagos are something else again. Ya got any more brilliant ideas? What the hell ya trying to do, get us killed?"

Al responded with his own disrespectful comment: "Come on, get your fat carcass up against the rear end and push."

The Overland rocked over the edge; with its headlights flashing in crazy patterns, it tumbled down into the depths of the canyon, pounding itself into a ball of junk. The crushing, crashing sounds subsided when it finally reached the bottom of the canyon. While staring into the darkened canyon with a tinge of horror in his voice, Fats exclaimed:

"Holy Christ! That car's almost new. What a shame . . . " Hesitating in a thoughtful manner, he added: "Somebody's gonna be awful unhappy about this, don't ya think?"

Al's response was not so sympathetic: "The hell with 'em, they asked for it. That'll teach those snitch'n bastards a thing or two."

"I'd watch my step if I were you, or you'll find yourself buying someone a new car . . . that is, after you get your ass kicked," said Fats with a final comment.

CHAPTER 7

Unwittingly, Al had scored some points with the Overland incident. Through the Oakland Police Department grapevine, news of the new driving force pushing its way into Oakland gained respect. Nobody, not even the recipients or beneficiaries of finger pointing really had much use for an "informer." Above all, they were known to be untrustworthy. Mike's escalated and generous contributions soon reached into higher levels of law enforcement authority. The word soon spread to the elite where, there was a willingness to pay top dollar for Mike's superb product, "Jackass Brandy." Aging proved to be a contributing factor in the development of its quality. So the need to locate storage facilities for the growing stockpile of aging barrels became apparent. Thanks to several newly made friends in Castro Valley, the problem of additional storage was resolved.

Fred Puls, a bachelor and owner-operator of a gasoline service station in Castro Valley that Mike did business with at the corner of Castro Valley Boulevard (Highway 50) and Lake Chabot Road, agreed to rent Mike his barn where he lived a few hundred yards from the station, just up Lake Chabot Road amongst a clump of eucalyptus trees. The seclusion allowed for the cumbersome handling of 50 gallon barrels.

Smaller 5 and 10 gallon barrels were also stored at Fred Hoffer's chicken ranch at the corner of Lake Chabot Road and Williams Street. Buried in chicken manure, it was found that the fermentation heat given off by the chicken manure added to a speedy aging process. A little messy, but nevertheless it did improve the product. Fred Hoffer and his sweet, charming wife's place could be considered a safe and quiet setting if it were not for the caged talking parrot they kept outdoors that insisted on calling out to one and all that came near the place. The bird's vocabulary and knowledge of the English language was by far in excess of most of the Italians living in the area. Mike realized that this arrangement would be temporary at best, since sooner or later the parrot would be calling out to visitors: "Polly wants a shot of 'Jackass,'" instead of asking for a cracker.

Another arrangement was made with Fred Crossman, whose place was located halfway up Castro Hill, also known as Pergola Hill (Highway 50), east of Crow Canyon entrance. The Crossmans and the Hoffers would never be suspected of having a hand in such illegal activities. However, the two Freds had little in common. Hoffer seldom drank the stuff, whereas Crossman indulged in it.

The need to establish himself permanently in Crow Canyon was also apparent, so the purchase of a four-acre parcel of land adjacent to the rented old yellow farmhouse was finalized. Upon so doing, construction of a new home was undertaken in the midst of its apricot orchard, with chicken ranch facilities as a front for the bootlegging operation.

Sworn to secrecy, a local Danish builder-carpenter by the name of Asmussen was hired, along with several carpenters to construct the new facilities. The main house was built with a full concrete basement and a car garage incorporated into it in a manner to enable the transfer of equipment and alcohol with ease. The basement, with its summer kitchen and garage, opened to a concreted rear yard connected to driveways on either side of the house, complete with brick pillars and metal gates at the entrances. Across the yard, a bunkhouse sufficient in size to accommodate several employees was built with a secret full-size concrete under-floor chamber, with a cleverly disguised opening. It was constructed to accommodate 50 gallon oak aging barrels. These charred oak barrels were so arranged that an electric copper heating element was inserted through the head at the low point. Loose charcoal was then added to the heated whiskey along with a daily hand rocking motion in order to keep the charcoal in suspension for better purifying and aging. The end product - Jackass Brandy.

Other adjacent structures provided the needed seclusion for handling alcohol and its related supplies. One chicken house with a workshop as the first stall, was also off the yard area. In the second stall of this same chicken house, a chamber carved under the floor into solid sandstone provided storage for several hundred smaller 5 and 10 gallon oak barrels.

Two additional large chicken houses were built across the parcel to the rear in a manner to leave a roadway extending from the yard area down to Crow Canyon Creek that made up the south border of the ranch. Before the construction crew departed, a swimming pool was also constructed. Yes, indeed, Mike had gone all out. He now had himself an Italian style villa, as it was now at times referred to, but it would not be complete unless it consisted of an accompanying vineyard. But the tedious job of digging out the remaining tree stumps was too slow for a man on the move such as Mike. So he decided to try dynamite, and since no one else dared handle the explosive, he chose to do the job himself. Experience gained as a young man while working on the Northwestern Pacific Railroad in Montana gave him the confidence to work with it.

Determined that it would work, he instructed a paesano employee to dig around the base of a stump resting in the proximity of the bunkhouse, while another drilled the proper size hole into the stump itself with a hand auger in preparation of setting the first charge. As they did so, Mike prepared a stick of dynamite by whittling out a hole in the end of it with his pocket knife. A piece of fuse with a blasting cap pressed on the end of it was then inserted into it. Loose dynamite shavings were pressed back around the fuse, making it snug and firm. As he walked up to the stump holding the dynamite in one hand and a box of stick matches in the other, the paesani employees scattered like cockroaches being exposed to light. The stick was then placed into the augured hole and using firm, damp clay mud, the hole was packed good and tight with the fuse dangling out ready for the match. As he torched the fuse, he yelled out "Fire!" This exclamation was more a reaction of delight on his part rather than a warning for the others that by now had taken refuge under almost anything that would protect them from falling parts of tree stumps, rocks and boulders.

Seeing what was about to take place, Livia, with her youngsters hanging on to her skirts, took refuge in the bunkhouse. Under normal circumstances, the bunkhouse could be considered a safe distance from where the explosion was about to take place. However, the instant horrendous shock waves from the explosion rattled the bunkhouse to near destruction. The overcharged blast of dynamite not only left a crater at the point of explosion, but the previous contents of the crater, which included the stump itself along with sizeable boulders, came crashing down on the bunkhouse and chicken houses, thus catapulting the chickens into instant fearful flight. The lingering cloud of dust and smoke shadowing the surroundings added to their plight. In a fit of rage, Livia came charging out of the bunkhouse to challenge her husband's unorthodox method of excavating tree stumps. With a trembling, high-pitched voice she sailed into him:

"You imbecile!" she screamed. "You'll wreck the place with your stupidity! Stop this nonsense! If you don't kill the chickens outright, they'll surely die of fright!"

Mike responded with a wave of his hand as he made his way to assess the results of his endeavor. Undaunted, she took after him, catching up to him about the time he reached the edge of the crater. The stench of burnt nitroglycerin lingered in the air. Staring into the hole, he inhaled a lung full of the acrid fumes then burst into hilarious laughter. But his wife wasn't laughing. She was aghast at the size of the hole left behind by the horrendous blast; she added to her earlier comment:

"We could have been killed," she said somewhat worriedly. But then in an escalated tone of voice, as anger within her was re-aroused, she lambasted him again: "Look at that! Brand new buildings and you're ruining them with . . . that . . . that . . . dynamite stuff!"

But the more she made an issue of the dynamiting, the more Mike enjoyed it. He responded accordingly:

"It worked, didn't it?" he said between chuckles. "And it was quick and easy. Did you notice how fast the stump came out of the ground?"

"No! I didn't, but I saw where the pieces landed—on the roof of the chicken house! And the bunkhouse!"

Mike glanced over to the closest chicken house and, sure as hell, a sizeable chunk of stump was embedded in the roof. He gleefully ordered the paesani to retrieve it and drag it clear of the buildings. He marched past his wife in long strides heading for the storeroom. She wondered, what next? He came striding back carrying a container of black powder along with a piece of fuse. Livia slapped her hand to her forehead, in despair, while exclaiming in horror:

"Oh my God! Not again?" then retreated to the main house to wait out the inevitable—another explosion.

Using "black powder" in a similar manner as the dynamite, he blew the stump into manageable pieces. Elated with the results, he repeated the process for days.

Booming blasts of exploding dynamite and black powder echoed throughout Crow Canyon from Mike's attempt to rid his newly acquired land of the remaining old apricot tree stumps. There was no question that the inhabitants of Crow Canyon, whether man or beast, were well aware of his presence, as well as others. Federal prohibition agents, having gotten wind of the flamboyant activity taking place in what should have been a quiet canyon community, soon began snooping around, asking questions, and observing activities at the new chicken ranch with interest. One of their favorite points of observation was up on Jensen Road that branched off of Dublin Canyon Road where it followed the top of the ridge above and east of the chicken ranch. From this vantage point, they spied on the goings-on below. They parked their car behind trees and brush, with enough cover for camouflage, but still sparse enough to see through with binoculars. It became a habit with them to keep a vigilant surveillance on the activities and goings on down at the new chicken ranch below. There was no question as to what went on in their minds:

"All other chicken ranchers in the area are struggling to survive," said the senior agent to his cohort, "but this immigrant with a bunch of fellow countrymen comes along and builds a villa, so to speak, and spends money like it belongs to the taxpayers. Hell, he's not a Congressman, he's supposedly a chicken rancher; where's he getting all the money?"

"Bootleggers, Chief. That's what they are, and Italians at that---sure as hell . . ."

"Exactly—and loaded with money . . . "

The federal agents were satisfied that they were on to something. There was money to be made here. All they had to do now was to get the goods on this enterprising immigrant called Mike, and before long they would be getting a piece of the action. They chuckled at the prospects of shaking the operation down:

"From this vantage point, within a short time we can gather enough knowledge about that bootlegging operation to shake it down for a piece of the action," said the senior agent.

"Sounds good, Chief. How about Crow Canyon Road below? We should patrol that as well, don't you think?"

"Yeah, you're right. But we may eventually need another unit if we're to find the still itself — we want it all."

Had it not been for the kids and the games they played with broken pieces of mirrors in and around the chicken house, they would have indeed succeeded in a matter of days to do just that—get it all.

The chicken houses, built level on sloping land, thereby creating areas under them where goats, ducks, pigs, and other farm animals were housed, also provided recreation for the kids. At certain times of the day, when the sun was right, they would flash sunlight by the use of mirrors into the darkened areas. As the sun started its decline towards the west, there was a point where the sun reflected in the same manner off the side windows of the federal agents' sedan, parked up on Jensen Road. This reflection flashed a bright beam of sunlight through the sparse brush aimed directly at the chicken ranch below. The kids were quick to recognize this phenomenon taking place that was sending the bright sunlight flash in their direction. As little as they were, they knew much about the illegal activities their elders were engaged in, and so reported their discovery. Once reported, the adults kept a close watch for the phenomenon to reoccur until they were able to determine that, yes, they were in fact under constant surveillance. They correctly assumed that federal agents were now on the scene. What they couldn't be sure of, was how long they had been watched.

Bootleg-related activities were immediately shifted to and restricted to nighttime. The presence of federal agents was now a matter of grave concern, since the paesani were not sure just how to deal with them. The rumor had it that they too could be bought, but just how do you go about approaching them? Rumor also had it that they could be ruthless in their methods of soliciting bribes. Mike decided to meet with Al and Julio to discuss this newly posed threat; however, the meeting was not to take place there at the chicken ranch, but rather at Fred Puls's barn during the night.

Fred's little black and white fox terrier jumped off his lap and ran to the back door. She cocked her head to one side as if trying to identify the sounds that were coming from the area of the barn across the yard. Her whining, yipping outbursts were indicative of her manner of advising her master of the presence of intruders. Since Fred was a bachelor, he found comfort and companionship in his relationship with his little dog. She understood him and what he expected of her. By the same token, he knew her habits so he could detect by her actions what could be expected to be found outside in the darkness. He set his book aside and removed his reading glasses before rising from his chair to make his way towards the back door. Picking her up in his arms, he addressed her in the form of a question:

"Are they out by the barn, girl?"

She responded with a whine and a whimper as if to say: "Yes, they're out by the barn, maybe you should investigate."

"No, you be quiet now, let's take a peek out the window and see." With that comment, Fred dowsed the light, pulled back the curtain, and looked across the darkened yard to see the familiar cars outlined against the light seeping from within the barn through cracks and knotholes. "That's our friend Mike; there's no need to go out there now, is there?" He then turned away from the window, while carrying and still talking to his little dog, made his way to the bedroom and prepared himself for a good night's rest.

In the barn, a kerosene lantern was sitting on the end of an empty barrel, casting shadows of three men against the walls. They spoke in solemn, sinister tones.

"Do you really think federal agents are watching us from up there?" asked Julio of Mike.

"Who else would be interested enough in us to spend day after day sitting in the sun if they're not federal agents? And for all we know, they may have been there for quite some time."

"Yes, I see what you mean, and they do drive black sedans."

"Mostly Hudsons," put in Al.

"Have you noticed anyone following you during your deliveries?" asked Mike of Al.

"I've seen suspicious looking cars of that description at times, but I didn't think they were following me."

"Did the occupants look like federal agents?" came the next question.

"Well, they were well dressed, mostly dark suits with felt hats, something like you always wear; generally two, sometimes three to a car."

"But you don't think they were interested in you?"

"I don't know that for sure, all I know is they didn't follow me, or at least I don't think they did."

"That's probably because they couldn't catch up to you, don't you think?"

"No, not really. Those Hudsons could overtake me when I'm loaded. These four-cylinder jalopies, loaded with Jackass, can't outrun a Hudson. No," said Al, thoughtfully, "not hardly."

The next question was directed at Julio:

"Have you noticed anything unusual around the still, like maybe someone watching or snooping around, maybe looking down on you?" The still Mike was referring to was located a half-mile up the canyon from the chicken ranch out of sight of Jensen Road above.

"No," answered Julio. "The only people that look at us with suspicion are the two old Amish bachelors that ride by in their black buggy. I can see them through their curtains stretching their necks while looking in our direction; they know something is going on up at the old house."

Julio was referring to the Amish bachelors and the boy they were raising, who lived three-quarters of a mile up the canyon from the still location. While coming down the canyon, the minute the buggy would approach the flattened mound to their left, where a saloon and stagecoach stop once stood, just up from the bridge and immediate driveway to the old house and still site, they would speed the horse up from a walk to a fast trot as if not caring to have anything to do with the place.

Bootlegging, saloons (whether functional or not), houses of ill repute, and other activity in the way of stimulating unnatural behavior in man, was frowned upon by these Amish bachelors. However curious as they were, they did mind their own business. They were not about to spy for anyone or point a finger at other's lifestyle.

What little was left of the old stagecoach stopover, once located on the mound, no doubt had something to do with their curiosity as well. The rumor had it that Black Bart, as well as other bandits of that day, frequented the little out-of-the-way saloon in order to appraise the wealth of stagecoach passengers before holding up the stage further up the canyon. After the holdup, the bandits would head up to Rocky Ridge and hole up in one of its many caves. The caves could be reached on horseback from Crow Canyon's spurs, Cull, Bellina (originally Bolena), or Bollinger Canyons, since all three spur canyons came together at the top of the rugged ridge where the caves were located. Trapping the bandits in this remote hideout was no easy matter since there were many escape routes.

"Maybe we should move you further up the canyon. What do you think?" asked Mike.

"I don't think we've been detected, at least not by the agents. As for the Amish, they won't say anything even if they know," answered Julio, then continued: "If you're going to move anything at all, you should move the smaller unit from the old place next door to you. The activity in and around the big barn is sure to catch the agents' attention, sooner or later. Like your place, they're looking right down on that place, too. You better keep those gasoline drums out of sight. Get them under cover or they'll soon be wondering about them, too."

Many stills such as Mike's were fired with gasoline pressure burners. Therefore, the presence of 50-gallon steel gasoline drums was an indication of the presence of a still. Federal agents watched for these signs as well as monitoring gasoline distribution. The suggestion was well taken:

"You're right, we'll move it and the drums. I think I know where to put the still so they can't see it from up on Jensen Road," said Mike.

Not more than a quarter of a mile up the Canyon, out of view of Jensen Road, lived a neighbor and bachelor friend of Mike's by the name of John Baron. The old, two-story house with rear access fronted on Crow Canyon Road, with the creek right up to the backyard. This was well within easy walking distance to the other still located at the old stagecoach stopover just upstream. From this location, men could simply cross the creek and walk up through the wooded area undetected to the other location without ever exposing themselves to the road itself. Both locations were completely shielded from Jensen Road up on the ridge behind them. And, if necessary to do so, 5 gallon tin cans of alcohol could be hand-carried down the creek to the chicken ranch for final processing.

John Baron was a large, rather tall, past-middle-age man with deep-set eyes and bushy eyebrows. He never married, or at least that is what was believed, since he lived alone. He was never known to have a job, but still he seemed to always have a few dollars in his pocket. Some believed that his partial Indian ancestry had something to do with his being kept supplied with money. However, there were a few that felt it was money recovered from a discarded safe that was thrown from a speeding getaway car while being pursued by the County Sheriff's Department. On the night of the incident, it was believed that while investigating the commotion, he came across the unopened heavy safe lying on its side in the brush near the bottom of the creek embankment, not more than 50 yards or so upstream from his house.

Assuming that someone would no doubt come back after it and attempt to blow it open on the spot, John decided to try his luck at opening it himself. He was handy with tools and very well versed on the use of nitroglycerin, thanks to past mining experience. After studying the safe carefully, he placed a charge into the exact spot necessary to blast the door open. Although the blast bulged the safe itself, as well as scattering its contents, it was assumed that the money it contained was recovered right down to the last silver dollar. Since others heard the blast, he, too, had to admit hearing it as well, and since he would talk about it while grinning through his big mustache, and eyes gleaming from under bushy eyebrows, folks couldn't help but wonder if it were not he that blasted open the safe.

John and Mike were good friends and neighbors, and did have at least one thing in common, they both liked to brew something. Since John's desire was to make beer (home brew) for his own personal use, the idea of having a good supply of fine whiskey on hand would enable him to enjoy the luxury of an occasional boilermaker (a shot of whiskey with a beer chaser). For an advance supply of whiskey, Mike felt that John would agree to allow the still to be set up at his place.

With business matters settled, the lantern was extinguished and the barn door locked behind them. The muffled sounds from the departing men caught the attention of the ever-alert little fox terrier sitting up at the foot of Fred's bed. No way would she have gone to sleep until they departed.

CHAPTER 8

The federal agents soon stepped up their surveillance, putting the heat on Mike's operation. Their motive was to gain full knowledge of the operation so as to be in a position to shake it down. What they wanted was to nail down the entire operation, starting with the raw material source and continuing to the stills; the warehousing; high-proof alcohol distribution (primarily transported and stored in 5 gallon tin cans); aging facilities where the cutting, coloring, filtering and purification took place in charred 50 gallon oak barrels; to the smaller 5 and 10 gallon oak barrels used for further aging, thus a better product revered by elite private clubs, high class speakeasies and restaurants.

Mike was now forced to shift various phases of his bootlegging activities so as to avoid a raid on the stills or interception of sugar and other needed supplies, gasoline included. The movement of alcohol was carried out during different hours of the day and night to coincide with the agents' movements. Since it was such a money-making, lucrative business, there was plenty of money to employ the needed help to handle alcohol and supplies, even to the extent of hand-carrying them long distances when necessary.

Deliveries to individual small consumers which was done by breaking the finished product down into 1 gallon glass jugs supplied by Pete's Hardware store in Castro Valley, the principal supplier of glass jugs for the area, was also restricted to nighttime deliveries.

However, the federal agents were reluctant to concern themselves with small-time peddling, and for good reason. It would be impossible to shake every phase of the operation down for bribes without it becoming common knowledge amongst the general public. Certainly, an unacceptable situation. At this point, they were not too sure what or who they were really dealing with, except for the fact that there was a sizeable concentration of bootlegging activity in and around the community of Castro Valley, no doubt tied into Mike's chicken ranch. As a whole, it was deemed to be a good-size operation, well worth their efforts to tie it all together in order to get a piece of the action. However, as much as they tried, they were to get no information from the local business community that was enjoying a brisk business, not only directly in its dealings with bootleggers, especially Mike, but also from the stimulated indirect boost in the local economy. Local authorities were of no help either since they admired this group of unarmed, nonviolent entrepreneurs with their charismatic leader who produced the finest Jackass in the entire Bay area. Again the agents sat in their car talking—working out a strategy.

"Going after them a gallon at a time isn't worth the effort," said the senior agent. "Besides, we'd be spooking them for mere peanuts."

"Yeah, you may be right. Not only that, if it ever came to light, we'd be in real trouble. We'd have to arrest just about everybody in the entire community in order to cover our ass—impractical."

"Hmmm! I never thought of that—good point. That settles it! We'll concentrate on this fellow Mike—he's no doubt the head Capo, keep an eye on the chicken ranch—locate the stills. There's where the big money is . . ."

Al, as the youngest and most aggressive, was suggesting taking violent action against the pesky agents, but Julio in his calm and sensible manner and Mike with his fear of violence did their damnedest to keep him at bay. Not an easy chore.

By now the stills had been moved further up Crow Canyon. The closest one being set up at Bill Boyd's place on the side of a wooded hill, at a good flowing spring between Jensen Road on the ridge and Crow Canyon Road at the bottom. The still could be reached via a narrow dirt road that led up the side of the hill from Crow Canyon to Bill Boyd's house and corrals above, or from Jensen Road through a wooden gate.

The other still was moved about a mile further up the canyon to Pasqual's place. Since the barn was built on the side of a sloping gully, the still itself was located under the heavy plank floor of the barn. Gravity feed from the fermentation tanks above on the main floor made this location an ideal setup except for the undependable water supply. Since a good source of water was required to operate a still, Mike was constantly in search of secluded locations with good flowing springs. There was plenty of water in Crow Canyon Creek itself, but for the most part, the still locations could not be well enough shielded from the main road, especially since they were getting to be sizeable installations considering the array of fermentation tanks needed to feed the still.

Needless to say, the expanding operation was beginning to draw too much attention, to the extent that one of the judges of the Alameda County Superior Court, during a get-together of local law enforcement agencies at their private club, while sipping Mike's velvet smooth, well-aged Jackass Brandy, expressed a desire to meet the man responsible for this fine product.

The Chief of the Oakland Police Department, to whom the request was made, turned to Captain Brown of the Eastern Station, since it was he who furnished the refreshments, and therefore passed on the Judge's desire in the form of an order:

"Captain," said the Chief, "you heard what the Judge said; make the arrangements!"

"Well, Sir," responded the Captain, "I've never met the man, that is, the actual distiller—only his man, a friend of mine." The Captain was referring to Al. "I'll ask him and see what I can do," he volunteered.

"Fine—you do that. But don't keep 'His Honor' waiting!"

Captain Brown immediately put out the word that he wanted to see Al at the station, "post haste." Knowing the connection between him and Fats, whom he also knew, and knowing where Fats could be found most anytime of the day or night (the pool hall), he was approached and asked to relay the urgent message to Al. The deed was done.

"Damn! I hope we're not in trouble over that 'Overland' car thing. Did they say what it was about?" questioned Al.

"Nothing was said—only that you be there—pronto!"

"Yeah, I guess I'd better. Captain Brown isn't one to play games with."

"I've been trying to tell ya; someday, you're going to get your ass kicked—but good! Friend or no friend."

Al had no desire to hash over his past conduct with anybody, especially Fats. There was only one thing to do and that was, follow instructions and face the music. He reported in to Captain Brown:

"You wanted to see me, Captain," said Al, nervously.

"Yes, I do—sit down," ordered the Captain while sensing Al's uneasiness. "Relax, it's not what you think—I need a favor." Being one to not mince words; he came right to the point: "Al, one of the judges wants to meet your . . . that is, . . . Mike. Can you arrange that for me?"

"Holy Christ!" thought Al, then stammered, " . . . what's the deal? Are we in trouble . . . ?"

"No, no . . . nothing like that—just the opposite. The Judge likes the Jackass you've been dropping off and would like to meet the man that's behind it. For that matter, so would I—that's damned good stuff!"

With a swallow of relief, Al relaxed. Tense muscles went limp; it was a noticeably good feeling. The Captain cracked a grin, then repeated his rather unusual request:

"Well, do you think you can arrange it?"

"Sure—hell yes—no problem. I'll check back with you tomorrow."

"Good! I'm sure nothing but good will come of it."

Al left the station, now cockier than ever: "To think, we've now got a Judge on our side!" The thought was staggering.

Shortly after the request was made, arrangements were made to bring the two men together. This was a proud moment for Mike and an interesting experience for the judge, and a feather in the cap for the Captain. The judge asked nothing of Mike, and in return, Mike requested no favors from him. Nevertheless, after that meeting, the judge was never to be without a reasonable supply of fine Jackass Brandy, and Mike was never without knowledge of the federal agents' movements. The respect and admiration for each other grew into a strong friendship.

"The Judge", as he was referred to, was much like Sheriff Kelly over in San Mateo County. He could tell the difference between the good and the bad that made up the bootlegging profession, as well as his own legal profession. So, as their relationship strengthened, the Judge took it upon himself to warn Mike that his operation was drawing considerable attention, and for that reason, it would be wise for him to slow it down if not shut it down completely, at least for a while. Obviously this was good advice, especially considering the source, but Mike felt that he was not in the position to shut the operation down at this time.

The paesani, Mike included, had transformed from a happy-go-lucky, carefree group of old friends, to a hard-driving organization hell-bent on making money. Needless to say, their attitudes towards each other also changed. Serious, to-the-point argumentative discussions were now becoming commonplace, rather than the usual clowning around horseplay they were so well noted for. A good, long vacation would have been in order, but a new high production continuous still was ready for delivery and scheduled to be set up in Bellina Canyon at Tony Soares' old 80-acre homestead. Therefore, any thought of vacation had to be set aside.

Traveling north up Crow Canyon, the Bellina Canyon spur was to the left, approximately a mile short of the Alameda-Contra Costa county line. A series of closed gates designated each property line, with John Soares (Tony's brother) being the first at the canyon entrance itself. The road crossed Crow Canyon Creek, then ran through John's yard before crossing Bellina Creek, then running along the west side of the canyon. Granspacher's (the original Bolena ranch) line gate was the second one up, although the ranch buildings were to the east of the creek. The third gate was Tony Soares old 80-acre homestead, where the road continued up the canyon by climbing up the side of the hill with Tony's driveway continuing along the creek to where it terminated at the old vacant house. This was referred to as "Tony's still."

Except for the cows, the place was vacant, since Tony lived just short of the entrance to Bellina Canyon in the adjacent spur canyon. However, the rear portion of his main ranch adjoined the 80-acre parcel at a point on top of the ridge, while the front portion adjoined his brother John's place with a road interconnecting the two ranches. Tony's main driveway came off of Crow Canyon Road proper just up from the Edenvale school, therefore offering an alternate route into Bellina Canyon.

The main two-story farmhouse housed the still itself. The fact that the column still was much too tall to fit in the basement made no difference to these enterprising bootleggers. They first dug a large hole in the basement which was referred to as "the pit," then they simply cut out sections of floor and ceilings to accommodate its height. Unlike most column type stills that were steam operated with the steam boiler as a separate unit, this one was fired by gasoline pressure burners at the basement level. Various sections and stages protruded up through the main floor, with the still cap extending into the attic. The "worm," or cooling coil attached to the still cap, worked its way back down again through the ceiling, spiraling through walls and back down to where the alcohol was caught down in the basement.

Precautions were taken in order to prevent a horrendous explosion which was not all that uncommon with these amateur distillery operations. The unit was also designed to remove poisonous "Fusel Oil" from the finished product by drawing it off at various stages. This by-product of the distillation process, if not dealt with properly, could "kill", and often did, when left in the alcohol in appreciable amounts.

Due to its chopped up condition and added vibrations set off by the roaring gasoline pressure burners in the basement that kept the windows rattling constantly, the house struggled to stay in one piece. But despite the makeshift manner in which the still was put together, on an around-the-clock basis it did put out close to its noted capacity of 250 gallons per day of 193 proof alcohol. Once cut 50% with pure spring water, an added dash of caramel for coloring and flavor, then aged in charred oak barrels, the superb finished product, "Jackass Brandy," soon attracted every rancher the length and breadth of Bellina Canyon.

Tony Soares was smart; he would take his quota of a 5 gallon barrel of Jackass which he was entitled to in addition to cash rent for the use of his old homestead, and with the use of block and tackle, would hoist it up high in a slender tree and lash the barrel to crotches at the tree's highest point that would support the weight, and let the wind and breeze do the rest. Not until the gentle swaying of the trees had aged the whiskey into a velvet-smooth, first class Jackass, would he let the barrel back down to drink it and/or sell it, when cash was needed.

Tony's brother John was also entitled to a whiskey quota, as well as cash compensation, since the road ran through his yard proper. However, the bulk of his cash revenue, as it was with Tony, came from the hauling services he was able to provide whenever the dirt road become impassable for trucks or loaded cars during wet weather. John would be called upon at all hours of the night or day to hitch up his team of draft horses to a sturdy freight wagon to haul sugar, mash or whatever supplies were needed up to the still. The two brothers would also haul alcohol back out. The fact that they were making money also induced them to keep an eye out for the federal agents who were frantically trying to get the goods on Mike in order to shake him down for a sizeable cut of the profits. However, the snoopy agents didn't get far with either of the two brothers. When it came to government men of whatever nature, John especially had little patience with them. His nasty disposition, when in their presence, reflected his dislike for them in no uncertain terms, thus bringing on unpleasant confrontations.

Tony and his brother John were husky, barrel-chested, tough, cowboy ranchers with an unyielding Portuguese mentality to match. Their two eldest teenage sons, the "cousins" as the paesani referred to them, shared their fathers' attitudes towards the federal agents and their taste for Jackass as well. In a fight these two husky ranch boys could prove to be a problem, especially the two working together. Challenging anyone of the Soares clan in an unfriendly or unsmiling manner could bring about a confrontation of extreme magnitude. The big black cowboy hats the Soares wore set them apart from other inhabitants of the community.

Charley Granspacher, known as Dutch Charley, the second rancher up the canyon, was also supplied with good sipping whiskey. He needed it to soften his grumpy disposition brought about by his being in the sheep business—the dumbest animal by far that is associated with the ranching business. Even on his best days, federal agents would have their hands full in dealing with Dutch Charley.

All-in-all, Mike and his paesani had a good thing going for them with the irate bulldog attitudes of these guardians of the canyon.

It was an easy matter to make friends with the Waldie brothers and Henry Mast, the other two ranchers, who together owned the land further up the canyon since their preference was to drink whiskey in the place of water. Their loyalty and friendship was cemented by inviting them to stop off at the still and pick up a weekly supply of whiskey. The ranchers were not about to pass up this invitation, and for the most part, drank it long before it would smooth out to be classed as "Jackass Brandy."

Henry had acquired several old homesteads, bringing his land holdings adjacent to and just over the fence from the still operation. This made it convenient to just tie his saddle horse up to a fence post and walk the few yards over to the still for a drink; this happened quite often. At times when he rode right up to the still, the paesani would stare up at him in amazement. Riding straight in the saddle, Henry took on the appearance of a bona fide western U. S. Marshal. He'd swing his tall frame out of the saddle, slap his cowboy hat on his pants a few times, then place it back straight on his head. Hat and all, he towered a good foot and a half over the tallest of the paesani. The fact that they spoke two different languages made no difference, since Henry was not much for words anyway. His level gaze expressed his feelings quiet well. He admired these little enterprising Italians; besides, to his liking, he soon found them to be good cooks.

CHAPTER 9

The horrendous amount of gasoline needed to fuel the roaring pressure burners soon became a serious problem. So far, the only practical way to keep up the supply was to pay jacked-up prices, but even then because of the federal agents' constant monitoring of distributors, shortages occurred. So the emphasis was as much on getting gasoline to the stills undetected as it was on cranking out and distributing alcohol.

At their next meeting during daylight hours at Tony's still, the matter of gasoline was discussed at great length.

"We have no choice," said Mike. "Either we pay through the nose for gasoline or we shut the main still down. There's no other way it can be fired."

"Damn it Mike . . . No!!!" snorted Al. "We'll do nothing of the kind! We'll get the gasoline in spite of those bastards!" He was making reference to both the federal agents and gasoline distributors alike.

Al's aggressiveness came as no surprise to Mike; however, being challenged in this tone of voice set him back on his heels. But rather than thrash out the issue of authority, he posed a logical question:

"What do you propose to do, steal it?" he said, not expecting the question to have much merit.

"No!" snapped Al. "We'll hijack it!"

"Hijack it? You can't be serious!"

"The hell I'm not!"

"For god's sake, Al, we're not common outlaws," protested Mike. "How could you suggest such a thing?"

"What's the big deal? Hijacking gasoline is no less a crime than hijacking wine or cranking out alcohol. . . is it!"

"You're going mad! Julio, for God's sake, help me out here," pleaded Mike, while turning away from Al.

But Julio, having been pondering both sides of the argument, was leaning in Al's direction and so stated:

"Well" he said thoughtfully, "if we could be sure the gasoline supply could be maintained by paying extortion prices, I'd go along with you. But I doubt it. Once the agents have traced the gasoline deliveries to us, they'll shake down the distributors as well as us."

"That's what I've been trying to tell ya," put in Al. "Either way we're screwed, so let's hijack it."

Mike's argument about the sinful thought of hijacking gasoline was put to rest with the reminder of their own unlawful activities. But he never viewed himself as an outlaw—just an enterprising businessman.

The meeting ended with the matter unresolved; that is, as far as Mike and Julio were concerned. But not to Al. He'd already given thought as to the prospects of hijacking gasoline, and how to do it. His intent was to hijack the tanker transports before they reached the distributors. He correctly surmised that the agents were monitoring gasoline deliveries going out of the distributors' facilities, but not so much coming in.

It so happened that the Lang Transportation Company's gasoline tankers, "Mack trucks", were routed through Crow Canyon, a shortcut from the Martinez refinery in Contra Costa County to the Bay Area in Alameda County. Crow Canyon Road being in the process of regrading and graveling in preparation of paving hadn't altered their schedule. Al's expertise as a mechanic that extended to Mack trucks gave him the confidence to pursue the matter. At one of his routine pick ups at Tony's still, Al once again brought up the matter of hijacking gasoline:

"I'm telling you, Mike, it's a natural. Those tankers can be taken. Take my word for it."

Julio, while sitting on an empty gasoline drum, beat Mike to the response with a question to Al:

"Who are you going to get to help you? These men are scared of gasoline. I'm having a devil of a time just getting them to handle these 50 gallon drums, let alone a gasoline tanker. For that matter, I don't like the stuff either, it's dangerous."

"You see," said Mike, "it's too risky. You better forget this crazy idea. It's outright madness."

"Don't worry about it. I've got someone in mind."

"Mechanics?" asked Julio.

"Yes, mechanics. Gasoline doesn't scare them."

"Who do you have in mind, and can they be trusted?" asked Mike, seeming a little more receptive to the idea.

"For one, my buddy Fats Meehan. He's helped me before and he'll do it again. He can be trusted."

Mike, being aware of Fats' involvement in the wrecking of the Overland, didn't question his loyalty. "Who else?" he asked.

"The two Portagees that have the service station down off 23rd Avenue. They'll swim in it for a few bucks, and they'll keep their mouth shut."

"I guess we can trust Portuguese," concurred Mike, then added: "All right, but keep the paesani out of it," he said firmly. He felt it was better to agree than face up to the possibility of watering down his authority.

"Okay, I'll get Guido with the International to haul these empty drums down to the old place."

"There's more over at Pasqual's," offered Julio.

Mike walked away gritting his teeth, stomped his cigar into the ground, boarded the Dodge Brothers touring sedan and sped down the rough dirt road away from this so-called "madness."

"Mike's not happy with this hijack idea," said Julio to Al as he was also about to pull out.

"Yeah, I know. But, damnit, we need the gasoline and I'll be damned if I'm going to stoop over for it." With these parting words, Al took off with his load of alcohol and to seek out his buddy, Fats.

When the idea of stealing gasoline was put to Fats Meehan, he responded with astonishment:

"Steal gasoline?" questioned Fats. "For Christ's sake, that's kid's stuff. Do ya need a tank of gasoline that bad?"

"I'm not talking about 'a' tank. I'm talking about hijacking a 'tanker' — 4,000 gallons of the stuff."

"Huh? 4,000 gallons . . .? Man, you can't be serious."

"The hell I'm not. Come on, make up your mind, I haven't got all day. Do you want in or not?"

"Yeah, I guess so, who else . . .?"

"The two Portagees down at the service station."

"Ya mean, Kanaka Joe and that screwball cousin of his, Blacky, the runt?"

"Yeah, that's who . . . what about it?"

"Nothing. I guess that's the kind of nuts ya need to pull off a crazy stunt like this."

All these East Oakland gang members went by nicknames. And for the most part, well suited.

Kanaka Joe's ancestors migrated from Portugal to the Hawaiian Islands before coming to California, thus the nickname "Kanaka." Although he insisted on being purebred Portuguese, his facial features especially indicated that some moonstruck Hawaiian had jumped the fence somewhere along the line. His Hawaiian blood strain tempered his tough Portuguese disposition.

As for Blacky, the runt, his nickname said it all. His dark complexion and short, tight curly hair indicated that his ancestors had dwelt along the

Ivory Coast of Africa before coming to California. He was short, muscular, and such as Al, a born scrapper. His aggressiveness made up for his size. He was always on the defensive, ready for a fight.

Al and Fats, as juveniles and members of the Fruitvale district gang, were in constant conflict with the Portuguese dominated 23rd Avenue gang which Kanaka and Blacky, also as juveniles, were members. However as the gang members grew up, their turf battles subsided and friendships developed among their respective members. However, their mentality as tough, cussing, scrapping, former delinquents was still with them. But what they were now about to embark on was a far cry from their days, as kids, sucking gasoline out of gas tanks, and scrapping over the spoils. As a team they would attempt what most would deem unthinkable: "hijack 4,000 gallons of gasoline under the very nose of snoopy federal agents."

They targeted the last Lang Company tanker of the day on its return trip from the Martinez refinery putting it coming through Crow Canyon evenings after dark. They spent several evenings monitoring the tanker's route and its driver's habits. Each evening, the driver stopped off at the roadhouse in San Ramon, Contra Costa County, for dinner before continuing his trip through Crow Canyon. It was the logical thing to do — let the truck cool down before tackling the grueling climb from the valley floor, up the east side of the ridge that split the two counties, Contra Costa and Alameda. This pause in the tanker's journey, and while the driver ate his dinner, gave Al an opportunity to study the Mack truck that made up the tanker. The truck's characteristics divulged its model and year of manufacture. He recognized it as an older model. Since it was chain driven, the size and type of its drive chains is what he was primarily interested in.

Armed with the necessary information, he next visited the paper company garage in San Francisco and with the blessings of his former boss, the shop foreman, searched through the pile of used truck parts for a set of drive chains to match those of the tanker. Having found them, the jug of Jackass left at the foreman's office more than compensated for the drive chains plus the master links needed to assemble them.

While riding the ferry back from San Francisco, Al gave thought to the planned hijack. All the available empty 50 gallon gasoline drums had been gathered up and placed in the big barn at the old place next door to Mike's chicken ranch. They would make the gasoline transfer from the tanker to the drums within the seclusion of the barn, under the very noses of the agents staked out up on Jensen Road. Although they did get things ready, neither Guido nor his brother, Lepo, Al's brother-in-law, would have anything to do with the transfer procedure. For that matter, Lepo especially balked at just about anything ever proposed that involved the least amount of risk. The point was argued constantly.

"But no matter," mumbled Al. "I'll check to make sure everything's set up, then they can both take a powder. We'll do without them."

Fats, having been instructed to be at the 23rd Avenue service station, was hanging around waiting for Al to show up.

"Here he comes now," said Kanaka to Fats, as Al wheeled up to the gasoline pumps.

"Fill'er up," ordered Al before asking: "Where's runt?"

"Ya better smile when ya call Blacky, runt, he's in a bad mood, he'll be all over ya," warned Kanaka.

"Oh no he won't. Where the hell is he?"

"Down in the pit wrestling a transmission. What the hell do you need him for? What's up?"

"You're shutting down. We're pulling it off tonight. Gas up Fats' car and your tow truck. I'll get runt out of the pit."

Al walked over to the adjacent garage and as he approached the car straddling the pit, called out to Blacky:

"Hey, runt! Come up out of there!"

With a blast of profanity, Blacky came scrambling up and out the opposite end of the pit addressing Al in a fit of rage:

"Ya goddamned Dago! Don't ya call me a runt," he swore as he came at Al in a crouched fighting position.

Having been through this sort of thing before, Al met the challenge by engaging Blacky in a sparring match.

"Damned, you're up tight today," said Al as he bobbed and weaved while giving ground. Although the smaller of the two men, Blacky was a good match for him. This had been proven time and again in their younger days.

Kanaka, knowing damned well what Al was getting himself into with his cocky remarks, came to the rescue:

"Blacky! Back off!" yelled his cousin. "He didn't mean anything by it."

"He didn't have to call me a runt, damn it."

As he intervened, Kanaka addressed Al: "Ya damned Dagos are all alike, always pushing."

"Who the hell're ya calling a damned Dago?" snorted Al as he now came at the taller of the two cousins.

"For Christ's sake! Break it up! Don't you wops ever grow up?" Fats' voice boomed from the garage entrance.

As far as he was concerned, just about anybody that wasn't Irish, was an immigrant, regardless of where they were born.

The jostling and sparring subsided before serious punches found their mark. The whole affair was really nothing more than a reenactment of some of their street fights as youthful ruffian gang members.

Having pulled up short of throwing a punch at Kanaka, Al said: "Come on, let's quit screwing around. We've got a job to do. You guys follow me out, we're heading for the roadhouse over at San Ramon."

Once in Crow Canyon, Al stopped the caravan.

"You guys head on up to the roadhouse. I want to check things out at the barn," he said. "And keep a couple of minutes apart so it doesn't look like we're traveling together. The Feds may be up on the ridge. I'll come up behind ya."

The stack of empty gasoline drums was giving off enough gas fumes from the tell-tale gasoline left in them to blow the barn apart. Upon announcing his intent of coming in with the tanker, the few remaining paesani hightailed it over to Mike's place. They had been forewarned that a forgetful striking of a match during the transfer of gasoline could level every building on the place.

Al's delayed arrival at the roadhouse in San Ramon found the Mack tanker already parked along the row of eucalyptus trees bordering the Dublin-Martinez Highway. Darkness had enveloped the valley. His cohorts were inside having a cup of coffee while the tanker's driver was eating his dinner. With a pair of diagonal snippers in hand, he brazenly walked up the left side of the chain driven Mack tanker. Feeling along the drive chains he located the chain's master link and snipped off the locking cotter pins. Continuing around to the opposite side of the truck, following the same procedure, he snipped the locking cotter pins off the master link on the right drive chain as well. The master links on both drive chains were now free to drift. He then entered the roadhouse and seated himself away from the others as did Fats from Kanaka and Blacky. Being he was wearing a leather jacket and cap, the driver looked up from his dinner in recognition of a fellow truck driver.

"What-a-ya hauling?" inquired the driver.

"Nothing," answered Al. "I didn't come in with a truck."

"Oh, I thought ya . . ."

"That's OK, ya didn't miss it by much."

Al glanced over to Fats with his fat carcass overlapping the stool he was sitting on while his chubby, fat hands cradled a cup of coffee. His battered stetson fedora hat did little to shield his pig-like ears and bull-like neck. It was obvious, his line of work, if in fact he ever did any, wasn't oriented to physical exercise.

The driver had already sized up Kanaka and Blacky. Their oily clothing and greasy caps were strictly that of auto mechanics. Besides he had seen them pull into the parking area with the tow truck. He rose from his stool, flipped a silver half dollar onto the counter to cover the cost of the meal and tip while addressing the waitress:

"Gotta get going. See ya tomorrow night."

With that he headed out the door. Fats dropped a nickel next to his cup and followed the driver out. Reaching in his shirt pocket, the driver came up with a pack of cigarettes, gave it an upward jerk, swung the pack towards Fats in a gesture to take one, then took one for himself. One match fired up both cigarettes.

"I envy you truck drivers," said Fats as they walked towards the tanker.

"Envy? Christ, there's better things to do than driving tankers, especially these goddamned brutes." The driver was referring to the Mack truck itself. "Ya looking for a job—driving truck—maybe?"

"I could use a job, all right, but I've never driven anything the likes of these things," responded Fats as they walked right on past his car.

"Hell, a guy like you would be a natural, providing ya didn't twist off the crank," laughed the driver.

Fats took the comment as a compliment to his size. As they approached the gasoline tanker, he followed the actions of the driver by dropping his own cigarette, then crushing it under the heel of his boot.

"That's one thing ya better not forget to do, or you'll blow yourself to kingdom come."

"Yeah, I can understand that."

The driver stepped up on the running board, turned on the ignition switch, set the throttle at about half speed, then stepped back down.

"Well, I gotta get this beast started and get going," he commented again as he slipped the leather strap off the crank handle. "Someday they'll give me a new model, one of those with a self starter, I hope."

In the darkness, he groped around for the choke rod as he worked the crank to a point of compression. In a simultaneous movement, he pulled the choke shut as he pulled up hard on the crank with a hefty grunt. The magneto fired off the cylinders in rapid succession.

"Hell, that didn't seem to be so difficult," commented Fats.

The driver responded to the comment as he hung the crank handle back in the leather strap:

"Ya gotta keep your thumb off the handle. Use only your fingers when ya pull up. These buggers'll kick like a mule. They'll bust your thumb if not your arm if ya don't do it right."

Back in the open cab, he switched on the lights as he positioned himself behind the wheel. In the absence of a battery and synchronized with the generator's rotation, the lights flickered brighter as the engine revved up.

Fats watched the tanker leave the main highway in a right turn and onto Crow Canyon Road. It made its way past the general merchandise and feed store, which it so happens, was closed for the night. Without shifting gears, it negotiated the eucalyptus tree lined short winding stretch of road, across the narrow culvert, straightened out and headed for the grade. The driver chose to stay with the lowest gear since the grade started but a few hundred yards up ahead.

Al took a last drag of his cigarette before flipping it in the direction of the highway. He addressed Fats, who was walking towards him:

"Okay, get going. Don't crowd him. No telling what might happen when the drive chains part."

"Jesus, I hope those chains hold together until he's down the other side. He's not all that bad a guy." Fats was expressing concern for the driver.

"As long as they're under pressure, they won't come apart. It's when he starts shifting into higher gears that they'll part."

"Boy, I don't kn . . ."

"Come on, get going. If he's a good truck driver, and I believe he is, he won't lose it —if not . . . well?"

As Fats parted, Al turned his attention to Kanaka and Blacky. Kanaka, such as Fats, expressed concern. He was aware that the only brakes on those older models were on the drive sprockets, directly at the differential case.

"When those chains part, he ain't got no more brakes. That ain't much of a road to hold a runaway truck on."

"I'm telling ya. They won't come apart until he's down the other side. Come on, let's get over to the general store."

They drove across the culvert and stopped. Al walked back as Kanaka was maneuvering the tow truck in position to block the road just past the culvert. Satisfied with the roadblock, he issued a final instruction:

"Now remember, nobody gets through—savvy?"

"Suppose it's a cop, then what?"

"Tell him you were ordered to close the road. Don't let him through! Regardless of who it is, stick with the plan! I'll see ya down the other side in a half hour or so."

The laboring sound of the tanker could no longer be heard as it topped the grade. Without further comment, Al left the scene in pursuit of the tanker. At the summit he got back out of the car, lit a cigarette and listened to the various sounds of the tanker as it descended into Crow Canyon. This would be his last smoke for the night; that is, if all went well. The engine's backfire while under compression and groaning of gears echoed throughout the canyon. Brakes alone couldn't possibly hold back the heavy tanker. Finally the backfire and groaning gave way to a variation of engine sounds and high pitched whirring of gears as the shifting proceeded. Al breathed easier. The tanker was now at the bottom of the grade picking up speed. The only other sounds to break the stillness of the moonless night were the occasional mooing of cows.

Suddenly, the sound of a free running engine, followed by a metallic clatter, reached Al's ears. He knew what that meant. At least one of the drive chains had let go. The truck's differential, responding to the left drive sprockets freedom of load, sent it into a sudden accelerated spin, causing the drive chain to whip through the air and slam against the truck's cab.

The driver also knew what had happened. Dictated by instinct, he came down hard on the brake, but with the left drive chain gone, only the right set of wheels braked causing the tanker to veer accordingly. In a near panic maneuver the driver tried to straighten out, but the loose freshly graded gravel wasn't giving him the front wheel traction he needed. The slack and pull sequence at the remaining master link caused it to also fail, thus dropping the second drive chain, a blessing for sure. Relieved of the one-sided braking, the tanker responded better to the steering efforts of the driver. Veering from side to side, the runaway tanker was churning its way through the freshly graded road bed, nothing like the plan of rolling to a coasting stop as Al had thought it would do.

The chilling sounds of the tanker's ordeal echoing up from the canyon below sent Al running for his car: "Oh Christ! He's going to loose it!" he exclaimed as he hightailed it in pursuit of the tanker. In an instant he caught up to Fats who had backed off once it was apparent the tanker was out of control. Fats didn't mind Al passing him and taking the lead. He wasn't all that eager to be the first one at the scene of a wrecked gasoline tanker. Buddy or no buddy, he had some choice words for Al as he shot past him like a bat out of hell:

"Ya dumb Dago!" he yelled. "I tried to tell ya . . ."

Back on the Contra Costa side of the ridge, the two cousins were having their own problems. As far as they were concerned, there was no plan. At least not one they could cope with. The first vehicle to reach the roadblock happened to be one of Peterson Trucking Company's Fageol trucks, with a Portuguese driver at the wheel, loaded with tomatoes destined for the cannery at Hayward. It came snaking around the twisting roadway, past the general store, made the tight left curve that put it on course to hump over the narrow culvert dead center. Its lighting and braking system, being no better than the Mack tanker's, came upon the darkened roadblock before the driver realized there was a roadblock. Fortunately for the tow truck, the Fageol wasn't traveling too fast when it plowed into the side of it. Nevertheless, the tow truck ended up straddling the road with its passenger side somewhat caved in.

Kanaka and Blacky came running up to their tow truck to assess the damage as the Fageol's driver leaped down out of the cab with only one thought in mind, and that was to beat the hell out of the two idiots that had disrupted his journey. The barrel-chested truck driver with a Portuguese mentality to match his unreasoning disposition, that puts fighting ahead of reason, came up behind the two cousins as they viewed the damage by the flickering light of the one still functioning Fageol's headlight. Recognizing the two cousins to be fellow Portuguese only added to the truck driver's determination. His to the point statement: "Ya dumb Portagees . . .," caused Kanaka to turn towards the voice, only to receive a stunning punch to the jaw that sent him sprawling to the ground.

Blacky responded by jumping up in a monkey-like fashion that put him up on the Fageol's hood. Not one to run from a fight, he leaped at the much larger than himself truck driver with the intent of knocking him to the ground. But, what he was dealing with here was not the usual street fighter. This man was a cattle rancher and hay farmer. Driving truck was only a seasonal job with him. He reached up with gnarled hands and grabbed the airborne Blacky like catching a bale of hay being let off a stack, thus tossing him over his head directly into the thick poison oak that bordered the culverted gully behind him.

Kanaka was back on his feet but with little desire to fight. He was caressing his fractured jaw while holding his other hand straight out, palm flagging a 'stop, I've had enough' gesture.

Blacky's frantic thrashing around in the patch of poison oak indicated that he'd be occupied for at least a few minutes, enough time to now get to the reasoning part of the confrontation.

"What're ya dumb jackasses doing with that tow truck strung out across the road?"

"I'd of told ya, had ya given me half a chance," answered Kanaka with extreme difficulty.

No more than a few words were spoken before Blacky came charging at the truck driver once again.

"Back off, ya little runt!" demanded his cousin while throwing a kick in his direction.

The size of his opponent wasn't much of a deterrent for Blacky as he looked for an opening to throw a punch. A series of punches were thrown before the truck driver, side stepping gracefully, was able to grab at Blacky's clothing and pin him up against the Fageol with some sound advice:

"Now you listen to me. I didn't come here to fight. But if you don't cut this out, I'm gonna beat the living daylights out of both of ya."

With the urging of his cousin, the message got across. Blacky calmed down just as a car appeared on the scene. The Contra Costa Sheriff's emblem on the side of the door negated an introduction. Apparently the proprietor of the general store had reported the incident.

"What the hell's going on here?" the Deputy Sheriff demanded to know as if he couldn't see for himself. "How'd that tow truck get across the road? Who does it belong to?"

Despite the pain in his jaw, Kanaka gave an explanation as to their reason to block the road.

"All right, you fellows get over to the wreck, I'll hold up traffic for a couple of hours," said the Deputy.

"You're not going to follow us?" inquired Kanaka hopefully.

"No. I'd be out of my jurisdiction once over the ridge."

Kanaka said no more. The two cousins boarded their crippled tow truck and headed out of there.

The zigzag pattern of churned up gravel indicated that the driver was staying with the tanker. Under such circumstances a less experienced driver would have jumped from the cab and let the tanker fend for itself. Al was having second thoughts as he raced through lingering dust and over churned-up roadway. Wrecking the tanker and putting the driver's life at such risk was certainly not part of the plan. The plan had sounded so simple when laid out to the others. Once having lost its chains, the tanker was assumed to coast to a stop, but apparently it had picked up too much speed before its drive chains parted. Fats was to then appear on the scene as a good samaritan. The object was to get the driver away from the tanker and out of the canyon, and to delay him while Al and the cousins hijacked the gasoline. A good plan, but apparently it wasn't working.

Reaching the end of the straight stretch, the driver had managed to stabilize the veering side to side motion. He hadn't jumped for fear the tanker would roll over on him. The turn at the schoolhouse that swung first to the left then around the school yard in a sweeping right turn didn't offer any better alternative but to stay with it. Hanging on to the vibrating steering wheel as much to keep from being ejected out the open cab as to maintain control, the driver skillfully negotiated the left turn. Had he failed, the tanker would no doubt have demolished the little schoolhouse dead ahead. Although slowing down some, coming out of the left turn and now swinging into the right sweep was a real bear. As the tanker leaned heavily in response to centrifugal forces, its sturdy wheels dug a trench to match the radius of the right hand curve. Yards of earth and gravel splattered against the embankment to the left. Not being able to hold the road, the driver intentionally let the tanker's left bank of wheels take the course of the shallow ditch. In doing so he lurched forward against the steering wheel as the deep gravel along the shoulder and ditch instantly afforded resistance such as a braking action needed to stop the runaway tanker.

Al, having slowed down for fear of running into the expected wrecked tanker, was relieved to see the stopped tanker's rear end loom up through the dust. He stopped short and to one side as Fats pulled up alongside asking questions.

"Holy Christ, is the driver all right? Did he ride it all the way?" he asked of Al worrisomely.

"I don't know. We better take a look."

They stumbled over what was once a smooth, recently graded roadway, peered into the open cab to see the driver slumped over the steering wheel. In his dazed condition, his hands were still firmly clamped to the steering wheel. Al scrambled up into the cab, grabbed hold of the driver and gently eased him towards himself. To lose his grip would send the driver tumbling out the opposite end of the leaning cab. Al's voice trembled as he asked the question: "Hey, fella, are ya all right? Are you hurt?"

Realizing the wind had been knocked out of him, Al shook him a few times as he laid him across the seat. The driver responded, taking deep breaths as he moaned and mumbled.

"He's coming around," announced Al in an unsteady voice.

"This whole idea was nuts," said Fats in no steadier a voice. "We could have blown this thing to kingdom come!"

"I'm beginning to think you're right. We'll talk about it."

As the driver was beginning to resume normal breathing, he also was beginning to make some sense with his mumbling: "Man, that was a close one," he said, hardly audible. "Did you see that?"

"Yeah, we saw it. But you're OK now. Just take it easy. We'll get ya out of here." The smell of gasoline was strong to the nostrils. Although it was oozing from around the cap of the truck's gasoline fuel tank rather than the transport tank itself, it was still worrisome.

Fats assisted the driver away from the tanker while Al hurried back to meet the tow truck that had just pulled up to the parked cars. Kanaka blurted out what had taken place back at the road block — a troublesome report.

"Huh? . . . A deputy sheriff???" Al thought for a second before commenting further: "Holy Christ, those buggers have radios!" he exclaimed. "While I think this out, take the chains and master links out of my car and throw them in your tow truck. Then drive up behind the tanker, and for Christ sakes, be careful. The gas tank's leaking."

"The big tank?" asked Blacky with a wide eyed expression.

"No, not the big tank. It seems to be coming from around the fuel tank's gas cap —I think."

"Oh . . . what the hell . . . I can stop that," volunteered Blacky.

"How? You don't dare take the cap off."

"Whittle a stick and push it in the vent hole. That's probably where it's coming from."

"You might be right," stated Al in agreement. "Okay, if you think it'll work — go try it."

In a matter of minutes, Blacky had the leak stopped.

The driver, having gained a measure of stability, walked back to the tanker. As he grouped around viewing the situation by the light of the tow truck's headlights, Al signaled to Fats and the others to walk back to their cars.

"Now listen," he said. "This whole goddamned affair isn't working out. That deputy sheriff across the line no doubt has a radio. No telling who might show up. We can't afford to take a chance; we're not going to take the tanker tonight."

Nobody argued the decision, but a question was asked:

"What're you going to do?"

"Something decent for a change," answered Al. "Let's get these drive chains over there and get them on. He doesn't have to know our reason for being here. It just so happens, you had a set of chains along with you."

"Okay, it's your show," answered Kanaka.

It didn't take much persuasion or explanation to convince the driver that he should accept their offer of assistance. As the work progressed, and still somewhat shaken, he kept repeating how fortunate he was to have made such new and concerned friends. In the course of the conversation, the driver volunteered his name, "Arty"; the others did likewise. Fats carried on the conversation with him while the other three men struggled with the drive chain assembly. Finally the announcement was made:

"Okay, she's ready to go."

The driver responded: "This thing ain't going to push itself over the top of that pile of gravel."

He was right. The bulldozer effect that took place when he hit the soft shoulder had created a barrier.

"We'll pull it out backwards," offered Kanaka. "I'll hook on to the rear end with the tow truck, it ain't much, but it might help. It's worth a try."

"Yeah, I think that might do it," agreed Al.

While Kanaka got turned around and Blacky got the tow chain hooked up, the driver got the Mack tanker's engine running again, but not until Fats volunteered to try his hand at the crank. The engine wasn't starting by a mere pull, the crank had to be spun, and the logical person to do it was Fats. With his strength, he was able to wind up the engine.

Coming up between the cab and the embankment, Al said to the driver: "Move over, I'll take it from here. I know these Mack's better than the back of my hand." He wasn't about to trust anyone else with the task of getting the tanker back on the road. Under such stress, there were several weak points that could let go. Only an experienced mechanic would know their limits.

"Who the heck is that guy?" the driver asked Fats as the two men stepped clear. "He seems to know what he's doing, and has a lotta guts."

"Huh!" grunted Fats. He knew the driver to be right on all counts, but the grunt was more to say Al had gotten his ass in a sling on this one.

With Blacky running to and fro shouting instructions, and the synchronized efforts of the tow truck pulling and the Mack truck's drivetrain under power, inch by inch, the tanker was back on the road proper. As best that could be determined by what lighting there was, it was roadworthy.

In a state of excitement, the driver went from one to the other shaking hands. When he got to Al, he dwelled a little longer. Al felt the driver's hand trembling, no doubt from the excitement. He called out to Blacky:

"Blacky, this guy's pretty shaky; I better take the tanker out of the Canyon for him. Take my car and follow us out."

The driver's resistance to the idea was weak. He climbed aboard on the passenger's side while Al addressed Fats:

"We'll meet down at Live Oak service," he instructed.

The service station and highway diner was located at the bottom of Castro Hill (Highway 50), a few hundred yards down from the Crow Canyon entrance. As they wound their way out of the Canyon, the driver dominated the conversation:

"You have no idea how much I appreciate you fellows getting me out of that mess. And those two mechanics with the tow truck—the company'll get them out a check for their services. They're real good about paying. They should be, with the money they're raking in."

That last comment drew a question from Al:

"Hell, I thought gasoline was cheap, and the hauling can't be all that expensive. Or is it . . . ?"

The driver in his eagerness to talk, cut Al short with further comment:

"Cheap! Yeah, to the distributors. But not to where some of these loads go. Ya can't beli. . . "

"Huh! Ya mean this stuff isn't being hauled for distributors?" interrupted Al inquisitively.

"Not this load," came the quick answer.

"Well, who the hell's getting it, if not the distributors?"

"Big still operators — bootleggers. Ya can't blame the company. Why deliver it all to the distributors for peanuts when they in turn break it off in the bootleggers by doubling the price. Our company finally got smart; for a nickel more a gallon, we deliver direct to them. The bootleggers get the stuff cheaper and our company picks up an extra $200 a load. Not bad, eh?"

Al's head was swimming. He couldn't believe what he was hearing. He risked his ass in this screwball scheme of hijacking gasoline when for a couple hundred bucks over the distributor's cost, it could be bought and delivered to where he so designated.

The tanker in the lead, the caravan stopped at Live Oak service. Al scrambled off the tanker. He first encountered Fats. "I'll catch up to you tomorrow. Beat it!"

"As usual," responded Fats. "Hired and fired."

"That's not what I meant. Don't worry about it. You'll get paid. Just do as I say."

He next addressed Blacky bringing in his own car, and Kanaka with the tow truck:

"Park it over there."

Blacky parked the car in front of the diner, then walked up to his cousin as Al was giving him final instructions:

"Throw another $40.00 on the tow bill for the drive chains and hand it to the driver. They'll send ya a check—no questions asked. Then beat it, I'll see you guys tomorrow.

The two cousins had earned more money that night than they had in a month. Well worth the fractured jaw and dose of poison oak.

Al threw his arm around the shoulder of his newly made friend, Arty, and waltzed him into the diner for a piece of apple pie and a cup of coffee. He had things on his mind. They sat at a table near the window overlooking the yard and station area, puffed on a cigarette while at the same time ate their pie. Al leaned back, blew a blast of smoke out his nostrils and came right to the point.

"I wanna buy a load of that gasoline."

"Ya what?"

"That's what I said, and I mean the whole load—all 4,000 gallons of it."

"Ya mean, this load—tonight?"

"No, it's too late for us to handle it tonight—tomorrow night. Is it a deal?"

"Holy cow, you're serious."

"You bet, I'm serious."

"Now hold it a minute—not so fast. The Company will want proof of your ability to pa . . ."

Al figured the matter of payment would surface, so he reached in his leather jacket and slapped a bundle of bills on the table, enough to choke a horse. As he shuffled the edges, bills of all denominations up to $100 flashed in rapid succession. The driver never finished what he had to say, he just gasped. Al rose from his chair, pocketed the bundle and as he departed, said:

"Have the load at the roadhouse tomorrow night. I'll be there waiting for ya. By the way, what'll the full load cost?"

"Well . . . ah, ten cents a gallon plus a nickel—$600."

"Okay, the cash'll be there. See ya tomorrow night."

CHAPTER 10

Nineteen hundred twenty-five had seen the election of Earl Warren as District Attorney for Alameda County. He was truly untouchable and known for his integrity. By the end of 1926 and early 1927, his presence was being felt; however, federal agents were being uncooperative in his efforts to clean up the county's bootlegging industry. He was dedicated to putting the industry out of business, while the federal agents' and newly elected Sheriff Becker's main objectives were to make a personal profit, rather than shutting the industry down. What the agents knew about the bootlegging enterprises they kept to themselves.

By now the federal agents had figured out that a sizeable still was being operated somewhere just up Bellina Canyon—naturally they assumed it to be Mike's; their assumption was correct. Now all they had to do was to sneak past the two Soares brothers' ranches, verify their suspicions, then put the bite on Mike.

The first attempt was to approach John Soares, the guardian of the main entrance. This proved to be an experience in itself. As soon as the Hudson with the two federal agents stopped in John's yard, it was immediately surrounded with irate ranch dogs with no better dispositions than their master's. The perfumed smell of these two city slickers was putrid compared to the pleasant barnyard smells these dogs were accustomed to. No way could either man step out of the car among that pack of barking, snarling, snapping ill-tempered dogs. The agents did what they thought to be the next best thing, and that was the mistake of sounding the car's horn to announce their presence. The sudden disturbance sent chickens and other barnyard animals scurrying in outright panic. John's reaction to the intrusion was a fist waving barrage of profanity in broken English and Portuguese, with a heavy accent on the latter:

"What the hell are you doing? Shut up that horn! You make my chickens die—you die too!" he said as he approached the Hudson.

"We came to talk to you—we need some information," responded the senior agent while ignoring the threat.

"What you need and what you'll get are two different things. Get out of my yard!"

"Sir, are you threatening me? I'm a feder . . ."

John cut him short: "I don't threaten you — I'm gonna kick your ass!"

"We're federal agents—watch your step, mister!"

"No, you watch your step—this is my property—not your property!"

The statement was followed by a smattering of Portuguese profanity. There was no mistaking that the abusing insults were directed at the federal agents, along with the warning that if either one of them stepped out of the car, he would not only be mauled by the dogs, but would also have his ass kicked all over the barnyard. The furious onslaught of unrecognizable Portuguese words, along with gestures of clenched fists, was enough to convince the agents to turn their car around and head back out of the yard, accompanied by John's parting words in his heavily accented best English:

"You goddamned sons of whores, get out of my yard and stay out! You hear me?"

Assuming they could expect a similar reception when approaching Tony Soares, the guardian of the alternate entrance, the agents decided to first snoop around his barns and outbuildings during the night in hopes of finding some incriminating evidence that could be used to pressure Tony into a cooperative mood. In this case, the dogs would not be a threat; they determined that they were kept chained close to the main house. However, the agents had overlooked the next best thing to a pack of dogs, and that was a flock of barnyard geese. They were parked at Tony's gate talking it over:

"The full moon should give you plenty of light—use the flashlight only to identify the evidence," instructed the senior agent. "In any event, if you arouse the dogs, don't abort the mission—lay low until they calm down," he said to his cohort.

"Yeah, providing the rancher doesn't come out to investigate. If he does—I'm gonna hightail it out of there! By what I see, these cattlemen are tough as hell."

"They're not that tough. They just make a lot of noise—you don't need to worry, I can handle 'em."

"Oh yeah, I didn't see you step out of the car the other night."

"That was different . . . come on—get with it."

The cohort managed to penetrate the vigilance of the chained dogs by sneaking in from the rear of the barn area, but found himself trapped among a flock of hissing ganders determined to protect the geese and their clutches of eggs. The cackling, warning sounds and slapping of wings brought Tony out to the corrals in a hurry. In the bright moonlight, the intruder was assumed to be a snoopy federal agent retreating from the determined feathered barnyard guardians. Tony did not mince words:

"Halt or I'll shoot!" came the order, along with the pronounced click of a six-shooter's hammer being cocked ready to fire. Either sound was enough to stop the agent in his tracks.

"What the hell're you doing around here?" came the question in heavily accented Portuguese. The intruder identified himself as a federal agent, but it didn't cut any ice with Tony. As for the gun the agent was carrying in his shoulder holster, it's a good thing he chose not to go for it, because he would have found himself trying to stop an acorn size chunk of lead coming at him at eye level.

As it was with John, Tony lambasted the agent mercilessly. His final message was brief:

"You get the hell off my land and stay off!" he barked in his best Portuguese-punctuated English. Thus, the intruder departed hastily without further explanation. He had heard about the fruitlessness of trying to reason with an irate Portuguese cowboy rancher. To speed up his retreat, Tony fired a couple of shots over his head.

Again, while parked on Crow Canyon Road just short of John's gate, the two agents talked the situation over while nipping at a pint of whiskey. It was a quiet night. The stench of distillation waste wafting up from the creek below was strong to the nostrils. The senior agent spoke first:

"Damned that stuff smells strong. The creek is literally awash with that putrid stuff." He then added thoughtfully: "I doubt the still is on these two brothers' ranches. It must be further up the canyon." The senior agent was referring to Bellina Canyon.

"Maybe so, but those two Portagees are in on it in some manner or other. Why else would they be so goddamned nasty?" put in the cohort before adding: "That bugger was shooting at me the other night."

"Yeah, I'm sure you're right. After all, the road goes right through their yards. If nothing else, they'd certainly be paid something for that alone."

"OK, so we know the still is somewhere not too far up the creek, and we're pretty sure it belongs to this Dago called Mike. So why not just walk in and put the 'bite' on him?" suggested the cohort.

"Right, we'll do just that, and we'll do it right now. Drag the Dago out of bed if we have to."

The Hudson took off down the canyon heading for the chicken ranch. It swung into the driveway and stopped short of knocking the iron gate down. Its headlamps illuminated the entire front of the house, lighting up Mike's bedroom as well. He woke up to the slamming of car doors and men's voices. No question, these were not his men. The senior agent, followed by his cohort, marched brazenly up to the front door and proceeded to pound on it demanding a response while announcing that he was in fact a Federal Prohibition Agent, an unnecessary introduction since only a peabrain such as he would pull a stunt like this at this hour of night. Surges of fear struck the hearts of the family as they, too, were aroused by the disturbance.

Mike responded by opening the door, then stepped out on the porch. He wasn't about to let the agents in the house. Without further introduction, the dirty business of soliciting pay off (extortion) took place. Paying off federal agents was something that he knew he would sooner or later have to deal with, but, recognizing the unmistakable smell of alcohol on the agent's breath, a sure indication that he partook to drinking, left some doubts in his mind. Could the agent be trusted? He avoided the issue by refusing to acknowledge ownership of the still in question, and therefore stuck to his being a chicken rancher producing eggs. Not being able to budge Mike, the senior agent issued a stiff warning:

"Who do you think you're kidding with this chicken rancher crap? You're a bootlegger; a still operator. Once we get the goods on you, you'll pay, and plenty—or else!"

With that final comment, the agents left, but the next day, while sober, they plotted to actually raid the still—set an example—teach Mike a lesson.

"That still's not too far up that canyon. It should be easy to find. And, the Dago's the owner—no question," announced the senior agent while scanning Bellina Canyon from John's gate.

"How about the D.A.—we'll need some help."

"He'll be the last person to hear about it—if at all. We'll borrow a couple of agents from the San Francisco office—use 'em, then send them back. Then we'll deal with the Dago . . ."

"I get it—good idea . . ."

The plan was formulated; they'd follow the creek on foot and let the distillation discharge lead them up to the still. This meant parking their cars in the vicinity of the Edenvale grade school, walking down to Crow Canyon Creek to the rear of the school, then walking up the creek, picking up the Bellina Creek branch to the left, then following the creek past John's place. They would then sneak by Dutch Charley's, continue upstream to where the distillery waste was being discharged into the creek, thus leading them to the still at Tony's. Since they were not too sure how far up the creek the still was, the raid would be pulled off late afternoon at dusk, while there was still enough light to allow the agents to pick their way up the brushy creek and arrive at the still right at dark.

The raid was well planned and on target. It would no doubt have had a better measure of success if the senior agent in charge had wiped his mind clean of the shakedown dollars he expected to milk from Mike, and had concentrated more on the traits of the young Portuguese students that attended Edenvale school.

Tony's eldest son, also named Tony, a husky teenager, was attending school the afternoon the raid was being planned and rehearsed. Young Tony knew without a doubt that the men he saw that day in the area were federal agents and not the familiar bootleggers. He knew the paesani well, since it was he who would ride horseback over the ridge and down to the still to pick up an occasional 5 gallon barrel of Jackass for his dad. He also knew Mike. It had been only a few days before that Mike was run off the road and into the ditch just across from the schoolyard in trying to avoid a collision with one of Lang Transport Company's gasoline tankers. The tanker came around the bend hogging the road, leaving no choice but for Mike to swing his loaded Dodge touring sedan into the ditch. He was not about to unload his cargo of illegal supplies there in the road without some help, so he asked young Tony if he would hike up to the still and let his men know of his predicament. But young Tony having had strict orders not to leave the schoolyard for any reason whatever until school was out, had to refuse his request. So Mike hiked the approximate one and a half mile distance to the still, leaving the loaded car behind and unattended except for the watchful eye of young Tony. With this background knowledge, on the day of the planned raid, young Tony knew what was going on and what to do. He hurried home after school to report his findings.

Tony Sr., having been alerted of the presence of federal agents, kept a watchful eye on that evening's activities along that particular stretch of Crow Canyon road. Sure enough, the agents returned. There were four of them, prepared to hike up the creek and to the still site. Satisfied as to their intent, Tony instructed his son to saddle up and ride over the ridge and warn the paesani at the still of a possible raid.

Young Tony arrived at the still well ahead of the raiders who were now making their way slowly up the creek. Having sounded the alarm which caused the paesani to shut the still down and scatter into the wooded countryside, young Tony took it upon himself to strap a 5 gallon barrel of jackass across the back of his saddle before he too galloped off into the darkness. Once well out of sight of the still, he let the horse pick its own way up the hillside and to the top of the ridge where it paused to catch its breath. With his leg hooked over the saddle horn in a resting position, young Tony watched the raid in progress at the old house below. In the shadowed darkness, flashlight beams could be seen flickering throughout the house and about the premises in general. He single-handedly had thwarted the agents' ill-intended mission.

In disappointment, the senior agent addressed his men:

"We missed them — not by much, but nevertheless, we didn't get a single one of them. How'd they know we were coming? They must have a warning or signal system of some sort. No question—we need to know more about their methods of operation."

"Yeah, I see what ya mean. The dogs would have come after us had they heard us coming up the creek," answered his cohort, then adding: "The still's plenty hot; it hasn't been shut down for very long. And look at this," the cohort was now referring to a big cast iron skillet left simmering on the stove. He lifted the lid off and commented as he looked at its contents: "What the hell, take a look at this stuff. What the heck is it?"

The senior agent peered into the deep skillet, then commented: "I don't know. Looks like some kind of stew . . . what the hell . . . baby chicks!" He picked up a ladle and stirred into its contents, a thick tomato-base gravy, bringing a mixture of various size birds to the surface as he stirred. Had they not been feathered, they would have been recognized as sparrows, quail, bluejays, robins, meadowlarks, towhees and even woodpeckers, all simmering together in the form of a stew. Alongside the skillet, a pot of cornmeal (polenta) was ready for serving. What they were looking at was a poor man's supper, but savored by kings, or at least those that appreciated Italian homecooking.

"I don't like the looks of it, but it sure smells good," commented the cohort, while sniffing the aroma.

The senior agent didn't answer; he was deep in thought. All this effort got him nothing. With no one to finger the head Capo, namely Mike, he couldn't very well shake him down. He finally issued an order:

"Well, there's no point hanging around. Let's head back."

"Shouldn't we break up the still—dump the high proof—the Jackass?" asked one of the others.

Having second thoughts about the whole affair, without further explanation, the senior agent answered:

"No, let's just leave things the way they are, but we'll take a couple of casks of Jackass." His thirst for it dictated his decision. He was sure it was Mike's still by the quality of the product, but he needed more proof than that. He then added to his instructions: "Don't anybody say anything about this still or this night's incident. We'll keep it to ourselves, understand?" Not realizing that he had an ulterior motive, the San Francisco agents wondered, but nevertheless agreed.

CHAPTER 11

After the raid at Tony's place, Mike's friend, the Judge, warned him and advised him to shut the operation down completely or face the wrath of District Attorney Earl Warren. By now Earl Warren had put together several teams of investigators, "prohibition officers," working directly out of his office with no connection whatever with the federal agency, although some of the investigators were former federal agents. Their orders were to bypass the federal agency and go after bootleggers and stills directly.

The judge also told him that Warren was getting suspicious of bootlegging activity in and around the Castro Valley area. This time he did take the judge's advice and, therefore, saw fit to shut down the operation.

Livia's reaction to the news of the shutdown of operations was a deep sigh of relief. The strain was getting to be about as much as she could handle. To add to her delight, Mike announced plans to spend the coming summer in Italy visiting their parents and relatives whom they had not seen since leaving the old country. The delivery of the new 1927 deluxe Buick sedan that was to take the family across country to New York, added to the excitement.

Julio and his right-hand man, Narciso, one of the still operators, were to also make the trip with Mike's family. Mike's brother, Natale, and another paesano named Pioli were to remain and stay on the payroll to look after certain designated responsibilities during Mike's absence. Even though Natale was Mike's older brother, Mike did not feel comfortable leaving him in charge during his absence. His trustworthy old friend Matteoli, Julio's cousin, was the man he left in charge of the chicken ranch, as well as overseeing bootlegging business matters. Matteoli was his surname. Seldom if ever did anyone ever address him otherwise, no doubt as a matter of respect since he was looked upon as a knowledgeable person. He was at present living in Healdsburg, in Sonoma County, some 80 or so miles north of San Francisco. He was in the process of winding up and getting out of a bad ranching deal. Mike's offer had come at just the right time. It was indeed good news that his good friend Mike had hit it good and was requesting that he join him as his chief counselor and ranch manager, with added duties that would extend to the bootlegging operation itself. The offer was extended to include the family—housing had been arranged. This now made it possible to be with his family while working with Mike, rather than leaving them behind such as he had done during the wine hijacking campaign headquartered in San Bruno.

For Matteoli, it had been bad enough that the wine grape ranching business had fallen upon hard times, but to make matters even worse, he had unknowingly taken on a partner with a bad unshakable gambling habit. Such as it is with a drunk who insists on driving the car, the man insisted on handling the business and money matters of the partnership. He would insist on delivering the grapes himself to their individual customers who made their own wine, primarily located in San Francisco. Once the deliveries were made and the cash collected and pocketed, the urge to gamble would get the best of him. Invariably he would return to the ranch a day or two later with empty pockets and expressing indignation when questioned about the matter of money. Needless to say, under the circumstances, the grape ranch was lost anyway, so Matteoli might just as well walk away from it and try something different.

It was an exciting emotional moment when the two families, the Butis and the Matteolis, were united. What came as an even greater satisfaction to Matteoli was seeing what Mike had accomplished since the last time the two men worked together at San Bruno. This now gave Matteoli and his family new hope, an incentive to apply themselves even more so to the task of getting a sound foothold; a slice of the American dream was within their grasp. Prohibition had opened the door to opportunity for them as well. They were to live in the main house during the Buti family's absence, with full privileges of all other available facilities. A credit line was set up with the local businesses to accommodate the needs of the family, as well as for ranch supplies. This, along with an advance in salary, put Matteoli in position to manage the ranch operation in a businesslike and orderly manner.

At this point in time he was not to concern himself with the still operation since it was now shut down. He would, however, oversee the process of converting the inventory of high-proof alcohol to drinking-grade Jackass Brandy. He was also to oversee the matter of distributing the finished product as well as high proof alcohol to the few select customers that were to be kept supplied during Mike's absence.

However, this overall authority being vested in Matteoli didn't set well with Mike's older brother, Natale. Such as it often is when the general manager of a company appoints an outsider to a responsible management position, the least qualified and less knowledgeable employee always seems to think he is the one that should have been appointed to the job, especially if he is related to the boss.

Unlike Natale, who was single, Pioli was married with a family and being a friend of Matteoli's, he and his family would also live in the main house during Mike's absence. His primary duty was as a salesman on a commission basis; certain designated districts of San Francisco were his territory. Pioli was a short, extremely overweight runt of a man, who always wore a baggy unpressed suit. His flabby jowls hung over his shirt collar giving the impression that his soup-splattered tie was growing out of a crevice between his chin and his chest. He wore his undersized stiff-brimmed felt hat jammed down on his bald head, giving further credence to his look of stupidity. He tried to present himself as a big shot, when actually he was the most dispensable of the lot. He, along with Natale, soon proved to be traitors.

Al, now on his own, wasted little time in getting back in business. His reputation as Mike's driver opened doors to a plentiful supply of wholesale whiskey. With his share of profits, he acquired a luxurious 1927 Cadillac Sedan. The car's sturdiness was ideally suited for converting it into a unique alcohol tanker. He constructed steel tanks of various shapes that once welded in place throughout the car's undercarriage became an integral part of the car. Cleverly placed ornaments disguised the filling and dispensing devices of the interconnected whiskey holding tanks.

The switching system of the car's carriage lights was modified so as to signal customers as to whichever side the car should be approached in order to get their containers filled. Money was slipped through slots in doors much like slipping mail through a mail slot. Curbside transactions could be performed fast and efficiently without the need to step out of the car or as much as opening a window.

Al's car with its unique delivery system, had become known as the "Jackass Express".

CHAPTER 12

It was early morning during the first week of May 1927, when the deluxe Buick sedan, with Mike at the wheel and Livia, the kids, Julio and Narciso, pulled out of Crow Canyon heading south down the central valley of California. The route, made up mostly of unpaved, dusty gravel roads that stretched for hundreds of miles across uninhabited deserts and up steep winding mountain grades that put the loaded Buick and its driver to the extreme test, was known as the Santa Fe Trail. It followed a course over the Tehachapi Mountains and across the Mojave desert to Needles, California; across Arizona and New Mexico to St. Louis, Missouri; then to New York where the Buick was loaded aboard a freighter and transported across the Atlantic to Genoa, Italy, while the family boarded the luxury liner "Roma," also bound for the seaport of Genoa.

The drive from Genoa to his hometown that bears the family name, the city of Buti, was to remind Mike that the narrow streets and cluttered roadways of Italy were not designed to accommodate the big sedan. Regardless of the difficulty of getting around, he reveled at the hospitality extended by his beloved Italy.

As the summer wore on, Mike's thoughts were far from the matter of returning to America, but as it usually turns out, eventually all good things must come to an end. The letter from America, postmarked in Hayward, California, that awaited him at Cascine di Buti, upon his return from a week's stay at the seashore with his family, brought about the abrupt end to a glorious, enjoyable summer vacation.

As he read the letter, his younger brother, Santi, watched Mike's face change from a pleasant, relaxed expression to an angered, worried look, accompanied by nervous tension within. Halfway through the reading, Mike looked up and away from the letter. His lips were trembling as he answered Livia's question: "Yes, the letter is from Matteoli."

"What does he say?" she asked in an alarmed manner.

Mike swallowed hard while trying to control his emotions. "My brother Natale, and the fool Pioli, have double-crossed me," he answered. "I will read the rest of the letter in the privacy of our room," he said as he turned from the others gritting his teeth. These few words spoken by his older brother caused Santi to commence trembling. He was well aware of what the eventual consequences of such an act of treason within an Italian clan could bring. So did their parents, the mother and father of these three brothers. They did their best to comfort Santi and Livia, but with clasped hands in the form of prayer, they could only extend sympathetic glances towards their son as he walked away.

In the confines of his room, Mike sat down in the chair at the window. By the light afforded through its lacy curtains, he proceeded to read the rest of the letter being held in his trembling hands. In order to better digest its contents, he proceeded to start reading it from the very beginning:

"Dear Mike,

It is with a depressed heart that I must report to you my inability to fulfill your expectations in administrating the responsibilities you have instilled in me. I did my best, short of using extreme violence in trying to thwart your brother, Natale, and our paesano, Pioli, from committing what I believe to be an act of treason on their part. Since the two men were in your employ, I advised against them joining Al and some of the others in setting up their own still in Sonoma County, and therefore engaging in an independent bootlegging operation. As your counselor, I can say that Al and the others are not at fault. Since they were no longer in your employ, this in itself could be considered justification for them to embark on such an endeavor. It should be considered an act of loyalty on Al's part that he chose to set up the operation in Sonoma County and well away from your territory. But Natale, and his friend Pioli, joining them is another matter entirely, especially since they were still in your direct employment."

The letter went on to say that in order to raise the cash for their share, the two men took liberties with inventoried alcohol. In addition to pocketing the proceeds from its sale, they also purchased supplies on credit in Mike's name, and helped themselves to his dwindling supply of sugar. Their intent, or at least the argument they gave Matteoli, was that they would pay it back from their share of profits from the new venture. This Matteoli did not believe. They ignored his demands to the extent of threats to his well-being if he were to intervene. They were crazed with the misconception that they, too, could duplicate what Mike had accomplished.

Mike read on:

"However due to unforeseen circumstances, the still was raided shortly after full production got underway. Neither Natale nor Pioli got caught up in the raid. As much as I would like to have seen them both go to jail, I do feel that this is for the better, since being traitors such as they are, they no doubt would have borne witness against you in order to save their own hides. Now they are left with a debt to pay, both to you and the sugar suppliers, which they cannot pay. I have been informed that the sugar, as well as other supplies, were purchased in your name on your account. Because of their conduct, I have refused to recognize them as employees and therefore suspended their pay accordingly," wrote Matteoli.

"Good boy," growled Mike in low, menacing tones. He was gritting his teeth as he read the next several pages that related to the two traitors' conduct on the night they realized their predicament. Having escaped the raid in Sonoma County, they had arrived at the ranch in Crow Canyon near midnight. The Dodge Brothers touring sedan they were driving was registered to Mike and could have been traced and connected to his own bootlegging operation, therefore implicating him in the Sonoma County venture. During these past few weeks, Matteoli was always relieved to be awakened by the car's chugging sound as it pulled into the backyard of the ranch in the middle of the night.

But on this late night, the night of the raid, instead of Pioli retiring upstairs to his room in the main house, to be with his wife and two young daughters, and Natale retiring to the bunkhouse across the yard, the two men followed each other into the basement of the main house. They now engaged in a heated discussion as they reviewed their previous activities that got them into this predicament; each accusing the other of being responsible for their going astray. The discussion escalated to a heated argument, then to actual blows being struck at each other. The thrashing sounds of the two men engaged in fierce battle aroused the rest of the upstairs occupants. Pioli's daughters were crying hysterically as their mother screamed down the long stairwell leading to the scene of the battle.

Matteoli, hearing her pleading and sensing what was taking place, took the time to dress and put his shoes on before descending the stairwell to the basement. Just as he was about to start down, he could hear the threats of death co-mingled with the crashing sounds of fists against flesh, and choking, gasping sounds of strangling, as each combatant momentarily got a grip on the other's throat in between the blows being administered. Matteoli hesitated; common sense told him if he were to intervene at this point, both fighting men in their fit of anger could very well turn on him. He therefore chose to call out as he slowly descended the stairs:

"Have you men lost your minds? Stop this nonsense! Now!!" Raising his voice to the pitch of a frustrated military commander, he called out again: "Fools! Stupid fools! Natale—Pioli! I command you to stop! Think of your families—the consequences!"

His repeated demands finally bore fruit. Pioli, splattered with blood about the head and shoulders, thoroughly thrashed to near death, stumbled and fell at the foot of the stairs. Knowing that he must now intervene, Matteoli stepped over the fallen man to face the oncoming Natale who, in his crazed frame of mind, would surely kill his opponent. Taking a fighting stance and in a firm, steady voice commanded:

"Stop! Or join Pioli—it's your choice!"

Aware of Matteoli's combat military training, and considering his own thrashed condition, Natale, uttering obscene profanity, turned and retreated to the bunkhouse across the yard.

What details of the fight that were omitted in the letter, Mike was able to surmise. He was indeed in a frame of mind to deal with the two men in a harsh manner upon his return to America. Livia and her mother-in-law were waiting at the base of the stairs as he made his way down to the living room, while still holding the letter in his hand. The worried look about their faces indicated that they had a pretty good idea of the contents of the letter. His face had an expression of disbelief as he thrust the letter forward while walking slowly toward his wife and mother. He shook the pages violently as he muttered: "How could my own brother have done this to me? I was good to him. Why did he turn against me, I don't understand it?" The answer was there, but Mike couldn't see it.

Among the Italians, the older brother is not to be surpassed by the younger brother. This applies to marriage, financial position, family affairs, and other matters, regardless of their importance. Whether or not the older brother is qualified to be on top or in command is neither here nor there; the pecking order must prevail. In this case, Mike being the younger of the two, and his accomplishing what he did, caused a deep jealousy and resentment to build up in his older brother. While the younger brother is pushing like hell to make a mark for himself, and hopefully to be looked upon with pride by his elders; the truth of the matter is, the more accomplished, the deeper goes the resentment, and in some cases even to the extent of vindictive vendetta-like clashes taking place within the family. Generally, you will see other older brothers and sisters take the side of the oldest of the two in dispute. However, the youngest in the family, being just as proud of his next oldest brother, may join with the younger of the two brothers in dispute. The Buti clan was no exception. In this case, Natale, taking advantage of his absence, jumped at the opportunity to outdo his younger brother, Mike. Santi, the youngest of the three, expressed his loyalty to Mike, especially since he was the one sending money back to the family in Italy.

The two most important women in Mike's life had good reason to express their distressed feelings. Italian women know their men, their egos, their ambitions and goals, as well as whatever else makes them tick. The women's job was not to try to patch things up between the two brothers because that would be futile, but instead, try to keep them apart in order to avoid an escalated argument that could very well culminate into a vendetta to the death.

In the remaining days that the family was preparing for their return trip back to America, Mike's mother, with Livia's blessings, dispatched a letter to her son Natale, warning him of Mike's present state of mind. As it is justifiably so with a mother, she will protect her children regardless of their misconduct or behavior. Mike also sent a letter, only it was addressed to Matteoli, advising him of his plans to depart from Italy as soon as arrangements could be made. Barring any unforeseen delays, the departure would take place shortly. Julio would once again accompany the family on the return trip. Narciso chose to remain in Italy.

All went well and there appeared to be no problem with the departure. However, Mike's cousin, a judge, insisted on accompanying the family to the seaport at Genoa, in order to assist in event a problem might arise that could delay the Buti's departure. The judge's presence proved to be a godsend, for Mike was detained without explanation, while his family, along with Julio, were hustled aboard ship and the Buick stored in its hold. Putting it bluntly to Mike, the officials in charge informed him that he would remain in Italy.

It was, of course, a scam concocted by persons in public office to shake him down for whatever dollars he had left. With his cousin, the judge's intervention, he was able to negotiate a settlement that insured his retaining sufficient funds to carry him through the journey home. The rage that boiled within him was now even more unbearable. The judge hustled his cousin aboard ship at the very last second of departure with some sound advice:

"Cousin Mike," he said, "you know what Italian public officials are like, surely American officials are not much different. Vent your rage on the seas, they will be more understanding."

Apparently in the days that followed, Mike did indeed communicate with the sea, for halfway across the Atlantic, one of the worst storms in history battered the ship and its passengers. The sea had joined with Mike in venting its rage as well.

As soon as the Buick was placed on the dock at New York, Mike hustled his family along with Julio into it and headed for home. This time he drove due west, picking up Highway 50 across the plains and Rocky Mountains, in as much of a straight line to Hayward, California, as was possible. The threat of early winter storms in the mountain passes were trivial matters compared to the storm that raged within him. Since Livia was a licensed and accomplished driver, they drove in shifts in order to cut the travel time. At one point, on a long stretch of rough gravel road, with Livia at the wheel, a tire gave way to the constant, relentless pounding of rubber on the washboard road surface. Outright disaster was avoided only because of Mike's quick instinct to grab the steering wheel away from his wife's grasp, who was struggling to maintain control of the heavy car as it careened from side to side scattering gravel in all directions. The cause of the blowout could be attributed to the same reason that was contributing to her shattered nerves—he was pushing too hard.

Julio calmly advised Mike to back off a little, lest he sacrifice his family for the like of settling a score with his brother. But it was not only the score to settle with his brother that was pushing him to the brink of disaster; it was also the eagerness to get back and reorganize his gang of paesani into an effective working organization.

The Buick pushed on, across the seemingly endless plains, up over the steep winding passes of the Rockies, bucked the winds that swept across the barren lands of Utah, then rattled relentlessly over the dusty washboard roads of Nevada. Steaming, it topped the high Sierras, the last of the tough grueling trip across country. Having held together remarkably well, the car descended the Sierras into the fertile Sacramento Valley, homeward bound.

75

CHAPTER 13

The two letters from Italy arrived simultaneously at the ranch in Crow Canyon. Matteoli handed Natale the letter addressed to him and proceeded to open the one addressed to himself. Stepping a few yards apart while still standing in the back yard, the two men proceeded to read the different messages of urgency contained in the two letters. As they read on, there would be an occasional pause, accompanied with a sharp glance and meeting of eyes, then without uttering a word, the reading would proceed. Once the contents of the two letters were well-digested, the two men faced each other as if preparing for combat. Natale, voice trembling, eyes expressing rage, was the first to speak:

"You . . . damn you! You informed my brother Mike of my unfortunate adventure while you pretended to be my friend. Given the chance, I could have explained the affair. He didn't have to know everything. Now look what you've done, you villain!"

Although angered at the inference, Matteoli expressed calmness in responding to Natale's fearful, vengeful outburst:

"Apparently the letter you have received has warned you of the inevitable consequences you can expect to encounter because of your act of treason towards your brother. As for my informing him of your's and Pioli's traitorous conduct, it was my duty to do so."

"Pioli had just as much to do with this matter as I," blurted Natale. "Why just me, how about him?"

Matteoli responded with a firm, to-the-point accusation:

"When dealing with traitors, the motive is as much of importance as the act itself. Pioli's motive was strictly confined to profit, but your's was as much to satisfy an ego to be the 'Capo,' which you are not qualified to be. Your intention was not only to set yourself up in business for profit by taking liberties with your brother's property, but his credit as well. It has also come to my attention that you had approached his customers with the intent to steal them from him." Matteoli now took several steps closer to Natale as if to prepare himself for physical combat as he added to his last comment:

"You are a vindictive traitor, motivated by jealousy and envy brought

76

about by your own shortcomings that cannot stand up to your younger brother's qualifications as a capo; and for that, I spit at you with a reminder that if Mike is not capable of giving you your just due, I certainly will." With this comment, Matteoli let fly a gob of spit intended to hit Natale in the face rather than fall short and splatter his trousers. He then added: "And as for Pioli, you can be sure he'll also get his just due."

This now unnerved Natale. He was well aware of Matteoli's Italian military training. Trembling nervously with a flushed expression, he retreated from Matteoli's slow, forward, menacing movement. He was well aware that he would have to pay the consequences for having committed one of the worst offenses imaginable against the organization, especially his own brother. Now he had Matteoli, with the ability and frame of mind to terminate his life if need be, moving towards him clutching a letter of confidence and authorization from the 'real' head capo. Natale backed off—headed for the bunkhouse—grabbed up a few of his belongings and headed out the gate on foot. His sudden departure from the ranch avoided a fatal conflict between the two men. The last that was heard of him was that he was on his way back to Italy rather than wait around to confront Mike.

As for Pioli, he had no choice but to remain in the vicinity since he did have a family to consider. It was no doubt his family status, as well as Matteoli's sympathetic feelings towards a fool, that would help temper Mike's rage when the inevitable confrontation did take place upon his return. There was little time to waste in getting the matter settled.

To spare their families the agony of witnessing what might turn out to be a bloody affair, the three angry men stomped past the chicken houses and continued down the roadway through the vineyard until they reached the creek. The three wives and children remained at the house to wait out the confrontation. The best they could do was to comfort each other in despair, and pray that their husbands would in some manner work out their differences without the need to engage in physical combat.

Livia's mental stability was shattered when Pioli's wife, in a statement of fearful desperation, announced that her husband was carrying a concealed handgun on his person. The three women made a sensible decision in not rushing down to the creek to announce the matter of the gun, for to do so could have triggered the pea brain of the idiot carrying it to react brazenly, with fatal results.

Matteoli's military training came into play once again. Sensing the presence of the handgun tucked under Pioli's shirt and into his trousers, he stepped behind him and grabbed at the gunman's coat collar and lapels with both hands, jerking his coat backwards and down, pinning both his arms in a straightjacket position. In a swift move, while still holding the coat collar firmly with his left hand, he then reached around Pioli's fat belly with his right hand and retrieved the handgun.

Mike was momentarily awestruck as he witnessed the fast maneuver that disarmed the unsuspecting gunman. A combination of fear and anger sent him into a rage as Matteoli let go of the collar and stepped around to face the now bewildered former friend. Putting himself between Mike and Pioli, while still clutching the pistol, he came up fast and hard with his right foot, planting his boot into the startled gunman's crotch. The smashing blow to his testicles buckled him. As he staggered forward, the butt of the gun slamming against his head sent him stumbling to the ground in agony. Now that Matteoli had his attention good and proper, he stepped aside to allow Mike to lambast the disabled gunman with insults, threatening gestures, and a fair ration of unmentionable sex-oriented vulgar profanity. Mike regained his composure long enough to allow the injured man to get back on his feet, retrieve his hat, and give a brief accounting of his traitorous conduct. It was apparent that the sums of money collected by Pioli from the sale of high-proof alcohol in his San Francisco territory had been spent. It was gone. There was, however, one load that was still owed on and, according to him, collectable.

With the rage within him escalated to near murder, Mike growled with unsteadiness:

"You knew better than to leave the alcohol without the money exchanging hands! What distracted you . . . ? A woman—a whore . . . ?

The question need not be answered. Pioli's sudden change of expression, an unblinking stare of astonishment accompanied with sagging, heavy jowls jerking his mouth open, told it all. Nevertheless, shifting his stare to Mike's feet, with trembling voice, he muttered in a pleading manner: "She was not a whore . . . a Sicilian woman . . . I beg of you to not ment . . . . "

Mike cut him short with a degrading comment:

"You simple-minded, bloated fool," he said in disgust. "What kind of woman but a paid whore would have anything to do with you? You were set up!! No! I won't mention your affair to your wife. She's too good . . . she'll be spared the embarrassment." He then directed an order to Matteoli: "See to it that this bastard stays out of my sight."

Once the interrogation was finished, Matteoli stepped in once again offering the traitor some sound advice, which was taken without argument. He agreed to move out of the area of Mike's influence and above all to keep his mouth shut.

Not trusting him, Mike wasted no time in getting over to San Francisco to collect the money still owed for the high proof. The person was unknown to Mike, but by following Pioli's directions and method of contact, he did manage to find the person at his place of business. This turned out to be an old shack of a building in the worst and toughest section of San Francisco. Since the man could only be contacted at night, that is when Mike paid him a visit. After having given the proper password, he accepted the offer to enter the dimly-lit building, only to be confronted by an unsmiling, unblinking, tough-appearing gangster. Nevertheless, he let it be known that he was there to collect the overdue payment in full. It was then that Mike realized the reason Pioli had not collected the payment himself.

While maintaining his stare, and with unblinking eyes affixed to Mike, the gangster calmly raised his right arm level with his line of sight while pulling the hammer back on the .38 caliber revolver he was holding. In his heavy, accented, Sicilian-Italian tongue, he called out to an accomplice in the background whom Mike couldn't clearly see:

"Nick, shall we pay him?" he asked.

"Yes, in full," came the answer, followed by a chuckle. The way it was said told Mike that he had made a mistake—he was in trouble. Sure enough, while steadying the gun, the gangster snarled:

"You heard him. How do you want it, in the head, or . . . ?"

"Forget it . . . what's a load of alcohol amongst Italians?" responded Mike nervously as he turned away from the gangster while stepping back through the door he had just entered. Needless to say, he left the scene empty-handed. These men were without question, 'Mafiosi.'

Facing the threat of guns coming into play in such rapid succession set Mike back on his heels. To add to his nervous state of mind, there was now news of machine gun-wielding hijackers moving into California from the Midwest. He had received word that a sizeable still operation in Sonoma County had been raided by submachine-gun wielding hijackers with mafia connections. The bootleggers were cleaned out of their stockpile of alcohol, whiskey, sugar, and supplies in general, as well as a bundle of cash. The bootleggers were found two days later tied up in the barn housing the still.

Other stories of truckloads of sugar and alcohol being hijacked along highways by armed gunmen, some believed to be renegade lawmen, were also being spread around. What peace of mind and easing of tension had been gained by Mike and Livia's summer vacation in Italy was by now completely wiped out.

"Michele," pleaded Livia, "give this bootlegging business up. Don't start up again. We have our family to think about. Can't you see what this business is doing to you?"

"The business is doing nothing to me," snapped Mike in anger. "It's the traitors such as my brother Natale and the fool Pioli that has upset the organization. We no longer have them to deal with, we'll start over again."

"There will be others," responded Livia, trying not to antagonize her husband. "And the many police officers you pay, do you think they can be trusted forever?"

"You worry too much. It would be best if you were to mind your household chores and leave business matters to me!" The response was firm, but the question went unanswered.

There was little point in her pursuing the matter much further, for it was obvious that his mind was made up. The dreaded thought of embarking on a full-scale bootlegging operation was heavy on Livia's mind. Despair was written all over her face. Her fear was displayed through sunken, hollow-eyed worried glances, glances directed at nothing in particular, as if she were scared to concentrate on any one particular thing. She talked out loud to herself, asking herself questions, then answering them in a like manner, as if carrying on a conversation between two people. To her, this whole bootlegging affair was shear madness, but such as it was among Italian immigrants, seldom if ever did a woman's feelings about such matters have much of an impact on their husband's ambitions.

Mike, Julio, Matteoli and Al got together again in hopes of picking up the pieces and getting back in operation. They would have to if they ever expected to recover their losses. Their meeting was in an atmosphere of old friends and business associates getting together to plan the needed strategy to set up shop again. Matteoli had already apprised Mike of Al's ill-fated venture in the bootlegging business. But, nevertheless, to put the matter to rest, Mike insisted that Al explain the affair in his own words for the benefit of all present, and so he did.

He went on to say how the still and all its related paraphernalia was offered to him by a dealer that dealt in such equipment. What he was not told was that the still had been raided and confiscated just months before from the very same location where he had chosen to set it up. Once confiscated from the previous owner by the Sonoma County Sheriff's Department, federal agents took possession of it; then, instead of destroying it, turned around and sold it to the dealer, no doubt pocketing the cash for themselves. So, no sooner had Al's operation gotten under way, the Sheriff's Department got wind of it and made its move.

The still was located in the approximate location of the rattlesnake-infested petrified forest, halfway between the communities of Calistoga and the city of Santa Rosa, approximately a half-mile up a dirt road that branched off the winding, mountainous main road. The paesani operating the still had been warned to be aware of rattling noises because the snakes had a habit of frequenting the old buildings in search of mice and rats. With this thought in mind, they made it a point to establish their makeshift privy well back into the forest and away from the buildings. They were not about to pull their pants down and squat close to the ground to relieve themselves, not with snakes around. On the particular night of the raid, a paesano sitting across the plank with his pants down, did in fact hear the rustling of leaves and an occasional rattling noise. But it wasn't a rattlesnake. It was the handcuffs hanging from a deputy's belt, coming from some distance back in the forest. In the moonlight, he could detect shadows moving along towards the still. The first thought that came to mind was that rattlesnakes do not cast shadows. Wiping his butt before pulling his pants back up was not on his mind as he cinched his belt while at a dead run in the direction of the others. Once in shouting range, he gave the alarm, which automatically sent the others scattering through the moonlit forest.

That is, all but Al, who jumped behind the wheel of his red racing roadster, followed first by Guido, then Lepo, who was doing his damnedest to squeeze in, but ended up half in, half out of the cockpit as the roadster took off down the dirt road with its lights out and at full throttle. The light of the full moon was enough for Al to make out the confines of the dirt road as it wound its way between the trees and embankments. Fishtailing around a sharp curve, the roadster came upon the sheriff's car with the sheriff himself at the wheel and a deputy at his side, moving slowly up the road, also without the benefit of headlights. Upon seeing the roadster coming at him hell-bent for destruction, the sheriff braked, but Al, rather than brake and chance a spinout, swung up the embankment to his right, ripping out barbed wire fencing on the way up, then again on the way back down, picking up the road again downhill from the sheriff's car. Outbursts of horror-induced profanity commingled with earsplitting sounds of snapping fenceposts and screeching barbed wire rising above the laboring sound of the roadster's revved up engine, echoed throughout the still of the night.

It was difficult to determine whether Guido's normally beautiful mop of curly hair was now straight as hog hair because of the wind blowing through it, or the fright instilled within him. Wide-eyed, Lepo, with one leg in the cockpit and the other dangling outside with his foot searching desperately for a foothold, was clawing at every crack and crevice of this streamlined racing roadster without benefit of running boards. His plight made little difference to Al. Once past the sheriff's car, he put the accelerator to the floorboard and that's where it stayed until they crossed the county line on the opposite side of the valley.

As for the rest of the paesani, when they encountered barbed wire fences in their head-long dash through the moonlit countryside, they hurdled them; those that could not, either went under or through them, ripping and tearing their clothing to shreds. In either case, they lost little time distancing themselves from the scene of the raid.

As serious as the matter was of reactivating the still, Al's report brought about a relaxing round of chuckles and laughter. Now back to the matter of business, Al was quick to remind Mike of the need for a fast, powerful car that could outrun the Hudsons and Essexes that were being used by the agents.

"Besides," he added, "we better concern ourselves with hijackers. There's some pretty rough characters operating out there, so I'm being told."

"Tell me about it . . . " responded Mike. "I'm convinced the man that put the gun to my head the other night was a Mafioso—one of Al Capone's men, a professional hijacker. And, by what I gather, he's not working alone. These men were sent out here for the sole purpose of hijacking us distillers . . ."

"Holy Christ! Capone—Mafiosi??" exclaimed Al.

"That's right. So tell me, what would you recommend?" asked Mike.

"A Buick such as yours," came the instant answer. "It would have the power to maintain speed under a full load. Yes, that's what we need—speed, or God help us . . ."

"Are you suggesting using my car for delivering alcohol— Jackass?" questioned Mike.

"No, I know of a 1925 Buick touring sedan that is in excellent condition, despite it being a used car. It's reasonable and it will do the job," answered Al in a positive manner.

"All right, then if this is your recommendation, we'll buy it. By the way, what color is it?"

"Dark blue with black canvas top and side curtains."

"Fine, a good color for night deliveries," responded Mike, then added: "Pass the word on to the others to report to work, we're back in business."

CHAPTER 14

The Natale-Pioli affair tended to accelerate Mike's changing attitude. There was now something tough about him; he was impatient and unyielding. Instructions were being given in the form of sharp orders, more of a bark, and much like a military commander. The paesani were responding like soldiers under siege; the clowning around gave way to stern discipline.

As Mike's friend the judge had warned, the heat was on. Reports from the news media were constant reminders that Alameda County District Attorney Earl Warren was on the warpath, as was Alameda County Sheriff Burton F. Becker, but for different reasons. Within 60 days of having taken office on January 1st, 1927, he put together a graft machine the likes of which had never been seen before. To stay in business, the bootleggers and still operators were expected to pay large sums of bribe money or take the risk of being put out of business, if not in jail. The news media was having a field day reporting the constant raids the sheriff's deputies (corrupt themselves) were pulling off against the hardheads that dragged their feet when it came time to pay up. And, the senior Federal agent, like a hungry hyena, had been constantly on the prowl, waiting patiently for the operation to start up again. He'd figured it right, and so boasted to his cohort:

"What did I tell ya, our friend Mike is at it again."

"How do you know—how can we be sure?" questioned the cohort.

"The truck. That International we saw the other night heading up the canyon was loaded; loaded with sugar."

"Hell, it could have been loaded with most anything. What makes you think it was sugar?"

"Because sugar is heavy, and if you hadn't noticed, it was moving along in its lowest gears. It was loaded with sugar, all right enough," stated the senior agent with confidence.

"Come to think of it, that clunker was steaming—pulling a heavy load for sure. Yes, you could be right."

"I know damned well I'm right! But, we'll stay clear of it—not interfere, lest we 'spook 'em.' We want them to get started good and proper before we move in for our cut."

However, unlike the federal agents, the Sheriff and his deputies were very much interested in sugar since it offered another avenue for them to shake the bootleggers down for more money; they'd confiscate it—legally hijack it, so to speak. So on the next night's schedule trip from Oakland, the deputies waited on the outskirts of Hayward for Guido Bronzini, Mike's truck driver, to come chugging up the highway with the sugar-laden International with the intent of intercepting the truck before reaching Crow Canyon. In the meantime, at the entrance to Bellina Canyon that branched off of Crow Canyon, just short of the Contra Costa County line, where the stills were located, John Soares, the rancher at the head of the canyon, was also waiting for the truck's arrival, but for a different reason than the deputies.

The heavy duty, chain driven International truck, with its solid rubber tires was ideal for hauling the heavy sugar since there was no concern for flat tires. However, it was not well suited for the hilly dirt road of Bellina Canyon, especially during wet weather. So the load of sugar sacks had to be transferred from the covered, canvas-draped truck bed to John's heavy duty freight wagon pulled by a team of five horses, and hauled up to the still. John, along with his oldest son, Antone, were waiting up for Guido to arrive with the load of sugar, since Mike was paying a premium for this service. However, on this night, the rendezvous was not about to take place as scheduled because by now the International had been intercepted by the sheriff's deputies.

Guido, having been schooled to act dumb, and to speak only in Italian, pretending to know nothing in the way of the English language, reached in his coat pocket and started thumbing through the stack of $100 bills that was carried purposely for such an event. However, the officers were not only taking the payoff money being offered, but they also wanted information. As they plucked $100 bills from Guido's hands, they asked questions. Guido stuck with the shuffling of money rather than talk. Besides he insisted he couldn't speak English. That would have been all well and fine had it not been for the fact that these two officers were well schooled on how to get an Italian to talk. It hadn't been too long since he had arrived in this country, so he was still wearing his Italian-made shoes with thin leather soles. While standing and bracing himself against the side of the truck, he was made to stand on one leg while an officer, gripping the pants cuff of his other leg, held it up in a cross position, exposing the soles of his shoe to the headlights. While standing aside so as not to shadow his target, the officer smacked Guido several times across the bottom of his foot with his billy club. The first couple of blows could be tolerated, but as a few more sharp whacks were added with additional force, he was able to muster up some knowledge of the English language. The interrogation now got underway in earnest. When asked again what he was hauling, Guido blurted out the word "zucchero" (the Italian word for sugar), along with a smattering of words in English. He was being taught the English language in a crash program.

"Now, that's better," said the officer, while slapping the billy club firmly in the palm of his hand. "So you're hauling sugar, how nice . . . where to?"

While keeping his eye on the billy club, Guido answered: "To the cannery, in Hayward."

"But you're going the wrong way. The cannery is on the other side of town. I think you're heading for Crow Canyon. There's no cannery in that direction, now is there?"

The officer knew damned well that the sugar was headed for Mike's still. The officer's knowledge of his destination with the sugar was no surprise to Guido. What did come as a surprise was that since these officers were so well informed, why were they bugging him? As far as he was concerned, they along with everyone else in the law enforcement business, was receiving their little cash-filled envelope on a regular basis. He asked himself the question: "What happened here, did the runner miss these two officers?" but, such was not the case.

The runner, an enterprising young man by the name of Billy Ralph, had not missed anyone. He was not only honest, but keen of mind as well. He had built up one hell of a money-making business among the bootleggers, acting as the runner delivering cash-filled envelopes to the predesignated proper authorities. At times the authorities would also entrust Billy Ralph to relay messages back to the bootleggers. For the most part, the return messages pretty much fell into one category, and that was asking for more money. The takers had no trouble finding all kinds of excuses or reasons for wanting or needing more money.

Apparently, Mike had been ignoring some of these return messages, so the sheriff had sent his official collector, a man by the name of Fred C. Smith, to advise him that a sizable contribution was long overdue. But, since the man was an automobile dealer and not a lawman, Mike ignored him as well.

After having swept the money out of Guido's hand, the interrogation resumed. With each additional whack of the billy club, Guido's vocabulary improved tenfold. If they'd kept it up long enough, he'd soon be reciting the Gettysburg Address.

"OK, let's go over this once again," said the officer. "Where are you hauling the sugar?"

"To Crow Canyon," came the immediate answer.

"Fine, that's better. And who are you hauling it for?" asked the officer as if he didn't already know.

"A man by the name of Mike." Guido felt there was no point in getting beat up for something they already knew.

"Ah, now we're getting somewhere. Where are the stills located?"

"I don't know for sure. They move them around." Well, at least this was somewhat the truth.

"Oh, then how do you know where to haul the sugar?"

Now that the whacking had stopped and the stinging feeling had subsided, Guido was able to think a little more clearly. He responded appropriately by saying:

"All I do is leave the truck there at the clubhouse. Where the sugar goes from there, I don't know." He was lying, but convincingly.

"You mean the whorehouse there at Norris Canyon?"

"Yes, that's the place."

The officers believed him, but not only did they confiscate the sugar, which was their intent in the first place, they decided to arrest him anyway in hopes of flushing out Mike.

Guido was hauled off to jail and held until Mike was able to get there and post bail, which amounted to paying a fine. That part was easy; the tough part was to get his truck back with the load of badly needed sugar that was being held for ransom in the name of "impounded evidence." However, getting the sugar back proved to be nothing more than a matter of buying it back from the sheriff.

When Mike appeared on the scene to rescue Guido and retrieve his truckload of sugar, he met the newly elected sheriff of Alameda County, Burton F. Becker, for the first time. Mike not only retrieved the load of sugar, but also a not-too-friendly piece of advice from the sheriff. Coming right to the point, he had this to say:

"The next time my confidential operator, Mr. Smith, calls on you, I want you to be a little more courteous to him. Do you understand me?" said the sheriff firmly.

"You mean the automobile dealer from San Leandro?" questioned Mike.

"Yes, that's who I mean," came the sharp answer.

"But I don't need a new automobile," pleaded Mike. "I told him that."

"He has something much more important than an automobile to sell you, hear him out."

The firmness of the sheriff's statement caused Mike to swallow hard and cut short his protest. The sheriff didn't have to add the "or else."

Not too long after this conversation, Mr. Smith showed up at Mike's place with something other than an automobile to sell; namely, "protection," protection from the sheriff's own department. This time Mike didn't rudely run him off; all he said was, "how much?" The answer was brief and to the point, "Five hundred dollars." Mike paid up. After that incident, sugar deliveries went uninterrupted, that is, from law enforcement agencies.

By now the original hoard of sugar had been exhausted, thus necessitating the need to purchase sugar from a well known supplier in Oakland by the name of Damonte—well known not only to bootleggers, but also to professional hijackers, thus posing an even greater threat.

So a couple of weeks later while working his way through the streets of West Oakland with a load of sugar, Guido, behind the wheel of the International accompanied by his brother Lepo, noticed a car following him. He glanced into the rearview side mirror once again to verify his suspicions, then announced:

"We're being followed. There's a car tailing us. Now what the heck do you suppose that's about?" inquired Guido as if expecting an answer to the question.

"What? Where . . . what did you see?" asked Lepo with a frightful question. The constant fear of police officers and hijackers during these late night activities kept him wide-eyed and jumpy. The fact that he was the older of the two didn't make him any braver. Not having a rearview side mirror on his side, he couldn't see anything behind the truck, so he had to rely on Guido. "Are you sure we're being followed?" he asked nervously.

"I'm sure. As far as I can make out, we're being followed."

"How many are there? Maybe it's the police . . . what'll we do?" Lepo was squirming around ready to jump.

"Calm down. It's not a police car. They're probably hijackers after the sugar." This was even worse news to Lepo.

"Hijackers!" he exclaimed in a state of shock. "Stop! Stop! Let 'em have the truck. Let's make a run for it. Holy Christ, hijackers!" he repeated while extending his foot out on the running board, ready to jump.

"For God's sake, quiet down. They haven't asked for it yet. Get back in the truck before you break your neck."

"Christ, I'm scared. I wish Al was here."

"You better wish he's not here. The way you're acting, he'd kick your ass, brother-in-law or not."

Guido made a sensible decision. As he approached Broadway, he swung to the left off 7th Street and headed up the well-illuminated boulevard. Driving past the pawn shops, he parked at the entrance of the all-night dance parlor, the "Dime Jigs." The tail car following made the same maneuver except that it continued up the street and parked in the next block up, within sight of the truck.

"Come on," said Guido to his brother, "let's go upstairs."

"That's a 10 cent dance hall. I'm not going in there. I can't dance," complained Lepo.

"It's about time you learned. Come on, let's go."

They left the truck parked under the street lamp. Guido, following his brother, hesitated long enough to see a police car pull up alongside the tail car up the street. The driver of the tail car appeared to be talking to the cops through the open window. It was obvious they knew each other.

"Look at that, they're talking to the cops," said Guido.

"No, you look. I'm leaving."

"And abandon the truck?" questioned Guido.

"The hell with it—why not?"

"Because your brother-in-law will catch up to us and kick our ass all over Broadway, that's why."

"The hell with him. I'm not going up against hijackers on his account." As a matter of fact, Lepo wouldn't go up against anybody, for any reason. Guido didn't feel much different, but the comment did give him an idea:

"Let's get upstairs; there's a telephone up there. We'll call Al. It's pretty late, he should be home by now."

The call was placed. Sure enough, Al was home, in bed, but no matter, he took the call. Having been dragged out of bed, he didn't give Guido much of a chance to explain his predicament before jumping all over him.

"Where in hell are you guys?" Hearing the dance music in the background didn't set too well with him either. The question was firm; it had to be answered.

"At the 'Dime Jigs', down on Broadway. We think . . ."

That's all the further Guido got before he was lambasted with a barrage of profanity, unbefitting a Madam in the slummiest whorehouse in town.

"What the hell are you doing in a dime jig? Where the hell is Lepo? Don't tell me he's dancing? Damn it, get that sugar up to the still!" Al wasn't mincing words.

"Wait a minute," pleaded Guido. "For crying out loud, listen to me. We're being hijacked . . . I mean, there's somebody following us. We think they're after the sugar, and . . ."

"Where'd you pick up the load?" cut in Al.

"At Damonte's."

"I know that—damn it! At his warehouse or at the railroad siding?"

Delfino Damonte was the proprietor of the California Beverage Supply Co. Not only did he deal in commercial and home brewing and winemaking supplies, but also sugar, and lots of it. He'd buy a carload of sugar which would then be spotted at a railroad siding in West Oakland and sold to boot-leggers directly from the railroad car by the truck load, or from his ware-house located at 6th Street, a couple of blocks west of Broadway.

"At the railroad siding. What difference does it make?" questioned Guido.

"Maybe it's his men following you, keeping an eye out . . ."

"No, they're not. Delfino himself was there with his son and another kid to help with the loading. These are not the same guys, I'm telling you . . . "

"What's Lepo think?" cut in Al in a more understandable manner.

"He's scared stiff and wants to abandon the truck."

"What?! Abandon the truck??" screamed Al unbelievably. "You tell that brother-in-law of mine that I'll kick his ass for even thinking of such a thing."

Bringing up the matter of Lepo wanting to abandon the load of sugar was a plus for Guido for Al assured him he'd be there posthaste. Just sit tight.

His wife's pleading to not leave the house at such a late hour did little to change Al's determination to get to the bottom of this hijacking threat. He was dressed and on his way in a flash. But he wasn't going alone. Knowing that neither of the two Bronzinis were much in the way of scrappers, he stopped off to pick up his buddy Fats Meehan, whose two great loves were drinking beer and brawling. Dragging Fats out of bed was like wrestling a bear having just emerged from hibernation. Grudgingly, he agreed to go along, but not until he let it be known that if he, Al, didn't someday get his ass kicked, he'd sooner or later do the job himself.

By the time they got to Broadway the police car had since departed, but not the tail car, a Durant sedan, with its two occupants obviously waiting for the International to resume its laborious task of hauling the load of precious sugar through the dimly lit streets of Oakland so they could hijack it.

Fats, having spent most of his youth in the Melrose district of Oakland among Italians, having gained enough knowledge of their language to en-able him to follow the quarrelsome conversation, interrupted the discussion by asking Al a logical question:

"Who do ya think they are?" he said, referring to the two occupants of the car parked up the street.

"Bootleggers . . . hijackers after sugar. Who else?" answered Al with an added comment: "Just because they were talking to cops doesn't mean any-thing. They could be in on it."

"Maybe they're Federal Agents?"

"No, not likely. In this town, the cops won't have anything to do with Feds. No question, they're hijackers, and since there's only two of them and they don't know who you and I are, maybe we can walk up and get the jump on them. We'll settle this matter here and now," said Al with determination.

Lepo had his own announcement to make: "I'm leaving; the hell with the sugar. They could be a couple of Capone's men!"

"Oh no you're not. You stay with Guido. Once we've got those guys occupied, pull out and head for Hayward. Stay on East 14th, there's more lighting—just in case."

Guido and his brother remained within the confines of the "Dime Jigs" while Al and Fats headed up to the next block. The pronounced fragrance of fresh gardenias emitting from corsages worn by the shapely dime girls (as much prostitutes as anything else) could be considered stimulating when practicing their trade but under the present circumstances, the exotic fragrance now wafting their way was nauseating to Lepo who related it to a funeral parlor rather than anything else.

"Let's get the hell out of here," urged Lepo. "I don't want to die in a place like this . . ."

"Why not?" quipped Guido. "I can think of worse places to die in. Jesus, look at the saddlebags on that one, will you."

"You say that because you're not married, but I am. I want to go home!"

"What for? You don't have anything like this at home," he quipped again as he pinched the butt of the dancing girl he'd just remarked about, as she whirled past him. An old Italian tradition. Actually she got a kick out of it, so the next time around she came in even closer. This time Guido literally grabbed at her buns. This now caught the attention of the bouncer.

"You damned fool," said Lepo. "Now look what you've done. The bouncer's coming after us . . . come on, let's beat it!" urged Lepo.

"I think we'd better," agreed Guido as he swept past his brother heading for the stairwell.

Lepo all but trampled his brother as the two men scrambled down the stairs with the bouncer hot on their heels. In a matter of seconds they were aboard the International just as Al and Fats reached the Durant. They were not about to wait around to find out how they intended to deal with the would-be hijackers. They departed the scene—'posthaste.'

"If they're Chicago hijackers, we're asking for it. They'll have guns," advised Fats as they approached the car.

"Not likely. If they're in with the cops, they don't need guns. The cops do the dirty work for them. You take the passenger side, and I'll take the driver side. If they're not hijackers, we'll back off."

"If they are, they sure as hell are not about to tell ya," commented Fats.

"Maybe not, but they may give some indication."

The strategy was to walk up casually. Al, coming up the driver's side with his hands tucked in the pockets of his leather jacket, while Fats, on the sidewalk, trudged along with his arms swinging freely.

"Well, what do ya know about that," snarled the driver of the Durant as he viewed the rearview mirror. He'd recognized Al as the one who had worked him over on the night of the Overland incident.

"You know that guy coming up your side?" asked his cohort, a barrel-chested man that appeared to be too robust for the size of his shirt.

"Yeah, I know that cocky little bastard," sneered the driver. "I've got a score to settle with that bugger."

"What did he do? This guy coming up on my side doesn't seem to be all that bad a guy."

"Not him. It's that cocky little bastard on my side. Now listen," he said hurriedly, "as soon as they get to the back fender, jump out and take them on.

Get the jump on them."

"OK, if you say so. I'll take the big guy."

The instant the two buddies were alongside the car, without warning the doors flew open. They were set upon instantly. Before they could react, they were taking punches. Fats' big belly was obviously a likely target, but his belt's massive decorative metal belt buckle tucked under the flap of his belly wasn't anticipated. The pile driver fist that smashed into it was pulled back in agony. The buckling over associated with such a punch didn't occur. This gave Fats a chance to catch his breath and take the initiative.

Al, caught with his hands in his pockets, took a hard left to the face followed by a right haymaker that spun him around and up against the back door of the sedan. The two devastating punches were followed by a spine chilling statement:

"Remember me, ya frigg'n dago," snarled the attacker through tight lips.

Al instantly recognized his attacker as the same man he'd beaten up during the Overland incident. At that time, he had the element of surprise in his favor; now the opposite ensued. He knew he was in trouble.

Not realizing Al's stunned condition, and thinking he'd turn and face him in an aggressive fighting stance, the attacker unleashed a battering-ram punch to Al's midsection in hopes of catching him dead center as he whirled, then follow up with a kick to the testicles such as he had received in their previous fight. It would have worked if it wasn't for Al being momentarily stunned. Rather than whirl around as anticipated, he cowered, hugging the car in a protective manner. Too late to abort the maneuver, the punch and kick took place, but with little effect. Recovering from the stunning initial attack, blood spurting from his battered nose, Al came out of his coverup position to face his tormentor. The second left hook that caught him on the side of the face reminded him that his opponent had the edge. Using the side of the car as a spring board, he lurched forward grabbing at the attacker in hopes of smothering his devastating fists. This unexpected maneuver caught the attacker off guard. He stumbled backwards. Al hung on; both men fell to the street. With regained confidence, Al took advantage of the diversion by changing his grip to a bearhug as the man tried to regain a standing position. With Al's arms wrapped around his chest from behind, and dragging him back to the pavement, his attacker's deadly fists had lost their effect. He couldn't pry his opponent's clenched hands apart, and neither could he reach back to grab at him. The constant pressure against his chest was impairing his ability to breathe, thus rendering him faint.

Al knew that his only chance was to apply pressure with the bearhug, and keep his head tight against the man's back. No matter how much they rolled around on the hard pavement, the two men stayed locked together. Al now had his legs wrapped around his opponent, stifling his thrashing motions. With the inability to heave his chest to breathe, the man was gasping for air, a weakening situation for sure.

Up on the sidewalk, things weren't so glum. Fats had little trouble keeping his opponent at bay. They were swinging and sparring with each other, but not with the vengeance of their buddies rolling around on the pavement. This was understandable since they had no ax to grind. There was nothing to gain by their thrashing each other. Amongst grunts and groans, Fats got the message across that it would make sense for them to talk this out. His opponent welcomed the idea, especially since he couldn't bring Fats down, and his friend was no longer on his feet. Concerned with what was going on in the street, the two big men stopped fighting and trotted over to their buddies and proceeded to break up the fight.

"Come on, break it up!" commanded Fats as he broke Al's suffocating bearhug. "It's all over, enough is enough!"

Al welcomed this interceding. He wouldn't be able to keep up the pressure much longer.

"Yeah, come on, break it up," said the other man to his friend while helping him to his feet. He then added a comment as he restrained him from going after Al: "I don't know what the hell it is with you two, but killing each other sure as hell won't settle anything."

There was little said as they parted company. No apologies; no explanations, and no glancing back.

As they walked back down the street, Al splattered with his own blood while holding his handkerchief against his bleeding nose, commented to Fats:

"Damn it, he got the jump on me. I had no idea it would be that same son-of-a-bitch from the other night."

"Maybe he set ya up with that tailing bit."

"I don't think so. There's no way he could connect me with the International. I go along with Guido; he was after the sugar, and he may try it again."

"I doubt that he will. Not after what happened tonight. He knows you're onto him . . . no way."

"I hope you're right. I sure as hell don't want to go through that crap again. That guy's tough—maybe a Mafioso."

The thought lingered on Al's mind: "Does he have Mafia connections?"

CHAPTER 15

Surveillance by the federal agents from up on Jensen Road was soon re-established, as well as the added occasional drive-by snooping of a second agent's car moving slowly along Crow Canyon Road out in front of Mike's place. Its occupants stretching their necks, looking down the driveways, trying to detect something going on other than a chicken ranch operation.

The place was obviously out of the ordinary, considering the new elaborate facility complete with twice as many employees as would normally be needed for a chicken and egg producing business. The senior agent was convinced that the chicken ranch was, in fact, a front for Mike's bootlegging enterprise. At his request, the two extra agents used in the earlier Bellina Canyon raid were permanently assigned to him along with a second car, an Essex. They, along with his cohort, were fully aware of his motive. Get the goods on Mike, and shake him down; they were all for the idea. He expressed his thoughts in a briefing:

"There's no such thing as a gentleman chicken farmer. A cattle ranch or fruit ranch, maybe so, but not a chicken ranch. A wealthy gentleman farmer is not about to walk around all day wading through chicken manure, that's for damned sure!" he stated with an air of arrogance, then added: "We'll keep a close watch on them; eventually we'll get 'em."

As the days went by, the more anxious the agents got. They were bound and determined to get a piece of the action come hell or high water. Besides, the senior agent was thirsty for Mike's Jackass Brandy. The few barrels they'd made off with from the still raid at Tony's were long gone. Surveillance was now to be extended far into the night as well as observations of unusual night trafficking in and around the area of Crow Canyon. But, with the experience and expertise gained from the days of working with Pucci, Mike and his gang of paesani were able to keep operating despite the surveillance. The agents found themselves always one step behind them. They were beginning to realize that although they were on the right track, they were being outsmarted, and this infuriated the senior agent beyond imagination. For one thing, because of their greedy nature, they dared not pass on to their colleagues the knowledge of the possible existence of a potential gold mine, so to speak. This group, made up of a Hudson and an Essex, along with two men in each car, were not about to share the proceeds of their shakedown take once they had it implemented. "No, indeed not!" They were not about to water it down by bringing in others. "We four can handle those dumb dagos; let's keep this to ourselves," they would tell each other.

The first thing these so-called dumb dagos did was to make it a point to disassociate the recently acquired 1925 Buick from the chicken ranch by keeping it garaged in Oakland. At the time of delivery, the car was taken directly to the garage where Al had previously been employed as a mechanic. The garage was located in the Melrose district of Oakland, not too far from where he lived with his young family. Al immediately applied his mechanical expertise in souping up the engine and gutting out the rear portion in order to accommodate 5 gallon alcohol tin cans and 5 and 10 gallon whiskey barrels. Overload springs were installed for carrying extra weight and to keep the car looking level and empty while fully loaded.

On a side street, just off East 14th Street next door to the garage, Al arranged for the rental of a warehouse to be used as a transfer point and for warehousing alcohol and the finished product, Jackass Brandy and plain whiskey, as well as garaging the blue Buick. Seldom if ever was the car seen on the streets during daylight hours. The matter of security, protection against hijackers or police interference, was about as unique an arrangement as anyone could ever expect or hope to find. Adjacent to and next door was the Oakland Police Department's sub-station referred to as the Eastern Station, fully staffed and manned 24 hours a day. Since every one of the members of this authoritative contingency of lawmen, Captain Brown included, were Al's friends, and sympathetic to his cause, they had passed the word along the line to other police officers that he was not to be harassed in his endeavor to supply the thirsty population of the good city of Oakland with the finest Jackass available that they, too, shared. Unlike the federal agents, they were satisfied with small favors and a supply of Jackass Brandy, and were willing to share their good fortune with others of their profession.

When Al first took Mike down to see the setup, a justifiably horrified expression crossed Mike's face, along with a choking gasp. While snuffing out his cigar on the sole of his shoe, he looked up at the front of the police station with the appropriate name assigned to it in bold letters above the door. With his eyes frozen on the sight of the Sergeant sitting at his desk behind the window, he uttered a few trembling words: "Al, you're crazy!"

The comment triggered a burst of laughter from Al, who added a comment in a clowning manner:

"Hey, Mike, what's the big deal? All they can do is throw us in jail!" he laughed, while Mike shook his head in disbelief.

His judgment to locate the relay and distribution point in this location proved to be a stroke of genius. In fact, if they were being targeted by Capone's hijackers, it would be quite handy to have the police on their side, and so close at hand. It got so that when Al pulled out of the warehouse, policemen on duty would comment with envy: "Damn, look at him go. Wouldn't you like to be in his shoes?"

Well, the city of Oakland's police department, for the most part, did join in on the excitement afforded by the presence of bootleggers. By day the City moved along about its affairs in a tranquil businesslike manner; but come nightfall, it jumped to life in a free-for-all scramble made up of almost every type of character, good or bad, trustworthy or untrustworthy, con artists and hijackers alike, that could have possibly been thrown together by the Prohibition Era. So the police department had to be thrown into this arena of misfits in an attempt to sort out the bad from the good, and try to maintain a measure of law and order.

The religious groups and churches in their well-meaning attempts to save mankind also played an important part in this three-ring circus. They constantly urged the bad to be good and the good to be better. For some of the religious organizations, the whole affair was indeed a challenging, difficult, if not an impossible task. However, since for the most part, the bootleggers were devout, dyed-in-the-wool Catholic believers, as were the Irish that were the principal consumers of this stuff called "Jackass,"a few minutes spent in the confessional cubical followed by "The Lord's Prayer," along with a smattering of repeated "Hail Marys" thrown in for good measure, and a final "Amen," in their minds cleared them of all wrong-doing of the past week. Now they were prepared with a clean conscience for a fresh crack at the following week's onslaught. The little gold crucifix, depicting Christ on the cross, that hung from the rearview mirror, was an added comfort. In a pinch, it could take the place of a fully sung mass. Held firmly in one's right hand while pressing it to the heart, with the added exclamation, "Oh, my God! Lord save me!" would tend to suddenly clear the mind, hopefully bringing forward the right decision.

Al had by far the best of all worlds. He had the support and respect of the police, thanks to Captain Brown; the thought of the latter lingered on his mind as he cruised along on his way to make a delivery at the North Pole Club. As he swung into the darkened alley behind the club, a police car immediately flooded his car with its spotlight, only to instantly douse it again once the blue Buick was recognized. There was no mistaking it, for his was the only one of its kind in town, and the manner in which he drove it, made it unmistakable.

"Oh oh," muttered Al, not being sure of the police's intentions. Rather than make a run for it and arouse suspicion, he decided to sit tight while viewing the rear view mirror.

The new police recruit sitting alongside his superior officer, correctly assuming the car to be delivering alcohol, called out eagerly:

"Hey, that's a bootlegger! Let's take him!" he yelled as he swung the car door open ready to jump into action..

"Hold it! Stay put!" commanded his superior officer. "That bootlegger is OK. I know who he is."

"What's the difference — a bootlegger is a bootlegger. What the hell goes here?" questioned the recruit.

"Kid," his tough veteran Irish superior office said, "when you've acquired the taste for good Jackass Brandy, and some day you will, you'll answer your own question. In the meantime, leave that Buick alone. Come on, let's work our way down to the waterfront and find ourselves a bad one; that is, if excitement is what you want."

"What do you mean, Jackass Brandy? I never heard of it. What's the difference?"

"Well, I'll tell you kid; depending on how it's made, and it runs 100 proof or better, it's generally referred to as Jackass Whiskey or Jackass Brandy."

"But why call it jackass?"

"Because, a couple extra belts of the stuff and you'll feel like you've been kicked in the head by a jackass! And another thing; don't concern yourself too much with bootleggers. Let the damn federal agents deal with them, that's what they get paid to do. Besides, the Captain's orders are to lay off that particular car."

Expressing a sigh of relief as the police car pulled away, Al muttered: "Thank God, and a salute to Captain Brown."

The senior federal agent was indeed a bastard, but not necessarily stupid. He surmised that a warehouse or distribution facility of sorts had been established somewhere in Oakland. Determined to find it, he now extended his activities and surveillance to the city of Oakland in hopes of catching up to Mike's driver as well. But Al's friends, the cops at Melrose, the Eastern Station, knew who the agents were, and kept him advised of their presence. The agents' Hudson, and its backup, the Essex, roaming the streets of East Oakland were quite conspicuous.

Terzo had also been alerted to the problem of snoopy federal agents being seen in and around the area of Castro Valley proper. He was urged to change his routing for he too, such as Al, was being targeted. He did in fact change his route by bypassing downtown Castro Valley entirely. He would now leave Foothill Boulevard (Highway 50) at San Leandro, picking up Lake Chabot Road at that point, chug his way up along Lake Chabot, then down to Seven Hills Road where he would make a left, cut across the valley to Redwood Road, make a right heading down Redwood Road to Castro Valley Boulevard (Highway 50), then head east again to Crow Canyon. This worked for a short while until the agents got wise to him. Having concluded that he was also tied into Mike's organization, the Hudson picked up his trail in San Leandro. Their intention was to tail him, thus leading them to the still location, or whatever, somewhere along the way. Terzo realized he was being followed when he made the left turn on to Seven Hills Road from Lake Chabot Road. There was no point in trying to outrun their Hudson with his Model-T Ford, so the next best thing would be to ditch them.

It so happened that his and Mike's good friend, Frank, a fellow Italian engaged in the chicken buying and selling business (a poultry peddler as they were referred to), had his ranch at the approximate base of the last hill just before it intersected Redwood Road. No sooner had he topped the last hill and before the agents came into view, he swung the Model-T to the right and into Frank's circular driveway, continued around to the rear and parked.

Lights out, he waited.

Frank's wife urged her husband to get out of bed and investigate the disturbance. Pulling back the curtains of the kitchen window, he could see the Model-T parked out in back in the moonlight. He recognized it to be Terzo's. The clear view of the intersection below revealed the presence of the agent's car stopped at the intersection, trying to figure out which way the Model-T had gone. Since they could see for a considerable distance down Redwood Road to the right, but not as far to the left where the hill obstructed the view, they concluded that to be the direction their quarry had gone since it led to the remote canyons and hills to the north. A likely spot for a still, so the Hudson swung to the left and headed over the hill at full speed.

Satisfied that he had given the agents the slip, Terzo first lit up a Toscanello cigar, then let the Model-T roll down the inclined driveway, starting it with the rolling momentum as he drove under and past Frank's observation window. Frank let the curtain return to its normal position, then turned away from the window and while shaking his head, mumbled: "What a strange way to make a living," referring to the occupants of both cars.

By the same token, Terzo, glancing up seeing the curtain drawn back, commented: "Why the hell anybody would want to wade ankle deep in chicken manure when a fortune can be made cranking out alcohol is beyond me."

Not being ones to leave any stones unturned, the agents started following just about every vehicle that came close to Crow Canyon and/or that functioned in a suspicious manner. Matteoli's frequent daytime trips to the Hayward Poultry Producer's Association in the Model-T Ford truck, accompanied by his son Orindo, also raised their suspicion. But by following the truck on several occasions convinced them that the Ford truck was engaged in hauling chicken feed and nothing else. The truth of the matter was that what appeared to be strictly chicken feed was, for the most part, brown sugar sacked to appear like chicken feed. What the agents didn't know was that the Poultry Producer's Association was in fact dealing in sugar as well as chicken feed. As a matter of fact, in the absence of grains, much of the chicken feed, in the form of mash, was also dumped into the fermentation tanks along with the sugar. It made a hell of a good whiskey but obviously, not the kind of product that fetched the high price such as Mike's "Jackass Brandy."

CHAPTER 16

To what extent the agents had expanded their surveillance was of concern to Mike, especially since the column still at Tony Soares' old 80 acre
homestead in Bellina Canyon was back in full production, and known to at
least the senior agent. He couldn't prove who actually owned it, but he knew
it was there.

Mike now had even more of a good reason to call for a strategy meeting.
He, Al, Julio and Matteoli met again in Fred Puls's barn on the night of
October 30, 1927. In the glow of the lantern, Mike, silouetted against the
barn wall, opened the discussion:

"If you haven't already heard, Santucci's big column still down at his
Russell City hog ranch has been raided."

"Oh Christ, when did that happen?" asked Al.

"Three days ago," answered Mike.

"I don't get it," responded Al. "It's common knowledge among us that
Santucci's bunch have been paying off the sheriff regularly the same as we
are. What did the bastard do, double-cross him?"

"It wasn't the sheriff or the federal agents that staged the raid. It was
Warren's men from the District Attorney's Office," Mike answered, then
added: "To make matters worse, they accidently set fire to the place while
dismantling the 600 gallon-a-day continuous column still. That, and the
smaller 200 gallon-a-day still, burned up along with the main building and a
bunch of hog pens. I suppose a few hogs got roasted as well."

"For Santucci to be caught red-handed while operating a still of that
magnitude could be tough on him," put in Matteoli, then added: "I'd rather
believe that Santucci or one of his men deliberately tossed a match into the
alcohol with hopes of destroying the evidence."

"Maybe not. It so happened that Santucci was not there at the time; only
Nello Fornacari and Domenico Martini, along with a couple of employees
by the names of Fuccari and Salo, were there. Martini insists that he alone is
the owner of the still. I know Domenico Martini, he'll keep his mouth shut.
But you know those pig men, they're pretty tough and mean. If, in fact, they
did torch the place, it was with the intention of roasting the prohibition agents

along with the pigs. If proven, they'll come down hard on the lot of them."

"I suppose we best concern ourselves with the same threat," commented Julio in his calm manner.

"Yes, I'm afraid so," answered Mike. "Especially since some of Warren's men were former federal agents. Those buggers know too much." Mike's friend, the judge, had apprised Mike of this when he notified him of the Santucci raid.

The four men talked the situation over. The decision was made to shut down Tony's still altogether, at least for a while, and set up a less cumbersome still up at the old Peters' place, the very last place up at the end of Bellina Canyon, just under the outcroppings of the granite bluffs that gave the ridge its name, Rocky Ridge. The structure, more of a ranch building than a house, served as a home for the Frank Soares family (no relation to Tony or John). But not for long. Its beds were nothing more than 1" x 12" plank shelves built along the outer walls that consisted of single vertical redwood boards. Fetching supplies necessitated leaving before daylight with horse and buggy to the city of Hayward, an all-day journey, and arriving back well after dark. On one occasion, Frank Soares returned to find his wife Rose had given birth to a baby girl while alone and unassisted. The child, named Lillian, was the youngest of a half-dozen children. Mother Rose was of hardy pioneer stock to say the least. When meat was needed, she simply put the double-barreled 12 gauge shotgun to her shoulder, stepped beyond the confines of the yard and shot rabbits on the run and quail on the wing. No doubt, Henry Mast's offer to rent the pasture and Mike's to rent the building was a deciding factor in their decision to abandon the place altogether. Henry eventually was to buy it.

Another still was to be moved out of Crow Canyon proper and set up at the old vacant Thompson place adjacent to and upstream from Tony's place. The Thompson place, also controlled by Henry, consisted primarily of a one-story yellow wood frame house, located on a flat knoll halfway up the side of the hill on the east side of Bellina Creek and among some poplar trees and an old apple orchard. The place was abandoned and ravaged by constant neglect. A good spring seeping from a higher elevation, thus supplying gravity flow water directly to the house where the still and its related equipment would be housed, was also a plus.

Having been previously decided that the column type still was not all that practical for setting up in these remote-out of the way locations, Duarte Sheet Metal of Hayward, the best known coppersmith in the area, had been commissioned to come up with a completely new continuous production unit that would be more suitable for Mike's operation. Mobility was needed, something that could easily be dismantled and moved on short notice, even while hot, unlike the big cumbersome column stills such as Santucci's that caught fire while in the process of being dismantled by Warren's prohibition agents the night it was raided. Duarte did come up with such a design, and under Mike's orders, was in the process of manufacture. It was, therefore, resolved that the new still, when ready, would be set up at the old Peter's place.

Since the oncoming rainy season would eventually render the dirt road for the length of Bellina Canyon useless for motorized vehicles, the Soares brothers would be called upon to continue to transport supplies by wagon from Crow Canyon Road to the new still sites further up the canyon, and haul alcohol back out again in the same manner.

The matter of moving into the new location settled, Al then raised the question of setting up a more elaborate signal system. The Soares brothers, along with their teenage sons as guardians of the canyon entrance, was all well and fine, as well as the blinking of headlights when moving up the dirt road, but an independent backup system was needed, especially since Al would have to concern himself with the threat that he might lead federal agents and/or Warren's men alike into the canyon. Al put a question to Mike:

"Haven't you been paying something to the okies over at the Habberney ranch? Maybe we can get them to work a signal system for us."

Al was referring to a destitute family from Oklahoma that lived on the old Hebering Homestead, now referred to as the Habberney place just a short way up Crow Canyon Road from the Bellina Canyon entrance. Mike had negotiated a lease for the place from a Portuguese by the name of Machado. Machado had acquired extensive land holdings in the area even though he could not write or read English, or for that matter, Portuguese either. He signed his name by scribbling hardly legible marks, and transacted money matters in an unbelievable manner. He used a circle such as an "O" to represent twenty dollars. A half circle represented ten dollars and a quarter circle five dollars. By using a smaller size circle to represent one dollar and with the same bisecting system, he would be able to perform his calculations in increments of 25 cents, "two-bits," "four- bits," and "six-bits." He never fooled or wasted his time with pennies, no doubt the reason for gaining such wealth, in addition to the fact that he was just plain smart. True, he was uneducated, but nevertheless, smart.

Mike felt the need to pass a few bucks to the Oklahoma family for two good reasons: The first because they needed it, and the second because the kids, as well as the father, were forever roaming around the area trapping small game for meat for the table and pelts which they would sell for cash.

In their wandering, they couldn't help but come across signs of an on-going bootlegging operation in the area.

"Yes, I have," answered Mike. "And for a few extra dollars, they'll do whatever we ask of them. They can be trusted. Now tell me, how do you want it set up?"

Julio interrupted with his own comment since he was quite familiar with the canyon area:

"You can see the hill behind and above the Habberney place from almost anywhere up Bellina Canyon. From the fence line along the crest of the hill, you can also see Crow Canyon Road for quite a ways in both directions. Signals from the fence line can easily be sent up the canyon without detection, as well as to the road below."

They all concurred that this was a splendid idea. Mike would approach the family and set up the signal system. Although not located on the Nunes' property across the road, nor did the Nunes have anything to do with it, the paesani now referred to the Habberney place as the Nunes place, no doubt because of its less complicated pronunciation.

The matter of moving the stills and setting up an additional signal system being resolved, the matter of bribing the federal agents came up for discussion.

"Mike, we must consider making a deal with the federal agents," advised Matteoli, who by now was being referred to as the counselor.

"Yes, that might have some merit, but we must be careful how we approach it, it could backfire on us," warned Mike. He hadn't forgotten the night the senior agent and his cohort had all but knocked the front door down to solicit a bribe.

"Something has to be done. The paesani working the stills will get a little nervous after they hear about the Santucci affair," added Julio. He directed the comment to Mike while studying Al's expression of anger.

"That's the point. Those were Warren's men, not the feds, that pulled that off. What makes you think you'll stop them by paying off federal agents?" questioned Al.

"Obviously not," answered Mike, "but so far, it's not Warren's men that are bugging us, because I don't think they know as much about our operation as the federal agents do." Mike was right; the federal agents were not sharing their information. He then added in a thoughtful manner:

"If we do make a deal, do you really think this harassment will end?" Mike put the question directly to all three men leaning against barrels casting grim shadows, the flickering light of the kerosene lantern highlighting their worrisome facial features. Matteoli was the first to answer:

"No, they will not! Those kinds of people are like wood ticks on a dog's neck — once attached, they'll suck blood until they burst or deplete the supply! There is no in between! Take my word for it!" he said sternly.

Since he was in charge of the stills, Julio expressed his concerns: "If they get to the stills, we'll be all through. All we'll be doing is working for them, and that is totally unacceptable. They must be held here, at the distribution end; if not, they will surely end up getting both."

"The hell with them, don't give them anything! If anything, we'll run them down the side of a canyon, put them out of commission once and for all!" insisted Al, then added: "I'll go along with paying off the sheriff such as we are; that's bad enough, but those damned federal agents are another matter all together. You can't trust the buggers!"

The scene of the devastating fatal crash between Primo's big Mack truck and the federal agents' Essex at Benicia several years before, had never wiped itself clean from Mike's mind.

"Wait a minute! Hold it Al! For Christ's sake, let's not go through that again! For God's sake, let's work out another way to deal with this!" The tremble in Mike's voice emphasized the graveness of the matter. Matteoli sided with him.

"I think the best thing to do is to try to hold them there at the ranch; offer them a regular monthly payment. Maybe they'll buy the idea that the chicken and egg operation is a legitimate, paying enterprise, and the Jackass peddling is just a sideline, and therefore not demand much. After all, they have no solid evidence we're operating stills in Bellina Canyon or anywhere else." This suggestion by Matteoli was the most favorable as far as Julio was concerned, and so stated. Mike concurred by directing a comment to Al:

"Yes, that makes sense. They may think we're just distributors of sorts and not the still operators. Once they're collecting regularly, they may seek greener pastures elsewhere. What do you think?"

"Mike," said Al, "anything is worth a try. If that's what the others agree to do, I'll go along with it. But don't let yourself get complacent; those guys are like a rattlesnake hypnotizing a squirrel to dance, then sinking its fangs into it without warning. I'm telling you, don't trust them! And, suppose it's not the money they're really after. Have you thought about that?"

"That's a good point," said Matteoli. "We'll see what we can do to call their hand and at the same time minimize the risk of being arrested for bribing a federal agent."

Mike agreed. Maybe they could flush the agents out with some sort of bait. If they take it, fine; if not, they may still not have enough to warrant an arrest based on attempted bribery.

"Talking about arrest, maybe we better plan for that as well, just in case." Julio's added comment in reference to an arrest was indeed something to think about. After much discussion on the matter, it was decided that the logical person to avoid arrest would be Mike. He would be in a better position to help those that might be caught and possibly jailed, if he was free to do so. The matter was resolved by Julio volunteering to be the fall guy. He reasoned that the others had families in America, and he did not. Besides, if the government was to deport him, that would be just fine with him, since his intention was to return to Italy anyway. It was therefore agreed that he would take an alias: Gelio Rossi, instead of Julio Matteoli. This too would disassociate him from his cousin Matteoli as a family member. And since he was in charge of the stills, he could be assumed to be the sole owner, and all others merely employees or associates peddling a little booze here and there, no big deal. The strategy was to keep as many others out of jail as possible, especially Mike.

If, in fact, the agents were to accept the offer of payoff, it would be assumed the pressure would be off and Al could then function with more freedom, even to the extent of using the Buick to pick up alcohol directly from the stills. The same could apply to Terzo. It was therefore agreed that the relocation of the stills would take place immediately while Matteoli and Mike devised a plan to approach the agents with an offer of a bribe.

The meeting ended with the extinguishing of the lantern and the closing of the barn door behind them. As they strolled back to the cars, Mike asked Al a question about the Buick's performance: "Are you satisfied with the new car? Does it do what you had hoped it would?" he asked while viewing the car in the darkness.

"You bet, even more so," came the answer.

"How about the brakes, are they as good as these new hydraulic brakes we hear talk about?"

Al's answer to the question came fast and to the point: "These are plenty good enough for me. Besides who gives a damn, I'll seldom be using them anyway."

They all knew what he meant by that comment. He no doubt would have to rely on the throttle more than the brakes to stay ahead of the agents.

The chuckles and low laughter did not go unnoticed, for the little fox terrier lying on the bed at Fred's feet, perked up her ears and gave a low menacing growl.

"That's all right, girl. Calm down. Be quiet, they're leaving now," reassured her master.

CHAPTER 17

"Chickens and eggs, that's all we have here," insisted Mike. "You want some, I'll give you all you want; this is a chicken ranch, nothing else," he said to the four federal agents who had driven into the yard with the Hudson and the Essex.

"Don't give me that bullshit, we've been watching you for weeks; we know what's going on here and it's going to cost you."

The senior agent wasn't mincing words, they were there to put the "bite" on Mike. They had been set up and were taking the bait, thanks to Matteoli's zest for coming up with the idea and strategy of flushing these agents into the open. On the night before this early morning visit, from up on Jensen Road, the agents had observed Terzo's Model-T pull into Mike's place, continue down the driveway and park at the end of the last row of chicken houses. Through their binoculars, and with the help of the bright, full moon, they watched what appeared to be small barrels of whiskey being placed under the chicken house at the far end adjacent to the hog pen. Through an opening, the hogs were allowed to quarter under this end of the building.

What appeared to be barrels were nothing more than burlap feed sacks, modified and resewn together so once filled and stitched, they took on the appearance of 10 gallon whiskey barrels. The best filler the paesani could think of that was light and not too obnoxious was horse manure, a plentiful commodity. The Essex had tailed the loaded Model-T on this laborious journey, which had come to be known as the "horse manure run" to its point of termination, Mike's hog pen.

Between the Hudson's stakeout up on Jensen Road and the successful tail by the Essex, the agents now felt they had the goods on Mike. For the time being, they would settle for what they had; tying the still to the operation would come next. When they gathered that morning to approach Mike for the "bite," they were strutting around like cock sage grouse in mating season, taking in deep breaths of fresh air, then exhaling in thundering, booming laughter. The four federal agents, on this crisp autumn morning were therefore standing before this supposedly startled and unsuspecting nervous bootlegger, pressing him for the "bite." They were there to collect, in installments, the proceeds from a paid-up annuity so to speak. All their weeks of hard work and vigilant surveillance was about to pay off. They were so confident that they didn't bother with formalities. They got right to the point:

"Sir, you're about to be sent to San Quentin. Now what do you say to that?" said the senior agent as if Mike was already convicted.

"But . . . but, I didn't do anything illegal," pleaded Mike.

"Come on now, cut that out, we know better," pressed the senior agent.

Unlike most of the other paesani, Mike by now had a pretty good grasp of the English language. Not only could he hold a good conversation in English, but he could also read and write as well. During the interrogation, from his overalls and shirt pockets he pulled out all kinds of documents including receipts for supplies and sales tags that pertained to the chicken and egg business. The senior agent looked the papers over carefully, readjusted them neatly, and said:

"We want the books; your records of dealings in jackass— moonshine— alcohol. Come on, let's have the records!"

"Well," stammered Mike, "I don't know, you see . . . ."

The senior agent cut him off short in a less than polite manner:

"Never mind the excuses! Let's see them or we'll take a walk down to the last chicken house," he said, pointing down the driveway where the Model-T had unloaded its cargo the night before.

The four agents' expressions and grins grew broader and broader as they chuckled with delight. Mike's fake stammering, while nervously pacing back and forth were a dead giveaway of his guilt. Yes, they had pegged him right, he was indeed involved in the illicit alcohol business. His squirming was adding joy to their game of cat and mouse. The agents then faked a thrust in the direction of the last chicken house; that is, all but the senior agent who called them back each time after they had taken a dozen or so steps.

"Boys," he called out pleasantly, "hold it a minute, give him a few minutes to think it over, there's no real hurry." He then turned back to Mike and calmly demanded that the records be delivered to him then and there.

If this federal agent had bothered to ask anyone that knew anything about immigrant bootlegging Italians, especially those engaged in this sort of business with partners, he'd find out that the records were being kept marked on the inside walls of the outhouse—the privy located near the stills. These facilities, in fact, were the offices. And for good reason—to discourage city slickers and strangers from sticking their noses into them. When a raid was inevitable, the paesani were instructed to torch the outhouse immediately before leaving the scene. If the heat didn't keep the raiders away from the office, the putrid stench it omitted sure as hell would. The paesani's theory on this matter of records was: "If they want them, let them dig for them."

Impatient, all four agents started down the driveway, only to be overtaken by Mike insisting that the hogs were dangerous. The senior agent responded by drawing his gun. "Don't concern yourself, my friend. We can handle the hogs," he stated, then instructed the others to do likewise.

"Wait! don't shoot the hogs," pleaded Mike nervously, then added: "Can't we . . . make a deal . . . I mean . . . you know . . . work something out?"

"Well now, that's better," said the agent dryly as he returned his gun to the holster. Figuring that he had pawed the mouse long enough, the agent made his final pitch while they walked back up towards the yard. "Mike," he said, "I'll tell you what we're going to do. We're going to let this matter of arrest go for the time being and only because you seem to be a pretty decent, understanding sort of fellow. But you know how it is, our time is worth money, besides we have expenses to consider as well, so we'll take—say, $50.00 each and be on our way. Now that's letting you off easy, wouldn't you say, all things considering?"

Being addressed in this manner came as no surprise to Mike, since by now the name "Mike" in the bootlegging business was well established. "You mean you're not going to check out the hog pen and you're not going to insist on getting the records?" he asked, with eyes wide open, raised eyebrows, and a look of pleasant surprise.

"That's right; I thought you would understand. We'll take the two hundred bucks now and be on our way."

"All right, that sounds fair enough. I'll see if I have that much cash on hand. Wait here a moment." Before he entered the basement, while holding the screen door open, he turned to the senior agent and asked: "Are small bills all right? I probably don't have anything else."

"Sure, that will be just fine; we realize you may not have been prepared for it this time, but you better be the next time."

Mike stepped into the basement summer kitchen, reached up on the top shelf of the closest cupboard, retrieved his cash box, and shuffled around through stacks of $100 bills trying to find enough small bills to make the $200 payoff.

The agent accepted the money with a final comment:

"Mike, we really thank you," said the agent dryly. "We'll see you again on the first of the month."

The pleasantries between the two men ended with each one looking at the other with tight lips, clenched teeth, and jaw muscles bulging from the pressure being exerted. Mike stepped back out of the way to let the two cars with their occupants complete the circle and head out the exit driveway. Once the agents were on the road, they waved their hats to each other in triumph. They had put it across, the annuity they had invested their time in was now paying off. However, the fact of the matter was, they had been bought; but unlike a prostitute, the alliance would offer no pleasure.

Once the sedans were off the premises, Matteoli stepped out from the bunkhouse where he had positioned himself near the open window, just a few feet from where the negotiations had taken place. With an exclamation, loud and clear, he yelled: "Viva!" and with that he sent his hat sailing into the air only to light in one of the few apricot trees left along the driveway. The two men, amongst boisterous laughter and chuckles embraced each other like the reuniting of long-lost friends. They had accomplished what they had set out to do. They had discreetly bought off federal agents, and since the agents instigated and solicited the bribe, in their minds the two friends were left with a clear conscience.

The first order of the day was to send a man down to the hog pen to let the hogs out from under the chicken house so they could roam freely outside in the pens. Their services as guardians of the phony kegs were no longer needed; they had done their hitch. Whether their masters could function as freely as they, remained to be seen, for their alliance with the federal agents was, at best, "unholy."

Warren's men, especially those that were former federal Prohibition agents, began to wonder how four federal agents assigned to a sparsely popu-lated area such as Castro Valley, teeming with bootlegging activity, couldn't possibly trace the source of the flood of readily identifiable Jackass Brandy. They correctly assumed the federal agents were indeed, for whatever reason, looking the other way. It was obvious; they were on the take. And who knew it better than they, since they, too, at one time, before joining up with War-ren, were brazenly solicited by bootleggers at every level. Taking advantage of their past experience, they soon started focusing their attention in the direction of Castro Valley and its outlying areas, including Livermore, at the east end of the county. It, too, was awash with alcohol.

The Prohibition agents from the D.A.'s office soon learned that a tavern owner by the name of Jack Gardella and his brother, Frank, both prominent citizens of Livermore, were what appeared to be deeply involved in alcohol distribution in the east end of the county. However, Warren concluded that they were not still owners, but instead were being supplied by one or more major stills operating somewhere in the area. It was apparent; putting the Santucci still at Russell City in the Mount Eden area out of commission hadn't stopped the flow of alcohol by much.

CHAPTER 18

The list of Italian names in the Book of Criminal Records was beginning to look like the roster at a bocce ball tournament. Mike's friend, the Judge, had been warning Mike to take precautions and to keep a low profile since District Attorney Earl Warren was putting more investigators in the field. No doubt the escalated bootlegging activities in and around the area of Castro Valley, Hayward and Livermore, would soon be scrutinized.

The Santucci raid at Russell City was sufficient proof that Warren was indeed on a rampage. It was apparent that unlike the federal agents or the Sheriff's Department, Warren's men could not be bribed. Alameda County's Sheriff Becker and his deputies were making raids on stills all right, but they were concentrating primarily on those bootleggers and still operators that refused to pay protection money. Therefore, friction did exist between the two agencies since one was pushing to shut the stills down while the other was encouraging production.

The front page publicity of the Russell City hog ranch raid being credited to Warren's men bugged Sheriff Becker, since he was aware of its presence all along. He was not about to want it shut down, since it was paying off handsomely to him and his deputies, as well as the still operators themselves. The local newspaper was covering that particular incident quite closely, much to Mike's concern. He read, with disturbed interest, the articles as they appeared. The fact that Warren was focusing on Castro Valley and nearby Hayward, he decided to set up a newly acquired modern continuous still somewhere away from the vicinity of Castro Valley. Livermore was ruled out completely, because being a competitor, Gardella's alliance with the Sheriff's department, made him uneasy.

Through a good friend by the name of Italo Pratali, a resident of Niles, Mike was introduced to Antone Garcia, a ranch owner in the Niles area (a small town 15 or so miles south of Hayward). However, he was introduced as a friend of a person interested in leasing Garcia's ranch. This purported friend of Mike's was mentioned as being G. Pasquale, but actually, an alias for Mike himself. Pratali knew that Garcia was heavily in debt and in need of cash, and therefore felt that an alliance with a bootlegger in need of a still site might be the answer to his friend Garcia's financial problems. By the same token, Pratali would be helping himself, since he would now have an alcohol-producing plant close at hand to better supply his own little moonshine peddling enterprise through his association with the Florence restaurant in the town of Niles.

Garcia's ranch was located southeast of the town of Niles in Morrison Canyon, also referred to as Morris Canyon. The Morrison Canyon Road that led to Garcia's ranch branched off the Niles-Mission San Jose Highway a couple of miles south of Niles. The dirt road turned east off the main highway, across the railroad tracks past the Overacker place, then through several closed gates where the road terminated at Garcia's place nestled back in the canyon out of sight. Not a bad setup, thought Mike; so he asked Garcia to have a lease prepared in the name of G. Pasquale as the lessee. Mike signed the lease as G. Pasquale out of the presence of Garcia. The $50 per month rental fee was to include the whole of the 30-acre ranch, including outbuildings and the old vacant house, but not the hog pens and other stock pens that Garcia retained for himself.

Garcia didn't mention that he had in fact already let out the farmable land on a share basis to a fellow Portuguese by the name of Caldera, who had already planted a patch of potatoes on Mike's supposedly leased land. Mike's first thought was that Garcia had been dishonest, but on second thought, his own conduct in using an alias to obtain the lease didn't leave him all that clean either. All-in-all, the potato patch affair wasn't that big a deal since farming the land was of no interest to him and the fact that once it was known, Pratali assured him that Caldera was trustworthy. Besides, "who knows," thought Mike—"maybe the anticipated potato crop could be thrown into the fermentation tanks along with everything else."

Garcia was delighted with the deal. He was now collecting rent in the form of cash, plus the potential sharing of a crop of potatoes, plus the reduced hog feed bill since the waste mash from the still was being fed to the pigs at no cost to himself. However, care had to be exercised in feeding the alcohol-laced mash waste to the pigs, since an overdose would cause them to act much like intoxicated human beings; that is, like a bunch of drunken pigs. In this respect, animal and man had much in common in their drunken conduct. There was another advantage, especially during the wet, rainy season; the pig pen aroma helped disguise the putrid, smelly discharge from the still and residue from the fermentation tanks.

All along, Garcia and Caldera thought the ongoing moonshine operation was under the ownership of two Italians: G. Pasquale, the signer of the lease, and Mike, since he was often seen in and about the place.

Unfortunately, the venture into Morrison Canyon soon came to the attention of Warren's investigators. How they found out about it was never known. Accordingly, a raid on the Niles still was scheduled. Through his contacts, Mike's friend, the Judge, became aware of the District Attorney's intention and the fact that the raid would take place that very same evening, January 6, 1928. The Judge passed the word on to Alameda County Sheriff Becker. Knowing well the existing friction between the two law agencies, the Judge left the option up to Sheriff Becker; either he raid the still ahead of Warren's men or warn Mike of the intended raid. As the Judge had hoped, the Sheriff chose the latter option; understandably so, since Mike was a heavy contributor to the Becker Organization Fund. The so-called fund was the vehicle set up by the Sheriff to handle the volume of protection money pouring in from all over the county. However, on such short notice, the Sheriff was not able to contact Mike in time for him to pull his paesani out of the still ahead of the pending raid. So, he did the next best thing. He dispatched a deputy to go out to the still ahead of the raiders and get Mike's men out of there. The deputy drove directly to Garcia's ranch in Morrison Canyon, and in his best sign language, explained the situation to the startled still operators.

The paesani were surprised to see a deputy sheriff appear at the still on such a miserable rainy evening. They had seen deputies in and around the still areas before, but had never had one hustle them into his car such as this one was doing. The urgency of the matter left no doubt in the paesani's minds that something big was about to happen, so they responded accordingly. There wasn't the time to explain much of anything, since hand gestures would have taken all night. After loading the men into the car, along with a few 10 gallon barrels of Jackass for himself, the deputy drove them into nearby Niles and dropped them off at the Wesley Hotel with instructions to the proprietor to hold them there until he heard from Mike. The Wesley Hotel was another contributor to the Becker Fund, but not just because illegal liquor was served on the premises, but more so because prostitutes were housed in the hotel rooms above the restaurant and dining room, of which Becker got a percentage of the take.

The Wesley Hotel proprietor, Pisa, or Pizzo, the latter being an alias, was referred to by his friends as Pisanino. The nickname was bestowed because of his small stature and little bald, shiny head. Pisanino agreed to accommodate the paesani as asked. The deputy then drove back up to the Garcia place in time to see the raiding officers go into the property, then come out again. He drove back into town, placed a call to Mike, and explained the situation.

In the discussion that took place, they arrived at the conclusion that since it was such a miserable, rainy night with the electric power out, the raiders may have assumed that the still operators had shut the still down for the night. Therefore, the raiders could be expected to return the next morning in hopes of catching the bootleggers at the still. In part this was true, but knowing bootleggers as they did, the raiders figured they'd be somewhere in town seeking some action while waiting out the storm. They had guessed right.

Mike's pulling the still out of there that night was out of the question, but the alcohol on hand was another matter. Matteoli, in the Dodge touring sedan, accompanied by his young son Orindo, immediately pulled out of Crow Canyon heading for Morrison Canyon to retrieve the alcohol, while Mike headed for the Wesley Hotel in Niles to rescue the stranded paesani. He was not surprised to find them in the hotel's back banquet room seated at a table consuming some of the finest Florentine cuisine imaginable, while sipping delicate imported claret wine from fancy straw-woven flasks. Pisanino was not about to allow Mike's paesani to leave his premises with an empty stomach. Besides, he knew he would be well paid for his efforts.

Although it did not surprise Mike to find his men wallowing in wine, he was not too pleased to find a contingency of well- perfumed prostitutes mingling with his men while helping themselves to the expensive wine he was paying for. This, along with his ulcer acting up over the impending raid, caused him to growl at Pisanino as he came bursting into the banquet room. While nervously wiping his hands with his apron, Pisanino had an announcement to make:

"Mike, listen to me! Prohibition agents are out front!!!"

"What . . . are you sure . . .?"

"Yes, it's them all right. I recognize the car!"

"Holy Christ!! They came back!! Quick—clear those tables! Goddamn it . . . get those whores out of here! I'll take the men out the back way!"

"No, Mike, they're wise to that. They'll nab you and your men sure as hell!" warned Pisanino as the Madam in charge of the prostitutes hurriedly breezed up to Mike with a sensible solution. Apparently she knew him quite well; maybe even too well, considering her actions and offer:

"Mike, calm down . . . come with me—get your men upstairs, the girls know what to do." She had something in mind all right, and it was surely not to have him and his men jump out windows.

Since there was nowhere else to go but up, he accepted her offer. A sharp command sent the tipsy men scrambling for the stairway in a panic. The prostitutes, with raised skirts held high above their panties so as not to impede their ascent up the stairs, led the way. The paesani followed close behind, nose to butt. Doors slammed shut as men and women disappeared into rooms. The prostitutes would take it from there. As for Mike, the madam, with a firm grip on his arm, jerked him into her personal quarters. He did not resist; a rainy, stormy night—Warren's men on his heels—an experienced madam at his disposal—"What the hell!"

Sure enough, no sooner was the banquet hall cleared, Prohibition agents appeared on the scene. Pisanino greeted them nervously:

"Good evening, gentlemen. I can seat you here," he said as he gestured towards the table furthest from the banquet room.

"We're not here for dinner; we want a room. As a matter of fact, two rooms, with twin beds if you have them." The statement was indeed solemn. They'd been scouring the town in the rain, looking for the still operators and, therefore, ready to sack in for the night.

Pisanino's heart jumped in his mouth. He swallowed hard as a horrible thought crossed his mind: "Between the prostitutes and Mike's men, most of the rooms were occupied, but who was in which room?"

"Well, sir . . . " he stammered, "Do you plan to stay the night?" A stupid question if one were ever asked.

"Of course. But we will be leaving quite early — we have business first thing come morning."

Thinking fast, Pisanino reached for the coffee pot while at the same time running his fingers through the handles of several coffee cups. Fumbling nervously with the cups, he again stammered while setting them down at the closest table:

"Please—be seated—help yourself to a cup of coffee while I check out the rooms."

This was indeed a welcome offer. Nothing like a hot cup of coffee when coming in out of the rain. As they poured themselves some coffee, Pisanino beat it up to the rooms hoping to find which ones were empty, while at the same time letting it be known that they'd have company for the night. The very first door he tapped on, a stark naked prostitute greeted him. While staring at her in astonishment, he made the announcement:

"There's men downstairs . . . ," but before he could finish the statement, she instructed in a slurred voice:

"Send them up." As far as she was concerned, and considering her tipsy, carefree condition, she'd take on all comers—one at a time or in bunches, it made little difference to her. The paesano she was assigned to had popped his cork the minute he dropped his pants. She never even got a chance to work on him.

At the next room, the occupants were in such a hurry to jump in bed they left the door half ajar. Peeking into that room, all he could see was a man's bare back straddling a pair of elevated legs. Beads of sweat broke out on his forehead as he quietly pulled the door shut; no point in making an announcement here.

Now treading softly, he tried the third room, but upon viewing and imagining the precarious tangled position the occupants might be in while gyrat-

115

ing under the sheets, he decided not to divulge his presence at all. The embarrassment of interrupting the action was more than he figured he could cope with. However, a thought did cross his mind: "If the wine I serve is that good, I'd better drink more of it myself."

Thinking it out carefully, he correctly concluded that everybody was in such a hurry to hit the beds that they headed into the first rooms they came across, so obviously the empty rooms were at the end of the hall. Feeling comfortable with that thought, he went back downstairs and announced that, yes, there were two rooms made up ready for occupancy. Upon signing the register, the prohibition agents followed Pisanino up the stairs and down the hall. The question was asked:

"What's with all these creaking noises emitting from the bedrooms?"

"Oh, that. Well you see," answered Pisanino as he hurried them along, "this is an old wooden building and when the weather changes, it squeaks and creaks."

"I guess you're right. That does explain it . . . after all . . . what with this bad weather and all."

It was well into the night and raining pitch forks and hayrakes (as the Portuguese cattlemen would describe a rainstorm of this magnitude) when Matteoli arrived at the first gate at Morrison Canyon Road. It was here that the lad, Orindo, was called upon to open the gates and let the car through, then close them again behind the car. The cows had an inclination to run up to any vehicle when approaching a gate in hopes of getting a handful of hay. Being nocturnal, their eyes reflected from the car's headlights. Wide-eyed with fear, the sight of starry-eyed figures coming at him through the stormy darkness hastened the procedure.

Matteoli made his way through the blinding rainstorm, through the cow pasture and up to the still. Once there, he proceeded to load the 5 gallon tin cans of alcohol, plus what few barrels of Jackass that hadn't been taken by the deputy. He didn't bother with alcohol in open containers or other supplies. With the car's side curtains securely strapped in place, nose dripping, rain-soaked Matteoli, with his frightened son at his side, drove the loaded-down Dodge back out the muddy canyon road and headed for Crow Canyon.

As predicted, the very next morning, Saturday, January 7, 1928, the raiders returned, only to find a cold still and the bulk of the alcohol and Jackass gone, and what they really wanted; the still operators, a disappointment for sure, since there was no one to arrest.

However, they did get a break; landowner Antone Garcia and a friend of his happened along as the raiders were about to start dismantling the still. Garcia was questioned extensively on the spot. He admitted being the owner of the property but denied any knowledge of the ongoing bootlegging activities. This, of course, was not a convincing argument, with the exception that he was not the still owner, and his purpose for being there at this particular time was to feed the hogs. Garcia mentioned nothing about the fact that he was feeding them waste mash from the still operation.

A short time later, Caldera happened along with his two sons. They were also questioned. Their story corroborated Garcia's in that the buildings were in possession of two Italians and possibly others. At first, both Garcia and the Calderas were reluctant to admit that the ongoing activities were of a suspicious nature. Caldera could get away with this, but not Garcia since he was the owner and a party to the lease arrangement with Mike. Even though he obliged the prohibition agents by hitching up his team of horses to a wagon and hauling out the still, along with other evidence, to a point where it could be loaded on a truck owned and operated by a drayman named Silva, hired by the D.A.'s office, the officers placed him under arrest anyway. It was hardly possible that Garcia could visit the ranch from day to day to feed his stock without detecting the presence of a still, since the smell of it even overpowered the hog pen aroma.

The officers questioned during the preliminary court hearing best described Garcia's reluctant but final admission to knowing just who G. Pasquale might be. He finally came forward and did admit having knowledge of the still. In so doing, with encouragement from the officers that he not take the rap as the still owner, if in fact he did not own the still, and finger Mike as the man purported to be G. Pasquale. By now, Garcia had a pretty good idea that Mike and Pasquale were in fact one and the same person.

The prohibition officers, Joe Brandon and Harry Piper, along with Alameda County Deputy Constable A. J. LaCunha, took Garcia over to Mike's home in Crow Canyon. There Mike was confronted with Garcia's accusations. He obviously denied being G. Pasquale, as well as denying even knowing Garcia at all, let alone owning the still. But, by this time, Garcia, in an act of self-preservation, had pretty well briefed the officers with enough of the details to incriminate Mike, alias G. Pasquale, as the still owner. A few questions were asked of Mike and a few answers were given with a final statement from Mike:

"This is no court—I won't answer no more questions until you get me before the judge. Take me if you want to, but don't forget, I am a sick man."

At least that much was true. Mike was suffering from a severe case of bleeding ulcers. Regardless of his illness, Mike and Garcia were both taken into custody. Two days later, the local newspaper let the community know that the D.A.'s office had scored big.

CHAPTER 19

Alameda County District Attorney Earl Warren was no doubt pleased with the fact that he had finally scored. He now had Mike (M. Buti), prominent bootlegger and gentleman chicken rancher of Crow Canyon on the hook, as well as the assumed partner-owner of the 600 gallon per day hog ranch column still, Oreste Santucci, the undisputed hog czar of Russell City.

Since Mike and Santucci were good friends as well as colleagues, Earl Warren was determined to send them both to San Quentin handcuffed together. And since the cases had similarities in their structures, both cases were assigned to Deputy District Attorney James C. Walsh, esq., a capable prosecutor. Of course, the two cases were being tried separately, but nevertheless, for all practical purposes, simultaneously. Actually, Santucci's trial was running slightly ahead of Mike's, thus giving the prosecutor somewhat of an edge in that techniques developed in the first trial could be applied to the second one following close behind. But this same advantage, to some extent, was to extend to the defense attorneys as well, at least to Mike's.

Attorney Sullivan, counselor for the defense of Santucci and his men, was smart and well seasoned. He was a good match for prosecutor Walsh. In Santucci's case, prosecutor Walsh was doing a good job in questioning his best witness, arresting officer Joe Brandon. His presentation was brief and to the point. He properly brought out the incredible, undeniable amount of evidence found on the premises that constituted an illegal, large-scale, distilling operation. He brought out the fact that the building housing the distillery did consist of one 600 gallon per day high-proof alcohol-producing continuous column still; one 200 gallon per day armagnac type still cranking out first class jackass brandy; one 70 horsepower steam boiler that fired the column still; fourteen 2000 gallon fermentation vats of wheat mash; another ten 2000 gallon vats of wheat mash in various stages of fermentation; plus one 2000 gallon vat partly full of waste mash that one of the still operators was busy shoveling out at the time of the raid; three empty 1000 gallon vats, plus three empty 2000 gallon vats; eleven 50 pound cartons of peerless yeast; twenty-nine 102 pound sacks of corn sugar; eight 5 gallon cans of 193 proof alcohol; and one 300 gallon copper-clad galvanized tank with 10 gallons of alcohol in it. However, the fact that Santucci was not on the premises at the time of the raid, or at least was not seen by any of the arresting officers, was indeed a plus for the defense.

Defense attorney Sullivan, in cross examination, went to great lengths in establishing the fact that Santucci was in fact operating a sizeable hog ranch in Russell City some three miles west of Hayward. In his questioning, he forced officer Joe Brandon into describing every detail of the place and the fact that there were some 1,000 hogs witnessing this event, there were hogs everywhere of which most died in the ensuing fire. There were also men above the pens standing on the edge of roofs shouting and hollering in their native Italian tongue as if warning others of the presence of strangers. It was not explained what the hired hands were hollering about or to whom they were addressing their remarks. Since the officers didn't understand Italian, it was unclear whether the shouting men's profanity was addressed to the pigs or the officers.

The questioning finally found its way into the sizeable distillery building: a wooden structure several stories high with a ramp leading up to the second floor. Swill trucks would back up the ramp so the swill could be dumped and guided into chutes leading to feed troughs below. It was here that officer Brandon politely said to the self-purported still owner in attendance, Domenico Martini:

"Domenico, I think you better shut it off." It was apparent that Domenico was no stranger to Brandon.

Knowing who Brandon was, and having been addressed by his first name in such an informal manner, Domenico reluctantly shut the smaller armagnac still down. The big column still was not in production at the time.

Brandon proceeded to handcuff Martini, as well as the other man present, Nello Fornacari. When asked then and there by Brandon, Martini admitted being the still owner; admitted that he paid Santucci $100 a month rent for that portion of the premises and admitted that the distilling equipment had cost him $12,000 to set up. He also stated that if left alone for three more months, he would just as soon go to jail for a while, then retire for the rest of his life. Since the column still was capable of cranking out 600 gallons per day of 193-proof alcohol, at the wholesale price of $5 per gallon, the revenue from it alone, amounted to $3,000 per day. The brandy coming off the armagnac still was worth some three times as much, thus adding another $3,000 per day to the take. Yes, indeed, if left alone, early retirement was foreseeable. If this comment was meant to be a hint for Brandon to play along, it didn't score. Neither did Brandon buy the idea that Santucci was not at least part owner of the stills.

When Sullivan pressed Brandon with the fact that Santucci was not on the premises at all, Brandon answered:

MR. BRANDON. His wife, not him.

MR. SULLIVAN. We are not trying his wife, sir.

MR. BRANDON. No sir.

Knowing something about Italians, neither man put much credence in the possibility that maybe the whole operation was being run by the man's wife. No question about it, the Italians were passing up a good bet by not putting their wives in charge. From an administrative standpoint, they were crafty with intuition-blessed foresight.

Sullivan also made quite an issue over the ensuing fire that came close to trapping Officer Brandon halfway up inside the still's column and Officer Flint down in the pit. As they were dismantling the main still, leaking alcohol accumulated down in the pit and for some mysterious reason ignited. As Brandon put it: "All at once, there was a blue flame of alcohol fire across the bottom of the pit. We yelled, and we all got out. We all jumped out of the pit, grabbed up our extra clothing, and got clear of the building to where we felt we were safe." The officers then simply stood around and watched the place burn down.

Sullivan pushed a little harder:

MR. SULLIVAN. So I understand you were a little bit accelerated getting out of there? I don't suppose by any stretch of the imagination that you happened to have a search warrant for these premises that day?

MR. BRANDON. Not to my knowledge.

MR. SULLIVAN. Except sledgehammers and such ladylike utensils—by way of a search warrant?

MR. BRANDON. That is all.

The officers had luckily managed to retrieve two 5 gallon tin cans of alcohol for evidence as they departed the burning structures. When the tin cans were produced as evidence in court, the question of whether it contained straight 193-proof alcohol or the finished product, Jackass Brandy, became the issue.

MR. SULLIVAN. That is holy water, Judge—I think.

Prosecutor Walsh also addressed the Judge with the comment:

MR. WALSH. If your honor pleases, at this time I respectfully request that, in view of what Superior Judge says, I want to find out what it is, whether it is Jackass or alcohol.

The Judge, in reference to witness Brandon, said:

THE COURT. He testified it was alcohol, and Mr. Sullivan says it is holy water.

As suspected, the cans contained 193 proof alcohol; considered to be holy water by some, but a devil's brew to others.

Walsh finally conceded to letting the two employees, John Fuccari and S. Salo, off the hook. However, the court held Santucci, Fornacari, and Martini to answer the charge of possession of, and operating, a still.

Struggling with the spelling of names, the recorder recorded and transcribed the final hearing.

MR. WALSH. No objection to John—I have no objection to Sala, but I think Santucci ought to be held to answer, and let the jury determine.

MR. SULLIVAN. Your Honor, If there was any evidence to show that Santucci, on the day in question, even owned the property, there might be some merit in Mr. Walsh's contention. The only thing that we have—and I examined the officers—and all they said at all, as far as Santucci is concerned, was that somebody had told them that this was Santucci's ranch. Santucci was not on the premises; Santucci was not even shown to have been in the vicinity over a period of time. The evidence showed that Martini, the gentleman who sits here, said at that time he had a lease on a certain portion of those premises, and showed them the lease. There is absolutely nothing to connect Santucci himself with that still.

MR. WALSH. Well, let me be frank.

An off-the-record discussion took place, then back on the record.

THE COURT. Let the Superior Court decide that when they present the evidence.

MR. SULLIVAN. Do you think they have other evidence?

THE COURT. I do not know — I do not know.

MR. SULLIVAN. All right, then. Sala and John are discharged.

THE COURT. Sala and John Fuccori.

MR. WALSH. Who is John Fuccori? Is that the man who was feeding the hogs when they arrived?

THE WITNESS. Yes, that is him.

THE COURT. That is the man—and Sala. The other three will be held over to answer before the Superior Court of Alameda County to the charge named in the complaint, to-wit, possession of a still. That means Nello Fornacari, Oresti Santucci, and Dominico Martini—they will be held over.

Fornacari and Martini, seeing the handwriting on the wall, jumped bail, each forfeiting the $2,000 bail they had posted. They fled to parts unknown, thus leaving only Santucci to stand trial. Now the prosecutor had absolutely nothing in the way of witnesses or solid evidence that tied Santucci to the still other than a lease that said he was receiving $100 per month rent for a portion of his hog ranch from a lessee whose activities he insisted were unknown to him.

Obviously, Santucci could safely say that he could smell nothing unusual about the place since the pig pen aroma of a thousand hogs certainly overpowered the distillate discharge and fermented alcohol-laced mash waste smells. But this stuff was being fed to the hogs along with the swill. How could he have not known that it was waste mash when it caused the hogs to stagger around like drunken sailors?

Prosecutor Walsh had apparently overlooked the one simple question that could have stumped the defense: "How do you account for all the drunken happy-go-lucky pigs that were staggering around the place?" But then, who would have thought of asking such a question even though pigs and men have so much in common; that is, act like fools when intoxicated.

The fact that Santucci had an interest in the property was not strong enough for a conviction. And rightfully so, because if that were the case, then Earl Warren would have been faced with the task of tossing just about every ranch owner in Alameda County into San Quentin. The jury, on March 7, 1928, acquitted Santucci by returning a verdict of not guilty.

CHAPTER 20

Mike's ongoing trial was not helping his health matters much. Now he too was finding himself in the court arena just as Santucci was. Setting up the still at Morrison Canyon certainly drew attention away from Crow Canyon all right, but it also was turning out to be a disaster for Mike personally. The loss of the expensive, newly acquired modern still was a substantial financial loss, and the trauma of the ongoing trial added to his already severe ulcer problem.

Prosecutor Walsh had learned something in the Santucci case in that by taking a "flock shot" in hopes of convicting all the parties to the case, he had in fact missed them all. So now in Mike's case he questioned the witnesses and the arresting officers quite extensively, as if building up a good case against his co-defendant Garcia, when in fact he was attempting to pile up the evidence only against Mike. His tactics weren't much different than the arresting officers' tactics in their attempt to badger Garcia into fingering him. A good solid, unshakable witness against Mike is what the prosecutor needed and wanted.

In this case Walsh was up against two separate, seasoned attorneys: O. D. Hamlin, Jr., defending Garcia, and Louis J. Hardie, defending Mike. It is possible, and therefore likely, that the two attorneys purposely nudged the hearing into concentrating on Garcia, first in hopes of establishing him as an immune witness for the prosecutor, but then disqualifying him later on a technicality.

The first witness that prosecutor Walsh called to the stand was officer George G. Hard. The prosecutor was being careful and thorough in questioning witness Hard. Walsh went through the whole routine of establishing the events of the morning of the 7th day of January 1928, that entailed the raid on the unattended still. The questioning did establish the fact that neither Mike nor any of his paesani were anywhere near the place on that day. The matter of the location of the buildings and the presence of hogs, chickens, and horses was well established—almost to the point of indicating their color and habits. Testimony indicated that the modern, up-to-date still was cold and that it was fired by kerosene burners. Reference was made to a copper boiler, coils, mash, jackass, alcohol, and implements of sorts.

The matter of the lease that Garcia surrendered to the arresting officers was thoroughly discussed: Garcia being the lessor and G. Pasquale being the lessee. The prosecutor touched lightly on the matter of G. Pasquale being someone other than the man he purported to be, since he was not quite ready to get into that matter.

When prosecutor Walsh finished with officer Hard, he offered him to Mike's attorney, Hardie, for cross examination, but Hardie wisely handed the questioning over to Hamlin, Garcia's attorney. Hamlin went after the witness hammer and tong. He not only covered the same ground that Walsh had covered a few moments before, but also insisted on getting every little detail worked out, even to the location of the fences, gates, and where each cow was standing in the pasture. Much of the questions and answers were repetitive to the extent that witness Hard became annoyed to the point that necessitated Hamlin stating firmly:

MR. HAMLIN. Will you just relate the conversation, all of the conversation you had in that three-quarters of an hour with Garcia?

MR. HARD. It has already been related.

MR. HAMLIN. I asked you to, Mr. Hard — did you hear me?

MR. HARD. Yes sir, I heard you.

MR. HAMLIN. Then answer it please.

MR. HARD. I have already told you.

MR. HAMLIN. I don't care what you have already told me. I am asking you to relate the conversation.

MR. HARD. I told you that.

MR. HAMLIN. You know, just because you related it once to a member of the District Attorney's office, does not mean I cannot ask you to relate that conversation.

After that altercation, witness Hard became more cooperative and again was asked questions relating to chickens, pigs, horses, and various smells being apparent as still smells and not barnyard smells. The loading of evidence on drayman Silva's truck with the help of Garcia was also covered. Hamlin then waltzed witness Hard through the matter of the officers having at least inferred to Garcia that he (Garcia) would in fact improve his position by fingering Mike. You would think that defense attorney Hamlin would try to suppress the facts at this point, but instead he was elaborating on them as if he were the prosecuting attorney instead of the attorney for the defense.

All the time Mike's defense attorney, Hardie, was playing it cool by not interrupting. It may have appeared that he was falling asleep, but he was in fact very much awake for he knew that sooner or later the name of M. Buti would arise. Finally it did arise with a question by Hamlin to Hard.

MR. HAMLIN. Did you know anything about Mr. Buti's connection with that still that day?

MR. HARD. No sir.

Now it was prosecutor Walsh that objected to the question on the grounds that it was not proper cross examination.

MR. HAMLIN. Did you?

Walsh objected again on the same grounds, then explained his reason: "So far we have not produced any testimony against Buti upon the direct examination."

With that statement, an argument between the two legal counselors ensued. One would think that prosecutor Walsh was Mike's defense attorney instead of Hardie, since up to this point Hardie had said nothing.

Once back on the record, Hamlin asked a particular question of Mr. Hard:

MR. HAMLIN. After you have listed the notes of what you did up there, I see the words 'Mr. Buti' appear. Did you write these?

Now Mike's attorney, Hardie, objected.

MR. HARDIE. I object to any examination of M. Buti.

Hamlin insisted he had a right to ask the question, but Hardie simply put the matter to rest by stating:

MR. HARDIE. He said he did not know anything about Mr. Buti at all - nothing.

The lengthy examination and cross examination of the witness, officer Hard, was finally concluded without Mike's attorney Hardie as much as asking him one single question. Hamlin had done it for him.

Apparently prosecutor Walsh started to sense that his quarry was getting away from him, so he put officer Joe Brandon on the stand in hopes of coming up with something better, or at least something new in the case.

In the course of the questioning, Brandon did add a few matters that were not brought out before, such as the fact that the officers had visited the still on the night before, January 6, at about 7:15 or 7:20 in the evening and found the still to be warm, but with the premises void of any personnel. Thanks to Sheriff Becker's deputy, the paesani were down at Niles enjoying a Florentine Italian dinner at the time, to say nothing of the fact that they spent the night wrestling a contingency of over-sexed prostitutes while they, the officers now testifying, slept in adjacent rooms. Brandon, as well as Hard, made no mention of the fact that someone had moved in during the night after they had left for the evening, staged a hijack, and hauled off the bulk of the jackass and highproof alcohol. The list of supplies he described as being there the morning after did include a full 5 gallon glass demijohn of red wine. This in itself was sufficient proof that the still was operated by a gang of Italians. Matteoli, in his haste to get loaded and out of there, apparently had missed the wine on the night he hijacked the place.

Officer Brandon's directions as to how to reach the Garcia ranch differed somewhat from officer Hard. Although the directions differed, they lead you to the same place.

Brandon also stated that he took Garcia out back for a walk to view the 8000-gallon water tank stuck up on the side of the hill and look over the potato patch that Garcia first said Pasquale was farming. This, of course, turned out to be untrue, along with a lot of other statements made by Garcia and others as well. Garcia was also badgered by Brandon into divulging the true still owner by Garcia's producing the lease and enough information to warrant confronting Mike at his home in Crow Canyon. Obviously Mike denied everything, answering: "I don't know," to all questions. But Garcia, to protect himself, rattled on and on letting it all hang out. He admitted that a friend of his, having known who Mike really was, once pointed out to him that G. Pasquale and M. Buti were one and the same person. Garcia even pointed out the one time he saw him up on the side of the hill near the still site hunting. Mike readily admitted that, but quickly added: "But I did it for the boys that were living at the ranch, not for myself." Fat chance. Under no conditions would he have parted with a couple of plump quail or a nice fat cottontail rabbit. These were a few of the things in his life that he did not share with anyone.

Prosecutor Walsh finally offered the witness Brandon, for cross examination, and Mr. Hardie, defense attorney for Mike, accepted the offer. He blasted officer Brandon with only a couple dozen short, sharp, to-the-point questions about the lease. Brandon answered in kind: sharp and to the point.

Hardie then wisely turned the witness over to Hamlin, Garcia's attorney for further cross examination. It appeared as though Hardie was trying to get Hamlin to do his job for him.

Hamlin, of course, knew what he was doing. Again he hammered away at the matter of Garcia going up to the ranch to feed the farm animals on that particular day, or for that matter, any other day. He hammered away at the lease between his client Garcia and G. Pasquale, and the fact that at no time did any of the officers see Garcia operating or in and around the still. He hit hard on the fact that Brandon, as well as the other officers, had in the way of inference agreed to let him go or clear him of the charges if he would find, identify, and point out the operator of the still, namely Mike.

Defense attorney O. D. Hamlin had made his point. He presented a brilliant defense for his client, Antone Garcia. With the exception of now being a witness against Mike, Garcia beat the rap.

Prosecutor James C. Walsh, was quite pleased. He now thought he had Mike dead to rights; the one he really was after. He now had a lot of testimony on the record from Garcia to work with, as well as testimony from the arresting officers. He should have been wary of the fact that Hardie, Mike's legal counsel, was allowing all this incriminating evidence to pile up without objection, or for that matter, little or any attempt to suppress or counterargue on his client's behalf. As a matter of fact, all during the days that Mike was being tried, Hardie did practically nothing in the way of any attempt to engage Walsh in courtroom theatrical hoopla to distract the jury from the horrendous pile of evidence accumulated through testimony of witnesses, Garcia and the officers. Prosecutor Walsh now carefully laid it all out before the jury in a meticulous manner. But when the final arguments by the prosecutor were presented to the jury, counsel for the defense, Louis J. Hardie, esq., came to life. He had in fact been doing his homework, not sleeping as one might have thought.

The trial had been extensive. It first started with a preliminary hearing on February 2, 1928 at 2:15 p.m. before the Honorable Joseph A. Silva, Justice of the Peace, then transferred to culminate in the courtroom of the Honorable Givin Gray, Judge, April 4, 1928. Louis J. Hardie addressed the court in the presence of the jury. The judge already had in his possession prepared instructions to the jury from which he could choose once Hardie made his last and final presentation. After briefly commenting about the previous testimony already heard, examination of witnesses, and presentation of evidence, Hardie stated:

MR. HARDIE. Now, I wish to call your Honer's (sic) attention to that section of the Penal Code (Section 1111) which reads as follows:

'No conviction can be had upon the uncorroborated testimony of an accomplice.'

'No conviction can be had on the testimony of an accomplice unless it be corroborated by such other evidence as shall tend to connect the defendant with the commission of the offense, and the corroboration is not sufficient if it merely shows the commission of the offense or the circumstances thereof.'

'An accomplice is hereby defined as one who is liable to prosecution for the identical offense charged against the defendant on trial in the cause in which the testimony of the accomplice is given.'

That, if your Honor please, is Section 1111 of the Penal Code of this state. Also, the law prevails in other states of the Union.

Now, I wish to call your Honor's attention to a passage in Section 130 of Underhill on Criminal Evidence, third edition:

'The evidence which the statutes require is corroboration and which tends to connect the defendant with the commission of the crime, must be such evidence as will independently of the evidence of the accomplice, tend to connect the accused with the offense,'

reciting quite a long list of cases;

United States vs Murphy, 253 Federal, 404,
Horn vs State, 15 Alabama App., 213, 72 So. 768,
Celender vs State, 86 Arkansas 23, 109 S. W. 1024,
Brewer vs State, 137 Arkansas 243, 208 S. W. 290,
People vs Desmond, 24 Calif. App. 408, 141 Pac. 632,
People vs Compton, 123 California 403, 56 Pac. 44,
People vs Coffey, 161 California, 433,
People vs Hoosier, 24 Calif. App. 746, 142 Pac. 514,
People vs Blunkall, 31 Calif. App. 778, 161 Pac. 997,

also, citing six cases supporting this fact from the State of Georgia.

Now then, if your Honor please, I am appearing here for this defendant, Buti. I am bringing this to your consideration for the simple reason that viewing this testimony as we all have, I believe that there is not a man here but what is fair. I don't believe, a man here, connected with this case, but don't want to see that justice is done, and I am including the learned Prosecutor himself. I cannot see how this defendant can be held on this testimony that has been forthcoming from the witness stand, in this case, as far as the defendant, I am repeating, is concerned, because there is not a single bit of evidence - there is not one scintilla of evidence from anybody that he was in any wise connected with the operation of that still, or in any wise at all connected with it except coming from this man here. Under the circumstances we know. Under the circumstances of how it came, we know all about that. So, I tell you that there is not one bit of evidence that in any wise connects this man with the commission of that offense other than the testimony of the man Garcia.

Now then, there should be no dispute to the question as to whether or not he is an accomplice. He is jointly charged with the defendant, and the law states here, and specifically and clearly defines what an accomplice is. Now, I will grant this; that it does say that no conviction can be had on the uncorroborated testimony of an accomplice. It doesn't say anything about a preliminary hearing or anything of that sort, but it does plainly state under law this fact, that no conviction can be had without corroborative testimony. So, should the men be held for further trial, no conviction can be had.

The judge did concur with Hardie and therefore submitted to the jury the one jury instruction that Hardie had hoped for.

THE COURT: The jury is instructed that a conviction can not be had upon the testimony of an accomplice unless it be corroborated by such other evidence as shall tend to connect the defendant with the commission of the offense; and the corroboration is not sufficient if it merely shows the commission of the offense or the circumstances thereof.

You are instructed that an accomplice is one who is liable to prosecution for the identical offense charged against the defendant on trial in the cause in which the testimony of the accomplice is given.

Penal Code Sec. 1111 of the State of Calif.
(Signed: Givin Gray - Judge)

The verdict: Not Guilty, was handed down by the jury on the same day, April 4, 1928.

Granted, Louis J. Hardie had done a brilliant job in defending Mike, but there was another factor that surely played a part in his acquittal besides Penal Code Section 1111 of the State of California.

Once the not guilty verdict was read into the records, prosecuting attorney Walsh asked the jury foreman, who happened to be a sensible middle-aged woman, as to why the jury returned the not guilty verdict. He thought he had a strong case against Mike.

The jury foreman, Edna R. Lawrence, answered the prosecutor with a to-the-point question of her own, while maintaining an air of elegance about her, she said:

"Why don't you throw the entire Italian community into San Quentin? Why only this person?"

Apparently, the Penal Code as referred to merely provided the jury the needed excuse to return the verdict they were most comfortable with.

The jury foreman had a good point, but had she known that all during the time the trial was in progress, Mike's gang of paesani were still busy cranking out Jackass from other units, she may have had other thoughts about the matter.

CHAPTER 21

Placing the one still all the way up to the end of Bellina Canyon to the old Peters' place had its drawbacks. The structure the men were housed in fell quite short of being adequate. The barn-like structure, with a couple of partitions and a wood plank floor, was set on chunks of sandstone that substituted for a foundation. Redwood boards were nailed upright to the frame, much like a barn. The cracks and knotholes in the floor eliminated the need for a dustpan. When sweeping, nothing in the way of dust or dirt ever got past the wide spaces between the boards so nothing accumulated for picking up. Gophers pushed mounds of dirt up through the large knotholes in complete disregard of the occupants. Such as it was with the rest of the canyon, electricity did not exist. The water system amounted to nothing more than a pipe extending from a ponded spring to the still site.

Coyotes living amongst the boulders and granite crags above and close by didn't help matters much either. The paesani knew nothing about coyotes; as far as they were concerned, they were wolves; they were scared to death of them. The constant yipping and howling during the night sent chills up and down their spines. Finally one night the coyotes got into a snarling, growling fight amongst themselves over dinner scraps tossed into the garbage pile, thus bringing the matter to a head. A spokesman for the group confronted Julio with what now appeared to be a serious problem:

"Julio," he said in a pleading manner, "we can no longer tolerate this. The men refuse to step out of the door even to urinate—what'll we do?"

The complaint was valid—a solution must be found. By the light of the flickering lantern, while in deep thought, Julio observed a gopher pushing dirt up through a sizable knothole in the floor. As he watched the gopher's activity, he jokingly stated:

"If they're afraid to step out the door, then let them urinate through the knotholes in the floor. Maybe it'll discourage the damn gophers."

The statement drew chuckles and laughter. They didn't take the comment seriously, but then, the more they joked about it, the more the idea seemed to have merit.

"Sounds like a damned good idea," said the spokesman finally, then added:

131

"Why not—what the hell . . . " With that comment, he unbuttoned his fly and positioned himself at a knothole in preparation for relieving himself through the floor.

"Hold it!" commanded a voice. "A quarter says you'll miss the hole!"

"You're a damn fool to make that bet," said yet another. "That's a big hole; anybody can ring a hole that big."

"Oh, is that so? A quarter says you can't do it either, not without splattering the floor."

The challenge was not only met, but a contest to see who could best urinate through a knothole without splattering the floor now erupted into a betting frenzy with others participating. Julio shook his head in disbelief at the sight of these grown men acting as kids, penis in hand, urinating through knotholes in the floor. He now wished he hadn't opened his mouth, but then— what the hell, the men needed some kind of entertainment to get their minds off the menacing coyotes and, under the circumstances, this was as good a way as any.

However, after several nights of this horseplay, they soon learned that where there's a colony of gophers, you can expect to find snakes— "rattlesnakes." They'd seen and killed a few around the place over the past few weeks, but didn't realize that all this time there was a den of them directly under their feet; that is, not until they started rattling every time the men urinated through the knotholes. Faced with this new threat —rattlesnakes under foot—they renewed their complaints. Julio, not liking the idea of snakes underfoot either, responded:

"There's only one thing to do, and that is run the buggers out of there!"

"Run them out? How?" questioned one of the men.

"We'll think of something," he said, then added: "Smoke 'em out, if we have to."

As thought was being given to the idea, one of the men lifted a 5 gallon tin can from over the top of a sizable knothole and peered down into it. A pair of snake eyes peered back at him. Slapping the can back over the hole, he announced excitedly:

"There's a big one right here! I just saw him—the bugger stuck his tongue out - staring up at me!"

"Quick! Pour some high-proof on him!" suggested another.

The suggestion had merit. A generous quantity of 193 proof alcohol was instantly poured through the knothole. Reacting to the burning effect of the highproof, the snake thrashed around under the floor, thus arousing others— hissing and rattling furiously. As other knotholes were peered into, more snakes were revealed so more alcohol was poured through the holes thus causing the snakes to start poking their heads up through the holes only to be drenched with more highproof. Using whatever objects were handiest, the men sealed the holes to keep the snakes confined. They could now be seen slithering out from under the alcohol-saturated floor area and across the yard. Expressing delight, the men stomped around on the floor in hopes of speeding up the snakes' departure. Thinking he could speed them up even more, a cigar-smoking paesano, without taking into consideration the consequences, announced in delight:

"I'll show you how to get them moving faster—watch this!" With that, he tossed his glowing stogie into a knothole with the thought of smoking them out.

"No! Holy Christ! No!" screamed Julio, just seconds before the whole underside of the structure erupted into a swooshing explosion, sending fingers of blue flames up through every crack and crevice in the floor like a huge gas burner. In a rattle of boards and creaking of stressed timber, the structure surged upwards off its foundation, then slapped back down. And, in so doing, extinguished the burning alcohol in a final swoosh, thus forcing smoke and dust up through loose boards and knotholes. The fact that the building was not on fire, or that a secondary explosion would not occur, did not register in their minds. Choking and gasping for air, they came boiling out the door, cursing and bitching. Fed up with the whole affair, Julio issued a firm reminder:

"You bunch of imbeciles better shape up, or God help you if you don't! Mike's not paying you $40 a week plus room and board to clown around blowing up buildings!"

"Julio," said the spokesman in a shaky voice, "for Christ's sake, talk to Mike—get us out of here. We can't work under these conditions. It's bad enough that there isn't a woman within miles of this God forsaken place, but to have to put up with wolves and snakes is too much!"

The mention of women gave Julio an idea. He assured them that he'd talk to Mike. Upon doing so, Mike agreed that Julio's idea to employ mobile prostitutes to service the men had merit, at least until they could make arrangements to move the still operation to a somewhat less remote location with better living quarters.

Since the prostitutes were already on occasion dropping in on the Waldie (bachelor brothers) ranch adjacent to and further down the canyon, it was a simple matter for Mike to proposition them into adding several more prostitutes to their stable, frequent the canyon more often, and to the delight of the two bachelor brothers, use their bunkhouse to carry out their duties, thus keeping them away from the still. Besides being well paid, both the Waldies and the prostitutes were assured that a generous supply of Jackass would be made available.

The plan went into action. The first two carloads of these well-perfumed women—ostrich feathered hats fluttering in the breeze, flowered skirts swirling with every move of the hips—scrambled out of their cars at the Waldie ranch, ready for action. The Madam (the prostitute in charge of these sex machines), knowing the Waldies from previous visits, and knowing them to be stone-deaf, yelled out:

"Well, here we are! Where the hell are those horny bootleggers?" Not seeing anyone around but the two brothers, Oscar and John, it was a logical question.

John, with a little better hearing then Oscar, answered the question while his brother passed around the jug of Jackass. Having already slurped up a fair ration of the stuff, in a slurred voice he responded:

"We sent a rider up to fetch them the minute we saw you coming up the road. In the meantime, you can start with us." As he said that, he started groping around her skirt. He was eager.

"Damn you, back off!" she snapped. "Mike's men come first! You'll get yours—last!" She and her girls had been paid more money for this job than they could earn in a month while working a double shift. Prostitute or no prostitute, she knew where her loyalty lay. No nonsense here. So they restricted their activities to passing the jug around—kind of priming themselves for the task that 'lie' ahead.

The rider (the Waldie hired hand) came galloping into the still site up at Peters' place, yelling at the top of his voice like Paul Revere to announce the coming of the prostitutes. Excitedly, he yelled:

"The whores are coming! The whores are coming! Bring more whiskey! Bring more whiskey!" With that announcement, he reined his horse into a tight spin and galloped off in a cloud of dust, heading back from whence he came, eager to join the Waldies.

Needless to say, production came to an abrupt halt. The still was shut down and devoid of personnel faster than if it had been a raid by federal agents. Taking a shortcut, crashing through patches of poison oak and brambles at a dead run, within minutes they arrived at Waldie's, ready for action. As hoped for, they were greeted with open arms and raised skirts.

By the time they got through with that Jackass-saturated contingency of prostitutes, shredded ostrich feathers and flowery skirts were strewn all over hell's half acre. The prostitutes earned their pay that day. But regardless, the decision was made to move the still anyway.

With the exception of Henry Mast having running water in his kitchen by means of a pipe stuck through the wall with a faucet at the sink, fed by gravity from a spring on the side of the hill above the house, conditions were about comparable to the old Peters' place across the canyon. He had gophers pushing dirt up through his floor as well, and since he occupied what little there was of the house, that location was ruled out. Henry never bothered to shut off the water that flowed in his kitchen sink. By so doing, the pure, cool spring water would maintain its fresh, cold temperature even though the pipe leading down from the spring above was laid on top of the ground and directly exposed to the hot sun. His saddle horse preferred to stick his head through the open window and drink out of the kitchen sink rather than drink out of his own warm watering trough.

During freezing temperatures, there was also the need to keep the water flowing constantly through the pipes in order to prevent freezing. This was fine, with the exception that the drain line from the sink to the outside would eventually freeze up and back water into the sink. When this happened, the entire sink would freeze up, causing water to overflow and cascade over the top, down the side of the sink and onto the plank floor where it would also freeze up creating a sizeable glacier extending part way across the kitchen floor. This didn't bother Henry much since he seldom drank water anyway, and Mike's Jackass kept him warm during the winter months; besides, he was accustomed to the hardships of rugged ranch life since he came from a clan of hardy pioneers.

The Waldie ranch was by far the best suited, and of course the owners were receptive to the idea. Having struck a deal, the still was finally moved from the old Peters' place over to Waldie's ranch, a more convenient location. The two bachelor brothers, John and Oscar Waldie, were delighted to have the still located there on their ranch, not only for the extra revenue it provided, but also for the generous supply of good Jackass so close at hand.

Oscar especially proved to be indispensable during the wet weather. With his huge muscular Clydesdale draft horses hitched to a sled or wagon, he was hired to haul loads of 5 gallon cans of alcohol down to Tony's relay house and haul back sacks of sugar, mash, and supplies of all sorts. Pulling stuck vehicles out of the mud was another of his functions. His only known real physical shortcoming was his deafness. You might say that he was stone-deaf, as were other members of the family. The deafness was apparently genetic. However, since the paesani were masters of sign language, with their habit of hand gestures and expressions, he had no trouble communicating with them.

Apparently he had lost all his teeth at an early age and had never bothered to replace them. This fact added to his already striking resemblance to Edward G. Robinson, the actor, even to the extent of talking like him. Since he was also built like the actor, he could very well have doubled for him, especially while smoking his ever present curved stem pipe.

John was a professional wagon maker and blacksmith so this too was extremely convenient since he maintained a well-equipped blacksmith shop at the ranch. Regardless of the type of material, be it wood or metal, John could repair it, if not build a duplicate when needed. Needless to say, the stills were kept in good repair.

The crew at the other unit, over at the Thompson place, halfway up the canyon, were extremely jumpy due to their knowledge of their being set up as the first line of defense. They felt like crickets impaled on a fish hook. They had been schooled as to what to expect in the event of a raid, even to the extent of the form of transportation that might be used by federal agents, which included various descriptions of automobiles and motorcycles. At the first indication of a raid, each one would be required to perform one or two specific functions in order to shut down and secure the still before departing the premises as fast as they could. They were told to run uphill, since the agents would no doubt be somewhat flabby and out of shape. By so doing, they would not be pursued for long on foot. Once in the high country, they could take refuge amongst the boulders and granite crags of the ridge above, for they surely would not be pursued at those higher elevations. The very early morning hours, at about daybreak would no doubt be the time a raid would be staged. This, therefore, would give the paesani the edge, since that hour is the quietest time of day. Any vehicle of whatever nature would unmistakably announce its arrival.

Once the schooling sessions were over, they then made a few practice runs of their own by giving each other commands of sorts and familiarizing themselves as to what warning sounds to expect. But such as it is with camp training, the many contingencies that surface when the real thing comes along are seldom considered or prepared for. This particular brisk spring morning, when the hay was ripe and ready for mowing, proved to be just one of those contingencies.

Oscar hitched up a team of horses to a hay mower, as did his brother John. The two brothers set out just before daybreak, riding the machines down the road to what was known as the Blue Gate, for its blue color. It separated cultivated land from pasture. The hayfield to be cut was in perfect earshot, but out of sight, of the paesani working the still down at the Thompson place across the canyon. The draft horses, having more sense than most men, needed little encouragement or verbal instructions from their masters, and being well able to find their way in the dark, they were given their head to guide the brothers to the hay field in the semi-darkness. The horses knew what was expected of them, so the caravan of horses, men, and machines, with the sickle blades in a neutral position, moved along down the road towards the hayfield, without as much as a spoken word or loud noise of any kind being emitted.

They arrived at the hayfield just about daybreak, lined up at the edge of the field one behind the other, and prepared to proceed with the mowing. Since the two brothers were both deaf, they seldom spoke to each other unless there was good reason. So both being quite familiar with the hay mowing routine, set their sickle bars down at the desired level of cut and climbed back up into the bucket-like seat of the mowers and prepared for the start of the hay mowing season. Of the two brothers, John was always the leader, with Oscar the follower. This was no doubt brought about by the fact that John was blessed with slightly better hearing than Oscar. John, in the lead, at the top of his voice gave the signal and command for the start:

"All right, Oscar!" he yelled back to his brother. "Let's go get it!"

Oscar in response and acknowledgment of the command, yelled back at the top of his voice as well: "All right, John! I'm ready to go! Let's take it!"

With that, the horses moved forward at a steady pace, pulling the mowers behind them, cutting a swath of hay. The reciprocating long sickle bar with blades shaped like so many shark's teeth, slid back and forth along the guide bar, sending off a loud chatter, much like a motorcycle in motion. The two machines working together did indeed sound like two powerful motorcycles, with sidecars attached, laboring at the chore of negotiating the road heading towards the still. The sudden loud sharp commands, followed by the constant chatter of the mowers echoed across the canyon on this quiet, crisp, spring morning to announce the start of the hay mowing season.

To the vigilant ears of the paesani at the Thompson place, however, it announced the start of a raid by federal agents coming in on motorcycles. These immigrants knew nothing of American hay mowing methods. In the old country hay was cut with hand sickles, by both men and women, with kids tagging along playing joyfully. It was a festive atmosphere with singing and laughter, certainly not loud military-like commands, accompanied by chattering machines that resembled military motorcycles. All their schooling, training, and dry run practice drills burst from their minds like so many bubbles, as the stark realization of being caught up in a raid, penetrated their brain cells. In a complete state of confusion, they were all to act simultaneously. The only thought that had not been dislodged from memory was to run like hell and head for the hills.

Those that were caught in their longjohns leaped directly from their bunks through the windows, as others crashed out the back door without bothering to shut the system down. The outhouse door, with its crescent-shaped vent hole emitting drifting cigarette smoke, burst off its hinges as the two-holer's occupants dashed out simultaneously, cinching their belts as they joined the others. However, they did at least remember to flip a match into the scattered newspapers in hopes of destroying the production records scratched on the interior walls. The one thing these immigrants knew how to do was to run. With the exception of purpose, the procedure was the same in America as it was in Italy. If there was any thought in their minds worth noting as they scrambled up the mountainside, it was the fact that now they knew what was meant by the fast-moving American economy.

The granite crags looming up on the horizon with the golden break of day behind them gave the impression of church steeples rising above the landscape below. To this ragtag group of God-fearing Italian immigrants, the thought and sight of church steeples caused them to stop long enough to catch their breath and make an assessment of their predicament. Huddled together, the decision was made to continue the ascent and deliver their souls in person to God waiting in the heavens above at the crags. The supposed federal agents in hot pursuit could then have the remnants of their physical being, and do what they wished with it. To add momentum to their already speedy ascent, the unsecured, unattended still blew up in a roaring explosion that echoed throughout the canyon. God need not wait long now for the hand delivery of the souls of these misguided immigrants.

The two brothers had just completed another round of mowing, and were resting the horses in the swath of the previous cut when the still exploded. The horses' keen hearing caught the thunderous roar, thus causing them to react to the disturbance with a stiff-legged, hoof-stomping shudder, just short of stampeding. Their intelligence and concern for their handlers' safety was the deciding factor in their holding their ground. Because of their deafness, neither one of the two brothers heard the explosion. Realizing that the horses sensed something wrong, they glanced around the swathed hay looking for the possible presence of a rattlesnake, but could not find one. As they walked back towards their mowers, wondering what caused the commotion, they glanced up to see the vapor and dust drifting upward from the still location across the canyon. There was no need for them to head back up the road to notify Julio of the mysterious goings-on over at the Thompson place, for he, along with several men, were already alerted to the incident and were therefore driving down the road as fast as conditions would permit.

Julio reached the point where the road branched off to cross the creek just as Mike appeared on the scene driving up from the opposite direction. From the high point of the road across the canyon he, too, had witnessed the cloud of dust with its accompanying rumbling blast echoing down the canyon. Apparently the explosion extinguished the still's gasoline burners thus preventing an ensuing fire. A cloud of dust was about all that was floating skyward.

"Julio, what happened?" asked Mike excitedly.

"I don't know," answered Julio. "More snakes, I guess."

"For God's sake, do they have to blow up the still to get rid of a few snakes? This has got to stop! That was quite a blast. We better get right up there—somebody may be hurt."

This made sense; they headed on up to the still expecting to find injured men, but there was no one to be found. They did note the outhouse ablaze, an indication that the intent was to destroy production records. Julio commented:

"They must have thought they were being raided. I wonder what made them think that?"

"I think you're right—they're all gone. They made a run for it, but why?"

The mystery lingered on his mind.

There being no reason for Oscar and John to join the rescue party, they gently slapped the reins on the big ham-like butts of the draft horses and urged them to recommence the task of mowing hay. The pronounced chatter of the two mowers again echoing across the canyon instantly told the rescuers what had happened. Despite the destruction of the still, the mystery solved, the group broke out in hilarious laughter at the thought of the paesani having heard the motorcycle-like chatter emitting from the mowers at such an early hour of day and mistaking it for revenue agents. The task of following the trail of the fast-departing men was not too difficult, but the task of coaxing them out of the sanctuary of the protective cathedral-like crags was another matter entirely.

Sending Julio and the others back up to the Waldie still, Mike took it upon himself to seek out and coax the men back down from the granite crags of Rocky Ridge, as it is known, that separates the two counties, Alameda and Contra Costa. It was near nightfall before he was able to catch up to them. He called out to his men to come on down, but his commands echoing throughout the crags only sent them crawling higher and higher. Bouncing from spire to spire, his voice had lost its identity, and so it was with his patience. He screamed in anger:

"Come down you fools or I'll skin you alive and feed your carcasses to the wolves!"

The thought of wolves gave Mike an idea. In silence he sneaked up without being seen to within shouting range of the paesani huddled on a ledge. Knowing of their fear of the beasts, he let out a wolf-like howl directed at an upright slab of granite that caused the echo to ricochet amongst the crags. The men heard it alright, and so did a nearby pack of coyotes that where just emerging from their den for an evening of howling at the moon. This was their territory this intruder was howling in, and so they responded to the challenge with a combination of howls, growls and yipping barks.

Horrified at the response to his actions, Mike, no braver than his men, hightailed back down at a brisk gait, but didn't get far before the men caught up to him. While at a dead run, with a note of urgency as they passed him by, they apprized him of the situation:

"Run for your life, Mike! The wolves are after us!"

Needless to say, he was doing just that. He wasn't about to be left behind considering nightfall was upon them with fierce beasts on the prowl.

CHAPTER 22

For a while the federal agents had backed off, leaving the paesani with the belief that maybe the scheduled payoffs satisfied their appetites. Their demands were always met without argument or incident. Unlike Al, Mike was satisfied that payoffs in the form of cash and an occasional barrel of Jackass was all part of the way of doing business.

Al disagreed. His handling of the Oakland police with an occasional favor, a complimentary all-night session in one of the many speakeasy whorehouse establishments that featured Mike's Jackass, was sufficient and not considered bribery. This was fine for the local authorities, but far from good enough for the federal agents. They wanted that too, plus a bundle of cash—outright solicited bribery. It wasn't long before the agents were back to their old tricks, only this time, correctly assuming that Tony's still may have been moved, appeared to be concentrating not only on finding the exact location of the stills, but also how to get to them. Instead of backing off, they were now hounding the operation even more.

"Now what the hell do they want?" asked Mike.

"More money," answered Matteoli.

"For Christ's sake! We've been raising the ante right along, aren't they ever going to be satisfied?"

"No, Mike, they'll never be satisfied until they get it all."

"What do you suppose their plan is?"

"For one thing, to locate the stills and how to get to them ahead of Warren's men, then we really pay off. I suggest you call a meeting immediately and alert the others of this newest threat."

The four men got together again. All-in-all, the news came as no surprise, at least not to Al. Never trusting the federal agents to keep their word in the first place, he reported that with attempts at tailing him now in progress, they could expect the senior agent to not only up his demands, but to also, eventually, doublecross them, and so stated:

"I said it before, and I'll say it again. These bastards can't be trusted. Believe me, they'll screw us."

"They must know that the main still, if not at Tony's, is still located some-

141

where in Bellina Canyon," responded Matteoli. "So why do you suppose they're tailing you?"

"They can no longer be sure of it. After all, it has been some time since the raid at Tony's. I think they have something bigger in mind."

"Like what?" asked Mike.

"Get the goods on all of us. Nail down the whole operation from one end to the other."

In his calm, thoughtful manner, Julio concurred with Al: "He's right. They're up to something big. What he says makes sense, so you better warn Terzo." The statement was directed to Mike. Trusting Julio's judgment, he agreed to do just that. The meeting broke up with a grim reminder: "You cannot trust a lawman on the take."

It never occurred to the agents to stake out the other end of Crow Canyon at San Ramon. So at times, when sugar and supplies were needed at the stills, to avoid the agents stakeout along Crow Canyon, Terzo was imposed upon to make occasional sugar deliveries by route of Dublin Canyon Road, heading east, then turning north at Dublin to San Ramon, therefore entering Crow Canyon from the opposite direction, the Contra Costa County side. He would then pick up his quota of alcohol in 5 gallon tin cans directly from the still and return by the same route. This would have continued to work fine, if it were not for the tedious, long journey, and Terzo's desire to nip Jackass as he drove along, which finally put an end to this method of operation. On this particular brisk night, after a chilling winter rain, his nips were more frequent, with an extra guzzle with each draw from the flask. By the time he reached the first gate at the entrance to Bellina Canyon, he was well-saturated. He worked his way up the canyon on the muddy, somewhat slippery road, managing to reach the second gate, then continuing to the third gate where a headlight signal had to be given to alert the lookout sitting in the man-made crow's nest high up on a sturdy madrone tree a good mile or so up the canyon at Waldie's. The proper code signals were given in the usual manner, even though the lookout would have recognized Terzo by his zigzag pattern of driving anyway. The lookout called to the paesani working at the still below:

"Terzo's down by Tony's gate."

"What does it look like, is he going to try to make it all the way up?" came a question from below.

"No, I doubt it. He's been zigzagging all over the road, it's probably pretty slick. He'll no doubt dump the sugar off there at Tony's place. We can go down and get it come early morning," came the answer. Had Terzo not had a snoot-full, he probably would have done just that, but since he was drunk and had made it that far, he saw no reason why he shouldn't continue the rest of the way. Once through the third gate, he staggered back to close it. Viewing the situation up ahead through blurry eyes, he decided to bypass Tony's place and take the load directly to the still. Sober, the hill up ahead could possibly be negotiated, but in his condition, it should never have been attempted. But such as it is with drunken drivers, the drunker they are, the better qualified they think they are to drive. He was no exception. Another jolt of Jackass under his belt would certainly help ward off the chill, besides it would help steady his nerves, he thought. So before starting off, he killed the rest of what was left in the flask, then searched around in his pockets for a fresh Toscanello cigar. Managing to get it lit, he then took off in an attempt to make the grade up ahead. His zigzag pattern was more pronounced than ever. Once again, the lookout yelled down to the men below:

"Holy Christ! He's making a run for the hill! He must be out of his mind! He'll never make it!"

"The hell you say! How's he doing?"

"He's zigzagging all over the road and he's not at the grade yet. He's got to be drunk!"

"He's drunk all right. You better keep an eye on him, that stretch of road is bad enough to drive sober, let alone drunk and loaded with sugar."

Halfway up the grade the headlights of the Model-T could be seen to change from a zigzag pattern to a tumbling pattern as the Model-T left the road to the right, and was now rolling over and over down the side of the hill until it finally came to rest in a clump of trees and thick brush in an upside down position.

"Holy Christ! He's rolled it off the hill!"

"He did what?"

"I said, he rolled it off the hill. I can see his headlights shimmering through the trees below the road."

"Come on down—let's get down there," shouted the man below.

Leaving a man behind to tend the still, they ran up the footpath to the main still at the big barn to announce the accident. Julio, along with a group of paesani, drove down to the spot where the Model-T was being held to the side of the hill by brush and trees in an upside down position. Being careful not to dislodge it from its precarious position, they proceeded to remove sacks of sugar until they were able to extract Terzo, unhurt, cigar still firmly clenched between his teeth, cussing the day that Ford invented the Model-T.

Relieved to find him unhurt, the paesani were quick to jokingly remind him that had he been as fit to drive as the Model-T was to perform its duties, the hill would have been negotiated without incident. Indignant about being referred to as drunk, Terzo demanded that he be unhanded while negotiating on foot the few yards below the clump of trees down to the roadway leading to Tony's place. He had something to add to his demand:

"I've had a few drinks, that I'll admit, but what makes you think I'm drunk?" he mumbled incoherently just before staggering and tumbling down head over heels the few yards left to go. As the men rushed down the embankment to gather him up out of the mud, he was to remind them of their mistaken diagnosis of his condition:

"Ha! You see, I beat all of you down, didn't I? And you think I'm the one that's drunk!"

CHAPTER 23

The constant tail on Al indicated that the federal agents were really getting desperate. The Hudson was now constantly popping up at various unsuspecting locations, pick up Al's tail, only to be outrun or outmaneuvered in some manner or other. After a number of attempts at trying to tail him, it appeared that the frustrated agents were actually trying to catch him if they could and arrest him. Confronted with the prospect of jail, they might get him to talk. So far, they hadn't come close enough to even see what he looked like. All they ever got was a fading look at the tail-end of the Buick as it outdistanced them. His racing instincts contributed to his ability to outrun and outmaneuver the Hudson. Also, the fact that he enjoyed what he was doing gave him an edge.

"That driver of Mike's is something else again," stated the senior agent to his cohort while on stakeout in Oakland on this miserable, rainy, drizzly night. "Maybe, just maybe, on this kind of night with the help of the Essex we can sneak up on him and trap him."

"I wouldn't bank on that, sir. I doubt that he'll be out on a night like this."

"You may be right, but nevertheless, we'll wait it out. Bad weather doesn't slow those kinds of guys down by much." And so the two agents, along with their backup, the Essex, sat out the drizzly stakeout.

As with professional racers, Al had built up a following amongst his many Portuguese cannery worker friends and buddies that lived and hung around the districts of 23rd Avenue, 29th Avenue, and Fruitvale Avenue (also referred to as "Jingle Town"), a short distance from the garage-warehouse next to the police station located at Melrose. The main artery, East 14th Street, was a broad street which ran from Oakland proper through these adjoining districts and continued through to San Leandro and Hayward. Two sets of streetcar tracks, typical of that era, ran through the center portion for its entire length, some 15 miles. On his return delivery trips, Al would leave Oakland by way of East 12th Street, make a left at 23rd Avenue, then a right onto East 14th, heading east again to Hayward-Castro Valley.

Despite the many fistfights and brawls that took place between these youths of Italian and Portuguese extraction, they did have much in common.

The fights that ensued were more for testing each other out than for any other reason. They addressed each other by calling out: "Hey, Dago, your old man's a spaghetti bender," or similar slurs that triggered a response such as: "What's it to ya, Portagee, where'd your old man jump ship?" With that kind of introduction, the fistfights and brawls would follow; nevertheless, they liked and respected each other for what they were, sons of immigrants trying to cut it in a new land.

Once Al started to show up on the scene with the Buick being pursued by the Hudson, his buddies made it a point to stand around the street corners waiting for him to put on a show. They loved the spectacular display of screeching tires, smell of burnt rubber, and revving up of engines. The high-pitched whistle of the Buick's fuel vacuum system added to their enthusiasm. However, care had to be exercised to avoid a collision with any of the Portuguese-owned parked cars that lined the streets for this event. To as much as dent a fender could bring about a thrashing of severe magnitude.

Al's wife, Ida's, call to supper didn't register as he stood at the bay window solemnly gazing out at the swirls of drizzling rain haloing the street light across the street. It was a bad night, but nevertheless he'd have to go out into it. A load of Jackass had to be delivered, rain or shine. The Terzo incident on the rain-soaked road a few nights before crossing his mind caused him to crack a smile. His mixed feelings as to the problems this bad weather was causing didn't go unnoticed. His wife's repeated calls to supper finally snapped him out of his trance. She worried about her husband's recklessness and antic capers, especially now that it became known that federal agents were out to get him, so she let her feelings be known:

"Are you taking a load downtown tonight in this drizzling rain?" she asked during the course of having dinner.

"That's right. Why do you ask?"

"It's a bad night . . . it's raining. Why do you have to go out tonight . . . can't it wait?"

"Wait for what? I'm not going up the canyon; I'm picking up a load at the warehouse."

"I know, but the federal ag . . ."

Al cut her off short: "You worried about that damned Hudson? Hell, it can't stay with me . . . no way!"

The answer was reassuring, but her woman's intuition gnawed at her inner feelings. He could sense this. This was one of those nights that caused her worry. Despite the fact that he spent many nights away from home, he loved and respected his wife; he understood her, so to put her mind at ease, he announced:

"Alright, if it will make you feel better, I'll pick up Fats. He ain't doing anything anyway. It'll do him good to get away from that crummy pool hall."

Ida felt better. Fats, as brawly as he was, was a good influence on Al. His slowness tended to temper Al's quick, aggressive reflexes, at times avoiding physical conflict.

As usual, Fats agreed to go along. But not until he was to berate his buddy in his usual manner:

"Now what the hell are ya up to? I damned near got my ass whipped over that Bronzini hijack affair! What're we up against this time? You looking to get yourself worked over again?"

"Dry up! It's nothing like that. It's a bad night. Ida'll feel better knowing you're along."

"Does she have any idea what you're up to?"

"Only that I'm in the alcohol business. She doesn't need to know anything else."

"That figures. You dagos are all alike—keep the women in the dark."

"In this business, the less they know the better."

"On second thought, maybe you're right."

Their first stop was the warehouse, where they picked up the load of Jackass. Fats knew about it, but had never been in it. He made comment about that as well:

"Holy Christ Al, you crazy dago! Next door to the police station! And Captain Brown . . . he's one tough cop . . . ? What the hell . . .? Look at all this stuff . . . unbelievable!"

Al chuckled. His buddy's surprised reaction was amusing. Fats now realized the extent of Al's involvement in this bootlegging affair. No question, the cops were in on it, or at least sanctioned it. He had more to say:

"Christ, I didn't realize the extent of . . ." he didn't finish the sentence before announcing: "Damn it! How about getting in on this? I could use a job . . . of this sort." He was careful not to mention work; just a paying job.

"Mike mentioned being shorthanded at the stills. I'll ask him, if that's what ya want. It pays real good."

"Sure! Hell yes!"

They headed in the direction of downtown Oakland, dropping off a keg of Jackass here and there. Their final stop was in West Oakland at the "North Pole," a speakeasy owned by an Italian who went by the name of "Francesco." The club had a reputation that lent itself to an exciting, wild night, especially for those that savored the exotic and unusual. The "North Pole," as its name so implied, also offered entertainment about as far out as one could possibly get, at least in Oakland. The featuring of Mike's superb Jackass Brandy attracted the "elite."

Now empty and heading back while travelling east on 7th Street, Fats commented:

"Heck, that was easier than I thought . . . like delivering sacks of potatoes . . . nobody around to bother ya."

"We ain't home yet," said Al as he glanced into the rear view mirror. The misty drizzle made for poor rear visibility.

"What do ya mean? Are ya expecting trouble?" asked Fats curiously.

"No, not really, just a couple of Feds in a Hudson. They've been bugging me lately," answered Al calmly.

"I knew it!" blurted Fats. "Goddamn you . . . why didn't ya tell me in the first place? So that's it!"

"Pipe down, it's no big deal. I doubt they'll be out on a miserable night like this anyway."

Where 7th terminated, as did other streets cut off by spur railroad tracks servicing industrial buildings, the Buick swung left, then a few blocks up, right again to pick up 12th, thus skirting the industrial area. Being dictated by habit, Al once again peered into the rear view mirror. This time he recognized the Hudson's big headlights following several blocks behind.

"Well, I'll be damned! I'd have never thought . . . "

"What is it?" asked Fats, twisting his massive body to see what had caught Al's attention.

"It's that damned Hudson, the one with the Feds."

"What's that mean?"

"It means we've got company." Glancing into the mirror again, Al had more disturbing news to announce—he'd spotted the Essex following the Hudson. He flipped his cigarette out the flap of the side curtains as he cursed profusely:

"You bastards! Don't you have anything better to do? And that goddamned Essex! What the hell is it doing here?" In answer to his questions, he surmised the reason for the two cars; the agents were intent on trapping him.

"Damn it!" he cursed. "Now what the hell are they planning? I guess we'll soon find out," he growled, as he made the left onto 23rd Avenue from 12th Street. Taking the turn at a fair rate of speed, he felt the car slip and fishtail on the wet pavement. "Oh-oh, I better watch it on the next turn," he reminded himself as he backed off.

Hanging on to keep from sliding from side to side, Fats offered some sound advice: "Swing out, take it in a wide swoop, and watch it on the wet tracks!" He was making reference to the upcoming right turn onto East 14th, with its double set of streetcar tracks.

The Hudson was experiencing the same thing causing the driver, the senior agent, to utter a sneering remark through clenched teeth:

"He can't hold it, he's backing off," he said to his cohort. "If we play our cards right, we can nail him when he makes the right up ahead," he added with a dry chortle.

"Stay on his ass. If he slips again when he makes the right, broadside him," advised the cohort knowing Al would make a right onto East 14th Street.

"How's the Essex doing?" asked the senior agent.

Glancing back, the cohort remarked excitedly: "They've dropped back a little but still with us!"

"Good, we'll need 'em."

The Essex was forced to back off on the turn; it was now lagging behind. It was new to this game the Buick and the Hudson were playing. They, being heavier cars, were better able to maintain contact on the wet street.

The cars came careening up the street. Al's Portuguese buddies were huddled in the doorway of the pool hall and peering out the plate glass window of the all-night diner. This was Al's scheduled night to pass through; they were waiting. Aside from a streetcar discharging passengers, and about to proceed across 23rd Avenue in the same direction Al would be traveling, East 14th Street was devoid of traffic. As Fats suggested, the Buick drifted left then right, taking the corner in a wide sweep while avoiding the slippery tracks. This was what the Hudson had hoped for, cutting the corner thus putting itself on a collision course with the Buick.

"So that's it—cut me off at the corner? You bastard!" swore Al at the same time changing course by veering left across the tracks to avoid their maneuver. In expectation of a possible spin-out, the instant he felt the front wheels slip he cranked the steering wheel, putting the car into a spin, fishtailed across the first set of tracks, regained stability, then in a split second decision, changed course again crossing the second set of tracks, veering left into the westbound lane. The Buick was now heading back across 23rd Avenue, an unanticipated maneuver for the Hudson. The sudden change in direction battered Fats from side to side. Directing his comments to no one in particular, he cursed and swore the day he ever settled within a community of Italians.

"Shut up and hang on!" yelled Al.

"To what?" barked Fats, grabbing his hat.

In trying to stay with the Buick, the Hudson went through a similar maneuver, skidding and rattling across the tracks. But the lag between the time it took the driver to determine what the Buick would do next, and the time he could react, caused the car to lose ground.

Accelerator to the floorboard, wheels spinning and engine roaring, the Buick charged past Al's awestruck Portuguese supporters who came racing to the sidewalk to better view this spectacular display of careening cars. Both the pool hall and the diner were emptied of patrons in no time flat.

The lighter Essex, having fallen back, came into the intersection as the streetcar was passing—bell clanging and clattering in despair, muttering profanity, the conductor not appreciating the car dueling going on out ahead of him, stomped his heel vigorously on the bell's button under foot while braking as the Essex swung into the right turn. The streetcar now disrupting the Essex's intended maneuver caused the car to skid. Its driver while fighting the wheel yelled to his passenger:

"We're going to lose it! Hang on!"

"Go with the spin! Go with the spin!" screamed the passenger in near panic. Heeding his advice, the driver cranked the wheel back desperately. Reversing the spinout, the Essex came around counter clockwise flashing its headlights across the side of the streetcar dead ahead, illuminating the horrified expressions on the passengers' faces. The driver of the Essex cursed the inevitable:

"Goddamn it! Oh no . . . ! Look out . . . !"

"Oh Christ!" responded the passenger as he threw his arms across his face in horror.

The spinning car slapped up against the side of and towards the back end of the streetcar. Fenders crushed as glass shattered. The impact spun the car back again to where it continued its journey to the rear of the streetcar spinning across both sets of tracks completely out of control, heading towards the spectators' parked cars just as the Hudson shot by in pursuit of the Buick.

The senior agent glanced over his shoulder at the sound of buckling metal and shattering glass in time to see the Essex come careening behind him across both sets of tracks, followed by a crunching sound as it plowed into the side of a parked car, a snappy-looking 1925 Chevy coupe.

"Holy Christ! Did you see that?!" yelled out the senior agent to his cohort who was spun around in his seat trying to follow the erratic course of the Essex.

The jarring impact popped the Chevy's rumble seat open, and snapped the radiator cap's decorative ornament, sending it skyward. The chrome-plated cast metal figure of an angel with arms outspread, wings simulating flight, sailed through the air landing at the car owner's feet in a swan dive, disintegrating upon impact.

The car owner, a rather short, stocky Portuguese cannery worker with jet black hair, as much on his chest as his head, was aghast at seeing his sporty little jewel, the spotless Chevy, plastered by an ugly black sedan. The man was so muscular that his hairy arms hung away from his body much like a gorilla. He understood English, but could hardly speak it. Typical of a tough Portuguese cannery worker, giving no thought to reasoning, he ran around to the driver's side of the Essex, cursing in his native Portuguese:

"You son-of-a-whore! I'll teach you to wreck my car!"

Jerking the door open, he grabbed the stunned driver and dragged him out while maintaining a cocked fist ready to turn his face inside out. In the process, he screamed in defiance of reasoning:

"I'm going to bust your face, like you bust my car!"

But, before he could strike a blow, the driver collapsed at his feet.

The senior agent having stopped up the street, came on a dead run, followed by his cohort. He came up to the Chevy owner fuming mad, thinking he had slugged his fellow agent. In an arrogant tone of voice, he yelled a blatant, ethnic insult at the Portuguese car owner:

"What the hell did you punch my man for, you stupid dumb portagee? You're under . . . "

Before he could finish the sentence, he was slammed in the face with a fist full of knuckles, and some sound advice spoken in pure Portuguese:

"Don't you ever call me that again, you son-of-a-dog!" he said, as he hit him again.

The senior agent rocked back on his heels, then fell forward into the arms of his adversary. In supporting him, the Portuguese car owner felt the .45 caliber automatic cradled in its holster.

"Holy Spirito Santo!" he exclaimed. "This man has a gun!"

At the same instant, the cohort jerked his coat back thus exposing his badge plus the butt of his own gun, and blurted:

"We're Federal Prohibition Agents! It's against the law to strike an officer of the law . . . "

The pool hall owner immediately stepped up and interceded on behalf of the Chevy owner:

"Hold it a minute," he interrupted. "That guy doesn't know a federal agent from a dog catcher. Button your coat up before this crowd gets nasty. And for your information, he didn't slug that guy—he collapsed on his own. And as for that other guy, there, he should have identified himself first. These people don't take too kindly to insults!" The pool hall owner did get the message across.

By now the diner's owner was on the phone frantically blurting out the happenings to Captain Brown up at the Eastern Station. The Captain wasted little time getting down there.

Upon his arrival, Captain Brown instantly got things under control. He knew how to handle this tough bunch of Portuguese, for he was even tougher than they. Once he had everybody calmed down, the pool hall owner proceeded to explain the situation as the Senior Agent was helped to his feet insisting that the Buick be pursued and its driver apprehended. But with what was reported and the fact that Federal Prohibition Agents were involved, Captain Brown surmised that it was Al they were referring to. The fact that it was the Essex that collided with the Chevy, and not the Buick, he was quick to put the Senior Agent in his place:

"I run things around here, mister!" he stated firmly. "I'll decide who is apprehended and who is not! In the meantime, I suggest you pick your man up off the street and get him to a hospital, like right now!"

"Who do you think you are, talking to a Federal Agent in that manner?" responded the Senior Agent, while flashing his badge to better emphasize his authority.

Captain Brown's badge being clearly visible negated the need to display it, but nevertheless, to emphasize his dislike for federal agents, he leaned into the Senior Agent's blood-splattered face and barked at close range:

"You can shove that badge up your ass . . . mister. And as for you and your frigg'n federal agency, you can go frigg a duck!"

It was this kind of spunk that gained respect amongst the tough Portuguese cannery workers that made up his district.

Luck, more than anything else, got Al out of that one. It was a close call. It taught him to be a little more cautious and not so brazen. Taunting federal agents, whether they be good or bad, could prove to be a mistake. In itself, high speed car duels in the congested streets of Oakland would sooner or later end up in disaster. Al now worked the Buick cautiously through the city streets until he picked up the main thoroughfare leading out of town. Fats, taking a deep breath, commented again:

"Damn, that was a close one."

"Yeah, that it was," responded Al in a sigh of relief, and then added: "Do ya still want the job?"

"Yeah, sure, but not driving. You can have it."

"How about riding shotgun with Guido on the sugar truck? He could use the company."

"I thought Lepo . . . "

Al cut Fats short: "Lepo ain't worth a damn on the sugar truck. He's scared of his own shadow."

"Scared of what?"

"Hijackers! They've been tailing both me and the truck."

Al fell short of mentioning the fact that the hijackers in question were suspected to be Capone's men—Mafiosi, trying to locate the stills. Regardless, Fats wanted no part of it.

"Nope, not interested. You can have it."

"O.K., you can work the stills."

CHAPTER 24

Now, an even more severe threat than the federal agents appeared on the scene. The sugar truck on its way to the stills was now being tailed by a couple of tough looking characters believed to be 'Mafiosi,' the same men that held a gun to Mike's head earlier in San Francisco. They fit the description perfectly. These were Al Capone's men from Chicago, assigned to the West Coast for the sole purpose of hijacking distillers. Their intent: locate the stills, then pull off a grand slam hijack—raid the stills and take the sugar, alcohol, money—the works. The 'submachine gun' was the tool of their trade.

Guido, having reported the threat directly to Mike, was aghast to learn that he, in fact, was being targeted by notorious Mafiosi.

"Have you reported this to Al?" asked Mike.

"No, not yet. You know how he is, always putting us down. I thought you best tell him."

"Alright, I'll take the matter up with him. In the meantime, keep this to yourself. Does Lepo know about this?"

"He knows we're being following but not that they're Mafiosi."

"Good. Don't tell him anything either."

On the very next day when Al pulled into headquarters, the chicken ranch, to turn over the previous night's collections, a money sack bulging with cash, Mike brought up the subject; the possibility of Mafiosi on the scene, something he already suspected. Concurring with the notion that they now had the Mafia to deal with, Al fired up a cigarette.

"Yes, I guess this spells trouble," he said while exhaling from a deep drag, then added: "We'll have to watch our step."

Mike posed a double question: "What can we do about it? Do you have any suggestions?" he asked worriedly.

The discussion that followed did in fact trigger a thought. Al responded: "Our best bet is to report this to Captain Brown; he should be told. After all, these are criminals we're dealing with here."

"And we're not?? Holy Christ, of all people to turn to—the police. Jesus, what's this business come to??" But regardless of his uncomfortable feeling, after some discussion Mike did give Al his blessing. The Captain would be approached.

It was now up to him to put the threat to rest, but how? Thus, he posed the question to Captain Brown as they sat talking it over on a stack of alcohol-laden tin cans within the warehouse next to the police station. The Captain, being fully aware of Al's aggressiveness, had some good advice, coupled to a warning, to offer:

"Al, listen carefully to what I have to say. Stay clear of these guys; they're more than you can handle. Federal agents are one thing, but by what you're telling me, and what I know about the mafia, what we have to deal with here now is something else again. If these men are in fact who we think they are, we've got problems. They play for keeps! They're tough to stop! In a shootout, they outgun us. If push comes to shove, we're not about to go up against them, at least not for a load of sugar—or for that matter—alcohol."

"Yeah, I follow ya," responded Al while nervously lighting up a cigarette. At least this once he felt uncomfortable; this Mafia affair was indeed scary—it showed. Exhaling from a deep drag, he added to his comment: "Captain, the last thing I want to do is to put you on the spot. My thought is that, maybe if they realized that there is a close connection between us and the police, they might just back off. See what I mean?"

The Captain gave serious thought to the comment. It had merit, but, how could they get the message across to these notorious characters without getting embroiled in a machine gun shootout? The thought of a confrontation with the Mafia, along with his friend's fidgeting with the cigarette, caused an uneasiness within. He'd never seen Al like this before. Flipping a cigarette up to his lips from his own pack, he asked for a light from his friend's cigarette. Holding Al's shaky hand steady while leaning forward to light up proved to be a task. "Christ, you're shaky. Is it all that bad?" he questioned.

"Damned sight worse than you think. You don't know these Mafiosi. They come damned near putting a slug in Mike's head," stated Al seriously.

"The hell you say! Recently?"

"Not too long ago, in San Francisco."

The response prompted the Captain to take a deep draw, and in the course of exhaling, chastened Al for his past conduct: "And another thing," he said in a to-the-point manner, "what the hell was that caper all about the other night down in Jingle Town? You come damned near getting a couple of federal agents killed! How long do you think you can get away with that sort of crap!?" Pausing for another deep draw, he then added: "As if that wasn't bad enough—now this . . . this . . . Holy Christ! Mafia hijackers—what next?!"

"Now wait a minute! That wasn't all my fault. The idiot in the Essex caused the problem. Everything was going fine until he bounced off the street car and hit the Portagee's Chevy . . . As for these hijackers, I just thought . . . well maybe—just maybe . . . you'd come up with some idea, that's all."

As he listened to Al's apologetic comments, thoughts flashed through the Captain's mind. "Maybe he has a point. Sooner or later I, too, may have to deal with these characters. Yes, now is as good a time as any. Maybe we can head off the inevitable." In the course of conversation, an idea crossed his mind: "Alright, I'll see what I can come up with," he finally said. "Until you hear from me, lay low; I have an idea." The two men parted with the heavy burden of the Mafia on their minds.

After sleeping on the matter, Captain Brown came up with a plan. However, before mentioning it to Al, he first paid a visit to his parish priest, Father Dominic, at the local Catholic church located within walking distance of the police station. The priest, of Italian ethnic background, and old enough to be his father, in receiving him knew in an instant that the Captain had something heavy on his mind.

"My son," said the priest, "you appear to be troubled. Come to the confession chamber and relieve yourself of this heavy burden you carry." As he made the request, he bowed his head and turned slowly while keeping eye contact, as if to say: "Follow me."

Captain Brown was aghast. It never occurred to him that, yes, indeed, the confession chamber was the ideal place to unfold his plan. In effect, this would be killing two birds with one stone; proposing a scheme that would involve the priest and the Church while at the same time confessing for having proposed such an unthinkable thing in the first place. Lifting his cap with his right hand, he held it over his badge and heart as if to shield both from the wrath of God for having dared enter his house with a devious scheme in mind, he followed the priest, entered the cubicle and waited for the panel between the confessor and the confessee to slide open. As it did so, the Captain, hat in hand, badge glistening, reflecting what little light filtered through the heavy curtain, broke out in a sweat—partly because of his being in full uniform in such tight quarters, and partly because of the anticipated scolding he was about to receive. Above all, despite his toughness, he was a believer. The panel slid open—the priest cleared his throat—the Captain instantly blurted:

"Bless me father, for I have sinned."

But the priest was not the least bit impressed by the statement. It was obvious; the Captain hadn't gone out of his way, while on duty, in full uniform, to call upon him simply to confess his sins. At least not all his sins. This was late afternoon. It would take the better part of a whole day to accomplish such a tedious task, to say nothing of penance. The Hail Mary's alone could very well run into the hundreds to clear his slate.

Suspecting that something big was in the works, the priest, dispensing with formalities, came right out cold turkey: "Captain," he said, "you didn't come here to confess your sins, not that you shouldn't. But it will have to be some other day when we have more time. Now tell me, just what are you up to? What do you have on your mind, and how does the Church fit in? Remember, this is the house of the Lord; please use discretion," he reminded him. The wise old priest wasn't mincing words. He wanted straight answers.

The Captain, near choking on his own saliva, swallowed hard, then laid it on the line. Yes, he was asking him, a priest, and the power of the church, both of higher authority than himself and, for that matter, the whole police department, to help get his friend Al, and maybe even himself, out of a tight spot. The priest listened carefully. Many times in his career he'd been asked to help members of his flock when in need. But this proposal was something else again—a real challenge—acting as liaison between sinners, all faithful Catholics—real believers, true, but, nevertheless . . . sinners!

After giving the matter much thought, the priest, while shaking his head in disbelief, responded: "Sinners are sinners. Whether they be Mafiosi, policemen or bootleggers, they are all God's children, and therefore, must be looked after such as anyone else. It is God's will that we, being ordained into priesthood, doing his work here on earth as he does in heaven, must not turn our backs on anyone." Now looking up as if to address God himself, he mumbled: "Oh Lord . . . " Leaving the statement unfinished, he bowed his head, turned towards the Captain and whispered solemnly: "Hopefully he'll understand."

Captain Brown pranced briskly out of the church. His hurried strides carried him back to the station in a matter of minutes. He felt good, God was on his side. "Mafiosi," he mumbled, "Sicilian or otherwise, are respectful of the church and what it stands for. Approached properly, they'll come around." At least, he hoped they would.

The next night when Al pulled up to the warehouse the Captain was there at the station, waiting for him. By the time the car entered and parked inside the warehouse, the Captain had also entered, pulling the doors shut behind him. Having disembarked, seeing the Captain walking briskly towards him, Al, wondering, posed a question: "What's up?"

Eager to unfold the plan, the Captain laid it on the line, finalizing it with the comment: "Father Dominic will be ready. When's your next sugar shipment? We'll pull it off then."

The whole idea hit Al like a thunderbolt; horrified, he exclaimed in horror: "Holy Christ! You can't be serious! How in hell are we going to get these guys in church? Oh, they may be there alright—for the funeral —yours and mine." With that statement he popped a cigarette between his lips and embarked on a smoking frenzy. It was obvious, he was uncomfortable with the idea and so stated: "This is nuts. They'll blow us away," he said as he flipped his cigarette across the floor in a shower of sparks, then hastily walked over to stomp it out.

"You better be careful where you flip those cigarettes. There's enough alcohol in here to blow this place to kingdom come," warned the Captain.

"Hey, that gives me an idea," responded Al thoughtfully. "Why not lead them in here then blow the joint up with them in it? It will appear to be their warehouse . . . what do you think?"

"I think it stinks. How the hell am I going to explain a warehouse full of alcohol next to the police station? Don't even think about it. Besides, we pull a stunt like that and we'll have not only their buddies from Chicago out here gunning for us, but District Attorney Warren on our backs as well. The District Attorney doesn't take too kindly to murder, and that would be in the first degree. No, damn it. We'll stay with the plan! Let them follow the sugar truck to the church; Father Dominic and I will take it from there. When's the next shipment of sugar?" he asked once again.

"OK . . . OK, calm down, we'll do it your way. We're picking up a load of sugar tomorrow night. How's that?"

"Fine. I'll alert Father Dominic."

"Holy Christ, wait'll Guido and my brother-in-law hear about this. They'll crap a brick."

"Don't tell them everything, they might panic," advised the Captain. "They screw this up and they'll crap a damned sight more than a brick, believe me."

The following night while the International chugged along on its way to pick up a load of sugar, the two Bronzini brothers worriedly hashed over the situation at hand. Guido at the wheel, annoyed with his brother's fidgeting, let his feelings be known: "For Christ's sake, quit squirming around before you fall out of the damned truck!"

Lepo responded: "I don't like this. Why are we taking the load to the church? Al's going to get us in trouble, you'll see. He's not telling us everything, he's up to something."

"We'll do as he says," said Guido as the rail car came into view. As he backed the truck up to the boxcar, the door slid open. Da Monte, his son and another young fellow were inside ready to transfer 100 pound sacks of sugar onto the truck. The loading went smoothly, money exchanged hands, and as Guido took his place behind the wheel, commented: "You see, nothing to it, nobody around, we're on our way." The truck pulled away from the railroad siding without a hitch.

But Lepo wasn't satisfied. He just couldn't understand why anyone would want to stalk them for sugar when there was a whole railroad car there on the siding with tons of the stuff so easy to take. Guido knew the reason but was not sharing it with him. What he did share with him was the fact that the sedan with the two sinister characters had by now picked up their tail. As he glanced in the rearview mirror, he announced:

"Well my dear brother," he said solemnly, "I hope to Christ your brother-in-law knows what he's doing. There they are again."

"I knew it, sure as hell this is it!" blurted Lepo. "He's going to get us killed, mark my words."

"Well at least there'll be a priest handy to administer last rights, as if it would do much good," remarked Guido.

"Damn it! Don't joke about it! I said it before and I'll say it again—we should never have gone along with this nutty idea—hauling sugar to a church—it's crazy!"

"Too late now. We might as well go through with it, or would you rather stop and have a chat with those guys back there?" said Guido as he backed off to make the stop up ahead.

"NO! Christ NO, go through the stop sign! Keep moving!"

Parked at the corner facing East 14th Street with the police station behind him, Al, in the Buick, watched the International chug on buy. Within seconds the tailing sedan appeared. The thought of who the occupants were made it a gruesome scene. "I hope to Christ the Captain has the guts to stay with us," he muttered as he took a deep drag on his cigarette before tossing it through the flap in the side curtain. "There ain't nothing here to stop a bullet," he added.

A couple blocks up the street the International took a left, now heading towards the church midway up the block to the right. Guido swung the truck out wide so as to better negotiate the entry into its driveway. Once in, the truck stopped, allowing enough room for the Buick to come in behind it. The sedan made the same left but to the surprise of its occupants, their quarry had disappeared. The driver commented in his native Sicilian tongue: "What the hell . . . where did it go?" he said, somewhat puzzled as he let up on the accelerator.

"Beats me," responded the passenger in the same manner, then added: "That's a long block; no way could they have made it up to the other end before we took the left." Although he had already done so, the driver was instructed to slow down. "Nick," said the passenger to the driver, "you keep an eye out on your side and I'll watch this side. It has to be somewhere between these houses."

"Or the church up ahead," came the response.

"What church? Where?"

"That church, up ahead, on your side."

As the car cruised by, the church came into full view and as suspected, the truck was parked alongside with a couple of paesani huddling inside, too scared to step out. "Oh God, there they are, right behind us," whispered Guido.

"Come on, let's make a run for it before it's too late," responded Lepo as he scrambled to exit his side.

"No! Wait a minute, they're going by. Let's get in the church," instructed Guido as he grabbed a handful of coat in order to restrain his brother.

"In the church? At a time like this? We'll be trapped! Goddamn it, let go of me! I'm going to make a run for it!"

By now the sedan had made a 'u-turn' at the end of the block, then parked facing the church on the opposite side of the street. The two occupants, puzzled, had to think this out: "How does the church fit into the scheme of things?" No sooner the sedan's headlights dimmed, Al came cruising in with the Buick in his usual carefree manner. Using the same maneuver as Guido, he swung out wide, swooped and bounced across the driveway approach amidst a rattle of tin cans that could be heard clean across town. As intended, it caught the attention of the sedan's two occupants. The passenger, while studying the situation, in his native tongue, commented:

"Well, I'll be Goddamned! So that's where the still is—in the church! I'd of never believed it. Can you imagine that—of all the places —a church!? Did ya hear those tin cans rattle? They're empty. The guy's coming back for another load. He's got to be carrying a bunch of cash. And the sugar truck— loaded. No mistake about it, this is it! Nick, what do you think?" he asked thoughtfully.

"I think they're damned disrespectful. It's an affront to God! And how about the priest—you can bet he is in on this. We're going to have a talk with him! I'll bet he's a Toscano like the rest of them. No Sicilian priest would pull a stunt like that—set up a still in a church! Let's go in there and clean the buggers out, Tommy-gun 'em," growled the man called Nick.

"Not so fast. Let's think this out. Our Sicilian counterparts would skin us alive . . . shoot up a church? No way. 'Big Al' won't sit still for it. He'll have our hides. Nick, think about it. These guys are not Sicilians, they're Toscani. They're not killers, they're talkers. Oh, they might talk you to death, but kill for the sake of killing? Not so. My guess is that they're not even packing guns, I'd bet anything."

"How can you be so sure?"

"Don't you remember when their boss came to the City to collect for the load of alcohol we conned that fathead salesman of his out of? When I put that .38 to his head, he was scared stiff—near crapped in his pants—took off like a stripe-assed ape."

As they recounted the San Francisco incident, they broke out in laughter. Once calmed down, the man called Nick added to the statement:

"That salesman—what a jerk! Catarina flipped out a tit and the guy went bananas. He pranced away from that load of alcohol like a young bull after a heifer. He had his nose up her ass all the time she climbed the stairs."

"Well Christ, Nick, the way she was swinging her buns as she worked her way up to the flat was enough to drive any man mad. But this Casanova falls in love with her. Can you imagine that? Falling for a whore —all tits and ass but uglier than sin. No, I don't believe we need worry. This will be a lead pipe cinch. But nevertheless, we'll take the Tommy-gun in with us— just in case."

They'd made up their minds. They'd hijack the church, clean these so-called bootleggers out of their money, sugar, alcohol and whatever.

In the meantime, as the Buick pulled in behind the International, Guido, loosening his grip on his brother, scrambled off the truck and hurried back to apprize Al of the situation.

"Get Lepo, he's coming up the other side," he called out as Al slammed the car door behind him. Taking a few fast steps between vehicles, he grabbed at his brother-in-law just as he cleared the backend of the truck at a fast trot.

"Hold it, damn it! Stay off the street! You'll get caught up in a crossfire! commanded Al.

"Crossfire? What do you mean 'crossfire'?" asked Lepo trembling. Horrified, Guido posed the same question. Somewhat nervous himself, Al put it to them bluntly:

"Stay off the street! Get in the church! This place will be crawling with cops any minute now!"

"What are we going to do in church?" blurted Lepo.

"Pray! Goddamn it! Pray!"

Without further explanation, the two brothers were herded into the church. The priest instantly greeted them, which didn't help matters by much. Guido's earlier comment in reference to 'last rights' flashed across their minds. Al's pronounced nervousness didn't help matters either. He needed a smoke and would give his right arm to be able to light up, but didn't dare. The priest remained calm, but then being fortified with faith and God so close at hand, this was understandable.

161

"Come, have no fear," said the priest softly. "You are now in the house of the Lord. Follow me and I'll administer Communion." As the statement was made, he started towards the alter, only to stop, turn and address the trio again: "When was the last time you had confession?" he asked.

In unison, the trio shrugged their shoulders as if to say: "I don't know."

"Hmmm . . . just as I thought. We will therefore dispense with formalities. Tell me, have you committed sin . . . that is . . . lately?" asked the priest as he hurried them along towards the alter.

Al answered for all three: "More so than we care to admit."

"Hmmm . . . well then, you must do penance before Communion. Kneel here in the first pew, in front of the altar, and start with the prayer, 'Hail Mary.' Repeat it until I tell you to stop."

Lepo panicked. Horrified, he blurted: "We're going to die, aren't we?"

"No my son—at least—hopefully, not this night," said the priest.

"Shut up and kneel, damn it!" commanded Al. "I'm sorry, Father," he added apologetically.

The priest said nothing. He then turned away, heading for the altar to prepare to perform the ritual, as unorthodox as it was. As the three kneeled, Guido, with eyes shifting nervously back towards the church entrance, whispered softly:

"Al, what's this all about? You didn't tell us . . . "

Cutting him short, Al whispered back: "Just sit tight and keep your voice down—don't look back. This is Captain Brown's idea; everything will be alright. If I had told you what he had in mind . . . well, you wouldn't have gone along with it. We needed you."

Without looking back, they heard the heavy church door burst open behind them. The sinister occupants of the sedan stood astride the entrance determined to carry out their mission. The bulky, heavy overcoat worn by the man called Nick was shielding the Tommy-gun. From their position, they scanned the interior of the church expecting to see men working a still, fermentation tanks, and whatever other paraphernalia needed to crank out alcohol. But the church was clean, no one there except the priest at the altar about to give Communion to the three men kneeling before him. With the exception of the mumbling sound of prayer, it was eerily quiet.

"It can't be! What the hell is this?" said the man closest to the vestibule with its door ajar. Having heard the statement, although said in Sicilian which he could not understand, the Captain, draped in a priest's frock, stepped out of the vestibule, startling his adversaries by responding firmly:

"This is a church—the house of the Lord. Please remove your hats—please." The man with the machine gun, having swung around to face the

Captain, was then addressed personally: "You have no need for that . . . here. That is a dangerous instrument. Please point it towards the floor."

Puzzled, and taken in by the Captain's calm but authoritative voice and manner, although somewhat skeptical, he obeyed. However the man called Nick, appearing to be frustrated, staring unblinking at the Captain, was wondering: "Who is this person—is he really a priest?" Bringing his right hand up ready to plunge it under the flap of his coat caused instant concern to Captain Brown. He, being thoroughly familiar with such a maneuver, and having concluded that they were indeed Mafiosi, and wise to him, raised both hands up to shoulder level, instantly peeled back the frock to expose his police uniform and badge while blurting:

"Wait! I'm Captain Brown, commander of the Oakland Eastern Police Station. This is not an arrest. I have a proposition to offer."

"Why you son-of-a-bitch," swore the Mafioso in broken English while plunging his hand under his coat, then pulling it back out with a fist full of metal. Snarling, he said: "You bastard! You've set us up!"

"No! Wait a minute, it's not what you think! We only want to talk to you," said the Captain hastily, while raising his hands even higher.

"We? Who's we?"

"Father Dominic—we must talk—please consider," answered the Captain while giving a nod in the direction of the priest.

The priest, seeing the confrontation taking place, aborted the sacramental procedure and hastily headed up the aisle. The man with the machine gun, having heard the fast shuffling of feet approaching, quickly stepped briskly around the holy water font to face the oncoming priest.

"Gentlemen . . . gentlemen . . . please, for God's sake, not in the house of the Lord!" pleaded Father Dominic in fluent Italian with an expertly placed tinge of the Sicilian dialect. Not only could he speak several languages, but also various Italian dialects, Sicilian being one of them.

Realizing that Father Dominic was indeed a priest, the man called Nick, in his native tongue, addressed his comrade:

"Put it away. This man is a priest. Keep an eye on that frigg'n cop while I talk to him." Stepping away from Captain Brown, he now addressed Father Dominic:

"Father, it is not our intent to offend you or the Church, but what's with this policeman—our being set up, what in hell is going on around here? We thought . . . "

"Yes . . . yes," interrupted Father Dominic. "I know—I understand your concern, but, there seemed to be no other way. I can explain it. Won't you come in and sit down so we can talk this matter over sensibly?" he asked

163

while beckoning the Mafioso to take a seat in the closest pew.

"All right, so we'll talk, but not in the church. Let's step outside where we can be freer to express ourselves," said the man called Nick, in his heavy Italian accent, as he turned away from the priest to lead the way.

"No! Wait!" called out the Captain urgently. "Let me dismiss my men first. They're armed . . . they have orders . . . "

"Your men?" questioned Father Dominic, surprised. "You have armed policemen out there . . . in front of my church, the house of the Lord? You hadn't mentioned anything about having armed men . . . Captain Brown!" It was obvious, Father Dominic knew nothing about that part of the plan. He was indeed irritated.

"Why, you bastard!" growled the Mafioso. "You son-of-a-bitch!" he swore as he jerked his gun out of its holster once again while turning to face Captain Brown.

Horrified at the sudden threat of violence, Father Dominic stepped between the two men; facing the Captain he commanded:

"For heaven's sake! Captain! Call your men off this instant or face the wrath of God!" After having made the statement, he turned his attention back to the Mafioso:

"I am asking you, in the name of God, to desist—abort your mission . . . whatever it may be. These men you see here are my parishioners," he said as he turned while directing attention by a wave of hand towards the now empty pew. To his and the others dismay, the trio had disappeared. The few seconds of silence that followed gave the Captain the opportunity to now make his own pitch. Somewhat uneasily he said:

"Might I add, gentlemen, that these men Father Dominic refers to are under my protective . . . shall we say, custody, and that I am, therefore, obligated if need be, to use extreme measures to protect them. So here is my proposition: you back off—leave them alone, and you can go about your affairs without my interference."

"So that's it," thought the Mafioso. "A crooked cop." Turning to his comrade, he asked: "What do you think? Should we go along with it?" he said in Sicilian.

"Why not?" came the prompt response with the added comment: "Cops on the take is nothing new. We've got plenty of them in Chicago."

A sign of relief from the priest told the Captain that they'd bought the deal. As he started towards the door to carry out the priest's earlier order, Father Dominic grabbed him firmly by the arm and while restraining him, issued another order in no uncertain terms:

"You be here—in church—tomorrow morning—at 6 o'clock sharp, and prepare yourself for a thorough confession, do penance, and receive Communion! Plan for the entire morning!" He'd need the entire morning for what the priest had in mind for him.

The two Mafiosi stood in awe. They were impressed as to the way Father Dominic firmly handled the situation. But, as for Captain Brown, the thought of coming within a whisker of being cut down in a hail of buckshot brought about a barrage of profanity directed at the Captain that blistered the ears of Father Dominic who reacted with a quick sign of the cross and a sympathetic glance towards the heavens on behalf of the Mafiosi.

As Captain Brown departed, the Mafioso called Nick asked:

"Father, those three men (referring to the missing trio), are they friends of yours—Italians?"

"Yes, not only my friends and fellow Italians, but also members of my parish. They're good people," answered the priest while glancing back towards the alter wondering what had happened to them.

"Toscani?" asked the Mafioso.

"Yes, Toscani," came the answer accompanied with a shrug of the shoulders as if to say, "'eh, what else?"

"That figures . . . well . . . all right, we'll not molest them."

Carefully scanning the street before stepping out the door, the Mafiosi viewed the departing shotgun-wielding policemen, led by Captain Brown, as they marched up the street heading back to the police station. The scene drew a comment: "That son-of-a-bitch wasn't bluffing."

Having had his fill of Mafiosi and policemen, Father Dominic locked the door, then hurried back to seek out the missing trio.

Lepo, having bolted from the pew the instant the priest had left them, hightailed it in search of a place to hide with Al, followed by Guido, in hot pursuit. The closest and handiest place to hide was the confession chamber, so Lepo plunged through the curtain. Since they had stirred up such a commotion, and realizing the consequences if they, too, didn't get out of sight, Al ducked into the center cubicle where the priest normally sat, while Guido plunged into the opposite side. With the intent of berating Lepo for having bolted such as he did, Al slid the panel open between them as a priest would do during confession. Before Al could open his mouth, Lepo, in his confused state of mind, instantly blurted:

"Bless me Father, for I have sinned."

Al, having been caught off guard by the statement, let fly the first thing that came to mind:

"Shut up, you idiot, or I'll kick your ass!"

Guido, horrified at the thought of being exposed by the two quarrelsome brother-in-laws, as tight as the quarters were, dropped to his knees in prayer. But since praying was never a big thing with him, he was having difficulty coming up with the proper verses to fit the occasion. Therefore, this necessitated creating new verses of which he started with: "Holy, holy, holy," but then suddenly realizing the extent of their predicament, blurted:

"Holy Christ! We're all going to die!"

Annoyed, Al now slid the panel open on Guido's side in order to set matters straight with him as well, Showing little sympathy, he barked:

"If you two assholes don't cut this out, we'll all die alright, and our souls will rot in hell for sure!"

They remained in the chamber until they heard the church door slam and the priest calling out for them while hastily coming down the aisle toward the confession chamber. As the priest came prancing by, they stuck their heads out in unison. Startled at the sudden display of heads poking out at him, Father Dominic exclaimed:

"What are you imbeciles doing in there? Not that you shouldn't be! Of all the stupid things . . . !" Without finishing the statement, he ordered the trio out.

Stepping out with hat clenched in hand, they stood before Father Dominic with bowed head, ready to be chastised good and proper. Rattling his index finger while pointing straight up towards heaven as if calling attention to God himself, he said sternly:

"Tomorrow morning—at six o'clock sharp—on an empty stomach —I want the three of you, to-be-here! At the church—lined up before the confession chamber—awaiting your turn at confession—along with Captain Brown! Do - I - make - myself - clear?!" he barked.

Gulping hard, the trio answered meekly: "Yes, Father."

"God help me, I'll cleanse you rascals' souls, come hell or high water!!"

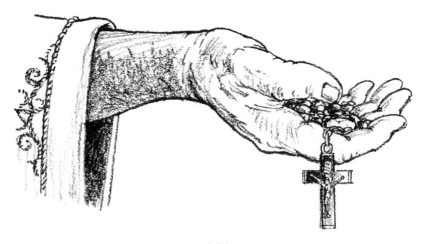

CHAPTER 25

Al also had to deal with Captain Louis Eike of the State Traffic Squad, "Badge No. 1," the squad's top cop. Not only out on the open highways, but around town as well. Actually, he and Officer Eike were pretty good friends and so you'd think they would try to avoid an encounter, but such was not the case. It was a challenge for Officer Eike to be known as the one person that could catch Al and an equal challenge for Al to remain the one person that, for the most part, the state's top-rated traffic cop could not catch. Of course, when on his motorcycle and around town Captain Eike had the advantage, but not so when in a patrol car. It would have been a simple matter for Officer Louis Eike to corner Al with the aid of other officers, but then that would not be very sporting; besides even when he did catch him, he didn't always care to give him a citation. Since neither one had any use for federal agents, they did have something in common. So, when Al was being pursued by federal agents, Officer Eike wouldn't interfere.

Frustrated with the adverse attitude of the Oakland police department, and now even the state police, the agents decided to change their tactics by attempting to intercept Al at Castro Valley, just west of town. However, by the time the two automobiles involved reached the town proper while traveling east, the Buick, with wide open throttle and high-pitched tea kettle whistle, careened through the deserted quiet little town at upwards of 75 miles per hour, widening the distance between the pursued and the pursuer until the Hudson was forced to back off in its futile attempt to overtake the Buick.

The federal agents' attempts at trying to be discrete about their intent had now become futile. They might just as well set up their stakeout in Crow Canyon proper and go for broke. Although they had seldom seen the blue Buick in and around Mike's place, they did come to the conclusion that there was a definite tie-in between the two, and that Mike was the head "Capo" of this entire, extensive bootlegging operation. To make matters worse, the senior agent was demanding more whisky along with the cash payoff. His habit of drinking on the job was soon to distort his sense of reasoning.

The senior agent had developed a dislike for Al and the car he drove, to the extent that he'd now play rough. At least for the moment, the matter of gaining full knowledge of the operation became secondary. Likewise, Al had made up his mind that in some way or another, he would get these bastards with their striped suits and neatly blocked fedora hats off his ass once and for all time. He was not a stranger to playing rough.

They now stationed themselves at the other end of the valley, parked alongside the Live Oak service station and garage at the foot of Castro Hill in view of Crow Canyon Road part way up the hill. The idea was to trap the Buick in Crow Canyon by following it in with the Essex stationed along the way to cut him off. But this was so obvious that Al's friends immediately relayed the information to him, so the next night out, one of the hottest evenings of the season, he watched for the Hudson and, sure enough, it was there, lying in wait. Having spotted them, he did not turn into Crow Canyon at all but instead accelerated up Castro Hill and into the driveway of the Pergola Inn (a speakeasy) at the top of the grade. Machine gun wielding guards held their fire — they'd recognized the car.

The Inn was located opposite Jensen Road and at the end of a long driveway. It was taken over and converted to a speakeasy featuring high-class prostitutes by a man who claimed the title of Colonel. What made Colonel White's prostitutes high class was merely the fact that the price was higher even though they performed no better. Since they worked on a percentage of gross sales, rather than paying a set rental fee for the use of the cottages that were spread about the premises, the prostitutes were, in effect, sharecroppers. The Colonel's military arrogance and presence of machine-gun armed guards stationed in an elevated guardhouse did add to the excitement of a wild evening for its patrons. Since the law enforcement agencies were all being paid off, the main purpose of the armed guards was to ward off hijackers. What the dealers and the stickmen didn't get at the gambling tables from their booze-drinking clients (suckers, at best), the prostitutes sifting through their billfolds did.

The Hudson, its occupants having recognized the Buick, immediately pulled out of its lair.

"That's him alright. This time we'll trap him in the Canyon for sure," said the senior agent with confidence.

"Hey, Chief, he's not turning into the Canyon . . . what the hell? He's heading up the hill," announced the cohort.

"That little bastard! Maybe he's loaded—making a delivery—let's go after him anyway."

The Hudson roared up Castro hill in hot pursuit. The federal agents saw the Buick's stop lights come on up ahead, then fade to the right as the car swung into the Inn's driveway.

"This is great. I've always suspected this place as being a speakeasy. Now we've got them both dead to rights. We'll arrest the whole damned lot of them, patrons and all. Better yet—we'll shake them down good and proper —take it all. That place has got to be loaded with cash, what with the gambling, whores and all. We can't miss!"

"You're sure as hell right, Chief. Maybe we should go get the others (the two with the Essex) to give us a hand."

"No time for that. We'll handle it alone. After all, we are federal agents, are we not?"

" Yeah, I guess you're right. The best bet is to jump out quick, draw our guns and scare the living daylights out of them."

The conversation was cut short as they swung into the long driveway in pursuit of Al who, upon seeing the driveway behind him illuminated by the Hudson, yelled up to the guards:

"Hijackers! I came to warn ya! Watch it!!"

With that, he gunned the car to the right onto a connecting driveway leading to the sharecroppers' cottages with the intention of using their driveway to make his getaway. As the car's headlights swept across the cars parked at the cottages in a right turn, a bizarre scene of half-naked women and men flashed before his eyes. "Holy Christ, business must be good!" he said to himself as he continued his right turn onto the picket fence lined driveway leading back to Dublin Canyon road.

Business was good, indeed. A bachelor party made up of a contingency of Oakland police officers was in progress at the Inn which by this time had escalated to an outright orgy that would even put the Romans to shame. Being a hot night, the prostitutes had shifted their activities from the confines of the stifling bedrooms to the moonlit freshness of the outdoors. Serving as love couches, the sweeping downward curvatures of front fenders were strewn with scantily attired lust goddesses lying on their backs gazing at the stars while the Johns hovered over them in precarious positions.

The unsuspecting agents had no idea what was in store for them when they stepped out of the Hudson with guns drawn. The instant rattle of machine gun fire sent them scrambling back into their car.

"Holy Christ! What the hell was that?" exclaimed the senior agent in chilling horror.

"Machine guns! It's an ambush! For God's sake, let's get our ass out of here, but fast . . . !"

"They can't shoot at us—we're federal agents!"

As the statement was made, a second burst of machine gun fire raked across the front end of the car, thus knocking out its headlights and punching a neat row of holes through the radiator. The cohort screamed in horror:

"For God's sake, can't you get this thing in gear? We're getting shot up!"

"Jesus, I've got to get turned around . . . "

"The hell with turning around! Head out across that field —over there— towards those houses!"

The senior agent responded instantly. The Hudson bounced across the field in the direction of the prostitutes' cottages, which the cohort had mistaken for houses. Without benefit of headlights, the connecting driveway was missed altogether as was the fact that a half-dozen automobiles were parked in the direction they were heading. The moonlight did allow for some sense of direction, at least enough to keep them on course towards the faintly lit up cottages.

The sudden burst of machine gun fire splitting the quietness of the night, then followed by the rumbling-rattling sound of the roaring Hudson coming at them, bouncing over rough terrain, sent the prostitutes sliding off the front fenders like seals off of wet rocks, once they lost the support of the Johns who were the first to leap into action. Sex is fine, and getting paid for it is even better, but who wants to die for either?

Gathering up their senses, which is all they had to deal with, the prostitutes made a bee-line for the cottages while the Johns jumped into their cars. They were police officers; they knew quite well the devastating effect of machine gun fire and were therefore not about to get caught up in a crossfire. Not bothering to gather up clothing or kiss the girls "goodnight," they hit the starters, snapped on the headlights and, with wheels spinning, churned up clouds of dust in getting turned around. The procedure startled the agents.

"What the hell!! Jesus Christ, we're cornered!" screamed the senior agent as the Hudson careened headlong into the confusion. Steam vapors spewing out through the punctured radiator added to the anxiety of the Johns. As far as they knew, the men in the Hudson might also be shot up. They wanted out of there . . . fast.

The cohort, peering through the dust, got a glimpse of the picket fence to his right and correctly assumed the driveway to be in that direction.

"Cut it to the right, cut it hard!" he yelled.

The senior agent cranked the wheel as instructed putting the Hudson on course with the driveway. However, by now, coming up on either side of it, the other cars with accelerators to the floorboards were heading for the same narrow driveway. In the ensuing frenzy, picket fences were mowed down like crisp, spring oat hay as cars with Jackass-saturated maniacs at the wheel came charging out the driveway, three abreast.

Al, having turned on to Dublin Road in the opposite direction as the maniacs, was now heading east toward the town of Dublin where he would then head north to San Ramon, thus entering Crow Canyon from that direction. Not knowing the chaos left behind because of his statement in reference to "hijackers," he was rehashing the events of the night, mumbling to himself as he cruised along. "Those pesky buggers are not going to get off my ass, that's for damned sure. And where the hell's the Essex—up the Canyon laying for me, I suppose? If that's their game, the next time out I'll have to take the long way around again . . . damn it!"

A couple nights later, having picked up a load of sugar after completing his alcohol deliveries, Al once again spotted the Hudson parked somewhat to the rear of the Live Oak garage. He knew in an instant what that meant—the Essex would be laying for him up the Canyon. He floorboarded the accelerator as he swore:

"Goddamned bastards! Of all times—a load of sugar."

The senior agent, along with his cohort lurking in the shadows, also swore as he started up the Hudson:

"There's that son-of-a-bitch now! And he's loaded!"

His cohort responded: "Hold it! Don't pull out now! Not yet! Let's see if he turns into the Canyon."

To their delight, he did not. He instead went past Crow Canyon, heading east toward the town of Dublin, just as they'd figured. The Essex, instead of being staked out in Crow Canyon as Al had surmised, was instead now cruising along Dublin Canyon Road as planned. He had been outsmarted. The Hudson took up the chase with a comment from its driver, the senior agent:

"If the Essex is where it should be—we've got him!"

By the time the Hudson topped the hill, the Buick was already down the other side negotiating the sharp turns of Dublin Canyon Road where it snaked its way along the creek and past Canyon Inn, another out-of-the-way speakeasy of sorts. The car continued past Canyon Service, a filling station and small cafe where in addition to gassing up your car and grabbing a bite to eat and cup of coffee, with or without a shot of Mike's Jackass Brandy, you could also play grab-ass with the proprietor's daughter. The atmosphere was always pleasant with an abundance of laughter.

Al continued east towards the town of Dublin where he intended to swing north following the same route as Terzo by coming in from the opposite end of Crow Canyon at San Ramon. But, the Essex was also cruising east on Dublin Canyon Road between Canyon Service and the town of Dublin, when the Buick, loaded with sugar, passed it up on the short straight stretch of highway in front of Harry Rowell's Rodeo grounds and horse-meat processing plant. Although a dark night, Al recognized it as the Essex. He swore at having found himself in such a predicament:

"Oh, Christ! Damn the luck! I should have known better—those dirty bastards . . ." He also saw the Hudson giving chase some distance behind.

The Essex took up the pursuit immediately. The two occupants were delighted that they were able to keep up to the sugar-loaded Buick as it was forced to give ground on the turns. But, once out of the canyon, instead of turning north at Dublin, Al floorboarded the accelerator and headed straight out across the valley in the direction of Livermore. The two vehicles were now engaged in a dueling match while traveling at extremely high speed. However, the two federal agents' delightful experience was short-lived once the Essex found itself directly in the path of an on-coming Greyhound bus. The bus, with its headlights mounted on the two wide-spaced front fenders put an abrupt end to this reckless game of chicken. Apparently the driver of the Essex, seeing the two further than normal spaced apart headlights coming at him from the opposite direction, thought the lights to be a pair of motorcycles traveling side by side.

On the other hand, Al knew the headlights coming towards him belonged to a Greyhound bus. There wasn't a motorized vehicle, whether it be a car, motorcycle, truck, or bus, that he was not totally familiar with. The Essex was right on the Buick's tail where the highway flattens out between Dublin and Livermore; both cars were traveling well over 70 miles per hour. He swore again:

"You bastards are asking for it," he growled as he prepared himself in those few seconds that he had to act.

Once the bus was too close to allow the Essex to pass the Buick, he abruptly let up on the accelerator while at the same instant momentarily braked. The Essex had a split second to either swerve to the right and roll over into the ditch alongside or rear-end the Buick. At the direction of its driver, it did neither.

"Hang on!" shouted the driver. "We'll run him off the road!" he added as he drifted to the left to get a better view at what was coming towards him.

The passenger, having seen the glare of headlights coming at them, issued a warning: "Watch it!"

"They're motorcycles . . . ! They'll move!" responded the driver with confidence.

Assuming the inside bike would move over if need be, he promptly swung to the left as if to pass and pull alongside the Buick. The bus driver could not act quickly enough to avoid colliding with the Essex as it swung out to pass.

"You stupid idiots!" yelled Al in astonishment.

One can imagine the horrifying thoughts that flashed through the minds of the two occupants of the Essex when they suddenly realized their mistake. The heavy front end of the bus ripped through the left side of the Essex in a sideswiping manner that sent it tumbling back across the highway to the Buick's rear, down the ditch and back up the other side, rolling over a number of times before coming to rest on its side ensnared in a tangle of barbed wire fencing.

The Hudson arrived at the scene of the accident about the time the bus driver was running back to assist the occupants, still trapped in the wreckage of their automobile.

"What happened?" asked the senior agent of the bus driver as they worked together to free the severely injured occupants.

"They sideswiped me," came the answer in an Oklahoma drawl.

"You mean you sideswiped them, don't you?"

"No, that's not what happened. They tried to pass another car they were following, and sideswiped me in the process."

A few exchanges along those lines transpired before the bus driver realized he was dealing with a federal agent and for whatever reason the senior agent was trying to infer that the driver of the Essex was forced into the bus by the Buick. However, the bus driver would not budge an inch. He stuck to his version as to how the accident came about.

"Why should I say different? I'm not about to twist facts by placing the blame on the other car when the fault lies with this one. What's the point?"

What the bus driver didn't know was that the senior agent was now trying to hang the accident on Al as an intentional, deliberate attempt at manslaughter, or an assault on a federal agent, or at least some related charge so he could obtain a warrant for his arrest. But it wasn't working out that way, because the bus driver was holding his ground and refusing to change his story. The agent's attempt to establish the driver as a witness in order to build a case against Al was fruitless. The agent lost his cool and blew his stack over his obvious failure.

"I'll get that goddamned dago, if it's the last thing I do! That dago son-of-a-bitch has had it! Him and that bunch of dagos he deals with are all going to get it!" With that opening statement, the senior agent let fly a barrage of profanity aimed at all the Italians that ever invaded the shores of America, along with blurting out a few latent ethnic insults with a generous reference to "Okies."

"Dang you, mister! Watch your dang tongue," responded the bus driver indignantly.

Having settled their differences, they managed to get the two injured agents placed in the back seat of the Hudson. It then took off back down the highway, leaving the confused bus driver standing there talking to himself, trying to figure out what this whole affair was all about. He was herding his startled passengers back on the bus when Al, coming back down the highway, stopped alongside the roadway pretending to know nothing about the incident.

"What happened?" he said, asking the same question of the bus driver as did the agent. Not having recognized the Buick and without answering the question put to him, the bus driver asked his own question:

"What the hell's a dang dago anyway?" he asked, his Oklahoma accent more pronounced than ever.

"An Italian Okie," answered Al with a grin.

"Oh, I get it, some kind of out-of-stater, is that it?"

"Yeah, way out of state," answered Al, as he slammed his door shut and took off, leaving the bus driver standing there scratching his head.

CHAPTER 26

The near fatal accident of the Essex prompted the senior agent to reassess his strategy. Replacing the wrecked Essex was not a problem, but he would have to wait for his injured men's total recovery before putting them behind the wheel again.

In the meantime, Al went about his business in the usual manner, offering little information to his partners as to the possible reason for the absence of agents in and around the area of Crow Canyon. He knew Mike wouldn't tolerate such shenanigans so he said nothing about it.

However, the senior agent made his presence known when it came time to pick up his payoff. Collecting the fistful of cash along with a fair ration of Jackass far outweighed the health and welfare of his cohorts. Since few words were ever spoken between himself and Mike, he offered no explanation in reference to their absence in and around the Crow Canyon vicinity. Besides he didn't want to take the risk of having Al pulled off the streets because he had a personal vendetta to settle with him, and sooner or later he would get his due. However, the senior agent had his work cut out for him, Al would see to that.

The senior agent now busied himself with going from one law enforcement agency to another to gather whatever information he could find as to Al's activities in the three counties: Alameda, Contra Costa, and Solano. Somewhere along the line, he'd trap him. But, he could use some help. In Alameda County, especially the City of Oakland, he was to discover nothing that he didn't already know. Neither would the local lawmen volunteer to help him in any way. It was obvious that whatever they did offer was not bona fide information that could be relied on. He stayed away from the District Attorney's office as much as possible, since he was fully aware of Earl Warren's tough reputation and dislike for lawmen on the take. It was common knowledge that the District Attorney would welcome the opportunity to nail a crooked federal agent as much as a bootlegger.

The Contra Costa sheriff simply told him that in no way could he concern himself with such trivial matters as a bootlegger passing through his county dropping off a can or two of alcohol along the way. What with the range of hills splitting the county as it did with bootleggers operating out of just about every canyon supporting a spring and clump of trees, to say nothing of the shoreline of the bay and the Sacramento River, teeming with rumrunners of all sorts and descriptions, he had his hands full.

But the senior agent was not to be discouraged; his next stop was the City of Vallejo, just across the Sacramento River in Solano County. It so happened that at the time of his visit to the city police department, the Chief of Police was in conference with another federal agent who was assigned to the North Bay District, which included Solano County. It seems that this agent was inquiring about the same matter of the blue Buick, but for different reasons. One of the bootleggers in his district was complaining about losing customers to an outsider that was offering much better moonshine than he could make or offer. Therefore, if this agent expected to keep collecting payments on the moonshine annuity he held from the bootlegger, the agent had better do something about it. It only took the Chief of Police a few minutes and a few dozen words spoken between the two agents to draw his own conclusion as to either one's interest in this so-called blue Buick matter. Politely interrupting the conversation between the two men, he asked them to please step out into the waiting room and continue their discussion there, for he had much better things to do than to listen to them.

The two federal agents struck a deal. "Fine," said the Solano district agent. "I'll leave it to you to run down the Buick and its driver, but remember our deal; if you can shake him down, I get a cut out of all the stuff he sells in Solano County."

"Agreed," said the senior agent, "leave that goddamned dago to me. Stay clear of him, I want that smart-ass little bastard all for myself."

Whatever made the senior agent think that he would have any better luck in dealing with Al on the north side of the river as opposed to the south side, was debatable. He was still short one car and two agents. Could it be possible that experience gained over the past few months would offset the odds? Not hardly, since Al also gained experience in dealing with the agents and knew more about their Hudson's ability to perform better than they did. What they really needed was some training in race car driving.

Al's mechanical expertise was being applied to getting peak performance out of the Buick. This same expertise was applied to knowledge of what the Hudson could or couldn't do. For one thing, as Al put it: "Once you get that pile of iron rolling, you can't stop it." This was said in reference to its poor braking system. Whatever the odds were, the dueling race between the two cars was about to resume. With the exception of having to deal with the Benicia-Martinez ferry, conditions on the Solano County side were not much different than the Alameda and Contra Costa county side for carrying out their deadly game of chicken.

Before the tailing had started on the Solano side, Al had, over the previous months, struck up a good relationship with the ferry crews, and the ramp and dock tender. The crews had their own little thing going down in the boiler room of the ferry. They had devised a small make-shift still of their own, using steam for heat, in what was referred to as a double boiler system. They were making alcohol for their own private consumption. To the crew, captain, and ramp tender, Al's activities were no mystery. They knew exactly what his purpose was in running around the county such as he was. Instead of trying to keep it a secret, he showed them how to make good whiskey. He supplied them with charcoal, a couple of small oak barrels, caramel for coloring and flavoring, and passed on cutting techniques. He also pointed out that the rocking motion of the ferry as it negotiated the constant turbulent river current was a benefit to the aging process.

"Don't be in a hurry to drink it," he told them. "You guys have the best conditions in the world for making good jackass, give it time."

The first indication that he was being tailed was one night on his round trip from Richmond to Vallejo, then to Benicia where he was to board the ferry and cross the Sacramento River to Martinez, then to San Ramon and Crow Canyon. As Al was waiting in line to board the ferry, the ramp tender walked up to him and said:

"I guess you know you've got a tail on you."

"The hell you say, I hadn't noticed," responded Al.

"Yeah, they're stopped up the street a-ways waiting for the ferry to start loading. They pulled the same stunt on your last trip, but were too late to board, they waited a minute too long and missed the ferry."

"What kind of car is it?" asked Al.

"A black Hudson sedan, with two men in it," came the answer.

"Those bastards!" exclaimed Al.

"You know them?" questioned the tender.

"Yeah, I know them, they're federal agents, they've been bugging me for months, but I didn't think they'd be on this side of the river."

"I'll tell you what, pull up to the front of the line, I'll talk to the first mate and see what we can do," said the tender.

Following the first mate's instructions put Al with the Buick right up in front of the ferry to the right. No sooner had the last car in line boarded, the Hudson came racing down the street, this time making it onto the ferry. The first mate purposely directed the Hudson to park to the left out of sight of the Buick surprisingly, to the agents delight.

"This is great," said the senior agent to his cohort. "He doesn't even know we're on the ferry."

"We've got him trapped; shall we take him?"

"No, hold it a minute. Let's think this over."

"Yeah, you're right. He'll lead us right to the still. We'll nail him there. Good thinking on your part chief," came the response.

The ferry made its way across the river and pulled into the slip on the Martinez side. As soon as the unloading ramp slapped down on the forward deck of the ferry, the Buick took off burning rubber. Once the right side was unloaded, the first mate started signaling the cars on the left side to move out, but in the process of doing so, he was to find all sorts of reasons for delaying their departure. The senior agent blew his stack. Commingled with the sound of the Hudson's blasting horn, profanity could be heard throughout the waterfront. From the back of the line he screamed:

"You damned idiot—move us out—we're federal agents!" as if the first mate didn't already know that. Finally the Hudson, the last car in line, came up to the first mate hesitating long enough to allow the senior agent time to address him in about every derogatory fashion and profane remarks he could think of. Needless to say, the agents were never to see the Buick again that night.

The next several attempts to trap Al at Benicia resulted in disappointment for the agents as well. They had missed their chance the one time they had him cornered. Now, they couldn't be sure whether their near misses at the ferry were intentional or not. Neither were they sure whether Al was even wise to them. Frustrated beyond reason, the senior agent was to throw all caution to the wind.

"Our best bet is to trap him on the ferry, only this time, we'll take him then and there."

"Right, no screw'n around," concurred the cohort, then added: "Get this thing tuned up so we can stay right on his tail."

"Good idea. I'll do that first thing."

Once again Al was traveling at breakneck speed across the same stretch of ups and downs from Vallejo to Benicia, such as he and Primo had done with the big Mack truck loaded with wine some years before that wiped out their pursuers in the process. The difference now was at that time he had the help of his paesano buddies to put his tormentors out of commission, to say nothing of a big monstrous Mack truck as a battering ram, along with the blessings of an old seasoned priest. A glance in the rearview mirror revealed the Hudson gaining on him.

"Those bastards must have tuned up their car," said Al, talking to the

Buick, such as a cowboy talks to his horse. "Come on baby, pour it on, I need all you can give. Don't let those buggers catch me with the goods. It's too late to dump the rest of these cans now," pleaded Al.

Talking to a machine is fine for your own comfort, much like whistling in the dark, but unlike a horse, it doesn't share your feelings. The Buick was putting out all that could be expected of it. As it was, he was holding his own, Benicia was dead ahead. But there was the ferry up ahead to contend with, would it be in the slip?

The growling of tires, the high pitched fuel vacuum tank whistle and blinking headlights as Al made the right turn into town, caught the attention of both the first mate and the ramp tender. He was on course with the about-to-depart ferry at the foot of Main Street. The ramp had already been raised. The two men yelled out to the captain above, who was about to work his way back from the pilothouse to the other end of the ferry to take the controls at the opposite pilothouse. The captain stopped and looked around to see the familiar Buick coming down towards the loading ramp at high speed. Quickly stepping back into the pilothouse, he gave the order to hold steady and stand by for full speed ahead. At the same instant he gave two quick blasts of the ferry whistle signaling the ramp tender to lower the ramp. But the slow motion of the steam engine that was holding the ferry up to the dock had already come to a halt in preparation of its reverse motion to move away from the dock. This now allowed the ferry to start gradually drifting away, even though the ramp was slowly coming down to its loading position.

The first mate flew into action. Without bothering to apprise the captain, he ran to the stairwell leading down to the engine room. As he descended the metal steps, he yelled urgently to the engineer on duty:

"She's drifting! Get 'er back up against the dock! For Christ's sake, move it!" he demanded.

The engineer, knowing nothing about the drama taking place above, followed orders but asked the question:

"What the hell's going on up there?"

"Al's in trouble! He's coming in full bore! He ain't going to make it unless . . . !" Without finishing the statement, and knowing that it was too late to correct the drift, he dashed back up to the deck.

Al saw the barricade chain drop as the ramp started its descent. His friends had seen his predicament and were assumed to be acting accordingly. He glanced into the rear view mirror. The Hudson had made the turn behind him and was bearing down. He swore:

"You bastards! You've got me! But you'll have to fish me out of the frigg'n river!" With that comment, he braced himself while maintaining pressure on the accelerator. There was no backing off now. The Buick careened towards the ferry.

"He's cornered!" yelled out the driver of the Hudson. "We've got that goddamned dago this time! Get ready to jump out and take him!" With the accelerator to the floorboard, the heavy car barreled down the street in hot pursuit hell-bent on destruction.

"That ferry don't look right," warned the cohort.

"They're holding it for us—we'll make it!" A misconception on his part.

The captain, the first mate, and the ramp tender could do nothing more now, other than to watch this spectacular display of reckless disregard for safety, and pray for a less than disastrous outcome.

The downstream drift of the ferry put the right side of the ferry in better alignment with the loading ramp than the left side. In the split second that followed, Al chose to aim for it, or risk climbing the stairs that led up the middle of the ferry to the upper passenger deck. The ramp was only part way down, with a couple of feet more to go, with the ferry still several yards out when the Buick shot across the ramp, then locked its brakes while still in midair, like a horse vaulting a ravine. Hitting the deck on all four wheels and bringing the car to a halt was a feat that only an aircraft carrier pilot could have duplicated. The pronounced thump and screaming of rubber against decking told the captain that the car had hit its target. Its condition unknown, he nevertheless shouted the order for full speed ahead, even though he was not at his post on the other end of the ferry. But the first mate, having appraised the situation, was already well on his way to the opposite pilothouse to take command.

Down in the engine room, a high pressure surge of steam to the engine put the vessel in full speed ahead. "Holy Christ, that was a heavy thud!" exclaimed the engineer. "He must have made it," he added, relieved.

The Hudson's driver panicked when he realized the ferry was not up against the dock as expected, but instead was moving rapidly away and out of the slip.

"Oh Christ! It's moving out! We're not going to make it!" he yelled, as he came down hard on the brakes.

"Brakes . . . ! Stop . . . ! Damn it . . . ! Stop . . . !" screamed his cohort in horror. They'd been applied, but with little results.

With eyes wide open, arms outstretched with sweaty hands gripping the steering wheel, right foot pressing down hard on the brake peddle, the senior agent watched the split second scene of being air-borne over the Sacramento River on a moonlight night flash before his eyes before plunging into the river, while the cohort buried his face in his arms.

As Al had said: "Once you get that pile of iron rolling, you can't stop it."
How right he was.

CHAPTER 27

"Mike, you better call another meeting," advised Matteoli once again.
"Yes, I believe we should," concurred Mike.

The meeting took place in the same location and in the same manner as the previous meetings.

Again Fred's little black and white terrier expressed her concerns of the presence of the paesani in the big barn. She showed signs of nervousness and was expressing her distress by whining and whimpering, jumping on and off the bed—pacing back and forth from the foot of the bed to the back door, ears perked—head cocked—listening.

"You don't like this, do you girl?" asked Fred of his little dog. She responded with worried glances, shifting her eyes from him to the back door. No she didn't like it at all, and she was letting her master know the best way she could.

"Well, I'll tell you what. Don't be concerning yourself because I'll be talking to our good friend Mike, and when he hears what I have to say, I'm sure that everything will be alright. Now what do you think of that?" asked Fred of his little dog as if he was talking to a human being. While he said that, she had her eyes fixed on her master, with her ears perked up taking in every word of what he was saying. She gave a sigh of relief, much as a person would do, then curled up at Fred's feet while he set his book down and dowsed the lamp at his bedside. Obviously the little dog couldn't possibly imagine the true reason his master would take it upon himself to quell her worrisome concerns.

On the very same day of this meeting, Pete Selmeczki, the owner of Pete's Hardware, more or less across the street from Fred Puls' gasoline station, had approached Fred with some disturbing news. Pete, a sincere man of impeccable reputation, never indulged much in conversation unless it was truly worthwhile. What he passed on to Fred was just that, nothing else.

"Fred," said Pete, " have you noticed a black sedan with a couple of men cruising around lately, especially after hours?"

"Yes I have. Why do you ask?"

"Well, I think they may be federal agents."

"Oh, and how do you know? What makes you think that?"

"Well, Fred, one of them came in the store the other day, just as I was closing up for the night. He said he wanted to look at some deer rifles, like maybe he wanted to buy one."

"And that makes you think he's a federal man?" questioned Fred.

"No, not that alone. I don't think he really wanted to buy the gun. Oh, he handled it like an expert alright, aiming it through the window at targets across the street and things like that, but he kept glancing over in your direction like he was looking for something."

"Pete, that still doesn't necessarily make him a lawman, does it?" questioned Fred again.

"When he'd throw the rifle up to his shoulder while trying it out, his coat opened up. I saw a badge and the butt of an automatic . . . "

"That's different. I see what you mean . . . hmmm . . . "

This now got Fred to thinking, Mike would have to be advised. Passing on this information is what Fred meant when he assured the little terrier. But it would not be done this night.

The three paesano partners, plus Matteoli, were resting their buttocks in a half-sitting and half-standing position against empty 50 gallon aging barrels. The flickering light from the kerosene lamp, setting on the end of an empty barrel, reflected against the stern faces of these once happy-go-lucky men. A stack of 10 gallon oak barrels full of Jackass was also being illuminated in the far end of the barn. The men's shadows were being cast against the inside walls like huge figures of an on-stage mystery drama. Mike had called the meeting so it was up to him to open the discussion:

"For some reason, the federal agents are getting rough, they're making life miserable for us there at the ranch. I can handle it well enough, but the family, especially my wife, Livia..." he hesitated for a moment before continuing: "She's having a hard time handling it. Their constant harassment during all hours of the night is beginning to tell. They bang on the door asking my whereabouts, scaring the life out of her and the kids with angry demands, insults and threats."

"Wanting more payoff, I suppose," put in Al while not letting on the full extent of his harassing of the agents. No doubt a contributing factor.

"Of course, what else? As I warned before, they'll want it all," added Matteoli.

Julio, knowing Livia's sensitivity, was shaking his head as if in disbelief of what he was hearing, but he knew it to be true. "Why can't they at least leave the women and children alone?" he asked himself. His expressions and head movements answered his own question. "No, they are not about to do that, that's Mike's weak point, and much like a pack of hyenas, there is where they'll hit him the hardest." Julio finally posed a question:

"Well, what do we have to do, pay them more money?"

"That will help for a little while, but they'll be right back demanding more," answered Matteoli.

"Too bad those bastards didn't stay down at the bottom of the Sacramento River with their Hudson. They're like rats, you can't even drown the buggers," commented Al in anger.

Mike wondered about that comment. Al had mentioned something about it, but . . . ? Once again he injected the family matter into the discussion.

"Their conduct is having a definite psychological affect on the family. I can see it in my oldest boy, my daughter, and the little guy. He dashes under the kitchen stove or jumps in his mother's arms every time they knock on the door. At least he has the protection of her arms to help him through this ordeal. If you think he cried when he was a baby, you should hear him now when those sons-of-bitches show up. They strut around the yard like they own it. When they approach the kids asking for me, they pull their coats back exposing their badges and the butt end of their automatics, then hold their coats open by jamming their left hand in their pocket like they were scratching their balls. Not only do they demand cash, but they also on occasion take a 5 gallon keg of Jackass with them. I keep one handy at all times just for them," said Mike while gritting his teeth.

"Goddamn them! Somehow we've got to get those damned hyenas off our backs! Kill the bastards if we have to! Make the buggers up a batch of methyl alcohol from that pile of horse manure Oscar has out at the barns and poison the whole lot of them!" said Al angrily. He was deadly serious.

Mike suddenly turned pale as a look of horror crossed his face. Knowing Al as he did, he might just carry out the threat, an unthinkable solution to the problem. Julio having noticed the expression, and with the same concerns, cut in:

"We're going to have to use restraint," he warned. "Getting picked up for bootlegging means a stiff fine and a short jail sentence at most, but to get an assault charge against us for working over a federal agent will mean a long jail sentence for sure." He was deadly serious about his comment, as well.

"Well, where do we go from here?" asked Mike, relieved that Julio put the killing matter to rest.

"Do you think they know exactly where the main still is located?" asked Matteoli of Al.

"So far, I don't think so, but they are narrowing it down. They can't help but know that it's in Crow Canyon somewhere," answered Al. "And since they once raided Tony's place, they could assume that it's still in Bellina Canyon."

Now the discussion shifted to what the agents might or might not know about the main still and its location. Mike expressed concern that all their activity around Crow Canyon would soon attract Warren's men and that could turn out to be very bad. Mike was still smarting from the four-month trial he had endured earlier in the year. Had it not been for Sheriff Becker's quick thinking and action, that incident could have turned out to be a real disaster.

One of the smaller stills was out of production altogether. It had been repaired and was now being kept as a standby unit so production could be maintained in the event the large unit might be down for whatever reason. So the concern was only the big unit up the Canyon.

"My suggestion is to develop an escape plan out of Bellina Canyon. In the event of a raid, get the men out and the hell with the still. We can always have another made up," advised Matteoli.

"You're right, the escape should be organized and orderly, not like what happened at Henry's Thompson place," put in Mike.

They now hammered out a plan that made some real sense; a plan that would give them plenty of time to clear out of the area if and when the proper signals were given. They figured the men could make it up the west ridge on foot and drop down to Cull Canyon through Gansberger's ranch or the Ramage ranch. Either one of these ranchers, if asked, would give the men a ride back down to Mike's place without asking too many questions. So the matter was settled; the men would be taken up to the ridge and familiarize themselves with the escape route.

The next order of business was an escape route for Al and the Buick.

"Al, are you familiar with Norris Canyon that swings off Crown Canyon to the right at the Country Club?" asked Mike.

"I know where it's at. What about it?" answered Al.

"Well, if its not too muddy, you can make it all the way into San Ramon," said Mike.

"Is that right? I had no idea that it went all the way through. I'll have to check it out and see what it looks like."

"You do that," said Mike. "It looks like a driveway into someone's ranch, but it does go through."

Al was pleased to know that there was another way out of Crow Canyon that could be used in a pinch. He would check it out first thing next day.

"I think it's a mistake to take the Buick into Bellina Canyon at all. The cans should be relayed down to the main road and transferred somewhere along the road away from the first gate," suggested Matteoli.

Al wouldn't go for the idea. He didn't like the idea of screwing around with transferring a load of alcohol along the main road. Once on the pavement and rolling he felt secure.

"No," said Al, "let's stick with what we've been doing. I'll pick up high-proof at the still. We can rely on the Okies' signals. They're doing a pretty good job." Al was referring to the renters across from the Nunez ranch at the Habberney place.

As for Mike's problem with the federal agents, there was little that could be done. Even if the agents knew for sure that he was in fact the boss and owner of the stills, they would have to prove it. And as long as he stayed away from the stills, that would be difficult to do. So he was to continue to play the part of a Jackass peddler and chicken rancher, hopefully minimizing the extent of the operation, as far as the agents were concerned. The meeting broke up without the usual last minute comments to raise their spirits. They departed with a solemn whispered goodnight.

CHAPTER 28

What surprised Fred Puls was Mike's casual concern over the matter of federal agents he'd reported. Although the news came as no surprise, and since Fred did express concern, Mike graciously put his mind at ease by agreeing to move his inventory out of the barn.

"Fred, don't concern yourself, I understand perfectly well," said Mike to his friend. "We'll have the rest of the 10 gallon barrels out of the barn by the end of the week. By the way," he added, "can you get me a new set of Goodyear tires for the Buick?"

"Don't tell me Al's gone through another set already? Christ, he's rough on tires!" commented Fred.

"Well, the way he's been taking the turns up the canyon does raise hell with the tires, and with the rainy season upon us, I do think he's ready for a new set."

"Yes, I guess you're right. I'll have them here for you in a couple of days or so."

When the tires did come in, Al had the Buick over at Fred's service station getting them mounted, while at the same time giving Matteoli a hand with the loading over at Fred's barn. Since he always drove around with the Model-T Ford truck during daylight hours hauling chicken feed, Matteoli decided to transport the whiskey barrels in broad daylight hidden amongst the sacks of chicken feed.

Once loaded, the truck made its way up Crow Canyon Road with the first load of camouflaged barrels, which appeared to be a load of chicken feed. The disguise was perfect; it looked authentic, even to the senior agent sitting alone in the Hudson parked undetected in the shade of an overhanging tree out front of Peterson's apricot orchard just up Cull Canyon road, within sight of the intersection where Matteoli had just passed. He knew the truck well, and had seen it make these trips many times before. This one appeared to be no different. He was not concerned because it was Al and the Buick that interested him, not Matteoli and the Model-T.

Guido and Contini were there at the ranch to help with the unloading. The barrels were to be stored in the secret chamber under the floor of the first chicken house. This meant backing the truck up to the small shop that faced the yard, walking through it and into the first chicken stall, where the secret chamber existed under the floor. It was agreed that, if all went well, Al would wait for Matteoli's return trip to once again help with the second load. Guido, having reported the absence of surveillance up on Jensen Road, induced Matteoli to return immediately for a second load. The sacks of chicken feed which were used for camouflage were left scattered around on the truck bed since they'd have to be rehandled anyway.

However, this untidy pile of feed sacks did not go unnoticed, at least not by the senior agent parked at Cull Canyon Road. Seeing the truck go past his stakeout, he asked himself the question: "Now, why should that truck be heading away from Mike's chicken ranch, with an untidy load of feed sacks, when it had previously been heading to the ranch with a full load—neatly stacked?" The only logical answer he could reasonably come up with was, maybe some other chicken rancher was to share the load. "Yes, that makes sense, no need for concern," he thought.

A short time later the agent's keen hearing picked up the laboring sound of what appeared to be the same truck straining under the weight of a second load of chicken feed heading back up the canyon. Like a hawk picking up the sound of rustling leaves, he sat up straight from his slouched position with his eyes trained on the intersection. Sure enough, it was the same truck chugging along with a full load of neatly stacked feed sacks.

"Those goddamned dagos!" he swore. "So that's it!" He started up the Hudson and took off with a scattering of gravel. The car was still in second gear when he reached the intersection; the truck had disappeared around the corner to his left and was now out of sight heading up the canyon to Mike's place. His cunning mind dictated a turn in the opposite direction, to the right instead of to the left. At the intersection of Dublin Canyon Road, the car made a left and charged up Castro Hill with the accelerator to the floorboard, and so it continued to the top, then made another left turn onto Jensen Road, where it stopped short of exposing itself to the eyes of the paesani down below at Mike's place. Sure enough the truck was just backing into position at the shop door.

Binoculars in hand, the senior agent stepped out of his car and walked several yards ahead of it, to the edge of a clump of shaded underbrush, and watched the unloading while it was in progress. He could only see the heads of the workers below since the roof of the buildings obscured a full view of the truck and its contents. He was watching and waiting for any further clue that might surface to strengthen his suspicions. Once the truck was relieved of its load of barrels, the untidy pile of remaining sacks of feed were left scattered around the bed of the truck as it pulled away in full view from above. He immediately concluded that it was whiskey barrels they were hauling—not chicken feed.

"So, that's where your big cache of Jackass is located; how nice. We don't have the still, yet, but we do have the second best thing to it." The statement parted the lips of the senior agent in audible tones, accompanied with the customary hissing sounds of a rattlesnake about to strike. He now realized that the paesani below had been aware of the agents' presence whenever they kept surveillance on the ranch from Jensen Road above. However, this time, the clever hunted had been outsmarted by the cunning patience of the hunter, constantly and patiently waiting for his quarry to make a mistake, then pounce on him. And pounce on Mike, the senior agent did do. The man was to waste little time. He showed up at the ranch that very same evening, and of all times, at supper time.

To jump a family while having their evening meal brands a man a beast of the worst magnitude. Even if it was for the purpose of making an arrest, which it was not, a more humane and decent time of day could have been picked. But, since extortion was the senior agent's stock and trade, and that's what he had in mind, it made no difference to him how he solicited his bribes. And now, to push himself into an even lower rung of the ladder of decency, he was double crossing his cohort and colleagues in that he would keep this newly discovered secret to himself and not share the extra "take" with them.

Needless to say, when Mike left the dinner table to discuss the terms of settlement out in the backyard at the entrance of the shop and chicken house, Livia became hysterical. The thought of seeing her husband, the father of her three children, being led off by a federal agent, that conducted himself more like a half-crazed, mentally deranged madman at the head of a vigilante committee, rather than a law enforcement agent, was more than she could handle. Her screaming tantrums, especially on nights that followed this and other similar episodes, were grim testimony to the heartaches she was forced to endure.

The bitter argument that ensued between the two men ended in Mike's capitulation to the agent's demands. The final words spoken by the agent were meant to be a part of the terms of surrender:

"I will expect an equal amount of cash to be paid to me, and me only, upon demand, which will be staggered in between our regular collections," said the agent, about as dry and to the point that one can get, before adding: "And keep your mouth shut! Do you understand me . . . ?" He didn't bother waiting for Mike's acknowledgment or agreement to this one-sided pact. He turned and walked towards his car while stuffing the freshly acquired bills in his pocket. Needless to say, whatever food the family had consumed that night was never digested. It was a relief to pass it out at a later time in about the same undigested form it had been when swallowed.

This was now a far cry from the pleasant, happy-go-lucky days of San Bruno. The many pleasant hours that were spent with Sheriff Kelly, and at times with his wife, were not to be forgotten. There were many law enforcement officers such as Sheriff Kelly who understood their jobs to be dedicated to maintaining law and order, but also to encourage people to obey the law, and to help them understand its intent and purpose. The laws of the land were not meant to be exploited by anyone, let alone the very persons who are assigned to uphold them. Granted, Mike was engaged in an illegal endeavor, a bootlegger, and a damned good one at that, but he did not resort to extortion, harassing women and children, or condone violence in any form, even though at times it might be justified. What the senior agent should have done was arrest Mike in a decent, orderly manner, to put him on notice that the law must be obeyed whether popular or not. Instead, this law enforcement scoundrel was encouraging him to continue breaking the law on the pretense that as long as he shared, the law could be flaunted.

Al was furious when told of the brazen shakedown. It was indeed fortunate for everyone that he was not present at the time of the incident. There would be no telling as to the outcome of such an encounter. Unlike Mike, he was a fighter; he would undoubtedly have engaged the senior agent in a free-for-all, despite the agent's being armed and his being a law officer. He would have no doubt received the payoff just the same, but he would have had to dig it out of his ass first in order to spend it, providing he could get it past his badge pinning his anus shut. So far, the accidents that had occurred involving the Hudson and Essex where not preplanned. But as far as Al was concerned, to set this particular agent up for a fatal accident was not out of his realm of thinking, especially now that Mike's family was being subjected to such brutal psychological tactics. He was restraining himself from retaliating against the agents, but given the opportunity, or if conditions were to develop whereas he could exploit them to their own demise, he would do just that. Unfortunately, the agents felt no differently towards him either. So far they had taken a beating brought about by their own actions more than anything else. Obviously, they would never admit to this, not even amongst themselves. If anything, they would use the same excuses that kids sometimes do when they say: "Look what you made me do!"

The agents were now confining their activities to cruising up and down Crow Canyon Road. At least for the moment, the senior agent restricted his cohorts from further surveillance by way of Jensen Road. He had a secret, and it was paying off handsomely. It was all his, and he wanted to keep it that way. What he wanted now was the main still location pinpointed exactly, and how to get to it. This would be the grand slam. He was envisioning the use of a wheelbarrow to carry away the $100 bills that he would collect from Mike and his paesani. Their fear of jail, especially being noncitizen immigrants, would keep them working the stills for him, so to speak. But such as it is with the strongest steel cable imaginable, sooner or later, with enough pressure, it too will snap.

CHAPTER 29

After receiving the all-clear signal from the okies, Al emerged out of Bellina Canyon and onto Crow Canyon Road loaded with 5 gallon tins of alcohol. He swung the Buick to the right and headed down Crow Canyon Road, leaving a trail of mud that had accumulated on the tires. At this time of year and this hour of night, cutting corners was no problem, for traffic was very limited. Nevertheless, he kept his speed down on the sharp turns until he reached the straighter section of road past the Edenvale Grade School.

The Buick started to send off its familiar whistle as it passed the Joseph Knowland (his prominence included the ownership of the Oakland Tribune) summer home to the right, an estate-like setting with a secluded study separated from the main estate, built high on a knoll and across the creek. It was a habit with Al to glance up at the quaint little cottage (Mrs. Knowland's retreat and study) reflecting its lighting from the curved window arrangement onto the sloping hill below.

But this time, something else caught his attention. A flash of light flooded the lower section of the next hill causing him to quickly turn his attention to the area from which it originated. The main road ahead at the junction of Norris Canyon and Crow Canyon Roads had a kink in it where a short stretch of it climbed, then straightened out again. The flash of headlights from an approaching car at that point was what caused the flash that he saw. This, of course, caused him concern.

"That flash came from a pretty good-sized car," thought Al. "I hope its not that damned Hudson again," he mumbled in concern. Sure enough it was, with the senior agent at the wheel accompanied by his cohort, his tormentors. Knowing damned well they would turn around and give chase, he tramped down hard on the accelerator. "They would have had to have recognized the Buick," he thought as the car went past. But, another thought crossed his mind: "Rattlesnakes come in pairs," he growled while adding a few choice words of profanity to garnish the statement. Rather than risk running into the unknown somewhere down the line, possibly a trap, he decided to swing into Norris Canyon (the alternate escape route) to the left and go out in that direction. At that point where the two canyons come together is where

192

the Colonial Country Club (nothing more than a glorified whorehouse) was situated. It was set back far enough to allow car parking out in front, off the paved road. To make the turn while heading south, meant he'd have to come around in a tight left turn and head back north again to enter the escape route. Crow Canyon Road had just been paved, but Norris Canyon was not and neither was the area in front of the Country Club.

Swinging around hard to make the turn while still traveling at a high rate of speed put the Buick into a spin. While the tires were in contact with the pavement, they screamed and screeched their defiance to the maneuver. When they came in contact with the rain-softened unpaved section of the parking area in front of the Country Club, the heavy load gave the tires one hell of a bite into the wet earth, thus splattering mud, dirt and gravel against everything and anything that was in sight. Short of breaking windows, the whole front of the Club on the north end that housed the rooms used for prostitution by the ladies of ill repute, was peppered as if shot at with cannon grapeshot. As the car straightened out to head up Norris Canyon, the johns, assuming a raid was in progress, came boiling out of windows and doors with their clothing bundled under their arms, running for cover. Al didn't have time to think of an appropriate comment to fit the occasion such as was his habit to do so.

Entering the escape route with engine revving and wheels churning, the car disappeared from view. At a point along the road where Norris Canyon Creek ran along the bottom of a steep embankment to his right, Al stopped the car, set the emergency brake, jumped out, raced around the right side, jerked the rear door open and started sliding 5 gallon cans of high-proof alcohol down the steep slippery embankment. The heavy cans pushed their way, one after another, through the underbrush, coming to rest in the creek bed below. The entire load dumped, he jumped back into the car and continued up the canyon. By the time he had reached the yard area of the ranch just short of the summit, he came to the conclusion that the road was too sloppy to make it over the top and down the other side to the San Ramon-Dublin highway. He had no choice but to turn around in the barnyard area and head back down the canyon. In getting turned around in the cattle rancher's barnyard, the disturbance brought out a pack of ranch dogs, the likes of which he had never seen before. They were a mixture of all sorts of breeds, crossbred, and interbred: hounds, shepherds, and mongrels alike. He liked dogs and dogs liked him, but this was an intrusion of their domain and as far as the dogs were concerned, they had no intention of tolerating his presence, friendly or otherwise. His first reaction was to let the dogs know how he felt about their interfering with his getting turned around.

"Get the hell out of the way you bunch of mangy sons-of-bitches!" he yelled out. For an instant they quieted down some; they were used to being addressed in this manner. They must have thought that this guy isn't all that bad after all, for they now started milling around the car taking turns at saturating the tires.

Other than the sexual drive that dominates their thoughts, ranch dogs generally fall into three categories. There's the mean, snarling and biting type whose nasty disposition is to be reckoned with. Then there are the habitual urinaters that at times will store urine for days, waiting to find something worthwhile to hoist their leg on. Last but not least are the car hoppers. The minute you open the door of a car, they are the first ones in. They would sell their souls for a car ride. This pack was made up of all three of those categories.

Al opened the car door to better address the mongrels that were interfering with his turning procedure, but the maneuver resulted in several car hoppers making it through the door before he could pull it shut again. One behind the other they leaped across his lap, wagging their tails, panting and slobbering all over him. They liked this guy. Again he addressed them in a derogatory manner:

"You sons-of-bitches—get the hell out of here!" he said as he kicked the passenger side door open.

But the dogs interpreted his statement to mean: "Get out of the front seat, not the car." So they leaped in the back in anticipation of getting a free ride. Rather than fight it any longer, he headed back down the road with these mangy critters riding with him. The stench of cow manure, commingled with ungroomed dogs, was overpowering, but he had no choice but to put up with it. The rest of the pack gave chase while barking up a storm. The dogs on the inside of the car were now barking back in response. He knew he had taken on a number of them because the commotion in the rear continued after two of them leaped back up front with him.

In the meantime, having recognized the Buick, the agents turned the Hudson around and were now racing down Crow Canyon Road in hot pursuit. They charged down the road until they encountered the Essex cruising the canyon in the opposite direction. The drivers of the two vehicles recognized each other and braked. The Hudson turned around and met the Essex in front of the Country Club. Their immediate presence, right after the disturbance that Al had created, sent the half-naked johns and skimpily attired whores, who were trying to coax them back into their quarters because they were yet to be paid, scrambling for the protective cover of the adjacent creek. The agents, now engrossed more in thoughts of sex than in catching Al, proceeded to assess the situation through their rolled down windows. The driver of the Essex spoke first:

"Holy Christ, look at that, will ya?" he said excitedly. "Damn, those are good looking broads. I could go for some of that."

"Me too," said his partner. Stimulated by the thought of engaging in sex, he added: "Come on, let's get in on that . . . "

"It'll cost ya. Women like that don't come cheap," warned the driver.

"Playing second fiddle, the best of them cut the price. I'm going for it!" In the mood he was in, he'd settle for third or fourth fiddle just as well.

"Hold it! You guys are not going nowhere. At least not until we catch up to the Buick. Didn't you see it? It was coming your way," asked the senior agent, somewhat puzzled.

"It didn't go past us. We couldn't help but have seen it if it had. The hell with it, let's grab a couple of those whores while the grabbing's good," responded the driver of the Essex. His partner, by now slobbering like a wolf in heat, concurred.

"No! Dammit I said no, and I mean no! That little dago comes first. The whores can wait. Besides, the later it gets, the cheaper they work." Apparently, sex was on his mind as well.

As they talked, they glanced over to where the cars were parked out in front of the Country Club. The glare from their headlights revealed the freshly mud-splattered cars and face of the building. A glance at the freshly churned up earth and fresh car tracks leading into Norris Canyon gave them instant answers to their questions.

"He's up the canyon, follow me!" commanded the senior agent excitedly.

The Hudson, followed by the Essex, took up the Buick's trail, which by now was traveling in the opposite direction. As the Buick came into view, the two agents' cars came to an abrupt stop, blocking the road; Al was trapped. The agents came running up to him with guns drawn, two around to his right side and the senior agent with his cohort to his left.

"All right, dago, come on out!" commanded the senior agent while holding his gun ready.

There was nothing that irritated Al more than to be addressed as a dago in that commanding tone of voice. Responding accordingly, he said in brief: "Up your ass, mister!"

"Pretty cocky, aren't ya! We'll see how you feel about it when I slap the cuffs on you!"

The signal was then given; all four doors were jerked open at the same time, supposedly to reveal the incriminating evidence the agents were so confident they'd find. But, instead of tin cans of alcohol, they were met head on by a pack of irate, snarling and growling dogs, hell-bent on keeping out the intruders. The dogs had got there first, and by God, they were not about to surrender their positions. While barking up a storm, the dogs held their ground. For once in his life, Al didn't mind having a snarling, teeth-gnashing, mangy mongrel stretched out stiff-legged across his lap between him and the steering wheel.

The senior agent's attempt to reach in and pull Al out while holding his automatic, could have resulted in a savagely ravaged hand if he had chosen to pursue the maneuver.

"Hold it boss!" warned one of the agents from the Essex. "There's nothing but dogs in here!"

At least some of these agents were aware of the rights of others and chose to respect them. It was apparent, this particular agent who issued the warning would not tolerate a complete disregard for Al's rights. The senior agent was aiming his automatic directly at Al's head as if ready to pull the trigger when the agent spoke again:

"Back off, sir, we can't take him!" he stated.

"Who the hell are you giving orders to . . . ? I'm in charge here!" responded the senior, about as angry and furious as he could get.

"I'm not giving you orders, sir, but neither will I be a party to what's on your mind!" said the agent quite dryly.

He then slammed the door shut and walked away from the Buick followed by his companion. The two men re-entered the Essex, slammed the doors shut and backed down the road to a point where they were able to get turned around and head back out the canyon. About that time the pursuing pack of dogs caught up to the stopped cars. Stiff legged, they suspiciously sniffed at the two remaining agents standing alongside, with guns in hand. Al was keeping his mouth shut for fear of provoking the senior agent. He knew the agent had it in for him, thus pulling the trigger of that .45 caliber automatic was not out of the realm of possibility.

The scene around the two cars had now turned into a bedlam of snarling, growling dogs, which forced the two remaining agents to retreat back into their car, but not until the dogs had hoisted their legs and marked the tires, as well as the agents' pin-striped trousers.

Al's riding companions, not wanting to miss out on the fun going on outside, rejoined the rest of the pack. Before any of them could re-enter, he reached back and pulled the rear doors shut, then his own. He now addressed the dogs appropriately: "Thanks fellows! Go get 'em!"

Getting past the Hudson by climbing part way up the embankment, he, too, headed out the canyon. Once onto Crow Canyon Road, he nervously searched around for a cigarette, lit it, and took a long drag before sending a farewell message back to the senior agent. It was brief: "Arrivederci — asshole!"

CHAPTER 30

"Matteoli, what do you think?" asked Mike of his counselor. "Shall we see if we can recover the high-proof Al dumped into the creek?"

"We certainly can't let him take the risk. You never know, the agents may have found it, and are just waiting for the person that dumped it to come back and retrieve it" answered Matteoli.

"All right then, what you're saying is we better go get it ourselves, or leave it there—which is it?"

"No Mike, not 'we,' you better stay out of it. I'll take care of the matter," assured Matteoli, then added: "You're too delicate a person to withstand the confinement and regimentation of a prison. I'll handle it."

"Your concerns for me are fine, but what about you?" asked Mike.

"You forget that when you were still a boy I served in the Italian army. I'm conditioned to that sort of thing, but you are not. The matter is closed; besides, I have a plan that I'm sure will work, or at least lessen the risk."

Mike was instructed to visit the rancher whose property the cans were dumped on. Since he knew the man he would ask for permission for the families to spend a day's outing in the pastures to gather mushrooms, and if it be permissible, the boys would bring their scatter-shot .22 caliber rifles and .410 shotguns to hunt birds and rabbits, while the adults gathered mushrooms and dandelions.

He took care of the matter that very afternoon and reported back to Matteoli that the request was granted, provided the kids restricted their shooting along the creek and not in the pastures where the sheep grazed.

"Fine, just fine," said Matteoli. "This will work out perfect," he added. Having anticipated permission to be granted, he, aided by Guido and Contini, had worked on the Model-T flatbed truck, removing three of the 1 x 12 planks from the center section of the bed. Then using heavy hog wire fencing as a cradle and boards for reinforcement, they arranged the area between the body frame to take the 5 gallon tins, leaving the loose boards for easy removal and replacing as a cover. They then loaded some chicken coops on the truck bed for an even better camouflage.

That night at supper, Matteoli announced the plans for the next day's outing to the family; they were elated. They would leave first thing in the morning, joined by Livia and some of her kids as well. Lunches were prepared and buckets for the mushroom picking were already loaded in the Model-T touring sedan that night.

Early the next morning, Matteoli pulled out of his yard with both families in the sedan, followed by Guido and Contini in the truck, loaded with several chicken coops, complete with chickens. The vehicles stayed together until they reached the entrance to Norris Canyon. At that point Guido and Contini were to wait until they heard the first shot fired from the .410 gage shotgun. This was the signal that all was clear.

The shot having been heard echoing down the canyon, they moved up the road to where Matteoli waved them down. "Contini, you come with me. Guido, get turned around and wait. We'll bring the cans up to you for loading," instructed Matteoli. Guido, remaining with the truck ready to place the cans down under the floor boards when they were handed up to him, could hear the two men in the creek below, arguing.

A few yards up the creek the two men were sloshing through the creek bed carrying 5 gallon cans of alcohol; one in each hand. Contini, not being much for rugged work, or any kind of work for that matter, was complaining:

"Surely you don't expect me to carry these cans up that steep embankment—through that poison oak—to say nothing of rattlesnakes, do you?" he asked, somewhat indignantly, while catching his breath.

"Yes I do," answered Matteoli politely before posing his own question: "Are you of such high esteem that work embarrasses you, or are you just plain lazy?"

This of course opened the door to a psychological debate as to what in the line of duty was to be considered demeaning and what was not.

Guido fidgeted nervously as the debate went on. He could hear them but not see them, so to get their attention he threw rocks in their direction. This action resulted in his being embroiled in the confrontation.

While this was going on, Al, with his brother-in-law, Lepo, Guido's brother, was coming up the Canyon as fast as his red racing Roadster could maneuver the turns. Having first stopped off at Mike's place, and noticing the absence of the families and the calmness that prevailed, he'd posed a question to Mike:

"Where's everybody at?"

"They're up Norris Canyon getting the alcohol back out. The families also went along to gather mushrooms."

"What?! Holy Christ!, I just passed the Hudson. It's down at Live Oak Service gassing up," answered Al with an air of urgency.

"That figures," said Mike, then added: "That son-of-a-bitch is on his way up here to collect his dues. It's about that time."

"I'd better beat it up there and get those guys out of there. Lepo, hop in—let's go!" commanded Al.

Knowing he'd be in for one hell of a ride, Lepo protested:

"Oh no . . . not me! I'm not . . . "

"Goddamn it! Get in!"

On second thought, Lepo decided to obey orders. He wasn't too sure which was worse, riding with Al or being present when the federal agents showed up.

The Roadster skidded to a stop face-to-face with the truck as Guido was placing the first four cans in place. Al jumped him:

"For Christ's sake! Is that all you got? What the hell's holding you up?" he demanded to know.

"Those two (referring to Matteoli and Contini) haven't stopped arguing since we got here," responded Guido.

Al turned to Lepo with the intention of ordering him into the creek to lend a hand down below, but then changed his mind. The horrified expression on his face negated the need to ask him much of anything, let alone scramble down the steep embankment.

"Lepo, you get up on the truck! Guido, you get down aways, and we'll hand you the cans! I'll go down into the creek!"

In the process of relieving Contini of the cans he was carrying, Al explained the urgency of the situation. Contini, as his jaw dropped, eyes popped wide, bushy eyebrows raised, expressing surprise, exclaimed: "What?!" The thought of federal agents appearing on the scene suddenly snapped him to his senses. Arms outstretched like a tightrope walker to maintain balance, he scrambled back over boulders, splashed through pools, and hurdled logs to get more cans back to Al's waiting arms. Amazed at the spectacle, Matteoli commented:

"Now we know what it takes to get Mr. Contini into high gear— federal agents barking at his heels!"

The truck loaded, it chugged its way back down Crow Canyon none too soon, for the Essex, not the Hudson, came around a turn hogging the road. The near miss caused the agents to take note of the Model T's cargo. Noticing steam vapor emitting from around the radiator cap, the driver remarked:

"That little truck's got a pretty heavy load. I didn't think chickens were that heavy. Maybe it's low on water."

Yes, it was low on "water," but high on "alcohol."

Al was pleased with the recovery of the alcohol, but he did express concern about that particular night's confrontation with the agents when he had dumped it.

"They didn't see you coming out of the canyon, did they?" asked Mike.

"No," said Al, "but like I told you the other day, they must have figured that I've been coming out of Bellina Canyon, otherwise they wouldn't have been that far up."

"How could they possibly have figured that out?" questioned Mike.

"By the mud and tire tracks coming out of the canyon and onto the main road," answered Al.

"Yes, that could be . . . what should we do?" asked Mike.

"Lay low for a few days . . . have the Oakies keep an eye out . . . report back to us."

Al's suspicions were warranted. By now, the Hudson was reported seen at the gate time and again, its occupants scanning the canyon with binoculars looking for telltale smoke or whatever that would indicate unusual activity up the canyon. The agents even went to the extent of questioning some of the nearby ranchers, but with little, if any, results. However, such as it is with a chicken scratching around in a horse manure pile, a few whole kernels of barley can always be found; you just have to scratch hard enough.

CHAPTER 31

Regardless of the amount of money being paid to the senior agent, he kept up his vigilance, as much to even the score with Al as gathering information. Hauling alcohol back out Bellina Canyon slowed to a trickle. Alcohol was backing up at the main still. Inventory was at an all-time high. So, the decision was made to shut the still down for awhile. This would also give the paesani a well-earned rest and vacation from this stressful around-the-clock moonshining operation. They were tense, needing to get away from each other. Thrown together under adverse living and stressful working conditions such as they were, brought about arguments amongst them with occasional pushing and shoving matches that could eventually result in a fist fight. The one non-Italian member of the work crew, Al's personal friend, Fats Meehan, was getting especially pushy. The paesani were relieved to get away from him for a while.

Some of them went home to their families, while others stayed at Mike's place visiting with each other in a more relaxed atmosphere. They clowned around enjoying the philosophical bouts between Matteoli and Contini, the masters of wit. This was also deemed to be a good time for a business meeting as well. So it was decided to make a festive occasion of the get-together since the weather was nice and the women folks were also eager to spend a Sunday together.

This event also brought together numerous children as well, and of course, each guest had something to contribute to their excitement and pleasure, especially Terzo. As tough as he was to do business with, he was by no means a tightwad. On the contrary, he was extremely generous, always making it a point to have a fistful of silver dollars to drop into the kids' pockets. The youngsters were taught not to request, reach out, or take anything, even to the extent of politely refusing to accept something offered that they really wanted dearly, such as apple pie. Terzo was aware of this, so while snapping their suspenders or whatever, he dropped silver dollars in their pocket. The dollars, to the kids, in comparison to an adult, felt like cast-iron manhole covers, thus causing their pants to sag, favoring the side carrying the load.

The chatter that emitted from the group of women gathered in the kitchen preparing the feast was beyond comprehension. This was their day to catch up to all the latest gossip and unload all sorts of trivial thoughts having accumulated over the past months.

To add to the laughter and festive atmosphere of this particular day was the incident of the cat making off with an uncooked steak from the platter setting on the table at the barbecue pit. A number of women chased the cat and so retrieved the steak. But not until it had been dragged back and forth across the yard a few times. They did their best to clean up the meat in preparation for the barbecue. Without it, a shortage would occur. Now the question was, who amongst the guests would get the cat-dragged steak. Al's wife, Ida, volunteered to give it to her husband, since he was not a fussy eater and would accept the matter as a joke rather than be offended if the matter was to come to light.

Once the feast was consumed, and while all the adults were still at the table, the matter of the cat-dragged steak surfaced. The women could not hold the secret any longer; they finally let it out to the delight of the others. Al added his dry humor to the incident, bringing about hilarious laughter that added to the already festive mood.

However, the festive mood was cut short by the wide-eyed, scared youngsters running into the basement where the dinner tables were set up. They were the bearers of grim news. The black Hudson with two federal agents had pulled into the yard asking to see Mike. Assuming it to be the senior agent and his cohort, Al was the first to rise to his feet. With clenched fists and profanity emitting from his lips, he started for the basement exit. He'd have it out with the two of them here and now. But before he could reach the end of the long table, Julio, aided by his cousin, Matteoli, blocked his exit while at the same time reasoning with him. They managed to slow him down long enough to give him time to re-think his intentions.

"Al, for God's sake, control yourself. Your involvement will only make matters worse for Mike," they reasoned. It took some doing to divest him of his "let me at 'em" attitude.

Terzo, seeing the need to act on the two cousins' behalf, as well as Mike's, seized the opportunity to volunteer to accompany Mike, who was already on his feet heading for the exit door in a fit of rage.

The women nervously started to clear the tables. Scared looks and glances between them indicated fear for Livia's mental reaction to these constant confrontations between her husband and the senior federal agent. In a fast-brisk walk, Mike made his way between the parked cars leading towards the Hudson parked at the far end of the yard. The smirking senior agent was half sitting and leaning back on its front fender with his arms crossed. Terzo was on his way to catch up to Mike. Whatever children there were, scattered every which way seeking a hiding place.

Mike saved his breath until he faced the agent squarely. This intrusion on this festive Sunday gathering of his most cherished friends was just about all he would take from this whiskey-saturated creature that called himself a law-man. By now the other menfolks were gathered in a group at the door of the basement with Matteoli and Julio restricting them from stepping out into the yard. They were to remain there out of sight while waiting out the inevitable confrontation between Mike and the agent.

"Hello Mike," said the agent in a slurred, sneering manner. "Just dropped by to pay you a visit. I was up the cany . . ." That was about as far as the agent got with his intended announcement when Mike cut loose on him:

"You son-of-a-bitch!" were the first words to part his lips in a trembling, furious outburst.

The senior agent's cohort, standing on the opposite side of the Hudson, suddenly realized that this situation should not have ever taken place on this particular day. Only moments before entering the yard, he had suggested to his boss that he was pushing Mike too hard:

"Why go in there when they're having guests for a Sunday dinner?" questioned the cohort of his senior.

"The embarrassment will bring him around all the faster," came the confident answer to the question.

Well, this time the senior agent might have wished he had listened a little closer to his cohort.

Mike didn't stop with the first outburst. Having set the record straight on the agent's ancestry, the next outburst was to berate him for his assumed sexual habits, with a generous smattering of sex-related four-letter words in order to highlight the barrage of derogatory insults that followed.

Such as it is with bullies when you stand up to them, the agent took on a sheepish look, like as if all of a sudden he wanted to be Mike's friend. The expression did not go unnoticed; it irritated Mike all the more. Continuing his aggressive assault, he added a final stern and to-the-point comment with a question:

"What the hell do you want?! Come on, get it out! Then get the hell out of my yard!"

The agent, in a sheepish, whipped, half-assed manner finally made a statement as he indicated his intention to leave. While grabbing the door handle of the Hudson, he said:

"My friend, you will regret this day!" The statement was intended as a warning, and Mike understood it to be just that, but nevertheless, he was to have the last word:

"I'm not your friend, and it will be you that will regret this day, along with many previous days!"

Under the circumstances, Mike could not have mustered up a better statement even if it were rehearsed. The two agents backed out of the yard rather than try to get through the parked cars to make the circle. As they drove down Crow Canyon Road, the cohort didn't dare look at his senior or make comment. It was obvious the senior agent was weighing Mike's parting statement: "Is he bluffing, or is he not bluffing?" A good question.

The cohort had some thoughts as well: "This man Mike is a man of influence. Who, higher up than his senior, does he know? Are our own questionable activities being monitored?" The thought left a lump lodged in his throat.

Terzo was the first to embrace Mike, followed by the others. They were pleased with his performance. In low, serious tones the paesani commented amongst themselves that this confrontation, putting the senior agent in his place, was long overdue. They continued to comment as they walked off and away from the others. The seriousness of the matter received top priority in their discussions. It was determined that the federal agents were intent on demanding a greater take, no doubt because they had not only narrowed down the location of the main still, but also how they might get at it. The presence of the principals closest to the bootlegging operation was a plus for Mike. Now they were able to see for themselves first-hand, what he had been up against all along.

"Mike," said his cousin, Terzo, "I suggest you pull the stills out of the canyon as soon as possible. Relocate them, maybe somewhere in town or in one of these many chicken ranches around here, or even another county, like the Jacklich brothers are doing."

Terzo was referring to the five Austrian brothers, colleagues of Mike's, who were operating a still in nearby Cull Canyon, as well as several other counties as far east as Amador County-Jackson. However, in the Jackliches' case, when a threatening situation would arise, they made no attempt to move the still components. They simply abandoned it and set up a brand new unit somewhere else. This was the job of the one brother, Frank, to see to it that there was always a new unit on hand ready to put in operation on short notice.

The name Jacklich was derived from the original family name "Jaklic", pronounced "Yak-lic". Such as it was with the Italians being called "Dagos", the Austrians were called "Bohunks." In either case, it was smart to smile when addressing them in this manner.

"How about the secret chamber under the chicken house? Shouldn't it be cleaned out as well?" asked Al.

"Yes, that too," answered Terzo.

Mike turned to Matteoli, seeking his advice on the matter: "What do you think about moving the operation?"

"I will give you my opinion," said Matteoli. "If it were up to me to make the decision, I would not move the still out of the canyon at all, at least not at this time."

"Why not?" asked Mike.

"Because there is too much pressure on us at this time. The federal agents may be planning on our doing just that. This whole affair may have been planned as their way of getting us out in the open." Matteoli's answer was on target.

He then mentioned the Jacklich brothers' method of operation, since at one time they, along with three Sonoma County men by the name of Pasquini, Catelli and Cottini, who's son, at the age of sixteen, was making the alcohol runs to Oakland, delivering the alcohol to the Jacklich brothers for distribution, had a still operating in a wooded section of Matteoli's old ranch in Sonoma County at Alexander Valley near Healdsburg. He was aware of how the brothers operated and their reason in so doing: more mobility with smaller stills scattered around rather than a big stationary one.

Julio, in his quiet, thoughtful manner, was nodding his head in concurrence with his cousin's comments.

"What he says has merit, all right," said Al, who then added: "They know the stills are located in Bellina Canyon; however, catching us all simultaneously would be tough, especially in the canyon itself, unless, of course, they figure out the signal system and lay for us, which they will also do sooner or later. And besides, here in Alameda County, hopefully we have Sheriff Becker on our side, although I don't trust him either."

"That's true, but if they are laying for us outside, and they will get us if we stay inside, maybe we should abandon the stills all together. Is that what we're saying?" asked Mike.

"No," answered Al, "let's just stay put and lay low for a while. You never know, miracles do happen."

If Al wanted to be truthful, what he should have said was: "I will attempt to perform a miracle," because that is what he had been contemplating right along.

CHAPTER 32

The recent confrontation that Al witnessed at Mike's gathering was, as far as he was concerned, the last straw. Besides, he was getting fed up with the constant harassment of being engaged in life-threatening car duels, while all along the agents were shaking the operation down for cash. Besides, the main still being forced to shut down altogether infuriated him beyond prudent reasoning.

The added thought of the senior agent having held his automatic pointed directly at his head during the Norris Canyon incident was still heavy on his mind. No question now. He would set out to demolish the Hudson. He put his thoughts into words:

"We'll kill that son-of-a-bitch, if we have to. And that creep that tags along with him. You're not Primo's big Mack, but you'll have to do," he said to the Buick as if it, too, had a score to settle with these so-called representatives of law and order.

The thought of the Benicia incident where the two federal agents met their maker by crashing their Essex into the back end of Primo's Mack truck was also lingering on his mind, and so stated:

"It would be nice to have that big Mack right about now, or even one of those gasoline tankers like the one we almost wrecked a while back." He was now referring to the Mack tanker he tried to hijack. You could almost set your watch by their daily scheduled trips up and down Crow Canyon. An idea was formulating:

"Yeah . . ., one of those monsters is what we need to demolish that Hudson, but we don't have one, do we?" He was asking the Buick as if expecting an answer. "Or do we?"

A thought flashed through his mind as if the idea was being implanted by some mysterious voice coming from God knows where. He stared in disbelief at the crucifix hanging from a gold chain dangling from the car's rearview mirror. It was swaying back and forth such as it does when the car was in motion, but it was not in motion; it was parked. "Jesus Christ!" he exclaimed in astonishment, then immediately clamped his hand over his mouth as if he shouldn't have said that. "The priest ... the old priest over at the religious order of winemakers—in Napa . . . ? Oh my God," he muttered. Every word of the old priest's blessings on that day when the big Mack along with everyone and everything in range was blessed was flashing across his mind as if a message was being beamed his way. He whispered softly as he turned the car's ignition switch in preparation to start its engine: "What must be, must be," he murmured.

From where he had been stopped was only a short distance to the warehouse at Melrose where he was to park the Buick for the night. He wasted no time in transferring from it to his red Roadster. Next door at the Eastern District Police Station, Captain Brown viewed the sudden departure with interest: "What the hell's he up to now?" he asked himself.

"Tomorrow you and I are going to be busy. Have you ever seen a Mack truck before?" Al was now talking to the Roadster as he had been talking to the Buick. "Well, you're going to see one tomorrow, loaded with gasoline. You know, the stuff that makes you so cocky. And, you're also going to see a Hudson, with a first-class asshole at the wheel. Now keep in mind, I want you to be on your best behavior. Don't do anything stupid that might expose our hand." The last comment was directed more to himself than the car. He didn't solicit or particularly care to have the opinions of others before carrying out the plan he had in mind. The fact of the matter was that alcohol was backed up at the still, and the senior agent was the cause.

Having stepped up their surveillance, the agents were maintaining a close watch on activities in the Canyon, not only from up on Jensen Road, but also from a position where the Hudson was constantly seen parked in the shadows of the Norris Canyon entrance. The car with its agents had to be flushed out of its lair and put out of commission in order to reinstate a free movement of alcohol down the canyon. It would be up to him alone to do the job. He felt comfortable with the idea, especially now that he believed he had received the go-ahead in the form of a message from the old priest, or maybe the good Lord himself. Either way, the swinging of the crucifix in its back and forth motion, like a pendulum on a clock, was a sure sign that a message was indeed being sent down from heaven. Being a believer, he chose to interpret the message as a go ahead to once and for all time, remove this creature, the senior agent, from their midst, and send him on his way to hell. "Surely the good Lord would have no objection to that; he couldn't possibly want him in heaven, that's for sure," thought Al. In his mind, he was doing everyone a favor.

Traveling up and down Crow Canyon in his Roadster, he carefully checked distances and timing, while fine tuning his plan to demolish the Hudson. He also traveled the narrow dirt road that wound its way up the wooded hillside from Crow Canyon Road below, up to and through Bill Boyd's ranch yard, that terminated at the ridge on Jensen Road. He was familiar with this seldom-used road since Mike at one time had a small still operating half way up the heavily wooded hillside at a good flowing spring. The road being clear, he drove through Bill Boyd's gate onto Jensen Road to seek out the known old wagon road that extended down the other side of the ridge onto Eden Canyon Road below, the better part of a mile from its junction with Dublin Canyon Road. Al was leaving nothing to chance. Everything had to be well timed and his escape route had to be checked for obstructions. The wagon road being clear, he headed back to the Melrose warehouse, satisfied that his scheme would work.

He immediately went to work on the Buick. There were modifications to be made in preparing it for the task it would be called upon to perform. The work extended far into the night—no surprise to his wife, Ida. She was accustomed to his late night activities. But, she couldn't help sensing the tenseness built up within him, more so this night than others. The few hours sleep he managed to get didn't do much to quell his anxiety. His embrace that morning before leaving the house was very emotional, like maybe . . . he wasn't sure he'd be back. She questioned him:

"Al, don't keep me in the dark—what are you up to? Are you in trouble?"

"No—I'm not in trouble," he snapped, then loosened his embrace.

"Will you be home tonight?"

"Yeah . . . I'll be home—maybe a little late—don't wait up." She shook her head and turned away with a frown.

The morning was spent fine tuning the Buick—the afternoon practicing maneuvers. With everything in order, and himself emotionally geared up, there was no reason to put off the inevitable: either destroy the Hudson, or himself in trying.

"If the Sacramento River couldn't destroy you bastards, one of those Mack tankers sure as hell will," growled Al as he headed east out of Castro Valley. He topped over Castro Hill and headed down into Dublin Canyon. The curves didn't slow him down much, in fact he was keeping pressure on the accelerator in order to better negotiate the turns that followed the twisting Palomares Creek.

The high-pitched whistle of the Buick's vacuum fuel tank caught the attention of Old Charley, as he was referred to, the proprietor of Canyon Service, as he was filling a customer's gasoline tank. He looked up from his task in time to see Al in the Buick roar on past as if being pursued. But there was no one in pursuit. The other odd thing he noticed was that the car's convertible canvas top was folded and strapped down across the back, and the fact that it was afternoon with a long way to go before sundown. The peculiarity of the situation caused him to raise a question:

"What the hell's he doing out here this time of day, and where the hell is he going in such a hurry with the top down? He must be empty," said Charley to his customer who was standing there with one foot resting on the running board of his car.

"Do you know that guy?" inquired the customer.

"Yes, I know him, but I have never seen him out during the day cruising around like a playboy," answered Charley. "My daughter has the 'hots' for that guy," he added, while reaching in his pockets for change.

Charley didn't bother using a cash register; he made change right out of his pockets, which were always bulging with coins that he'd constantly keep rattling with his hands while talking. His bib overalls contained his entire bookkeeping system as well. Every pocket was stuffed with money or receipts, invoices, records and notes. He even kept the deeds and documents to his property in his pockets. For him to lose his pants would literally wipe him out, since the records of whatever he possessed would be lost along with his overalls.

The mention of his daughter brought about a comment from his customer which caused Charley to wince:

"Charley, if you ask me, your daughter has the 'hots' for most any good-looking guy that can hang onto a vibrating steering wheel with one hand."

"Especially truck drivers; she likes them even better," snapped Charley in acknowledgement.

However, Al's thoughts were far from being a playboy, nor did he have Charley's daughter on his mind. His mind was occupied with the strategy he must apply to the planned destruction of the Hudson, and the demise of its occupants; hopefully, the senior agent for sure. Today was the day, and it had to be done right the first time, because to fail could very well mean destroying himself in the process. Each maneuver and timing, to the split second, would have to be executed precisely. There was no room whatever for a bad maneuver or a misjudgment. For this reason, he had once again spent the previous day cruising up and down Crow Canyon Road with his Roadster, studying the various sections of the road, the driving habits of the Mack tanker's driver, and the position of the Hudson as it lurked in its shaded den-like setting at the mouth of Norris Canyon. The action its driver would take was anticipated; hopefully, correctly.

In addition, he had practiced several hairy maneuvers, including putting the Buick into a complete spin. This was done on roads other than Crow Canyon, but with similar characteristics. He felt confident that the car would handle the escape route over the Jensen ridge as well as the Roadster did, because he had to concern himself with the Essex that was once again monitoring traffic on Crow Canyon Road while maintaining vigilance on Mike's ranch from up on Jensen Road. For the Buick to be seen traveling down out of the canyon after what he had planned for the Hudson was something that he did not care to deal with. All these thoughts were being hashed and rehashed in his mind as he was now traveling north towards San Ramon from Dublin on the Dublin-Martinez Highway.

The sloshing sound of the eight water-filled 5 gallon tin cans that were neatly laid down and tightly secured to the floorboards in the rear section of the Buick was pronounced. The added tarp, stretched tightly and secured down, not only disguised the cans, but also muffled the rattle and sloshing sound, as well as keeping them confined. By experimenting during his rehearsal spinouts, he had determined the exact weight needed on the car's rear wheels in order to maintain stability. The top had been purposely folded and tied down in order to give him an instant, unobstructed view in all directions. He could not afford blind spots for the maneuvers he would have to execute this day. Only the windshield and his head and shoulders protruded upward from the car's body.

The Buick was now approaching San Ramon where it was to make a left turn onto Crow Canyon Road, then head up the steep grade where the road topped over the summit at the Alameda-Contra Costa County line. The car cruised gently over the summit giving him a few seconds to view the setting sun, and to gaze down into Crow Canyon with its many spurs so magnificently shadowed. He viewed the scene admiringly, then mumbled as the car made its descent down into the canyon: "I hope to Christ this isn't the last time I see it."

The movement of the car as it followed the winding road was causing the crucifix dangling from the rearview mirror to sway gently back and forth as if to catch his eye. "You again," he commented, with a lump in his throat.

At the bottom of the grade, he slowed and turned right onto a dirt roadway that led down to the creek, across a wooden bridge, and up the other side where the road terminated amongst a group of cow corrals. Turning the car around, he now headed back down to the creek and parked out of sight. Barring no changes in the schedule of the Mack gasoline tanker coming from Martinez, his wait would be short.

Ten minutes had gone by, enough time to allow him to finish his cigarette, when he heard the loaded gasoline tanker making its way down the grade using compression on the engine to hold it back. The accompanying backfire from the engine's efforts was coming in loud and clear. At the bottom of the grade, the shifting of gears could be heard. With pressure back on the accelerator, the tanker roared on past, amidst a slapping of drive chains and whining of gears. The huge tires were sending off the sounds of grappling with pavement, a sure indication of a heavy load. In this particular case, the load was gasoline.

Al bided his time. He waited until he was satisfied that the tanker would be out of sight before emerging from his hiding place. He then pulled back onto the road and proceeded to follow the tanker at a distance so as not to be conspicuous. The tanker rumbled on past Norris Canyon to the left where, sure enough, the Hudson, containing the senior agent along with his cohort, the 'creep' as Al referred to him, were sitting in their car keeping up their vigilance while sipping Mike's Jackass. The tanker went on past, then less than a minute later along came Al with the Buick.

"There he is," exclaimed the creep in a slurred manner. "And he's loaded." The Jackass he'd been drinking was having its effect.

"Yeah—that's the little bastard all right," concurred the senior agent, in a slurring-like manner.

The Buick did appear to be loaded, since the set of overload springs had been removed purposely so as to give that impression. The senior agent wasted no time in getting the Hudson underway in hot pursuit of the Buick. The Hudson had to negotiate several sharp turns shortly after its departure before coming in view of the car and the tanker some distance up ahead. This stretch of road was rather straight before it entered the narrow part of Crow Canyon where the road picked up the creek again to its right, then followed its twisting course.

The tanker rumbled along at some 30-35 miles per hour as it passed Pasqual's ranch to the left, the last place before entering the narrow portion of the canyon. The Buick was halfway through the straight stretch just as the tanker disappeared from view. Through his rearview mirror, Al could see the Hudson come into view at the upper end of the stretch. This brought on a snarling comment:

"You son-of-a-bitch! You think I'm loaded, don't you? And you've got me cornered. Well, let me tell you something, Mister Federal Agent! I have a big surprise for you, so hang in there!"

The Buick responded to added pressure on its accelerator. It would now have to catch up to the tanker as it made its way through the narrow twisting section, then across the first concrete bridge where the creek flowed to the road's left for the better part of a quarter of a mile in a somewhat straight course. At the end of this straight stretch, the road left the steep embankment to its right and crossed the second concrete bridge that formed a sharp

"S" turn. If Al's plan proved to be successful, all three vehicles were to meet at this second concrete bridge. The introduction would not be pleasant.

No sooner had the tanker rumbled over the first bridge, the Buick was right on its tail, almost bumper to bumper. Once over the bridge, the Hudson came roaring into view, pouring it on, its occupants excited.

"We've got him!" yelled out the senior agent. "He's trapped! Shoot the tires out from under him! Better yet, blow that cocky little dago's head off!" he added with an alcohol-induced statement.

"You got it, Chief!" answered the creep, while slamming the bolt closed on the submachine gun he was cradling. It was now ready for action.

Al hadn't contemplated having a Thompson submachine gun pointed at him with the intent of killing him. But he sure as hell got the message when he saw the creep holding the gun out the car window trying to get a bead on him. Upon so doing, he swung the Buick to the left, putting the shooter's line of sight directly in line with the back end of the tanker. What the shooter now saw through his sights was the big letters painted in red: "Danger! Gasoline! Flammable!"

The creep momentarily pulled the gun back into the car as he addressed his senior: "Holy Christ, boss, that's a gasoline tanker!"

"That's OK, he ain't going nowhere," assured the creep's boss. "Get ready, I'll get on his tail again!"

Al kept the Buick along the left side of the tanker while flashing his headlights to catch the truck driver's attention, indicating his intention to pass. The tanker hugged the right-hand side of the road while keeping up its speed. There was room to pass. The Buick quickly pulled up alongside the tanker, then momentarily held its position in the driver's blind spot. The truck driver glanced into the side mirror again such as he had done seconds before only to see the Hudson starting to pass. For the moment, it never occurred to him that he was, in fact, looking at a second car.

"You better get the lead out of your ass, buddy, if you expect to make it before we get to the bridge up ahead!" said the truck driver as the end of the straight stretch was coming up fast.

Al held his position just long enough to look down towards and across the upcoming bridge. Through the alders, whose foliage was sparse enough, he could see that the road was clear as it continued on past the bridge.

As anticipated, the tanker was maintaining its speed. It reached the marker that Al had predesignated. Now the Hudson came up directly behind the Buick. The creep hung the submachine gun out the car window once again.

"There's that frigg'n machine gun again!" cursed Al. At that instant, he put the accelerator to the floorboard, then added a comment as the car surged forward. This one was directed to the old priest back in Napa. Hopefully he was still there: "Father, I need you now! Holy Christ, do I need you!"

The truck driver did get a glimpse of the Buick as it shot on past the cab then swung in front of the truck. However, the truck driver was primarily engrossed in what he saw in the side mirror. The chatter of the machine gun was holding his attention. Bullets were zipping past him directed at Al, who by now was no longer in the line of fire.

"Hijackers! Damned gasoline hijackers!" growled the truck driver. "The dirty, frigg'n bastards are after this load of gasoline sure as hell!"

The truck driver, being well aware of the stepped up activities of gasoline hijackers, interpreted the machine gun burst as a signal for him to pull over at whatever wide spot in the road should happen along. Fortunately, for Al's plan, there was no such place along that particular stretch, so the truck driver kept right on going. The thought did occur to the truck driver to run the Hudson into the creek, but the bridge was coming up too fast.

The fact that there were now two against one, the Buick and the Mack teaming up together against the Hudson, was an added bonus for Al, but he had not planned it that way, and neither did he need it. Timing was perfect and conditions were superb; he was doing fine just as it was.

The Buick pulled away fast, now making the sharp left turn onto the bridge. Al glanced over his left shoulder to see the Hudson clear the front end of the Mack as they were about to reach the bridge approach. The Mack had backed off on power, but was not braking; it would coast onto and over the bridge, then pick it up again, once emerging and straightening out on the other side. The slapping sound of drive chains verified it.

Having cleared the bridge and into the sharp right turn, Al came down hard on the clutch and brakes simultaneously, at the same instant cranked the steering wheel hard around causing the Buick to spin clockwise. The car continued around, then momentarily came to a dead stop broadside across the road facing the opposite direction he was traveling, some 20-30 yards up from the entrance to the narrow dirt roadway leading up to Jensen Road above. Slamming the car in reverse, he growled during the few seconds he waited before releasing the clutch: "Alright, you bastards, let's see how ya handle this one!"

The Hudson came onto the bridge at just as high a rate of speed as did the Buick, but its driver had not rehearsed these maneuvers and neither had he prepared his car to maintain stability under the conditions such as Al had done. Seeing the Buick up ahead stretched across the roadway caused the driver of the Hudson to react by instinct rather than a planned maneuver. Misinterpreting the situation at hand, the senior agent exclaimed:

"He lost it! We've got him!"

"Watch out! You'll hit him!"

The creep's urgent statement caused the senior agent to come down hard on the brakes, sending the car into a spin, slapping its right rear end against the side of the concrete bridge, then bouncing back into an opposite spin, smashing its left rear end against the opposite side of the concrete bridge past midpoint. It was obvious, the Hudson was completely out of control with the Mack tanker bearing down on it.

Al came down hard on the accelerator, while at the same time letting up on the clutch. Wheels spinning, the car lurched backwards covering the distance needed to enter the roadway within seconds. Braking to a halt, a quick maneuver put it in low gear then shot up the narrow dirt roadway, leaving behind a plume of acrid blue smoke generated by spinning rubber against pavement, along with a cloud of dust.

The Mack appeared on the bridge just as the Hudson finally crashed head-on into the concrete bridge railing, thus remaining broadside directly in the path of the on-coming tanker.

"Oh my God!!!" screamed the creep in the few seconds he had to view the monstrous, ugly, massive front end of the Mack looming up—bearing down on him. Accentuating his look of horror with screams of certain death, he buried his face in his hands awaiting the inevitable, while the dumbfounded senior agent remained frozen to the wheel in disbelief.

Before the truck driver could respond to the horrifying scene he was instantly confronted with, the Mack's massive front bumper was already crushing in the passenger side of the Hudson, pushing the car with its occupants ahead of it until the whole mass of iron was plastered up against the embankment just below the road the Buick had just traveled over on its way up the side of the steep, wooded hillside. Smoke generated by the Hudson's own splattered oil over hot engine parts was being sucked up in the Mack's air blower, located directly behind its engine, then forcing the smoke up and out the side radiators, giving the Mack the appearance of a mad, snorting bull.

It was not the truck driver's intention to let this happen, but since he thought he was being hijacked, he could cope with the thought of having put the threat to rest. Instinct had caused him to push the clutch to the floorboard, while putting as much pressure as he could on the truck's braking system, for whatever it was worth. If the clutch was not disengaged before locking up the chain drivers, the engine would die. This meant having to crank it to get it started again, since the electrical system depended on a magneto rather than a battery. These older model Mack trucks were not all equipped with electric starter motors.

With the truck's engine still running, the truck driver attempted to back away from the demolished Hudson. But the mangled car was impaled on the huge tow hooks bolted to the truck's front bumper. Looking at the carnage from a dog owner's point of view, it took on the appearance of a huge, ugly fierce-looking bulldog with a mangled rabbit clenched between its teeth. It was fortunate for those involved that the Lang Transport Company had chosen to mount its gasoline transport tanks on these sturdy Mack trucks, or the occupants of both vehicles would have been cremated on the spot. It would have made little difference to the creep, since he was killed instantly on impact. He died cradling his Thompson submachine gun.

Al made his way up the hillside, satisfied that the horrendous crushing sound of compressed iron and steel that echoed throughout Crow Canyon had put an end to the pestilence that plagued the canyon. Having difficulty controlling the nervous reaction building up within him, he hesitated long enough to light up a cigarette. Trembling hands were soon calmed as deep drags of nicotine-laced smoke filtered through his lungs. The sound of the truck's laboring engine echoing up from the canyon below soon faded as he worked his way to the top. The silence was welcome, but there was nothing to rejoice about. The whole affair was gruesome business.

Once reaching the top, the Buick skirted Boyd's cow corrals, passed through the wooden gate, turned left onto Jensen Road and traveled in the direction of the Jensen ranch proper where the road terminated. Before reaching the ranch yard, it passed through a second similar gate to the right marking the entrance to pasture land, then made its way down the east side of the ridge. Al worked the car down and onto the old wagon road leading to Eden Canyon below. As he approached Eden Canyon Road, he ran into an unexpected situation; the Davilla brothers were herding cattle up the road, blocking the entire canyon. However, the delay gave him the needed time to put the convertible top back up and snap the side curtains in place before leaving the wagon road. Once the herd passed, the Buick high-tailed it down the canyon, splattering fresh cow manure throughout the entire undercarriage of the car.

As he headed west on Dublin Canyon Road towards Castro Valley, it so happened that Old Charley was once again pumping gasoline into a customer's car as the Buick roared past his place of business, only now heading west rather than east, as Charley had seen it do earlier in the day. The familiar high-pitched whistle once again caught his attention.

"Look at him go," he said with a grin.

"I'd say he's driving a little too fast, wouldn't you?" commented the customer in response, then added: "Damn he stinks! What the hell's he been doing, herding cattle with a car?"

"Well, yeah, but he's a damned good driver. As far as I know, he's never had an accident, and as for the cow manure, they don't set up stills in the parks," stated Charley with a chuckle.

Yes, that was true. Al never had an accident, but he sure as hell managed to leave an awful lot of wreckage along the way, with or without the benefit of cow manure.

Coming down Castro Hill, he turned right onto Crow Canyon Road and headed back up Crow Canyon, terminating his journey in Mike's yard in full view of the two agents in the Essex parked up on Jensen Road. The wreck being further up the canyon and in the opposite direction from which he came gave him the perfect alibi. Stepping out of the car, he was greeted by Mike and Julio as Matteoli walked up from the egg room to join them. Having recognized the car, and hearing Al's voice, Livia interrupted the men's conversation by calling down from the kitchen above:

"Al, supper is about ready. Will you stay?"

"No, Livia, it's best I go home," he answered emotionally, then added:

"Ida will be wonder . . . " Without finishing the statement, he fired up a cigarette and took a long drag, the second since he had put his plan in action at the upper end of the canyon. Noticeably, is hands weren't all that steady, and neither were his lips, as he held the cigarette between them.

The initial comments pertaining to the greeting procedure behind them, Mike noticing Al to be somewhat nervous, posed a question:

"Al, what's the matter? What happened?"

"No big deal, Mike. Just needed a smoke," answered Al, while trying to calm himself down with another deep drag of the cigarette. He then added: "I've got some news for you."

"Bad news?" asked Mike.

"No, I wouldn't say that. Tomorrow we start hauling alcohol out of Bellina. Let's get everything we've got and go up and get the stuff out of there." Al's announcement caught everyone by surprise.

"Al, you better think that over carefully. That son-of-a-bitch in the Hudson is still watching us pretty close," advised Mike, while the others listened attentively for Al's response.

"Not any more he ain't."

"What do you mean, 'not any more'?"

"Just as I said, not any more. Or at least not for awhile—take my word for it." He couldn't be sure whether or not the agents had survived the wreck; however, he was sure of one thing, and that was the matter of the Hudson. That thing might just as well be towed directly to the junk yard.

Mike hesitated before asking any more questions concerning the Hudson or its occupants. Al, much calmer now, asked his own question:

"What's the matter, don't you believe me?"

About that time, the sheriff's car, with red lights blazing, caught their attention as it sped past the ranch heading up the canyon. Behind the sheriff's car, an ambulance, also with red lights flashing and siren wailing, charged on by heading in the same direction. Last, but not least, a tow truck came along, also heading up the canyon.

Al was leaning back against the side of his car, not bothering to stretch his neck such as the others were doing in the direction of the passing caravan. Once it had passed, the others turned back facing him, still leaning there, wondering whether or not the souls of the two federal agents had by now checked into hell.

"What do you suppose that's all about?" asked Mike.

Al took one more deep drag of the cigarette, then flipped it out across the yard in a shower of sparks. He held the smoke in his lungs for a few seconds, then exhaled through mouth and nose simultaneously. Before he could answer the question, although he had plenty of time to do so, Mike fired another direct question at him in a to-the-point manner:

"Did you have something to do with that?"

"You saw me come in from the opposite direction, didn't you?" responded Al with his own question as Guido walked up just in time to catch the tail end of the conversation. "Guido here saw me come in; he was trimming the hedge up front when I turned in."

"That's right, he came up from down below. I was standing there when he turned in."

Matteoli was scratching his chin while pursing his lips as if trying to identify what had left such a bitter taste in his mouth. He looked at Mike, then away, as if looking for something in the distance. His brilliant nose was telling him that Al had been up to something. But, "cow manure?" It just didn't fit.

Mike now put a question to his counselor:

"Matteoli, what do you think?"

"About the caravan that just went by, or the matter of hauling out the alcohol?" Matteoli had answered the question with a question.

The fact that Al had not fully answered Mike's question as to his involvement in whatever happened up the canyon did not get past Julio. Up until now he had said nothing, but there was something about Al's behavior that caused the name of his good friend, Salvatore DiCulteliari, to flash across his mind. Like Sal, did he settle a score with his tormentor? Julio was to ask his own question of Al:

"What about the main still, do you think it's all right to activate it again?"

"Sure, Julio, why not?" came the brief answer.

"Fine, I'll pass the word on down. My men will be ready to start up again tomorrow while the rest of you haul out the stuff."

"Now, wait a minute, Julio. Let's talk ab . . ."

Julio cut Mike off short, something he had never done before. But before he could comment, the wail of the ambulance coming back down the canyon caught everyone's attention. They viewed this carriage of mercy in extreme silence as it streaked on by. Hesitating for an instant, he once again picked up the conversation, purposely avoiding mention of the ambulance:

"Mike, what's done is done. Al here says we can get started again, so why drag our feet?"

"I agree," said Matteoli, then added one of his many witty quips: "Since the boat is in the water, why not row it?" He, such as Julio, was satisfied that in some manner or other, Al had cleared the way.

"All right, I'll go along with the majority," conceded Mike. "Come on, let's get ready for supper." But, he wondered—it was unusual for Al to decline an invitation for supper.

Matteoli, followed by his cousin, Julio, headed out across the vineyard towards the old yellow house next door to join his own family for supper.

Contini, lantern in hand, having completed his chores, which consisted primarily of seeing that the hogs were well cared for, joined Al and Guido as they were going over details for the next day's activities. Since the day had given way to night, the headlights of the Essex up on Jensen Road were seen to come on. The car moved slowly along the ridge where it was to disappear, turn around, then reappear heading back towards Dublin Canyon Road. Lately it had been standard practice for the occupants of the Essex and the Hudson to meet down at the bottom of Castro Hill at the Live Oak service station, garage and cafe. Of course, on this night, there would be a Hudson in the form of a pile of junk to greet them, less the occupants. As Contini approached the two buddies, he dowsed the lantern, then commented:

"Did you see the Hudson up on the ridge? It just turned around. It's been up there all afternoon."

"That was the Essex, not the Hudson," assured Al.

"How can you be so sure?" questioned Contini.

"Because I am sure. The Hudson is elsewhere."

"Ha, you see, you're not much different than the others. You rely on assumptions and rumors, rather than basic scientific fact," said Contini. He was about to continue into the miraculous inner workings of the sciences, when the tow truck coming back down the canyon could first be heard, then seen, towing the thoroughly demolished Hudson, with one rear wheel turning freely, while the other twisted, cockeyed wheel was dragging rather than turning, screeching and screaming its defiance to the pavement.

"Contini," said Al, at the same time jerking his head towards the passing tow truck, "that's the Hudson—do you see anything scientific about it?"

CHAPTER 33

It was the better part of two weeks before federal investigators were able to interrogate the near fatally injured senior federal agent. He was still hospitalized when the interrogation took place. The two federal investigators were not only interested in the accident itself, but also in the senior agent's activities as a whole. Since there was a general housecleaning under way, every local federal agency was being scrutinized. So far, these particular investigators, as well as others in other parts of the country, had yet to find a thoroughly clean sub-agency. They weren't too surprised to encounter the mess they found in Alameda County.

The two-week waiting period had not been wasted. In the interim, the investigators had interviewed the driver of the Mack tanker truck, as well as checking his driving record with his employer, the Lang Transport Co. His driving record was excellent, and his story very credible. They had also thoroughly questioned the two agents with the Essex. They were not all that clean either since they, too, had at least accepted some of the extortion proceeds as offered by their supervisor, the injured senior agent. The investigators were satisfied that the senior agent they were about to question was, indeed, shaking down a sizeable bootlegging operation, and extorting money from the operation rather than arresting the principals and shutting the stills down permanently.

The senior agent, propped up in his hospital bed, was about to be questioned by two of the toughest federal investigators one could possibly imagine existed within the framework of the prohibition enforcement system. Only one would ask the questions, while constantly reviewing his notes, while the other would take notes as the questions were answered. They started with the accident itself by asking:

"Are you aware that Jim Daley, your co-agent, was fatally injured in the accident that occurred in Crow Canyon?"

"Yes sir, I was apprised of that fact, and I am sorry that he was victimized by the bootleggers."

"The bootleggers!" snapped the interviewer. "He was killed in your car with you at the wheel, thoroughly saturated with whiskey! Would you care to explain that?"

"We were chasing a bootlegger loaded down with alcohol when this trucker . . ."

The investigator interrupted. "I'm asking you to explain the ruptured whiskey barrel found in the wreckage, and the fact that you had consumed a fair share of its contents yourself! For your information, the autopsy report on Jim Daley clearly establishes the fact that he was drunk at the time of death, and tests on you were no better! How do you explain it?"

It was now apparent that these investigators were after his hide. They already had the answers. Now they wanted to hear him admit to his own wrong-doing, which could very well include manslaughter charges brought against him. He asked to be heard.

"Go ahead, I'm eager to hear your side of the story. You don't mind if I interrupt you whenever the need arises, do you?" asked the investigator.

No, the senior agent didn't mind, so he proceeded to pick up the event at the point where he had caught up with the Buick:

"We had caught up to him, (referring to Al), just as he was trying to escape us by passing the tanker."

"Isn't that particular stretch of road precarious for anyone in his right mind to attempt to pass a gasoline tanker, of all things?" commented the interrogator.

"Well, yes, but he was loaded with alcohol and . . ."

"Hold it a minute—not according to the truck driver, who happened to glance into the open touring car you are referring to as it passed him. From his high position he could see the entire interior of the car and it was empty; there was nothing."

"Well, then, why was he so hell-bent on getting past the tanker? Answer me that!"

"Wouldn't you get your ass out of there if someone was peppering you with a Thompson submachine gun? Wouldn't you?"

"Well, yes, I suppose so, sir."

"You goddamned better believe you would!"

The senior agent knew he was in deep trouble. He was not about to display his cockiness with this man.

"How do you account for the accident itself if you were not in fact too drunk to drive?"

"Sir, you keep bringing up the subject of the whiskey. That was solid evidence."

"Evidence! Since when were you supposed to drink up the evidence? How you got it, where you got it, and why you got it, is a matter we will get into later. Right now, explain the accident!"

The fact that his fellow agents had done a lot of talking in order to save their own hides was unknown to the senior agent. They had already been transferred out of the area, with sharp reprimands. The senior agent proceeded to answer the questions asked:

"Well, once we passed the tanker, we found ourselves staring at the side of this blue Buick touring sedan that we have been trying for months to take. We know it belongs to a local notorious bootlegger."

"You mean it was in the middle of the road, broadside?"

"Yes, right there on the other side of the bridge. It was at a dead stop blocking the road."

"If that's the case, why didn't the truck driver see it as well, and why wasn't it demolished along with the Hudson? Considering your saturated condition, are you sure you weren't seeing things?"

Just as Al had figured, the truck driver would be concentrating on his driving because of the Hudson immediately in his path. Besides, the Buick was already out of sight by the time the tanker swung onto the bridge.

The senior agent snapped back with his own question:

"So you think I was seeing things. Ask the two guys in the Essex —from up on Jensen Road—they had a clear, unobstructed view of the road below. They couldn't help but see that car coming down the canyon. Why didn't you ask them?"

"We did ask them," said the interrogator, dryly. "They were parked where you say they were, and they did see the Buick you just described."

"Well, then, what's with this seeing things bullshit?" cut in the senior agent angrily.

"They both have sworn, and we believe them, that the Buick came into the canyon from the opposite end—traveling in the opposite direction — drove into the yard of the chicken ranch below, and parked in full view. No way could it have possibly been the same car that you say was involved! And mind your tongue when addressing me . . . Mister!"

The senior agent stared wide-eyed, mouth open in disbelief.

"I don't believe it—it can't be—the Buick had to have continued down the canyon. The truck driv . . ."

The interrogator cut him short.

"For your information, the truck driver is not sure what kind or color of car it was. The guys in the Essex did see a car come down the canyon at about the same time of the accident, but they swear it was not the same car you refer to."

"They're lying—and so is the truck driver! We were shooting at it while we were passing the tanker. He couldn't help but to get a good look at the Buick—it went right past him."

"He was too busy trying to avoid an accident, and since you idiots were rattling that submachine gun, understandably he was concentrating on you. He assumed, with good reason, that a gasoline hijack was in progress."

This investigator was more than just an investigator for the sake of investigating. It so happens he was the chief honcho, sent out from Washington to take care of the various local federal agencies and clean out the nest of rabid rats such as this one propped up in a hospital bed before him. He was making his authority felt in no uncertain terms:

"You, sir, are responsible for the demolition of two automobiles; putting a third one in the bottom of the Sacramento river; causing the near fatal injuries of two federal agents, involving them in a greyhound bus accident that endangered the lives of innocent passengers; contributing to the death of Jim Daley; threatening to kill a man over his transporting dogs; causing a submachine gun to be fired with the intent to kill an unarmed man whose only crime was possibly speeding, which under the circumstances, was justified! And that ain't all! You are also being accused of soliciting bribes; collecting monies from persons under duress; practicing extortion; and last but not least, being derelict in your duties to say nothing of being an outright son-of-a-...!" The chief investigator caught himself, paused long enough to regain his cool and take a couple of deep breaths before adding: "Do you have anything to say to that?"

"No sir," came the meek answer.

"All right then, you have one of two choices. Either you walk out of this hospital next week and behind bars, or you walk out of here and into my office where you will receive instructions that you must follow to the letter! We will expect your full cooperation in our endeavor to put that Crow Canyon bootlegging operation out of business! Which will it be?"

The answer was to the point: "I don't want to go to jail!"

"All right, then, we'll see you in my office next week!"

CHAPTER 34

The senior agent had received his orders and would follow the instructions given to him to the letter. He was assigned a new Hudson and co-agent, as well as two replacement agents using the same Essex as before. His new instructions were to continue his association with Mike, stay on the take, but to back off on the harassment, and last but not least, stay sober. He was also to stay away from the so-called "Blue Buick," lest someone else be killed. The chief investigator made no bones about his pleasure of seeing him end up on a slab, but there were others to consider. The stash of Jackass Brandy at the chicken ranch was known. Also known was that the Buick, with its incredible driver, was tied into the Crow Canyon operation, and that a major still was located and being operated up the end of Bellina Canyon was also a known fact. However, without full knowledge of the signal system, there was no way to raid it and catch the operators red-handed—another known fact! So his job now was to get the information needed so that a successful raid could be executed. He was to go back and try to accomplish what he had been trying to do right along, only for a different, more legitimate purpose and to save his own hide.

The chief investigator was asked by one of his colleagues: "Why send that no-good bastard back out there?"

The chief answered:

"Because sometimes it takes a thief to catch a thief. With his already accumulated knowledge, it will save us many months of time, and since he is already on the take, he can stay close to the still operators. Besides, hopefully the bastard will get himself thrown into a fermentation tank and come out in the form of alcohol."

"You mean you're going to rely on that jerk to come through for you? An extortionist at that?" questioned the colleague. "A corrupt federal agent that would just as soon double-cross you as not. What the hell do we have here but a bunch of crooked jerks, one no better than the other, and you're going to rely. . . ."

The chief cut his colleague short. He didn't care to hear about the type of people he had to deal with.

"Keep in mind, there is only one so-called jerk to deal with. The others are just plain smart Italian bootleggers who know their business." He then added: "Hopefully, that so-called jerk can get us the information we need to put that bunch of Italians out of business, so we'll give it a try."

As the days passed, the senior agent did not appear to be as aggressive as he was in the past; he appeared to have backed off some. But when he did reappear in Mike's yard with his hand out, he retracted it with a handful of cash, shoved it in his pocket, then drove off without as much as saying: "thank you." Mike was now resigned to the fact that he would be paying the agent on a regular basis or be forced to shut down altogether, an unacceptable situation. Wary of the agent's actions, the paesani talked the situation over. They were not about to be taken in by the improved atmosphere. It was apparent the payoffs would not deter the agent from his endeavor to pinpoint the main still, or develop a method of raiding it. So they decided to also back off, and wait things out for awhile.

But the senior agent was patient; he was also willing to wait, much like a python resting motionless on a tree limb overhanging a jungle trail, waiting the passing of a meal below. He knew it to be too lucrative a business to stay shut down for long. Sooner or later they would start up again. Sure enough, they did, and so reported his findings:

"Yes, Sir, I'm sure. They're at it again," answered the senior agent to a direct question. "And it appears to be escalating."

"Is it the same outfit?"

"Yes, Sir, apparently it is."

"Fine. Now, here's what you do . . . " The chief instructed him to back off. "Lead them to believe they are no longer under surveillance, however do continue, but without detection—concentrate on finding a method to crack the signal system."

Renewed bootlegging activities in and around Crow and Bellina Canyons were certainly apparent. As a matter of fact, very apparent, since during the lull, the Santucci bunch, the "pig men" as they were referred to, having been burned out at Russell City, saw fit to move their operation into Bellina Canyon as well. So now there were more signal codes flashing throughout the canyon that had nothing to do with Mike.

Setting up their new still at Dutch Charley's sheep ranch close to Crow Canyon proper appeared to be a good first line of defense. Besides, the extra cash now pouring into Dutch Charley's pockets also tended to soften his grumpy disposition brought about by his tending sheep, no doubt the dumbest animals on earth.

But this wasn't all. No sooner it appeared that things were settling down, the community of Castro Valley and its surrounding area were awakened during the night to witness a spectacular, out of control forest fire engulfing Cull Canyon, within a mile or so of its confluence with Crow Canyon. Fred Pulse, having been awakened by his howling little dog responding to the ear-splitting wail of the Castro Valley fire department siren, slipped into his pants, and in slippered feet ran down to the firehouse, arriving just as the fire engines were pulling out, they, too, with sirens screaming.

"Where's the fire?" he yelled out somewhat out of breath.

"Out at the 'Silveira' ranch—in Cull Canyon—there's been an explosion. The whole canyon is ablaze . . . " yelled back a fireman while hanging on as the truck roared past.

"Silveira ranch! Explosion! Holy Christ!" he exclaimed. "That's got to be the 'Jacklich' brothers' still. I'd better call Mike, and let him know. Prohibition agents'll be crawling all over the place."

Fred did place the call, but he might just as well have saved the effort because Mike, Matteoli and Contini, having been working throughout the night processing Jackass, were already up on the tank house viewing the spectacular display of flames spurting above the ridge that separated the two canyons. such as Fred, they had a pretty good idea that it was the Jacklich brothers' still that caused the inferno.

Several days later, Frank, one of the brothers, the one that Matteoli knew quite well, appeared there at the chicken ranch. By now the word had pretty much been spread around that "Yes, indeed," their still had been raided by Warren's prohibition agents, and in the process, assumed to have been blown up intentionally.

After having formally introduced Mike to Frank, eager to learn more about the details, Matteoli pumped Frank for information: "What happened the other night over at Silveira's?" he asked with a grin.

"Warren's men. Officer Hard and another agent sneaked in the barn and caught Joe off guard while Rudy was up on the loft. When he heard the order: 'Get 'em up and come up out of there!' Looking down, he could see Officer Hard pointing a gun at Joe. He had no choice but to climb up out of the pit—they had the drop on him."

By now, Contini walked up carrying a bucket of eggs, also eager to hear the details. Obviously, Frank hadn't dropped by just to explain their run-in with the law, but it did appear that he didn't mind talking about it, so Matteoli pressed on: "Did they get Rudy?" he asked inquisitively.

"No, he beat it to the rear—jumped off the loft into a pile of poison oak. They never knew he was even there, that is, until he blew the place to kingdom come. Christ, what a blast."

"How'd the fire start—the explosion?" The question was asked even though the answer was surmised.

"Well, after handcuffing Joe, instead of one officer staying with the still, they both took him up to the house to arrest Silveira. Seeing what was taking place, Rudy sneaked back in the barn, kicked over tin cans, opened valves, punched holes in the still itself, and, before you know it, the place was awash with alcohol! There was so damned much of it that it was running out the barn and down the gully out back, finally reaching the creek below."

Frank was never one to dramatize much, but regardless of how serious the matter was, he couldn't help but to grin and chuckle as he told it. The matter could have been dropped there, but Matteoli was not satisfied; how the fire actually started had not been touched upon. Considering that it took two days just to get it under control, say nothing of the damage to buildings, endangering lives, especially where law officers were involved, Frank obviously didn't care to go into that part of it. But then, since it was expected of him, he did continue:

"Rudy's intent was to just burn up the barn in order to destroy the evidence. So in leaving the barn, not realizing the total consequences, flipped a match through the door, and swoosh! The whole damned place went up in flames!"

"Still and all?" inquired Mike.

"Hell, there was enough alcohol left in it to blow the top clean through the roof. Then the gasoline drums . . . they started exploding. Some of them landed clear across the canyon—flaming hot—setting brush afire. And the gully—flames raced down it following the flow of alcohol like a river of fire. Jesus!—what a mess!"

Contini, having taken all this in, found the need to inject his two bits' worth: "That's the trouble with you bootleggers; you don't approach these matters scientifically enough. Alcohol will absorb water whereas gasoline will not . . . "

"For Christ sake, Contini!" blurted Matteoli, knowing damned well what he was leading up to—a long-winded, dragged out narration of the scientific nomenclature of alcohol. "Will you give the man a break? Frank knows more about alcohol than all of us put together!"

Fuming with indignation, Contini dropped the egg basket so that he could use both hands to better gesture in retaliation. The crunching sound of breaking eggs opened the door for another blast from Matteoli:

"You egghead! (making reference to Contini's baldness) Now look what you've done!"

Having added insult to injury, Contini blasted back: "Egghead, am I! You should talk with that nose resembling an aardvark. You should get into the business of tunneling for sewers!"

Somewhat to the point, Mike sailed into both men: "Frank didn't come here to watch you two make a spectacle of yourselves. Contini, you get back to work—go tend the hogs! And you, Matteoli, go fetch a jug of 'Jackass.' I'm sure our guest here could use a drink!"

The orders were obeyed, but as for Contini—reluctantly. Grumbling as he made his way to the hog pen after first dropping off the egg basket with the better part of its contents cracked, his devious, scientific mind was formulating a scheme to even the score with Matteoli.

Interrupting his guest's laughing jag, Mike asked Frank: "Do you have that kind of problem with your men?"

"Hell, no," he answered grinning. "We don't put up with that kind of shenanigans." That figured, since they were Austrians and not Italians. Frank now got to the matter of his visit—setting up a still in Bellina Canyon, Mike's domain.

"Mike, I understand you once had a still set up in Tony Soares' old place, there in Bellina Canyon. Why'd you pull it out? It was never raided, was it?"

"Oh, it was raided alright, by that senior federal agent, but not to shut it down. That bastard had 'blackmail' on his mind even though he's already on the take. So, we pulled it out and moved up the canyon." Wondering, Mike added: "Why do you ask?"

"Well, we made a deal with Tony, and we're wondering why you pulled out—maybe the water supply, or whatever, but that explains it. How do you feel about our moving into the canyon?"

"That's fine with me, but how about Santucci? I guess you know he just set up there at Dutch Charley's. You'd be smart making peace with those ornery 'pig men;' they're pretty tough."

"No problem—we're good friends—my old man slaughters his hogs." Frank's father was the proprietor of the slaughterhouse down on Davis Street in San Leandro near the Bay. His business was to buy and slaughter hogs and Santucci, being in the hog business, brought the Jacklich and Santucci family together. "As for the federal agent you're referring to, like you, we pay him off, but he's been warned to stay away from our stills, or get busted up." (Frank was a professional prizefighter with 23 knockouts already to his credit.) "Sooner or later, that crooked son-of-a-bitch is going to get his due. I understand your driver, that fellow Al, has been raising hell with the bastard. I'd like to meet him" (Al).

"Yes, but I'm afraid someday he will go too far and . . . " Mike couldn't bear to say the word. He didn't have to; it was understood.

"Yes, I know what you mean," responded Frank, then added thoughtfully: "We'd better get together so's we don't get our signals crossed." This matter would have to be worked out since now there'd be a third set of signals flashing throughout the canyon.

"Although they stay pretty much to themselves, I'll pass the word on to the Waldies," volunteered Mike. "But you'll have to watch out for Henry Mast. . .do you know him?"

"Well, I know who he is . . . what do you mean—watch out for him?"

"He likes whiskey. He'll be walking in on you, no sooner you get started. Ties his horse back away from the still, then walks in while snapping his suspenders—that's how you'll know who's coming in. Hardly talks. You push him, he'll push back—can handle himself, drunk or sober," warned Mike.

The warning was justified. Frank's reputation as a boxer was well known, but so was Henry's ability to stay on his feet. He demonstrated this on at least one occasion when he had been visiting Tony Soares. He liked his homemade wine, which Tony was quite generous with. Having drunk a fair ration of it, and while holding a half-empty bottle of wine in his hand, he staggered down to the wooden bridge that spanned the creek to relieve himself. His intent was to urinate over the edge of the bridge and into the creek below, but instead, while fumbling to unbutton his fly with his free hand, stepped off the edge of the planked bridge and tumbled into the creek below, landing feet first in a foot or so of water while still holding the bottle upright, without so much as spilling a drop. His comment on the incident was brief: "This is where it would have ended up anyway, so what the hell." With that, he proceeded to relieve himself.

While the conversation was going on, Contini, having tended the hogs, had now retired back to the egg room. Having concocted a devious scheme to settle the score with Matteoli, was busying himself with sucking the ingredients out of a half-dozen eggs. The process was simple—a small hole pricked into each end of the egg, then sucking from one end, resulted in an empty egg shell. With the aid of an old coffee can filled with high-proof alcohol, he skillfully refilled the egg shell with alcohol by gently pressing it into the alcohol. The top hole vented, while the bottom hole filled—the reverse of sucking the egg. A paste made of white wheat flour was then used to seal both ends. The job complete, he gathered up the six alcohol-laden eggs and hurriedly made his way through the vineyard to deliver them to Matteoli's wife to be set aside for Matteoli's breakfast. Being a daily routine to deliver six fresh eggs in this manner failed to raise suspicion to their being altered.

As it was both men's habit to be up long before daylight, the following morning Contini, with his kerosene lantern and gunnysack slung over his

shoulder, was working his way through the vineyard rows gathering dande-
lion roots and tender milkweed for the pigs' breakfast, while Matteoli busied
himself firing up the cast iron-wood burning kitchen stove, both for heat and
cooking his breakfast. In his usual manner, he sprinkled a little olive oil in
the frying pan, and as a sausage sizzled, cracked the first of a couple of eggs
(alcohol-laden) on the edge of the frying pan. In an instant, high-proof splattered partly in the pan, but most of it onto the stove, finding its way into the
firebox and igniting with a swooshing blast that rattled the old stove, sending a column of blue flame high into the darkened sky in full view of Contini,
by now down at the far end of the vineyard. Knowing what to next expect, he
set his lantern on a fencepost, empaled a note on the barbed wire fence, and
hightailed down into the confines of the creek, while Matteoli, dumbfounded,
grabbed the flaming frying pan by the handle and headed, cursing, out the
kitchen and into the backyard lest the house catch fire. While still clutching
the frying pan, with its flaming contents spilling along the way, he headed
toward the bunkhouse next door in search of Contini. But then, attracted by
the glaring flicker of the kerosene lantern sitting on the fencepost, turned
and in a dead heat, cursing the day Contini was born, ran the fence line in
search of him. "You imbecile! Stupid idiot! I'll smash your head like an
egg!" he screamed as he ran. Waving the frying pan above his head as he
came running up to the lantern as if to smash it as well, but noticing the note,
stopped short. Ripping it off the fence, moving closer to the light, fuming
mad, he read its brief message:

"Good morning, Sir Matteoli."

CHAPTER 35

Al first met Frank one evening when he was heading up Bellina Canyon, while at the same time Frank, in his nifty powder blue Studebaker touring sedan loaded with alcohol, was on his way out. They couldn't get past each other so being empty, Al chose to back the Buick to a wider point in the road. The two men, already knowing who each other were, formalized an introduction with an extended handshake across from one car to the other as the cars hesitated alongside. The hand clasp was firm — that of two powerful men. Frank was impressed. He'd heard of Al's exploits and therefore admired him, as did Al of Frank. The handshake expressed genuine admiration for each other.

The following week they met again, only this time, it was at John Soares' gate. Frank was coming out of the canyon, and in a hurry. He acknowledged Al's presence with a brief "hello."

"What's the hurry—what's the problem?" asked Al somewhat concerned. He felt there may have been a problem back up the canyon.

"Nothing I can't handle! Those frigg'n hijackers have hit us again! But now, I know who the bastards are!"

"Hijackers . . . the hell you say?"

"Yeah, but they're about to get their due."

"Need some help?" volunteered Al.

"No . . . thanks anyway. I'm picking up one of my best men along the way . . . we'll get the buggers!"

"Ya better watch it—hijackers can get rough," warned Al.

Frank responded with a positive answer:

"These so-called hijackers are nothing more than a bunch of common thieves, that is . . . if they're who I think they are."

"OK, but remember one thing: Don't let them get past or behind ya, and watch out for tire irons. Hijackers don't play by the rules." No one knew this better than Al. It was good advice.

Frank was a boxer, a fair fighter who went by the rules, but nevertheless, he'd heed a street fighter's advice. Thanking Al for his offer and advice, he headed for Clayton, a small community located at the edge of the Delta. It seems that four hijackers got wind of the stash of alcohol being stored in a building behind a walnut orchard not far from where one of Jacklich's stills was located. In pulling off the hijack, branches and leaves from the walnut trees growing along the roadway got caught up in the hijacker's truck's side-racks and were noticed by an acquaintance of Frank's, who knew who the truck belonged to—a hoodlum associated with three others of his kind—immediately reported his findings.

Throwing caution to the winds, Frank and his man drove brazenly into the hijackers' yard and confronted them with the accusation of hijacking his alcohol. While his man remained back close to the car, Frank stepped forward and said:

"You no good bastards have hijacked my alcohol! I want it all back! Every bit of it!" he barked aggressively while holding his ground.

Without responding, the leader of the four, an overweight fat man of some 300 pounds, made a downhill rushing charge at Frank, with the intent of doing him in. Frank stepped quickly to one side to avoid the threat and, in so doing, expertly planted his right fist deep into the man's fat belly, knocking the wind clean out of him. The fat man's legs buckled out from under him as he went on by falling flat on his face, gasping for air amidst grunts and groans.

"Cocky bastard, aren't ya," said the fat man's backup as he, too, charged Frank in a fighter's stance while the remaining two, one an adult teenager (a kid), skirted the fracas with the intent of getting themselves between Frank and his man; but it didn't work.

"Hold it ya son-of-a-bitch!" commanded Frank's man while holding a revolver leveled at the older of the two who, in his attempt to abort his charge in the face of the gun, skidded on the loose graveled sloping yard, landing flat on his ass. Now he heard the second command:

"Stay down or I'll blow your frigg'n head off!"

With the gun not more than inches from his head, he dared not look into its muzzle; he stayed put.

The sight of the gun caused the kid (speechless and horrified) to also stop short.

Ducking a thrown right, Frank countered with a right to the midsection followed by a stiff jab in the face of the fat man's supposed backup, then as the man's head snapped back gushing blood from a smashed nose, a stiff right on the tip of his chin put him into a deep slumber—out cold. With his three elders down, the kid back-tracked as Frank's man quickly handed him the pistol he was holding which, in turn, was used to keep the hijackers at bay while they heard him out. Breathing hard, Frank said in a commanding tone of voice:

"Now listen to me, you no good bastards! You leave this alcohol right here where you've stored it, and make goddamned sure nobody takes it! I'm coming back to get it 100 gallons at a time, and it damned well better be here or I'll kill the whole damned lot of you!" The statement was punctuated by the definite "click" of the gun's hammer being cocked ready to fire.

The hijackers didn't argue the point. They must have known that Frank was the one brother that their father, the owner of a hog ranch and slaughter-house in San Leandro, had commissioned to shoot the hogs in the head as they were led into the killing chute. They must have felt that it would make little difference to him whether he put a bullet between the eyes of four-legged pigs, or two-legged pigs. Needless to say, Frank did come back and retrieved his alcohol, 100 gallons at a time, and at his convenience.

But this sort of aggressiveness does make enemies. The leader (the fat one) of this gang of inexperienced hijackers was determined to get into the business big time, and since the Jacklich brothers were amongst the biggest producers around, they were the ones targeted. Besides, their dislike for Frank developed into a festering sore. So, plans were formulated to raid one of their stills directly. Through the underworld pipeline, they learned of the Jackson still located in a remote rugged canyon of Amador County with nothing but a rocky, rough trail leading into it. The fact that mules and jack-asses had to be used to haul supplies in and alcohol out didn't deter the fat one from his intended mission. He spent the better part of a week in Jackson casing the Jacklich still operation before finally driving back into town (Jack-son) followed by the others (the kid included) with a truck to haul out the anticipated bounty. The fat one had done his homework. As they milled around in their hotel room waiting for word from a hired informer, a local prostitute, he briefed the others:

"If all goes according to schedule, we'll hit the still this evening about sundown."

A question was asked: "How can we be sure of Frank's schedule? We sure as hell don't want him walking in on us!"

"I already told ya. The whore says he'll be in town today. He hikes up to the still, checks production, then pulls out at about dusk. That's when we move in."

"The whore? How in hell can we trust a whore? By the way . . . did you make out with her?"

The question, put in a sly form with a tinge of mockery, inferred that he, because of being so obese, could not perform.

"That's none of your goddamned business!" snapped the fat one, then added: "She's been well paid. We can trust her!"

"Well paid? Oh, so you did make out . . . how was it?"

"Goddamn you! Shut up!" The fat one was obviously annoyed with the inferences made.

"She damned well better not cross us!" warned the second man. To emphasize his statement, he let slide the bolt on the "Tommy" gun he was fiddling with. The action automatically injected a live round into the machine gun's firing chamber, ready to fire. The submachine gun was a new acquisition as were the revolvers being carried by the others, the kid included. After the beating they had taken in Clayton at the hands of Frank, they weren't about to engage in the business of hijacking alcohol without being armed. The move brought about a word of caution and a question from the fat one:

"Be careful with that damned, loaded Tommy gun. Do ya think ya can handle it? That things dangerous."

"Don't worry about it. It ain't all that complicated," came the assuring answer. But it was apparent he'd never fired the thing before; they'd just acquired it. The gunner likened it to a deer rifle, something he was quite accustomed to firing.

The kid, already nervous about the whole affair, squirmed at the sight of it. He'd fallen in with a bunch of common thieves who were now about to move into the big time, hijacking alcohol directly from a still operation, a place he didn't belong.

By mid-afternoon the prostitute showed up at the hotel. She reported that Frank had just left her and was on his way up to the still. The fat one was pleased at the news.

"There, ya see? What did I tell ya?" he said as he peeled off cash from a roll of bills and handed it to the prostitute. Holding another $20 bill in his hand, he added: "As long as you're here, and we do have time to kill, ya might just as well make yourself a few extra bucks . . . how about it?"

She was pleased with the offer, but raised a question that infuriated him. The added comment didn't help any either:

"These guys are easy, but you . . . I don't know . . . " She snickered with a chuckle as she added: "I couldn't find it the other night."

With that comment, all hell broke loose. As suspected by the others, he in fact hadn't been able to perform. It was impossible, at least not in an orthodox manner, and she'd have it no other way. At least this much could be said about the prostitute—she was straight. The others literally laughed the fat one out of the room. Fuming with indignation, he stomped out with a final stern instruction:

"Damn it! Get with it—get it over with—we haven't got all day!"

"How about the kid?" the prostitute called out as he was about to slam the door.

"Him too! Make a man out of him!"

With that parting comment, he trudged his massive body down the hall; he needed to get a breath of fresh air.

Frank, having parked his Studebaker at the corrals, hiked up to the still. An easy hike for an able man. He preferred walking to the trouble of saddling up a mule and riding up. The animals sensed his dislike for them and, therefore, reacted accordingly—ornery'er than ever. Both the mule skinners were up at the still preparing to lead out a pack train of jackasses loaded with 5 gallon cans of high-proof alcohol upon his arrival. But as soon as Frank stepped into the still site, he witnessed a sight he didn't like. One of his men had been struck in the leg by a timber rattler. Having slashed the fang punctures, the one man in charge of the operation was attempting to suck out the venom. Despite the effort, the man's leg continued to swell up into his thigh.

"Holy Christ!" exclaimed Frank. "We'd better get him down to a doctor—pronto!"

"Yeah, I guess we better," concurred the one administering the emergency procedure. He then issued an urgent order to one of the mule skinners: "Saddle up the two jacks. We have to get this man downtown. Frank, how about you riding down with them," he asked, inferring that the mule skinner would ride double with the injured man, and he'd ride along to drive him into town.

"No, you two (referring to the mule skinner closest to him) take him out. Here, take my car," he added as he handed him the keys to his Studebaker. Frank wasn't about to ride an ornery mule back down the trail, especially now that the sun had dropped below the ridge. He'd stay and tend the still until they returned. The fact that he wore expensive dress clothes didn't deter him from soiling his hands when needed.

"OK," responded the still operator. He then issued another order to Jake, the mule skinner that was hurriedly tying down cans on the jackasses. to make up the pack train consisting of four of the critters: "We better not take the time to take the pack train out now. You stay here with it until we get back." With that final comment, the three men riding two mules headed down the trail.

Satisfied that Frank hadn't pulled out yet, the fat one, now parked in seclusion along the main road, was talking to his men whose truck was also parked nearby, out of sight:

"He'll be pulling out before long," he said while they waited around. Sure enough, the Studebaker came swinging onto the main road leaving behind a cloud of dust it had gathered from the dirt road that led to the head of the trail. It came out of the canyon in second gear and so it remained until it roared past the waiting foursome.

"Goddamn . . . he's in a hurry," remarked the Tommy gun wielder, then added: "He can't be loaded?"

"That means there's more up there than he can haul. He'll be sending back a truck," answered the fat one.

"Do ya suppose that's the reason for the other guy riding with him, to bring back a truck?"

They couldn't see the third man stretched out across the back seat sweating out the feverish blood-thinning effects of the snake venom, so the fat one concurred:

"We'll have to make it quick . . . this is it—let's go!"

Both vehicles headed up to the end of the road to the corrals. They'd leave them there while they hiked up the trail. In viewing the trail leading to the still, a logical question was asked of the fat one:

"You sure as hell didn't hike up that rough trail. How the devil do you know what's up there?"

"The whore hikes up there once in a while—that is . . . when Frank's not around. He'd kick her ass if he ever caught her up there. She explained the whole layout."

"That makes sense. Bootleggers don't like whores hanging around their stills; they talk too much. But how'd you get her to snitch on him?"

"Paid her money—lots of it. Whores'll do anything if you pay them enough—that is, almost anything." The explanation was logical.

Following the well-defined trail as it meandered above the stream, they made their way up the canyon. It was dusk. The sun was down but the sky above the ridge to the west still glowed orange. The fat one paused; he'd have to catch his breath. It was understood that there was no way he could make it all the way up. The others would continue up to the still site, do what they had to do, then meet him on the way back along the trail. He reminded them:

"Remember, don't shoot to kill, unless you have to! Splatter the ground at their heels with machine gun fire. Those bohunks will scatter like a flock of quail. Once they're scattered throughout the forest, all you have to do is load the tin cans of alcohol onto the jackasses, and lead the pack train back down the trail. It's as simple as all that!"

The three hikers, having reached their destination, viewed the still site from the forming evening shadows. Two men were up the slope at the fermentation tanks. One was inside a tank shoveling out fermentation sediment into a wheelbarrow while the other busied himself with lighting up a kerosene lantern hanging from a tree limb. A third man was tending the still with his back to the hijackers. The glow from the gasoline-fired furnace outlined his features. For whatever reason, he appeared to be wearing expensive clothing, but then, this was a lucrative business. The hijackers didn't recognize him to be Frank. Obviously, they assumed he'd gone out with the Studebaker.

The fourth man was busy strapping down 5 gallon tin cans of high-proof alcohol onto the pack harness of the jackasses. Four animals made up the pack train, each carrying six cans, three on one side and three on the other—a heavy load, but then, it was all downhill. Ears drooping, heads bowed, they waited for the signal to move out down the trail led by this cursing, foul-mouthed mule skinner.

The Tommy gunner grinned. "Sitting ducks," he whispered. "Look at

238

that—the alcohol is all loaded and ready to go." He had more to say: "I'll scatter the frigg'n lot of them and keep 'em running. The minute I open up, you guys get to the pack animals and head 'em out. I'll cover our retreat. It'll be over within a matter of seconds; they won't know what hit 'em."

If it were Mike's men, a bunch of paesani, it no doubt would turn out as they planned. But these men were tough Austrians, and of all things, Frank was amongst them.

The Tommy gunner stepped into the clearing with his gun aimed between the mule skinner and Frank. His intention was to sweep back and forth in short bursts restricting the concentrated fire into the ground. If any one of them chose to resist and produce a gun, he'd not hesitate to concentrate his fire on the aggressor.

Trigger pressed, the machine gun chattered. The first few projectiles hit the spot where aimed. But then the bucking action of the gun in inexperienced hands, and the shooter not leaning into it, caused the gun barrel to raise with each round fired, sending lead slugs splattering upward, working their way up the slope, punching holes into redwood fermentation tanks, and finally into the overhead tree canopy, chewing bark, leaves, acorns, and pine cones like a Kale Chopper processing chicken feed. For a few seconds the gunner hesitated in astonishment. Gun smoke spiraled upward from the end of the barrel like a snake from a Hindu's basket responding to the sound of music. The sudden thought crossed his mind as it did his companions' that he didn't really know how to handle a machine gun. This was no common deer rifle he was firing. But he'd try it again.

The men at the tanks took cover behind them. They were not about to run around trying to plug holes to save the juice pouring out of the tanks like a spaghetti sieve. Certainly not while that submachine was in action.

The mule skinner was doing his damndest trying to control the bucking jackasses who's heads raised and ears snapped to attention the instant the first burst of machine gun fire hit the dirt. He screamed at them: "Whoa! Ya frigg'n critters — whoa! . . . damn ya, whoa . . . !"

Frank at the still whirled in disbelief when he heard the chatter of machine gun fire above the roar of the furnace. He knew in an instant that the burst of machine gun fire was announcing the presence of hijackers. Instead of running for cover, he ran to the stack of sacked sugar to retrieve a fully loaded, six shot 12 gauge shotgun and, in a crouched position, took a defensive stand against the gunner. The Winchester pump shotgun was normally used to run bears out of camp, attracted by the alcohol-laced fermentation waste dumped over the slope. In their drunken stupor from ingesting intoxicating waste, they'd brazenly charge into camp after the clumpy corn sugar.

The long-barreled shotgun, loaded with goose load pellets, was about the only thing that could run the bears off. The shotgun barrel glistened from the glow of the furnaces as Frank swung it around, throwing it up to his shoulder while at the same instant yelling out to the frustrated mule skinner:

"Duck, Jake! Duck! You're in the line of fire!"

Jake suddenly realized that, in fact, he was in the line of fire. The machine gunner was trying to get a bead on Frank, who was weaving in a crouched shooting stance while trying to get a shot off at the gunner. "What the frigg'n hell . . . " he uttered as he let go of the lead rope and hit the dirt.

Again the Tommy gun chattered, but with about the same results as before. Only this time, the projectiles emitting from the gun barrel were coming closer to hitting their target, in this case Frank. As lead slugs ricocheted off piping and the still itself, a blast of shotgun pellets swooshed over Jake's flattened body. He didn't make a move or dare look up; he'd rather get it without seeing it coming. The jackasses tugged at their restraints—they panicked—stampeded. The pattern of pellets from the modified chock shotgun barrel spread out catching the trio in a flockshot. Another charge was on its way, then another and another as Frank pumped the shotgun as fast as he could take aim. The distance between the shooters favored the Tommy gunner, but the stinging peppering he was getting was more than he could deal with. Frank wasn't playing games; he was shooting to kill. The deadly, accurate volleys of lead pellets tore through clothing and flesh, drawing blood.

The Tommy gunner's pistol-packing comrades also found out that a .38 caliber revolver has some peculiar characteristics in itself. In emptying their guns, they didn't hit a thing; they were taking on lead instead. The shotgun being used against them was something else again.

In the ensuing confusion, the kid damned near shot himself in the foot. He was plain frightened, flabbergasted to say the least. The first several pellets that got past the others and penetrated his clothing sent him on a dead run back down the trail. The other two weren't long in coming. They aborted the hijack attempt in a burst of profanity, cursing the fat man mercilessly as they ran at a brisk gait:

"That stupid son-of-a-bitch and that frigg'n whore!" swore the Tommy gunner. "That was Frank behind that shotgun! When I catch up to that fat bastard, I'll ram this frigg'n Tommy gun up his fat ass!"

But there wouldn't be the need for that; the stampeding jackasses having no other direction to run were also coming down the trail at a full gallop. They, too, wanted out of there. As tie-downs gave way, they were shedding tin cans of alcohol along both sides of the trail. The more cans they shed, the lighter the load, the lighter the load, the faster they galloped. All four of them, nose to tail, caught up to the runners halfway down the trail. The question of a right-of-way never entered their cotton pick'n minds as they all but trampled the three men to death in getting past them.

The fat man, not too far down the trail, was taking in the sounds of machine gun fire in delightful glee. He was talking out loud:

"Give it to 'em . . . ! Goddamn, listen to that thing, will ya? Holy Christ, that Tommy gun is something else again! We should have bought one of those things long before this! And those .38 caliber revolvers, Jesus Christ, what a blast!"

But it wasn't the report from the revolvers he was hearing; it was the shotgun blasts that were roaring down the canyon above the sound of machine gun fire. Soon he heard the clatter of hooves shatter the silence that followed the barrage of gun fire. He was elated. He continued his conversation with himself with even more enthusiasm:

"They got it! By God, they've managed to bring down the pack train! Damn—a truck load of alcohol! What do you know about that? I can hardly wait 'til they get here!" He was bellowing like a seasoned bull in a corral full of heifers.

In the ensuing semi-darkness, his eyes were fixed on the rocky bend in the trail just ahead. The sound of clattering hooves over chunks of granite was rising to an earsplitting crescendo. Wide eyed, he stood facing the direction of the escalating sound echoing across the canyon. Again he expressed pleasant thoughts in the form of spoken words:

"They're coming down at full gallop. They must be riding the pack train!" But then added in horror: "Holy Christ . . . here they come!" he exclaimed upon seeing the lead jackass round the bend nose to the wind, frothing at the mouth, ears pinned back flat on his neck with hair bristling down the length of his backbone. He had no idea that a domesticated animal, as docile as a jackass, could move so fast or look so horrifyingly frenzied. If it wasn't for the chunks of granite being pounded to bits beneath its flailing hooves, you'd think the animal's hooves never touched the ground. The fact that he was straddling the trail with his massive body therefore blocking the escape route didn't slow the critter down one bit, nor those following nose to tail. He stood there dumbfounded with arms outstretched as if he intended to hug the animal. Being knocked down by the lead jackass, his last vision before being trampled into unconsciousness, was their white bellies as they passed over him.

The four men did survive, and it can be said with certainty that they had served their apprenticeship and could now be classified as journeymen hijackers.

CHAPTER 36

The three consecutive raids by Warren's men: Mike's still at Niles, Santucci's still at Russell City, and now the Jacklich brothers' still at Cull Canyon, really infuriated Alameda County Sheriff, Burton F. Becker. When his appointed collectors approached the three prominent bootleggers for the usual protection payoff, it was obvious that questions were raised as to the worth of his protection guarantee. Besides the sheriff was now beginning to wonder if, in fact, the D. A.'s office was not wise to him and the protection scheme he had so profitably masterminded.

But it was too late for the Sheriff to undo the monster he had created because, by now, he was also deeply entrenched in the illegal gambling industry that flourished throughout the county, especially Emeryville and the San Pablo strip in general. As stated in subsequent indictments by both the Grand Jury and District Attorney Warren, Sheriff Becker, along with Deputy John L. Davis of his office, conspired with his chief bribe collector and co-ordinator Fred C. Smith, and an attorney by the name of Cromwell L. Ormsby, a go-between, acting on behalf of his clients, the lottery operators, to not only look the other way as to the illegal gambling, but to also give advance notice of at least 24 hours to the operators in the event a phony raid be staged in order to appease the D. A.'s office. By getting the advance notice of the pending raid, the operators of the gambling dens would have sufficient time to remove incriminating evidence from their establishments.

Those that paid for protection and advance information—lottery and slot machine operators, bootleggers, hijackers, and still operators— were allowed to operate unmolested; those that did not pay up, were constantly harassed. No question about it, a profitable conspiracy indeed, but not without its hazards because, for the most part, the gambling element especially, was controlled by Chinese with connections to the notorious "Tong" mob, an organization even tougher than the Mafia. Once involved, Becker and his henchmen found themselves obligated to stay with it or risk getting their skulls split open with a cleaver. However, in dealing with them, the Chinese, they soon learned how lucrative the gambling business really was. And so, in the face of the overshadowing threat from District Attorney Earl Warren, Sheriff

Becker's organization proceeded to set up a schedule of payments based on the projected gross income of their victims. A start-up fee (if an outright bribe can be referred to as such) in the amount of $10,000, was agreed to be paid to the conspirators by the Mills Novelty Company alone for the privilege of setting up slot machines in Oakland. The company was already running slot machines throughout the county under the protection of the Sheriff's Department, but the Oakland deal was to also pay the start-up fee in addition to the already exorbitant 10 percent of the take from the machines.

Cash payments in the form of bribes from good-sized operators such as large still operators, and out-of-county rum-runners, as they were sometimes referred to, ran anywhere from $500 up to $3000. The fee for small operators to stay in business generally ran anywhere from $25 to $100 per month, depending on the extent of the operation. From his Bellina Canyon operation, Mike was paying out sums of cash upwards of $500 to Smith, the sheriff's collector-solicitor.

These sums of bribe money were being collected by, and paid to, appointed division heads who, in turn, skimmed 10 percent off the top for their efforts. Cromwell L. Ormsby, the attorney for the Chinese lottery and the slot machine industry was right in the thick of things, acting as a go-between seeking protection for his clients which also included several large still operators. Two men by the names of Ernest Q. Norman and Jack Garbutt were appointed to oversee the gambling industry. They dealt directly with Ormsby and solicited bribes accordingly. They saw the potential for the alcohol business within the gambling establishments and therefore worked out a deal with Deputy Sheriff John L. Davis to corner the alcohol end of the business by developing and offering protection to the source of alcohol supply that was paying off. Any bootlegger delivering to the gambling establishments that did not obtain his alcohol from a predesignated still operator would simply be knocked over by the sheriff's department. At the suggestion of Deputy Davis, a man by the name of Pi Vierra was appointed as head of the alcohol ring as it related to the gambling industry, and since it was so lucrative, paid $1000 at the outset for said privilege.

Other bar and restaurant owners, such as tavern owner-bootlegger of sorts Jack Gardella, and his brother Frank, of Livermore, were solicited to act as co-conspirators in passing on the word that protection was available for small bootleggers and still operators for a fee. In their case, the fee for this service was paid in the form of their being allowed to stay in business.

To bring the Gardellas into the alliance, Sheriff Becker commissioned two of his deputies (cohorts in crime), John L. Davis and John J. Collier, to approach auto dealer, Fred C. Smith (his civilian collector), with a proposition to include the community of Livermore into his collection territory. Davis had made contact in Livermore, but the contact, Jack Gardella, was being coy about getting involved with crooked lawmen. So far, all Deputy Davis knew about him was that in some way, he was involved in alcohol, as was his brother, and that they were well known and respected in the community of Livermore. To gain Jack's trust especially, meant bringing others into the fold. So, rather than spook him by use of threats, etc., and flaunting their badge of authority, it was felt that civilian Smith, acting as a liaison, might get better results. The strategy worked in other areas and with tougher characters than the Gardellas.

Auto dealer Smith agreed. So Deputies Davis and Collier hauled Smith out to Livermore, and introduced him to the two Gardella brothers, Jack and Frank. The Gardellas, being aware that the Sheriff's Department was onto their bootlegging activities anyway, agreed to listen to the proposition being offered:

"I assure you, there'll be no problem," said Smith. "Others are well pleased with the arrangements. Take my word for it. It's OK—this is a matter between civilians."

The deputies stepped away, out of sight but still within earshot, as Smith badgered the Gardellas into submission.

It soon became apparent; the brothers' options were limited. Either deal with Smith and pay up, or close down. As anticipated, feeling more comfortable dealing with a civilian rather than a badge-toting lawman, the Gardellas paid up. The first monthly payment of $75 was paid on the spot, which Davis, Collier and Smith would later split three ways. Subsequent payments would be funneled into Sheriff Becker's so-called "Becker Organizational Fund." This, of course, was chicken feed compared to the thousands of dollars being extorted from the gambling industry centered in Emeryville and San Pablo, but then, every little bit helps, and a lot of little donations do equal one big one.

Before departing, Deputy Davis, in order to expand the racket rapidly, was quick to badger the Gardellas into soliciting, through Smith, other bootleggers for bribes with the thought of using their place of business as the focal point for collections. Thus, in effect, adding extortion to their already illegal bootlegging activities. Deputy Davis made no bones about having witnessed the payoff to Smith:

"I suggest you go along with this proposal, and keep your mouth shut!" said the deputy unsmilingly. "Civilian Smith will check back with you on a regular basis!" he added, while leaning slightly forward in an intimidating manner.

This part of the deal was not to the Gardellas' liking, but having already paid the payoff money in the presence of witnesses, sheriff's deputies at that, they found themselves trapped between a rock and a hard spot. They were left with no other choice but to cooperate. In effect, they were being black-mailed, by no less than the law itself.

Smith worked fast. He'd already had a taste of easy money, now this new territory held the promise of adding hundreds of dollars more to the Becker Fund, of which he shared. This certainly beat selling automobiles. He badgered and hounded the Gardellas constantly. They in turn responded by selling protection to other bootleggers, with some small operators paying as little as $25-$35-$50 per month. The Gardellas then introduced Smith to a bootlegger by the name of Croce, who in turn introduced him to owners of businesses that catered to the alcohol industry. To name a few: The Livermore Hotel, Schenoni's, Ma Fiscus, Sweeney's, Santa Rita Inn were now all donating regularly into the so-called "Becker Fund." From there, the list kept growing as more contributors were solicited.

While Smith was beating the bushes in Livermore, Deputies Davis and Collier joined forces with Deputies Shurtleff and Parker to organize an array of civilians, several attorneys, and God-only-knows who else, to extort more bribe money from the lucrative gambling industry.

It can be said, their efforts paid off handsomely. By now the Becker Organization Fund was bulging with money. Like a giant octopus, the extortion ring was prying into every crack and cranny, sucking the juices out of the criminal industry which was being dwarfed by the criminal element within the county's law enforcement agency. Sheriff Becker, in a relatively short time, had ingeniously masterminded one of the most efficient extortion rings imaginable. But yet . . . not perfect. Standing tall and unswayable, District Attorney Earl Warren's shadow plagued the sheriff's empire.

Such as it is with these types of unholy alliances, it wasn't long before all these established overseers, collectors, enforcers (deputy sheriffs), and so-called division heads, started preying on and milking each other. Deputy A. R. Shurtleff, with the help of Deputy Davis, managed to con auto dealer Smith out of a new automobile. It was getting so the conspirators were now paying for protection themselves. The whole affair could be related to a flea-bitten scroungy coyote gobbling up meat for subsistence while fleas, ticks, tape worms, and heart worms drained him of life supporting juices.

Sheriff Burton Becker could no doubt see this situation developing within the inner workings of his lucrative graft system. But to undo the monster he had so skillfully created would be no easy matter; besides he was by now well accustomed to the massive flow of cash that was flooding his pockets. The only big threat was District Attorney Earl Warren. Unlike all the other law enforcement agencies that were pushing and shoving for position in the hog trough, the District Attorney's Office was considered to be untouchable, and was getting a lot of good favorable publicity. So now, Sheriff Burton Becker, in order to offset unfavorable rumors, started to push for more favorable publicity. It appeared as if the news media was being called upon to evaluate the two competing agencies. As could be seen from news media articles, it now appeared that the Sheriff's Department and the District Attorney's Office had embarked on a campaign to try to outdo each other.

To the eager readers of newspapers, the federal agents were no longer of much interest simply because they were being outdone. That is to all but the big still operators who were being caught up in this free-for-all between law enforcement agencies. Although they were not getting much news media play, the federal agents were still there hounding the still operators just the same. With the other two agencies now being distracted because of their battle over publicity, the still operators became more and more complacent and, therefore, more vulnerable.

CHAPTER 37

The local federal agency, now under direct supervision of the chief investigator, was intent on taking advantage of the situation, but not as it pertained to, or interfering with, the other two law enforcement agencies, the D.A.'s office and the Sheriff's Department, because he had his hands full trying to clean up the mess within the ranks of the agency he represented. Since all the focus was on the battle raging between Warren and Becker, this gave him the opportunity to sort of sneak up on his main target—Mike and his gang, putting them out of business. However, his underlying investigator didn't necessarily agree with him and so stated:

"It's a mistake to not extend our investigation to the goings-on within the Sheriff's Department," he argued.

"Why? Don't you think we have enough to do? The whole damned county is awash with just about every criminal activity imaginable, including within our own agency. Since we can't cover all the bases, let's see if we can clean up our own mess—first!"

"Chief, I agree, but by getting involved, we may learn more about some of our own agents' misconduct."

"What more is there to learn? Some, you say. Are you kidding— they're all as crooked as a dog's hind leg, not just—some!"

"If that's the case, then why is the D.A. recruiting federal agents for his office as Prohibition agents?"

"Good question. I suppose it's for the same reason we're tolerating that no good . . . so-called . . . Senior Agent. It takes a crook to catch a crook— use them, then throw the buggers in jail along with the rest!"

"Yeah, I guess you're right—they know their way around. Well, then— the Crow Canyon gang—what's our next move?"

"For the time being, we do nothing— just keep our eye on things."

"Nothing, sir?"

"That's right—nothing. The more leeway we give them, the more complacent they get; the more complacent they get, the more they expand their operation; the more they expand, the more they become vulnerable. That's when we nail 'em!" said the chief sternly, then added: "Incidentally, according to the senior agent, that's already happening. Bellina Canyon is humming with activity."

"I sure as hell wouldn't take that guy's word for it. Sooner or later, he'll fall off the wagon and be back to his old tricks again."

"I'm watching him," assured the chief.

But, what neither he nor the senior agent were aware of was, both Santucci and Jacklich were now also contributing heavily to the so-called "activity." And of course, each entity had its own signal system. Obviously, eventually they learned to interpret each other's signals, which worked to their advantage. But, on any given busy night of activity, the signal flashing within the canyon took on the appearance of a flotilla of battleships at sea flashing signals back and forth while maintaining radio silence.

Gasoline burners firing the stills within the Canyon roared day in and day out. All through the night, alcohol-laden vehicles traveled up and down Crow Canyon, always being assumed to be Mike's doings. The thought of how much money could be raked off of an operation like that was driving the senior agent mad. Doublecrossing his supervisor was constantly on his mind, as it was with his newly appointed cohort. Before long, they were discussing just this possibility:

"You know, a guy could make a fortune shaking down an operation like that," said the senior agent as if the thought just occurred to him.

"You better believe it—I was thinking the same thing."

"I kind of thought you were. Maybe we ought to try it—what do you say?" said the senior agent without letting on that he was already on the take on direct orders of the chief.

"Do you think we can get away with it? I mean . . . how would we do it without getting caught?"

"Sure we can, provided we keep our mouths shut." In explaining his strategy, the senior agent was being careful not to divulge the fact that he was now proposing to doublecross the chief—go back on his promise. His plan was simple: pinpoint the exact location of the stills, crack the signal system, devise a plan of attack (such as he was commissioned to do), and delay passing the information on while they milk the industry. They agreed to go for it, and use the Essex and its agents when needed. So now both the Hudson and the Essex were once again making their presence known in Crow Canyon.

While sitting in the Hudson up on Jensen Road, maintaining surveillance on the chicken ranch below, the senior agent and his cohort witnessed a billowing cloud of black smoke inundating the yard area followed by a muffled swooshing blast of a sound, just short of an outright horrendous, distinctive explosion.

"What the hell?!" exclaimed the cohort in astonishment.

Without responding, the senior agent immediately put his binoculars up to his eyes and viewed firsthand the chaotic scene below.

"What do you suppose happened? What is it . . . can you tell?" asked the cohort eagerly.

"It's an explosion of some sort—sure as hell! Can't really tell, I see a couple people running around down there . . . "

"I'll bet that was a still blowin' up—that's where it's been right along — inside that building," stated the cohort eagerly.

"No, that wasn't a still . . . there's no still in that building. I . . . " The senior agent caught himself before divulging the reason for being so sure. He'd been there, in that very same building—the work shop—part of the chicken house where the cache of whiskey barrels is kept under the floor. More than once, while stuffing extortion payoff into his pocket, he'd marched into the chicken house, kicked the straw aside and demanded a keg for his own personal use.

"Well then, what the hell was it?" asked the cohort.

"My guess is—dynamite . . . no, I take that back—black powder. Dynamite would have blown the whole place off the map."

"Sir, you've got to be mistaken. What would they be doing with either? Don't you think . . . "

Before the cohort could add to his comment, the senior agent explained: "Our friend, Mike, is a real nut for dynamite and black powder. That's how he cleared the land of tree stumps — blasted 'em clean off the place. We watched him do it—like a war zone—crazy like."

The senior agent was right about the source of the explosion being black powder, but how or why the explosion came about, or the circumstances surrounding the incident, he did not know. What they were witnessing was Guido's misfortune of being caught up in a horrendous black powder explosion. While sharpening an axe in the shop, a red hot spark emitting from the grinding wheel bounced up and under the flap of a box of blasting powder that was stored on a shelf nearby.

The resulting explosion caught Guido with full force, showering him with burning black powder. Instinct caused him to dash out the door, along with the billowing smoke that preceded him. His clothing was on fire and so was the interior of the shop behind him. Orange flames and dense black smoke could be seen boiling within the shop. To some extent, the fire contained itself because of lack of oxygen. The smoke that preceded Guido's departure through the door had pretty much engulfed the immediate yard area. Remembering that Bruno, Livia's youngest son, no taller than a man's belt buckle, was there with him in the shop, in disregard for his own safety, dashed back into the smoldering inferno in search of the boy, screaming his name. However, the effort to find him in the shop was futile, since the boy had just stepped out the door seconds before the explosion. The initial blinding flash and searing heat had to some extent impaired Guido's vision, as did the cloud of black smoke pushing out ahead of him therefore obscuring the boy from view. Realizing his possible mistake, he came stumbling back out of this hell's inferno choking and gasping for air—life's supporting oxygen being rapidly consumed about him by the very flames that were roasting him alive.

Livia, followed by Contini, came running out the basement door only to be confronted with blinding smoke. Hearing her son's name being called out in vain within the cloud of smoke sent her into a state of screaming hysterics. But as Guido emerged from the billowing clouds of smoke, his gruesome appearance and the agonizing verbal expressions of a man being roasted to death, quelled her hysterical screaming. The horrifying sight before her eyes plus the sudden shocking thought that her son would emerge from this searing inferno in a similar condition froze her vocal chords into speechlessness. With her hands to her face to shield her own horrifying appearance, she heard Contini interrupt his own blurting, frenzied chatter:

"I hear him—he's over there!" Without hesitating, he dashed headlong into the billowing smoke towards the hysterically crying and disoriented boy in hopes of keeping him from running in the wrong direction. Finding him unharmed, he grabbed him up in his arms and, to Livia's relief, announced his findings.

As disoriented as Guido was, his senses dictated what he must do —save himself by plunging into the swimming pool which was not more than a dozen yards away. Obviously he ran, which of course fanned the flames, thus adding to his unfortunate disaster. But he did make it. The instant, chilling effect of the cold water stopped the deep heat penetration into vital organs, thus plucking him from the searing tines of Satan's fork.

The senior agent, still glued to his binoculars, announced:

"Somebody's hurt down there. I see a woman fishing a guy out of the swimming pool. He was on fire when he jumped in."

"Holy Christ, chief. Let's get down there. Maybe we can be of help—call the fire department . . . " The statement drew a sharp command:

"We'll stay put!"

The hardness expressed caught the cohort by surprise, but then he wasn't aware of the reasoning behind it. His senior did not care to have a fire crew discover the cache of whiskey stashed under the chicken house floor adjacent to the burning shop. He'd allow the place to burn to the ground with everyone in it before allowing that to happen.

Livia, snapping back to her senses, ran to Guido's aid while Contini, in his state of shock and confusion, mistakenly retrieved a large spaghetti colander from the kitchen with the intent of extinguishing the smoldering flames. Water pouring from the nearby faucet was running out the colander faster than he could fill it. Realizing his blunder, he dashed back into the kitchen and came back out with one of Livia's biggest spaghetti pots, which of course served the cause much better. His continued splashing of water through the shop door did slow the fire down enough to give him time to get a water hose connected to a nearby faucet. With the concentration of water, and the fact that the fire was choking on its own lack of oxygen, he did manage to get the fire under control.

Livia, in her state of near hysteria, managed to help Guido out of the pool. She was confronted with a sight that appeared more like a creature oozing out of the depths of a swamp than a human being. Guido's beautiful mop of curly hair, along with his eyebrows and eyelashes, were singed to the skin, which itself was peeling off in dangling strips and pieces, exposing raw flesh. No doubt his state of shock was shielding him from severe pain. He remained conscious; the incredible pain would soon come. She pulled herself together; since Contini couldn't drive, he did assist her in getting Guido into the back seat of the green Buick sedan. Being an accomplished driver, she drove out the circular driveway, hesitating only long enough to determine if the road was clear. From then on, the three- to four-mile drive to Hayward was a nonstop affair. The high pitched wailing whistle of the Buick's vacuum tank fuel system remained well-defined throughout the journey. She pulled up to the emergency entrance of the Hayward Hospital with her gruesome cargo. Guido was in the back seat thrashing around in writhing pain.

A snake skinned alive would well fit the description of his actions.

All this time the two agents remained at their post.

"The fire's out," announced the senior agent finally. "I guess that's the way it is sometimes with a confined fast burning substance like black powder. It consumes the available oxygen so rapidly that it smothers itself. Lucky—just plain lucky . . ."

Luck—maybe so. Certainly no thanks to him.

Around the clock attendance by dedicated nurses could be credited to Guido's near normal recovery. He was constantly being swabbed with medication, and at the same time roasted dead skin was peeled off, allowing for new skin grafting. It was at Mike's insistence that the cost of such care not be considered for he wanted his paesano friend back to as close to normal as was humanly possible. To lose one of his men's lives or to leave any one of them disfigured for life was unthinkable.

With an incredible will to live, Guido did survive. Once recovered, he left the hospital and the bootlegging business behind him. Considering the extent of his burns, he had recovered without too much disfigurement. His sense of humor and love for children and people was still with him, as was his love for life. So gathering up his wages and bonus money, a total of $9,000 in cash, and in July of this same year, 1928, departed for Italy to marry his childhood sweetheart, with the intent of bringing her back to America to share in the so-called "American Dream."

However, the ill winds of 1928 did not cease to blow. Dianda, Guido's close friend, severed his ties with the bootlegging operation as well. Mike did his best to change his mind about leaving, but apparently Guido's unfortunate accident weighed heavily on Dianda's mind. He was not to be convinced that the accident had nothing to do with bootlegging, so he left with the intention of seeking a less risky job, like working on the night shift at the cannery, within walking distance of the Melrose District where he lived. But why walk when you can ride, especially when it's with friends that have much in common and things to talk about. There were three such friends, one being the owner and driver of the car.

The light sedan, with its three passengers, followed its usual route down 54th Avenue, where it would cross the double set of train tracks before turning left at San Leandro Boulevard which ran parallel to the tracks. However, upon reaching the tracks, a slow-moving freight train blocked their path; they waited. While carrying on a three-way conversation, the driver, growing impatient, injected his concern of being late to work:

"Damn it! Of all the luck—now we're going to be late, sure as hell!" Aside from a fearful scream of horror, these were the last words he was ever to speak.

No sooner had the caboose cleared the crossing, the car surged forward directly into the path of a fast-moving freight train traveling in the opposite direction. The locomotive smashed into the sedan with terrific force, thus impaling it on its huge cast iron fender. The fender, also referred to as a cow catcher, and for good reason, had now snared a sedan and was dragging it along ahead of it, churning it into a mass of junk.

Dianda, sitting alone in the rear, was thrown clear of the wreckage, but sustained near fatal injuries. The driver, along with his other rider, remained trapped within the wreckage as it was being dragged along the right-of-way for the better part of a quarter of a mile before the train came to a halt. The two bodies were mangled beyond recognition, with gravel and debris pressed into their flesh. Their eyeballs were popped out of their crushed heads, their tongues dangling from blood-splattered mouths.

The sight and thought of his friends' misfortune was a shock to Dianda. He was now having to cope with the loss of these two friends, as well as Guido's sufferings. So he refused to return to work at the cannery, but instead accepted a job offer at the macaroni factory. Now this was a job more to his liking. For an Italian to be amongst all those tons of pasta was as delightful as a frog in a lily-choked pond. The good Lord had not only looked after him on the day of the fatal train wreck, but had now showered him with flour and dough as well. Whenever a discussion was to arise in reference to his good fortune, he would justifiably kiss the crucifix attached to the gold chain around his neck and boast about his close relationship with God.

However, while carrying out his duties at the macaroni factory, Dianda, in an attempt to clean an obstruction in the extruder, got caught up in its mechanism. No one saw his plight, so the machine continued its process of extruding dough until it became obvious that something was wrong. The machine was stopped immediately. Dismantling commenced instantly, but it was too late to save him. He was already jammed into the extrusion screw. All an autopsy could add to the already known facts was that he had suffocated to death before reaching the extrusion screw. This in itself was a merciful act of God. His efforts to avoid death or injury at the trade he detested, the bootlegging business, set him up to die at the thing he liked to do best, working with pasta.

It is understandable that the good Lord would be anxious to transfer such a devoted worshipper and follower such as he into heaven, but to use the method or vehicle that He chose to make the transition, is certainly not understandable.

CHAPTER 38

Guido's near fatal accident followed by Dianda's fatal mishap at the macaroni factory added to the paesani's already overtaxed anxieties. It was stressful enough that they were being called upon to perform extra duties now that they were shorthanded, but now discord amongst them started to crop up.

Contini was reluctantly taking on added duties at the chicken ranch so that Matteoli could spend more time up at the stills. The extra duties which cut into his time to read and philosophize made him all the more grumpy.

Bianchini, a short, rolly-polly bald-headed paesano with frog-like eyes, that when concentrating without blinking resembled shelled, hard-boiled pigeon eggs, was a close friend of Livia's side of the family, a bachelor with a pleasant disposition, and witty mind, was now assigned to helping Contini with ranch chores. But since the two men were each witty and smart in their own right, they could never work together for long before they'd have a fall-out for whatever reason. Their differences climaxed when Bianchini claimed that Contini had in fact tricked him into drinking discharge effluent from the septic system storage tank. The humiliation of the incident caused Bianchini to pack up and leave, for Contini would never let him live it down.

Problems were also developing up at the stills. Mike had received word that Fats Meehan was agitating his co-workers. Except for Julio, he was developing the habit of pushing some of the others around. Rather than get Al involved, Mike made a special trip up to the stills for the sole purpose of adjusting Fats' attitude. He straightened him out by telling him of the incident he witnessed while working in a lumber camp at Eureka before coming to San Francisco. Just as Fats was conducting himself, a big Swedish lumberjack had developed a similar habit of constantly harassing and kicking around his fellow workers, a group of little Italians. On a one-to-one basis, the Italians didn't stand a chance against the Swede, but organized as a group was another matter. So one night as the Swede was making his way back to camp from town, a group of Italians jumped him and proceeded to beat the living Jesus out of him. While still conscious, they stood him up on his feet and propped him up against a tree. As he was being held, the spokesman of the group slashed across the Swede's belly with the backside of a knife, thus leaving a bruising crease without drawing blood. With this gesture, the knife wielder warned:

"The next time the blade will be turned the other way." At the same instant the story concluded, Mike with the same movement as the knife wielder he had just described, slashed his index finger across Fats' belly. He got the message.

To add to Mike's developing nasty disposition, his close Italian friends and associates were implying that he was a fool for not jumping into the stock market frenzy that was pushing stock prices forever upward. However, once it was apparent the stock market was getting out of control, the banker, A. P. Giannini, warned his Italian depositors not to withdraw their money out of his Bank of Italy to buy stock, not even in his own Transamerica Corporation. But they paid no heed; new issues, whether they be bank stocks or whatever, were being snapped up as fast as they were offered. Italian investors especially, were grabbing at anything and everything Giannini was associated with even though he advised against it. The more he advised them not to buy, the more they grabbed at it, claiming he had an ulterior motive for so advising them. Savings were being depleted and homes were being mortgaged in the frenzy to raise cash. At the encouragement of stock-brokers, margin buying had become commonplace.

Mike answered his critics by quoting Mr. A. P. Giannini:

"The stock market is a gamble. It's not for commoners such as yourselves. You don't understand it . . . stay out of it." But since they would rather talk than listen, many Italians paid little attention to the banker.

Stockbrokers were close on the heels of their clients as they came out of the bank with borrowed money to hand over to them for margin buying of stock. Values were being set on their word rather than the worth of the company they were investing in. An intricate field of business that few investors really understood.

Mike chose to heed his banker, Mr. Giannini, and stay with the business he understood—moonshining, cranking out alcohol. And since chicken ranching proved to be a good front, he encouraged the Waldie brothers to also get into the chicken and egg business in order to better justify traffic activity in and out of Bellina Canyon. They agreed, and since the brothers already had a fair-sized chicken house on the ranch, Mike agreed to loan them the necessary chick brooders to get the flock started. But once underway, the chick brooders were no longer needed so it was thought best to haul the brooders back out rather than have them laying around where they might become damaged. Therefore, Matteoli made a special trip up to the Waldie's to haul out the brooders.

Since there was no need to be secretive of this operation, he came out of the canyon at midday with his loaded down Model T Ford truck. However, the load consisted of more than just the metal brooders and their component parts. As long as he was at it, and as a favor to the Waldies, the load was also made up of a dozen full crates of eggs destined for the poultry producers in Hayward. In addition, he had decided to haul out a discarded, damaged double boiler, a copper vat used in the mash brewing process of moonshining. This unit, about the diameter of a 50 gallon steel drum, but somewhat shorter in height, was stashed away among the brooder parts that made up the load.

After having closed the main gate at Crow Canyon Road and while walking back to the truck, Matteoli noticed one of the truck's rear tires going flat. He did have a rim-mounted spare tire, but no jack. He quickly jumped in the truck and headed down the road with the intent of reaching Bettencourt's dairy farm, a short distance away, before the tire went completely flat. As soon as he came to a stop in the dairyman's yard, the Hudson pulled in behind him. The senior agent, along with his cohort, had been on stake-out up the road, and seeing Mike's Model T come out of the canyon and then speed down the road with a suspicious looking load, caught his attention.

"We might have something here," stated the senior agent before disembarking the truck.

"That's Mike's truck all right. What the hell's it doing coming out of Bellina Canyon with all that stuff? You're right, boss; it's worth a look."

"If we can get the goods on one of his men, he'll talk. Then we've got him. Come on, let's give it a try."

The confrontation and argument that ensued between Matteoli and the senior agent, coupled with the barking of irate dogs, aroused Bettencourt, the dairy owner, from his midday resting period. The dairyman was an unshaven, grouchy, burley, ill-tempered immigrant Portuguese who wore rubber boots without socks all day and every day of the week. This was not only out of habit, but from necessity, since every square foot of his place was covered to some degree with cow manure. Depending on its moisture content, the consistency of the stuff varied somewhat, but no less putrid.

Bettencourt's midday rest was important since his first milking hours were well before daylight and again in the late afternoon, extending well after dark. Having been aroused halfway through his rest period, the dairyman came slam-banging out of the house in a fit of rage. He stomped his way through the cow manure, both fresh and seasoned, on his way to charge into the fray. His approach was more like an irate bull than a human being and smelled just as potent. He recognized Matteoli in his bib overalls, but not the perfumed city slickers he was arguing with. Without bothering to reason why the agents were there, with his stubby index finger pointing straight out in the direction of the entrance to the yard area, he addressed the senior agent in a mixture of Portuguese and English demanding that the agent remove himself and his cohort off the premises.

"You city people in the fancy pants, get off my property, right now!" he snorted angrily.

The senior agent brazenly took up the challenge:

"We have business with this man. We are Federal Prohibition agents. We'll do nothing of the kind."

He might just as well have been talking to one of the dairyman's bulls, for the only word of significance that old Bettencourt comprehended was "Federal." He, therefore, mistook them for milk inspectors.

"You lie!" he blurted. "You have no business with this man. He is a chicken man. You come to spy on my cows. I know your kind . . . get out!" He emphasized the statement with a raised fist in a threatening manner.

As the shouting got louder, the dogs barked louder, with added growls and snarls as they snapped at the heels of the retreating agents.

The cohort hurriedly backed off, distancing himself from chunks of cow dung splashing around as the men stomped in anger while engaged in argument. The cohort was in concurrence with his senior's suspicions as to the possibility of the egg crates camouflaging 5 gallon tin cans of alcohol, but he was somewhat concerned about trespassing onto the dairy farmer's property, especially since the man was making such an issue over the intrusion. He could also understand Matteoli's reason for turning into the dairy yard to change a flat tire and not necessarily to avoid being pulled over.

Bettencourt's bull-like rushes, while the dogs circled menacingly, finally backed the senior agent away from the truck. Realizing the futility of arguing with a Portuguese dairyman, the agents agreed to leave the premises even though they did not succeed in searching the truck. By leaving, they were at least to get some relief from the stench of churned-up cow dung.

Matteoli by now had calmed down since his friend, the dairyman, had unintentionally taken the initiative on his behalf. With his help, he managed to get the tire changed and on his way again, only to be stopped along the road by the same agents. This time, they escorted him down the road to the Country Club (speakeasy) yard area at the junction of Norris and Crow Canyon roads. As Matteoli stepped out of the truck, the Essex, along with two more agents, pulled up to join the Hudson. Waving his hands up over his head in a gesture of "all right, all right, go ahead and search the truck," he pulled off one of the side racks and set it leaning against the truck so it could be used as a ladder.

Within the speakeasy, the whores, thinking them to be customers, along with the Madam leading the way, rushed out in their skimpily clad attire to greet them. Of course, the Madam reached out for the senior agent since he wore the most expensive suit and drove the most prestigious car. She'd service him, personally. While tugging on his arm suggestively, she let her intentions be known:

"Come on, big guy," she said coyly, "I've got something nice to show you." Why she made the statement was indeed puzzling since her thin, see-through, lacy attire clearly showed whatever there was to be seen. You could see it all at a glance. And, of course, the overpowering scent of perfume wafting through the senior agent's nostrils, flushing his nasal membranes of the lingering putrid smell of cow manure, stimulated him beyond reason. Glancing down at his crotch, she figured he was ripe–ready to go for it. "For God's sake, not out here," she purred. "Please . . . come inside," she urged, while snuggling her sensitive, pronounced breasts up against him. But in so doing, felt the hard metal of his gun cradled in its shoulder holster along with the badge pinned on his vest. Before the senior agent could respond, she immediately backed off, cussing: "You're a cop! A damned frigg'n cop! You bastards never pay! You want it all for nothing! Well, let me tell you something mister! You can go frig a duck! Come on, girls," she ordered. "Get back inside. They're all cops—cheapskates!"

Dumbfounded and somewhat embarrassed, the senior agent, in a shilly-shally manner, turned to the other agents who were expressing disappointment with the way things had turned out with the whores.

"Well, don't just stand there," he finally said. "Let's get with it."

"Get with what?" questioned the driver of the Essex.

"Search this damned truck . . . that's what!" came the answer in the form of an order.

"Search the truck . . . ? What the hell for? All this is . . . is a bunch of junk—anybody can see that!"

Expressing indignation with the rebuttal, the senior agent marched up to the truck as he announced:

"All right, damn it! I'll do it myself!" With that final comment, he, along with his cohort, climbed aboard and proceeded to gently remove layers of carton-supported eggs in search of alcohol. Satisfied that the egg crates contained no alcohol, the cohort stepped back down off the truck to join the other two agents who were leaning back against the Essex awaiting the verdict: "There was no alcohol." However, in his rummaging around, the senior agent detected the copper double boiler stashed in amongst the brooders. Since copper was associated with stills and their component parts, the senior agent was to take a closer look at his discovery.

"Fellows," he called out, "come on over and give me a hand with this stuff. I think we may have something here."

Rather than further antagonize their superior, the others responded. With two men on the truck and two on the ground, they proceeded to unload the galvanized metal brooders. The removal of the umbrella-shaped, 6-foot diameter brooder canopies, revealed the damaged, nonfunctional cooper double boiler. The agents proceeded to search through the rest of the pile of brooder remnants, but could find nothing else to go with it. It alone could hardly be construed to be a still since it could have other uses besides making alcohol.

The senior agent studied the brooders carefully in hopes of associating them with the double boiler. Having come to a conclusion, he addressed Matteoli:

"Well, sir, we've got you this time," he finally announced in an authoritative fashion. This announcement came as a surprise to the other agents. They were wondering what else he'd discovered of significance.

As for Matteoli, all he could do was to ask the obvious question, which he did do more by gestures and expressions than words: "Got me for what?"

"For being in possession of still components for the purpose of manufacturing alcohol! You, Sir, have committed a felony! We place you under arrest!" came the sharp retort in answer to the question.

"Those are chick brooders, can't you see that?" pleaded Matteoli, applying as much Italian as English to the statement.

The senior agent slapped his right hand down hard on the copper boiler as he angrily asked him to explain this particular unit, and how it related to raising chickens.

"Oh that," he answered. "We use it to cook grain—potatoes— for the pigs." The answer was appropriate.

"In a pig's eye, and don't try to tell me you just happened to find it. This boiler is a part of the still you dagos are operating up there, isn't it!" accused the agent.

"No, Sir," answered Matteoli, positively. At least this statement was true, since the new continuous stills did not require the use of such a boiler.

One of the other agents walked up to his senior and asked him if he would step back out of earshot and explain to him just how he figured to make a case with only a damaged, out-of-commission boiler.

"Just because it's made of copper doesn't necessarily make it a still," stated the agent calmly.

"You fellows are overlooking the possibilities here," said the senior agent in response. "If we can get the D.A. and a judge to go along with us, this guy will crack. I know who he is. He works for Mike, and he does have a family. The threat of possible incarceration will induce him to talk."

"You better be right. You know the Chief—he won't tolerate a blunder," advised his junior agent.

Matteoli, looking on, had good reason to be nervous. He couldn't make out what they were talking about, but it was obvious the senior agent was doing his damnedest to build a strong case against him.

"We'll impound the whole damned load except for the eggs," said the senior agent, "then we'll list all this other stuff as separate distillery parts and turn in our report accordingly. Who's to know for sure what parts are a brooder and what parts are remnants of a still. We'll build our case around the double boiler with the kerosene brooder heaters as the source of heat." He had a point there, since kerosene was also used to fire stills.

"How are we—or should I say you—going to explain those umbrella-shaped metal canopies?" asked the driver of the Essex, who was somewhat annoyed with the whole affair. "And don't we need some alcohol—Jack-ass—to submit as evidence of a still?" he added.

"Getting him on possession of an alcohol manufacturing device might break him down, don't you think?" asked the senior agent of the others.

The senior's question was answered with a question: "If we had a still, yes, I would agree. But we don't have a still, do we?"

"I'm banking on the fact the D. A.'s office can be sold on this idea. Our report must show the brooder canopies as a new simple method of condensing alcohol vapors caught under the cone-shaped canopies, condense against the cool metal, then drop off the edges as alcohol. See how simple it is?" said the senior agent, trying to be convincing.

The Essex driver, the second highest in command, simply shook his head in disbelief. But rather than antagonizing his superior, he finally agreed to give this bizarre idea a try. Their attempt to break Matteoli down there on the spot had obviously failed. What little bit of English he knew, he conveniently forgot. Waiving his arms around with added hand gestures told the agents nothing, other than he possibly had some expertise in directing a symphony orchestra. The interpretation of his gestures and expressions always boiled down to hauling fresh eggs, brooder equipment, and a hog feed cooker. However, under the circumstances, he felt it to be smart not to antagonize the agents, even to the extent of offering to haul the load down to the courthouse at Hayward.

Responding to his cooperativeness, the agents allowed him to drop off the eggs at Mike's. As Matteoli handed down the egg crates to Contini, he instructed him in their native tongue to let Mike or Al know of his predicament. When the caravan, made up of the Hudson in the lead, the Model T Ford, and the Essex bringing up the rear, finally arrived at the courthouse, Al was already there waiting for them. The procedure of booking, impounding the evidence, and posting of bail completed, a date for a preliminary hearing was set to be heard within a few days. The repeated offer to drop charges in exchange for the information the senior agent was seeking fell on deaf ears. The posting of bail posed no problem since Al was prepared to peel off one hundred dollar bills from a roll of money like peeling leaves off a head of lettuce.

The two agents in the Essex hadn't bothered to disembark. They sat in their vehicle talking it over: "This is stupid," commented the driver, then added: "Did you notice anything strange about him (the senior agent)?"

"Yeah, he's lost his marbles—an alcoholic if I ever saw one."

While pursing his lips and nodding his head, the driver concurred with an added comment: "We're sure as hell going to get our ass chewed on this one, mark my words."

The D. A.'s office was therefore faced with the task of taking the matter before Judge Jacob Harder, Jr., a well-seasoned judge that knew the difference between a still and a chick brooder. He also knew the difference between an educated jackass and an intelligent immigrant that never made it past grade school because survival dictated otherwise. Before the day of the hearing, the prosecutor met with the judge to discuss the matter of the bizarre evidence, and to apologize beforehand for having to submit the case before the court at all. But since there were federal agents involved, it was decided to let the hearing proceed, if for no other reason but to appease the federal agency.

Matteoli appeared in court for the hearing accompanied by Al and legal counsel. The senior agent was present, as was the prosecutor from the D. A.'s office. The prosecuting attorney made his opening statement in the usual manner, finalizing his presentation by introducing the obviously unworkable, bulged-out, copper double boiler, as evidence with an explanation that a whole load of other possible incriminating evidence did exist. At this point, the senior agent asked the court's permission to address the matter of evidence, stating that he was prepared to have it carried into the courtroom.

The judge advised him that he had already viewed the so-called evidence, and therefore had no desire to have his courtroom cluttered up with chick brooders, alcohol-oriented or otherwise. In a fiery, to-the-point manner, he let it be known that the only evidence worth submitting was the copper double boiler.

Sitting in the courtroom towards the rear and close to the door, the other three federal agents were standing by to cart the brooders into the courtroom when called upon. They winced upon hearing the tone of voice with which the senior agent was being addressed. Speaking directly to the senior agent, the judge asked:

"Is this the best you have to offer in the way of evidence? He then added a second question before the first one could be answered: "How do you make alcohol with only a ruptured copper boiler? Don't tell me you use chick brooders because I won't buy it. It's an insult to the Court!"

"Well, your honor," stammered the senior agent, "it could be done."

"Could be done, my foot!" snorted the judge. "What do you take us for, outright fools?"

"No, your honor, but we are convinced that the man here (referring to Matteoli) is an employee of a prominent bootlegger operating in the vicinity of where he was apprehended," answered the agent. This, of course, was true, but Matteoli didn't look the part of a bootlegger, so the judge would not buy it and so stated:

"That may be so, but you've failed to produce sufficient evidence to substantiate it."

The counsel for the defense took advantage of the judge's frame of mind by asking for a dismissal of all charges against his client. The request was granted on the spot. The senior agent's protest was put to rest with a sharp reprimand from the judge:

"The trouble with you, Sir, is that you can't tell the difference between a still and a chick brooder, let alone a bootlegger from a chicken rancher."

The failed attempt at gaining knowledge of the signal code by way of this incident didn't help matters much with the chief investigator. He offered nothing new in the way of instructions, but the senior agent was reminded that District Attorney Earl Warren would like nothing better than to get his hands on him.

CHAPTER 39

The senior agent went back to the task of breaking the signal code. He was on the right track and knew it, especially after seeing the two Soares cousins, Tony's and John's two oldest boys, riding out of the canyon one evening about sundown. They had apparently visited Mike's still at Waldie's and were now on their way home. When they reached the fork in the road where one would go one way and one the other, they dismounted to relieve themselves. Unbeknownst to them, they were being watched through binoculars even though they were close enough to be viewed by the naked eye, since they were just across the creek not more than 400 yards or so by the way the crow flies from Crow Canyon Road proper.

The first cowboy to dismount stumbled to the ground. In so doing, his hat tumbled off his head and to one side. The second cowboy dismounted to help his cousin onto his feet, which he did, despite the fact that he, too, was staggering somewhat. Bracing themselves against each other, they managed to relieve themselves, then prepared to remount. It was noted that the fallen cousin being helped back in the saddle rode off without his hat, very unusual for a cowboy, young or old. The second cousin, being somewhat more stable, noticed the cowboy hat laying on the ground. Thinking it was his, he staggered over to it, picked it up, beat it on his jeans a few times in order to rid it of foreign matter, then grabbing it firmly by the rim with both hands, attempted to jam it down over the hat he was already wearing, only to realize he already had a hat on his head. There was good reason for the senior agent and his cohort to view this whole episode as quite unusual, to say the least.

"Those cowboys are tipsy, if not just plain drunk," announced the senior agent. He then added: "So, you've been drinking Mike's jackass, have you now. Or maybe even the high-proof stuff hot out of the still. Yeah, that's it all right, isn't it now?" He was talking and grinning as if the cowboys were standing right there in front of him.

"What do you say, chief? Shall we go over and talk to those two young fellows?" asked the cohort.

"No, that wouldn't do much good in the state they're in; besides, we've got plenty of time, we'll be back."

"They've got to know something. There's no way in hell they could get that drunk if the still weren't up the Canyon and not know how to get to it."

"Yeah, that's the way I figure it too. At least we know now for sure; the still is somewhere up Bellina Canyon. By the looks of traffic around here, it's either a big one or maybe even more than one. Our friend, Mike, is quite an operator."

With the exception of there being three stills operating independently, it didn't take the agents long to verify their findings. They were now concentrating their efforts much closer on the movements in and out of Bellina Canyon. It became obvious to them that a system of signals that could not be detected from Crow Canyon was definitely being used by those associated with the still while coming in and out of the canyon. Somehow, they must learn the workings of the signal system. But, there were three systems, not one. Having given this matter top priority, they first questioned the two cousins they had seen drunk some days before.

The two young cowboys, when questioned about their conduct the evening they were seen staggering around, took offense to the intrusion into their private lifestyle. The insinuations made by the senior agent were in bad taste; he apparently had never dealt with Portuguese cowboys before. He came within a whisker of getting the hell beat out of him, then being dumped into a manure pile. Had he not backed off when he did, that's exactly what would have happened. As Al, who knew the Portuguese well, had said at times: "Don't try pushing a Portagee around unless there's two of you." There were two federal agents all right, but there were also two young, tough cowboys, to deal with, in addition to their fathers.

But, the agents were persistent. There were other cowboys around that could be approached that were nothing more than ranch hands with no interest in the bootlegging that was going on up the canyon.

"Our friend Mike hasn't bought them all off, I'll assure you of that," said the senior agent with satisfaction. "Maybe we can do some buying ourselves; a couple of $20 bills amounts to a couple of months' pay to these ranch hands. Someone will take it. Yes, you bet someone will," he repeated. "As a matter of fact, maybe we can even buy off one of these cowboys; who knows?" The senior agent was now referring to one of the Soares boys.

"I wouldn't try it on those two Portagee cowboys if I were you. They'll throw you in a manure pile, sure as hell."

"Maybe not. We'll give them time to settle down, then we'll talk to them again. They're young, they'll respect a lawman. In the meantime, let's explore the possibility of sneaking up on the still—from some other direction."

The canyons on both sides of Bellina, Cull to the west and Bollinger to the east, as well as Bellina itself, all branched off of Crow Canyon. Although the entrances to the three canyons were several miles apart from each other, they did come fairly close together at their upper reaches, with only a ridge between them.

The senior agent had studied the geographic and topographic layout of the three canyons and their relationships to Crow Canyon proper. The possibility of staging a raid by coming in over these ridges from either Cull or Bollinger would be extremely difficult. It was rough terrain that only an experienced hiker could undertake. By night, not even such a hiker could do it unless he had a defined course such as a fence line or cow trail to follow. Therefore, a raiding party was ruled out, but getting one agent up to the ridge to detect the signals being flashed back and forth from the still site and the canyon entrance below was not ruled out. So this endeavor was embarked upon.

The first attempt to get an agent up the ridge from the Cull Canyon side failed, primarily because the two Ramage brothers, the working operators of the family ranch at the end of Cull Canyon, would not permit it. The Ramage brothers came across the agents snooping around their place while trying to map a course that would lead them up to the ridge. The brothers ran the agents off the place with a reminder that intruders were not welcome, night or day!

The Ramages were not only friends of Mike's, but their live-in employee, a six-foot-plus strapping young Canadian in his late teens by the name of Bruno Tognotti, was Livia's nephew. This cow punching job was somewhat of a summer job for him since he was here staying with his Aunt Livia and Uncle Mike while attending college. He loved to fight and would do so at the drop of a hat. He could throw punches with lightning speed—thus earning him the nickname, Speed. Obviously, having witnessed confrontations between his uncle and federal agents, he'd developed a dislike for them.

Bob Ramage, being aware of Speed's love to fight and dislike for federal Prohibition agents, was doing his damnedest to keep the agents away from his place for fear of their being assaulted.

"Why don't you go ahead and let them try it . . .after all, they are the law." commented Speed cynically.

"Like hell I will," answered Bob.

"What's bugg'en you? They'll never make it to the top of the ridge, if that's what you're worried about."

"No!," said Bob. "That's all we need is to have you tangle with one of those agents to add to our troubles. We have enough problems without that."

"I can handle them, don't worry about it."

"That's just the part that bothers me," snapped Bob.

"I promise you, I won't hurt them much," pleaded Speed. "All I'll do is send them back down with a bouquet of poison oak sticking out their ass." Regardless, Bob wouldn't hear of it.

Not getting anywhere with the Ramages, the senior agent then approached the next adjoining ranch back down the road—only to meet with the same results. The Gansberger ranch also had a brushy, wooded gully that extended down to the road with cattle trails leading up to the ridge. Such as it was with all these cattle ranches, the cow trails terminated at the corrals in the rancher's backyard. For different reasons than the Ramages, no way would Gansberger allow his place to be used for the agents' intended purpose.

Since the two ranches afforded the closest route to the ridge, the senior agent decided to try getting a man up on the ridge, regardless of the opposition, by following the fence that separated the two ranches. The fence ran from Cull Canyon Road below all the way up to the ridge and down the other side to where it intersected the Waldie line fence. The fence followed a course bisecting occasional patches of bull thistles, crossing small gullies and washouts as it made its way up to the top. In the absence of a well-defined cow trail, the fence could be followed in the darkness.

It was late afternoon when the attempt was made. The sun had just set behind the opposite ridge to the west. Cull Canyon itself was shadowed, darkness would soon engulf the canyon. Bob and Speed, on horseback, were bringing down a half dozen cows off the ridge when they spotted the agents' Hudson stopped down on the road below at the fence line. The agents could be seen standing alongside the car pointing and gesturing as if plotting a course up the hillside along the fence that would lead them up to the ridge.

"Look at those bastards, they never give up, do they?" said Bob. "I guess you know what they're up to, don't you?"

"Yeah, I suppose they're after Uncle Mike's still," answered Speed, then added: "Why else would they be plotting a course up this side of the ridge?"

"You see the one down there with the khaki pants and hiking boots, the one pointing up along the fence line—no doubt he intends to follow it all the way up to the ridge," said Bob.

"That guy in the dress suit sure as hell isn't about to hike up the hill. That means there'll only be one of them coming up to snoop on Uncle Mike's still," Speed said thoughtfully.

The two cowpokes sat in their saddles watching the agents down at the road below long enough to see the one dressed in khaki start hiking up along the fence.

"That guy can't possibly make it up here by nightfall. It'll be a while before he reaches the top. That'll give you time to ride over the ridge to the

Waldie ranch and let your uncle's men know what's going on." Speed's boss was saying this as an order to get riding, but Speed didn't respond. He wasn't saying anything, just watching the hiking agent and studying the fence line as it wandered down the hillside, disappearing into washouts, across small gullies, then bisecting an occasional patch of bull thistle as high as the fence itself. The order was repeated:

"Come on, get with it, get going!" commanded Bob. "It's getting dark on us. I'll take the cows in. Hey, aren't you listening? What's with you? Come on, get going!"

"It won't be necessary to ride over to the Waldies," answered Speed finally without taking his eyes off the hiking agent. "You go down with the cows and take my horse with you," stated Speed as he swung his 6-foot plus frame out of the saddle. "Leave the dogs here with me, they can have some fun too." He was referring to the two mixed breed cattle dogs, his constant companions when hunting or roaming the hills.

"Now listen, damn it! I don't want you working over that federal agent on my property!" Bob's statement was firm and to the point. "And don't forget, you work for me, damn it! Now get going!"

"He ain't on your property. He's coming up on Gansberger's side of the fence," answered Speed, without taking his eyes off the hiker. The comment was true, but in no way could the agent work his way up to the top without having to cross the barbed wire fence on occasion to get around thistle patches and washouts. Figuring that to be the case, he was studying the route the agent must take and at what point he would cross over.

"Hey, I'm talking to you. . ."

Speed cut his boss off with the announcement: "I quit! Take the damned dogs and horse with you. I'll drop by later to pick up my stuff from the bunkhouse."

"All right! All right! Have it your way. Keep the damned dogs with you; I'll see you back at the ranch, and if you get the hell beat out of you, it'll serve you right."

With this parting comment, Bob rode off, leading Speed's horse, but stopped some distance down the trail. Twisting around in the saddle, he extended a farewell wave of hand to his young cowhand, who by now had sat himself down with his two companions at his side. As perturbed as he was, Bob had no intention of accepting his resignation.

As eager as the dogs might be to follow the course down the trail along with their true master, they preferred to stay with their buddy, for as usual, he would provide them with excitement. Besides the scratching strokes of Speed's long fingers extending along their backs and up behind their ears was, in itself, worth being late for supper.

The agent soon found out that he was not in good enough shape for hiking. The fancy khaki pants he was wearing did not put muscle in his legs. He was now stopping quite often to catch his breath. The climb was getting steeper; progress was slow. The washouts and thistles were much more severe than what they appeared to be when viewed from the road below. Darkness was closing in on him, but regardless, he was determined to reach the ridge where he could position himself to study the supposed signal lights being flashed from both ends of Bellina Canyon. The agent was relying on a certain amount of moonlight, as well as the fence, to keep him on course after dark. He had contemplated the overcast clouds that would be coming in from the west at about this hour; however, with the full moon rising later in the night, some light would extend through the cloud cover. The two federal agents had planned everything quite well, with the exception that at these high elevations, the overcast cloud cover did not clear the ridges. Therefore, the upper portions of the hills would be engulfed in swirls of dense clouds such as a thick fog.

Speed, on the other hand, knew of this phenomenon, so he therefore waited patiently near the top of the ridge. Once the agent was engulfed in darkness and into the fog zone, he would not be able to see from one fence post to the other. It was then that Speed figured on taking him on. Being thoroughly familiar with the terrain and these adverse conditions would give him the edge, to say nothing of his superb physical condition and the element of surprise.

At a point where the terrain flattened out into a bowl-like depression, some ten yards across, where the fence cut through a thick patch of bull thistle, Speed took a position. Knowing that the agent would have to skirt around the thistles, he backed himself into it along with the dogs. Responding to commanding whispers, the dogs remained quiet. They were not only trained as cow dogs, but also as deer hounds as well. They knew the need to remain quiet when commanded to do so.

A band of coyotes roaming the top of the ridge on their evening prowl were howling and yipping, establishing their claim to this particular territory. In the near total darkness, the swirling fog and howling of coyotes created an uncomfortable feeling.

Noting the dogs' ears perk up on occasion told Speed that the agent was coming. They were picking up the sound of barbed wire screeching through loose staples as the agent crossed the fence at various points; something undetectable to the human ear. Soon they were trembling nervously with each incident, indicating the agent was getting closer and closer. As thick as the fog had become, through the dogs' keen senses Speed was still able to monitor the agent's progress. From the opposite side of the fence, the agent crossed over for the last time just below the thistle patch. This time, the screech was well pronounced. Both dogs and master were tense, ready to spring from their position.

The crunching sound of hiking boots announced the arrival of the agent as he made his way around the bull thistles. With a firm grip on the dogs, Speed let him go past, then released them, took a long step out of the thistles behind the agent, while at the same instant grabbing him by the collar, jerking him backwards, and planting his right fist into his kidneys. The gasp emitted by the agent was as much from fear as it was from the smashing blow he had received. Pulling collar and coat down to waist level, he pinned the agent's arms in a straight-jacket position and out of reach of his gun. Spinning him around, Speed hammered him with lefts and rights while the snarling, snapping dogs slashed at his khaki pants and hiking boots. Any attempt to speak was muffled by grunts and groans as punches found their mark. But then, Speed wasn't the least bit interested in what the agent might have to say anyway. Stumbling to the ground, the dogs were on him in a flash, tugging at his clothing. Speed intervened. Grabbing him by the gun harness, he helped him back up on his feet, only to slug him repeatedly before giving him a hefty heave-ho, thus sending him tumbling down the hillside amongst the bull thistles. The thought of pulling his gun crossed the agent's mind, but then: "to shoot at what?" All he ever saw through blurred vision was an image of a man beating the hell out of him, and now with the fog thicker than ever, he couldn't even see that.

The dogs rushed in for the kill, something Speed had not counted on. The growling sounds of mad dogs mingled with human pleadings caused him to scamper down through the fog to pull the dogs off, lest they kill him. But there wasn't the need. The battered agent had picked himself up and with the dogs snapping at his heels, ran down the hillside in a headlong stumbling charge that at times sent him crashing into the barbed wire fence. The screeching of barbed wire as it was jerked through the staples that held it in place finally subsided. The blows to the body and head, along with the puncture wounds inflicted by the dogs, clothing and hiking boots, torn to shreds attested to the efficiency of ranch dogs and barbed wire as a deterrent to trespassing. Not until the sound of the Hudson could be heard roaring out of Cull Canyon did Speed and the dogs start their descent from the fog-shrouded ridge.

CHAPTER 40

The senior agent had come to the conclusion that the ridge at Cull Canyon was being patrolled by some tough characters, along with a pack of killer dogs. At least the condition of his cohort that had the misfortune of being worked over by Speed and his companions, the cattle dogs, left that impression. The agents' fears of making any further attempts via Cull Canyon were well founded. Speed's presence in the canyon was all that was needed to keep the agents off the ridge.

To re-approach the two cowboy cousins at the head of Bellina Canyon itself was not too appealing either. The two cousins had it in for the agents for having meddled in their private lives. Whether or not the agents had anything to do with it made no difference. The fact is their once-abundant supply of jackass was now being restricted to a mere trickle; no doubt at the request of their parents. The thought of being tossed into a pile of fresh cow manure crossed the cohort's mind. It, too, was within the realm of possibility. Besides, he was still uncomfortably sore and so was not about to tangle with a couple of husky teenage Portuguese cowboys, with or without dogs.

Bollinger Canyon to the east was deemed to be the senior agent's next best bet. Maybe there he could find a cowboy with a somewhat better disposition and who was in no way influenced by Mike's bootlegging enterprise. Hopefully they could get to such a cowboy without the knowledge of the ranch owner who undoubtedly would be a friend of Mike's.

While driving up the dirt road that lead up to the end of Bollinger Canyon, where the Meuhler ranch nestled, the agents came across a despondent young adult cowboy sitting on the road embankment flipping small stones onto the road while his horse grazed nearby. It was obvious, this lanky suntanned cowboy was in deep thought.

The truth of the matter was, he was contemplating quitting his job and returning home. His thoughts were concentrated on the time he had left home years before as a mature teenager. Without as much as a dollar in his pocket, and a few clothes rolled up and tucked under his arm, he had bid his weeping mother goodbye and set out to find work. After many days had gone by, he finally sent word back to his mother. The day she received the letter, she was sitting on the front porch eagerly waiting for the mail. The mailman rode up out front and called out to her:

"Here's a letter for you. It looks like it might be from your boy, Bill." For her sake he was hoping it would be, for day after day he had been disappointing her.

"Oh . . . thank the Lord!" she cried out as she jumped up out of her chair and hurried up to retrieve the letter from his extended hand. Her mind was too occupied to even think of thanking him. She was holding the letter in her trembling hand while she ran her little finger under the flap of the envelope. Her eyes were moist with tears of joy to have finally received word from her beloved son. He would have much to say, she thought. She unfolded the single page letter and looked at it in disbelief. The message was brief and to the point. It read:

"Dear Mom, I'm punching cattle, send me my saddle." That's all he had to say, nothing more.

"At least he's alive," she finally murmured. Fortunately there was a return address on the envelope so she knew where to send the saddle.

Since receiving the saddle several years past, he had never written back home again, or received any word from his mother. He figured he'd been wandering around long enough; he was homesick and wanted to go home.

The senior agent shattered the despondent cowboy's thoughts as he walked up to him while extending a cheerful "hello." He then proceeded to engage the young man in cattle-oriented conversation. It wasn't long before he realized that he had found his man. So he propositioned him.

"You mean you'll pay me $20 to ride up on that ridge tonight?" asked cowboy Bill.

"That's right, cowboy," answered the agent. "And I'll pay you another $20 when you get me the information I need. You are familiar with the ridge, aren't you?" The agent was pointing west to the rocky ridge above that separated the two canyons.

"Yeah, I ride up on the ridge all the time; not so much at night though," answered the cowboy.

"How much of Bellina Canyon can you see from up there?" inquired the agent hopefully.

"Most all of it."

"Good. Now here's what I want you to do." The agent proceeded to instruct the cowboy as to what information he needed—what to look for, and if he was not successful the first night, to keep up his vigilance each night until he succeeded. He explained that the signaling may not take place every night. Once the details were worked out, the senior agent handed the cowboy a crisp $20 bill before departing with a final comment:

"What say I see you here, same place, same time, in four days. Let's see now . . . that'll be Monday, agreed?"

"Yes Sir," answered the eager cowboy.

"Fine, I'll see you then. In the meantime, tell no one . . . not even your boss—understand?"

"Yes, Sir—as you say—Sir."

Sure enough, on the fourth day the cowboy was waiting along the road as agreed. He was eager to report his findings, and collect the extra $20 as promised. Along with the back pay he had coming, this windfall of money would be more than enough to get him back home.

The senior agent drove up, stepped out of the Hudson and proceeded to address the cowboy:

"Well, did you see anything in the way of signals being flashed from one end of the canyon to the other?" he asked eagerly.

"Yes I did, for what part of the canyon I could see," came the answer proudly. "I could see what appeared to be a lantern come on and off just above a glow down in the trees and brush just this side of Waldies' ranch house, between it and the old Peters wagon road."

What the cowboy had seen was the lookout flashing signals from a perch high up in a madrone tree just above the smaller still location. The paesani had picked the location purposely for its abundance of fresh water from the spring-fed creek, and the presence of this tall madrone tree towering above the rest of the wooded area. Cleats of wood were nailed across its trunk to form steps that led up to the crow's nest, which was also made of wooden boards. From this vantage point, one could see the entire canyon below, all the way down to the okies' fence line and Tony's gate, a mile or so distance as the crow flies. From this same crow's nest, signals received could be relayed to the main still located up at the big barn. The two still locations were interconnected by a foot path.

The agent was all ears as the cowboy continued:

"This seems to happen every time a car comes up the road and stops at about the third gate—at Tony's."

"Could you see if the car's headlights were blinking on and off, like maybe signaling?" The answer to this question was critical.

"Yes, there was blinking at the third gate, just before the car came through."

"How many times did the car blink its lights?" another crucial question.

"Because of some tall eucalyptus trees, I really couldn't tell for sure, but I think they blinked about three times. Like I said, I can't be sure."

This answer caused the senior agent to grin. At least he now had something concrete to go on. He had surmised that the logical signal method would be by blinking headlights on and off, somewhere along the way. The flash of the lantern once the headlights were blinked was an acknowledgement of recognition. He also surmised that the main still had been pulled out of Tony's and moved further up the canyon.

The agent questioned the cowboy further, but couldn't definitely be sure that other smaller individual blinks he reportedly detected flashing between the third gate and the main entrance to the canyon, had anything to do with the stills at the upper end of the canyon. The cowboy did state that ranchers do at times wander around with lanterns or flashlights in amongst their corrals for whatever reason.

Satisfied that the cowboy had gathered about as much information as could be gained, the agent reached into his wallet, retrieved a crisp $20 bill and handed it to the cowboy. A generous payment, and why not? It was Mike's money he was handing out.

CHAPTER 41

Not one to be discouraged or put out by previous insults and threats leveled at him by the two Portuguese clans, the Soares, the guardians of the canyon entrance, the senior agent decided to try them again. Hopefully they might just say something that could add to what he already knew. He knew damned well that somebody in the Soares' clan knew the exact signal code. Living at the head of Bellina Canyon while riding herd, driving cattle up and down the canyon at all hours of the day or night, to say nothing of their apparent visits to the stills themselves, they couldn't help but know something. However, careful thought would have to be given to the method used in approaching these no-nonsense ranchers.

The senior agent was doing just that; taking his time, probing around in the folds of his twisted, cunning, conniving mind for an idea that would lead to formulating a plan. So as not to cloud his mind, he even backed off on his drinking—stay on the wagon and approach the problem dead sober. He was satisfied that the two young cowboy cousins would be the best ones to work on first. No doubt their fondness for Mike's Jackass outweighed their loyalty to law and order, especially to being informers. But in some manner or other, they must be tricked into divulging the signal code.

He concluded that it would take something other than bribery in the form of money or patriotism to get one or the other to talk. The next strongest driving force he could think of was jealousy, envy, and resentment. These feelings breed vindictiveness and spawn vengeance— not uncommon amongst families, especially those of Latin extraction.

"Yes, that's the answer. I'll work on them separately, one at a time, pit them against each other," the senior agent was telling his cohort while on stakeout.

"You better watch your step. These cowboys are pretty tough," suggested the cohort. Since his encounter with Speed over at Ramage's ranch in Cull Canyon, he could be considered an authority on such matters.

"Have you noticed lately that the two young cowboys haven't been riding out the canyon drunk? As a matter of fact, they seem to be quite sober. Have you noticed that?" repeated the senior agent as they sat in the Hudson viewing the canyon entrance.

"Yeah, I've noticed that. All the more reason to watch your step," advised his cohort again, then added: "The guy up on the ridge that worked me

275

over was also sober, that you can be sure of. Every punch he threw found its mark, coming in hard and fast, too goddamned fast and accurate for a drunk—believe me."

As the cohort said this, he repositioned himself, wincing as he did so. His kidneys were still bruised and sore. The urge to urinate every half hour or so had not yet subsided.

"For some reason, their booze has been cut off. I have a hunch, and I'm going to push it for what its worth," said the senior agent, ignoring the warnings. "I'm going to approach one of them alone, kind of unofficial like."

"Fine, you get your kidneys worked over for a change. Once is enough for me." The thought of it caused the cohort to step out of the car, unbutton his fly and urinate as he hung onto the door, groaning in pain. He had another warning for his senior as he was getting settled back in the car: "Don't forget what happened to the agent up in Sonoma County last month. He, too, went in alone, and that wild rancher, Kelly, got the jump on him—strung him up from a cottonwood tree with barbed wire. He's no longer around to tell about it."

"Yeah, I know, but that was a freak incident."

"Maybe so, but nevertheless, the agent is dead, and so will you be if you keep screwing around with these Portagee ranchers. They're tough!"

The senior agent expressed a sly grin as he contemplated the results of bringing these deep-rooted traits to the surface which are so inherent with Portuguese families. He was determined to exploit these traits regardless of the long-lasting, devastating fallout that might split the families forever. Their misfortune was of no concern to him. He wasted little time in implementing his plan.

It was pretty much common knowledge that just about every federal agent in the district was on the take. For this reason John Soares wasn't concerning himself too much with the presence of the senior agent. The agent was now acting and talking more like a member of the team rather than a determined lawman. After the first several visits, John would acknowledge the agent's presence with a gesture of hand or head nod; however, without the benefit of a smile. He still didn't like the bugger.

So now that the senior agent could drive into John's yard without getting thrown out, he pulled no bones about his being on the take. He was letting John know that, yes indeed, Mike was making money, and he didn't mind sharing it. Although John was keeping his mouth shut because he didn't trust the agent, the kids' sheepish grins, however, told the agent that they, the Soares, were being paid as well. It was a guess on his part, but he did guess correctly. He also guessed that Tony was being paid more than John since

Mike at one time had the still located in Tony's old house and, of course, crossed the whole of Tony's ranch to get up to the Waldies, whereas, just as Jacklich and Santucci were doing, Mike was merely paying John to look the other way. Of course, both the Soares families benefitted by their supplying drayage services with teams of horses, but that was another matter. In this case, they were being paid according to the services rendered. The senior agent knew nothing of this arrangement, and neither did he realize that all the traffic in and out of the canyon was not necessarily Mike's.

The first step was to let it be known to John's son that his father was being shortchanged or, putting it bluntly, screwed. The second step was to start supplying Tony's son with a generous supply of Mike's Jackass. Soon it became obvious to John's son that his cousin was getting whiskey while he was not. The senior agent kept planting seeds of dissention in his mind until the seeds were successfully germinated. When the time was ripe, he made it a point to encounter the one cowboy cousin, John's son, down at the cow corrals at about sundown as he was winding up his chores. He handed the cowboy a jug of Mike's Jackass along with the comment:

"If Mike won't give it to you, I sure as hell will. Why should your cousin be given whiskey but not you?" questioned the agent in a friendly, buddy-buddy manner.

With a grunt of satisfaction, the cowboy took a long drag from the jug, then handed it back to the agent, who to be polite, also took a long drag.

The cowboy commented: "Damned, that's good stuff. It don't taste like plain whiskey. Where'd you get it?"

"Cowboy," answered the agent, "you're drinking Jackass Brandy; Mike's best. Like I said, you've been getting the short end of it, and your old man is getting screwed to boot." No question; he was scoring points.

Like an old pro, the cowboy drank again. He could handle it. For the agent, however, this would be the first step to falling off the wagon. After another similar draw from the jug, the agent handed it back to the cowboy. As the cowboy drank, the senior agent injected into their conversation the already festering matter of differences in monies being paid the two families, as well as other trivial matters he was guessing at:

"Yeah, your Uncle Tony is sure making a killing. He'll soon be rich," said the agent slyly as he reached out for the jug again.

The cowboy's response was a generous use of profanity commingled with slurred words. The long draws from the jug were beginning to have their effect. By the time they passed the jug back and forth several more times, they were both well on the way to complete intoxication.

"But I'll guarantee you one thing," slurred the agent to his eager listener.

"I'll get up there and bring you back some more Jackass — the good stuff. You can bet on that." The statement was made as if it was a habit with him to visit the still.

"Damned good idea," answered the cowboy, then added in an equally slurred cursing manner: "Make the buggers give it to you hot from the still, and don't let them dagos give you any bullshit." With that comment, he took another long drag from the jug, then handed it back to the senior agent insisting that the man drink up to fortify himself for the drive up to the still.

The senior agent by now had lost complete control. He kept sucking on the jug like a content baby nursing in his mother's arms. The cowboy, who had been leaning against a corral post, was finding it difficult to stand, so he just slid down along the post until his butt met the ground, and there he remained, leaning back against it with his hat tilted over his face.

John came walking down to the corrals to see what the ruckus was all about. As he approached the scene, the agent staggered over to greet him. While holding the jug in his left hand, he reached out for a handshake, but instead of responding to the greeting by extending his own hand for the handshake, John stepped quickly aside, causing the agent's outstretched hand to miss its target. The unimpeded forward motion caused the agent to stumble and stagger, falling flat on his face. While attempting to pick himself up out of the fresh cow manure, first on his hands and knees, then up on his feet, while still bracing himself with his hands flat on the ground on all fours, the agent made the mistake of expressing his true feelings towards his Portuguese host:

"You goddamned bunch of Portagees!" he blurted in an insulting, contemptuous manner.

He hadn't straightened out yet when John, cursing in his native tongue, took several steps forward and gave him a hard boot in the ass that sent him sprawling back into the cow manure. Every time the agent tried to get up and straighten out, John would curse him and kick him again, constantly sending him tumbling towards the Hudson. The agent, thoroughly saturated in fresh cow manure, finally made it into his car. Once he got it running, he headed out of the yard minus his hat and his ego.

As for the signal code, the agent had figured it right; the Soares did know it, but they were keeping it to themselves.

CHAPTER 42

"**H**ello, Tony, where're you going with the load of cow manure?" asked Mike of his friend, along with an extended greeting, welcoming him as he stepped down from his truck. Tony's slow, swaggering walk could be attributed to his short robust stature more so than his lack of desire to be in a hurry. He responded in a slow drawl:

"I'm bringing it to you, Mike, where do you want it?"

"To me!" exclaimed Mike in surprise.

"Yes, to you. Tell my boy where you want it and he'll unload it. I know you have lots of chicken manure around here, but cow manure is better for your vegetable garden. Besides, we must talk."

It was now apparent that the load of cow manure was just an excuse for Tony to be visiting and wanting to talk. So, without further question as to his need for cow manure, Mike directed Tony's son as to where it should be placed, then posed a question:

"What's wrong, Tony? Is there a problem?"

"There may be. Lately there's been a federal agent, the one with the Hudson, spending a lot of time there at the canyon, mostly at my brother John's place. He's been talking to my boy and also with John's boy, asking a lot of questions. I thought you should know."

"What kind of questions?" asked Mike.

"It seems that maybe he's trying to figure out where the still is or maybe how to get to it," answered Tony.

"He already knows it's up the canyon. I can't see why he has to bother you people."

"I don't know, but he's after something."

"Did he find out anything?"

"Well . . ." drawled Tony, "he found out that my brother has a mean temper. John didn't take too kindly to the man's drunken insults. He kicked his ass good and proper."

"Holy Christ!" responded Mike. "Do you think he learned anything?"

"Yes, he did that all right," answered Tony with a grin. "He learned that you get rolled around in cow manure when you insult a Soares."

Mike couldn't help but chuckle with satisfaction in response to Tony's comment. Knowing John such as he did, it came as no surprise that the agent got worked over. He now added his own comment.

"That damned fool had the guts to stop Frank Jacklich one night not too long ago. He figured Frank was hauling a load of alcohol so he followed him thinking he could shake him down. At first Frank thought he was being followed by hijackers, so he pulled into Harry Rowell's rodeo yard and waited. The Hudson pulled up alongside. Frank jerked the door open, grabbed the son-of-a-bitch, and laid him out cold with a couple of punches, then drove away, leaving him there on the ground."

"You don't say," said Tony inquisitively.

"Those Austrians are not to be fooled around with. Maybe he found out they're operating in the canyon and intends to get even," stated Mike.

"No, it's your still he was inquiring about."

"Damn them! I pay them good money, say nothing of the whiskey they take, to stay away from us, and look at them, they're up there looking down on us right now. Do you see them up there on Jensen Road?"

Glancing up, Tony answered: "Yes, I see them. That's them all right. Doesn't that worry you?"

The question was well put. It did indeed worry Mike and so did the news of the agents renewed intensive snooping around Bellina Canyon. Surely they were up to something.

"There's one more thing. The boys are being supplied with whiskey again, and I don't think that's good."

"They're not getting it at the still," responded Mike.

"I'm pretty sure the federal agent is giving it to them, but don't you worry about it. I'll take care of it," assured Tony.

"That son-of-a-bitch!" exclaimed Mike in anger. His stomach tightened up in a nervous reaction, thus irritating his yet to heal ulcer.

No sooner had Tony left then Livia walked over to her husband. She had been puttering around in the flower garden a short distance away. She had picked up enough of the men's conversation to cause her concern.

"Michele, there's going to be trouble, isn't there?" she inquired in their native tongue.

"What makes you say that? You don't know anything about these matters!" snapped Mike.

"Can't you see why that government man—that federal man you pay so much money to, is being so friendly? He will trick you. He's not one of us, he cannot be trusted." Livia's response was on target, but ...

"As long as they're being paid, they'll leave us alone." Mike was saying it, but hardly believing it himself.

"That's just the point I'm trying to make," pressed Livia. "You say you're paying them, but you're paying only one of them. There are others, what about them? And that crooked sheriff you trust so much, do you think he can protect you forever?"

Mike had no answer for these questions. His thoughts flashed back to the comments made by his friend, the judge:

"There are rumblings coming out of Washington, and remember, District Attorney Earl Warren cannot be bought."

Mike hadn't forgotten. He was still smarting from the near miss over the Garcia-Morrison Canyon affair over at Niles. The thought of that trial caused his stomach to tighten up. He also knew that women's intuition was not to be scoffed at. His wife was doing her best in trying to convey her concerns and feelings that maybe all was not well. To his dislike, she pressed the point:

"Why would Tony go through all that trouble to load and haul cow manure all the way down to a chicken ranch of all places? Isn't it because he feels that all is not well, and that something is about to happen?" her questions were indeed difficult for Mike to answer. She added firmly:

"The Soares are good people, they have families and work hard to get by. I hope you're not making trouble for them!"

Livia's concerns for the Soares families was also of concern to Mike. For that reason, Mike had ordered the paesani up at the still to restrict the two cousins' whiskey supply. They were good, hard-working young adults with minds of their own and very well capable of making their own decisions. But to make whiskey so readily available to them could influence or impair their better judgment and therefore, lead them into a way of life where they didn't belong.

The paesani had been giving it to them in reasonable amounts in the spirit of good fellowship, but the federal agent was giving it to them in unrestricted amounts with the intent of tricking them into divulging valuable information. There was a difference.

Her final comment hit a nerve with Mike:

"You should have listened to Pucci," she snapped.

"Go back to the house! I've heard enough for one day!" he responded. With that final commanding comment, he plunged the pitchfork he was holding into the manure pile and walked away nervously angry.

Livia headed for the house trying not to acknowledge her inner feelings. Her woman's intuition was telling her: "There's an ill wind blowing our way." Needless to say, it had arrived earlier in the year and was not about to subside just yet.

CHAPTER 43

To some extent, Mike was putting his trust in a crooked federal agent on the take without knowing that the agent's bribe-soliciting activities had been discovered and were now being carried out as a part of the strategy being used by higher-ups within the federal agency.

The chief investigator, too, was putting his trust in the same crooked agent, using arm-twisting tactics to keep him in line. Not only was the chief relying on an agent gone sour, but on an alcoholic at that. The puffiness around the man's neck and face, referred to as whiskeyfat, along with his cooked sausage-like complexion, should have been a dead giveaway. The fact that he could hold his liquor and was not apt to be staggering around, was deceiving. Nevertheless, he was still an alcoholic. The chief apparently didn't realize the extent of the man's drinking and that it would affect his better judgment.

Several days had passed since Tony's visit when the Hudson pulled into Mike's yard, followed by the Essex. Two federal agents stepped out of each car, pulled their hat brims down to shield their eyes from the early afternoon sun, and with the senior agent in the lead, the group approached Mike as he stepped out the basement door. Having recognized the familiar sound of the Hudson, he first thought the senior agent was coming after his payoff. But seeing the yard full of federal agents standing before him meant there was something else in store.

The senior agent opened the conversation in a very formal manner. With his badge pinned to his vest so it could clearly be seen, along with the butt of his automatic exposed to further signify authority, he announced firmly:

"Mr. Buti, you are under arrest! We are taking you into custody for the possession of alcohol, the manufacture of alcohol, the sale of alcohol, and the possession of and operation of a distilling device!"

He was making it sound as if they had never met before and that he had, in fact, all the evidence to substantiate the charges.

Mike's jaw dropped; blood draining from his face, he swallowed hard, but said nothing. He had heard these words before, only now they were coming from the lips of a man who supposedly he could trust—on his payroll, so to speak.

The agent proceeded to spew out a jargon of legal terms and language that went right on past Mike. He was so engrossed with his thoughts after he

282

heard the announcement about arrest and custody, that everything else being said meant little to him. The sheriff's conspirator and collector, Fred Smith, flashed across his mind. He had stated and promised that Sheriff Becker's protection plan included being forewarned of such an event as was taking place this instant. But no warning had come. As Livia had pointed out, none of these crooked law enforcement jackals on the take could be trusted.

Once the senior agent had finished his speech, he turned and marched towards the shop door at the end of the first chicken house, followed by two other agents, while one, his cohort, remained with Mike. They proceeded through the shop, hesitating long enough to view and wonder what brought on the strong stench of burned powder, and how the interior had become so charred and blackened. The senior agent knew, but was saying nothing. They passed through the second door that led to the first section of the chicken house proper. The sudden, unannounced intrusion sent the flock of white leghorn hens flying in all directions, banging up against the chicken wire, walls, and ceiling. As low on the scale of intellect the chickens were, they nevertheless could sense the threat of the intruders. These men did not radiate the same warmth and kindness as did their caretakers, the paesani. These men knew nothing of how a flock of chickens would react to a sudden intrusion, so the agents momentarily froze in their tracks wondering what was taking place. The hens finally beat it out to the chicken yard.

The senior agent strutted to the center of the room and, with the shuffling motion of his feet, cleared away the straw exposing the trap door. The closest man to him handed him a crowbar which he was carrying to be used for prying open the trapdoor. The senior agent was well versed on the procedure since he saw it done on many an occasion when he came after his quota of whiskey. The trapdoor was pried open.

The chamber below revealed a cache of 10 gallon oak barrels of whiskey, the likes of which had never been seen before by the two junior agents.

"Holy Toledo! Look at that, will ya! How'd you know . . . ?"

Rather than answer the question, the senior agent made the announcement that the raid was indeed a success. He all but climbed to the top of the tank house to announce to the world that he was the greatest. Like an army general, he proceeded to give authoritative orders:

"All right men, start hauling these barrels out to the yard. Stack them over there in the driveway in the shade of those apricot trees. Count them and log them in the report."

While the barrels were being carried across the yard, he strutted back and forth with an occasional glance in Mike's direction, but, at least for the most part, avoiding eye contact. He was finding it difficult to face up to the man he once extorted hundreds of dollars from, and now doublecrossed.

The barrels, some two hundred or so of them, were neatly stacked in two rows back-to-back, pyramid style on the ends of the rows, then flat across the top some five feet high, resembling two stacks of logs. As many as could be loaded in the two cars were to supposedly be taken in as evidence.

The next step was to locate the so called distilling device and/or related equipment, along with some high-proof alcohol that the senior agent felt cocksure he would find. And, of course, records. These were needed in order to build a good case against Mike. The senior agent knew the main still was not located at the ranch, but he felt sure that enough paraphernalia could be found to serve his intended purpose. In his dreamworld, he could picture himself being carried around on his colleagues' shoulders while being praised for having apprehended almost single-handedly the head capo of the Crow Canyon Paesano Gang. This was the great prize, the glory, and the recognition of having masterminded and accomplished what Earl Warren's men could not do: bring in the head capo himself.

He was not a team player and, therefore, was not about to let someone else share in the credit of having smashed one of the largest bootlegging rings in the area. For his sake, it was just as well that he did not seek the assistance of the Sheriff's Department for the sheriff himself might have put a bullet in his alcohol saturated brain for having put one of his best contributors out of business.

"All right men, spread out and search every inch of the place," the senior agent ordered. So the search for evidence proceeded even to the extent of the little pump house down at the creek where the roadway terminated from the yard area above.

Orindo, Matteoli's son, and Bruno, Mike's youngest son, were at the creek screening out trout, when the one agent showed up at the pump house. The agent, being well-dressed and authoritative-looking, struck fear into the hearts of the two lads. Their first thought was that the agent was a game warden. They quickly dumped the bucket of trout back into the stream, then hurriedly slipped their shoes back on. Their hearts stopped pounding once the agent completed his search of the pump house and headed back up the roadway. True, they were kids, and should not concern themselves with such matters, but they now knew that the agent was not after them. They concluded that something else of a major proportion was going on up at the house. They waited until the agent was out of sight, then hurriedly scampered out of seclusion and made their way up the roadway. They could see activity up at the yard as they walked along. Two streams of whiskey were flowing down the tire ruts in the roadway. Orindo, the older of the two boys, knew in an instant what this meant; a raid was in progress, and lawmen were busting up barrels of whiskey. At the rate it was flowing, it would soon reach the creek.

The boys walked up to the yard area while the smashing of barrels was in progress. Two agents, one on each side of the stack of barrels, were simultaneously smashing the barrel heads with long-handled axes. Whiskey was cascading down the stacks of barrels, inundating the entire yard area. The mere smell and fumes of it was intoxicating.

The agents searched high and low but found no evidence of a still nor records of any sort. Since the chicken ranch did not feature an outhouse, no records were kept there. The senior agent fussed and fumed, demanding to know where the records were kept, but to no avail.

"Mr. Buti, you either surrender your records or we'll haul you to jail in handcuffs." Mike refused to answer. Addressing his cohort holding a camera, the senior agent ordered:

"Take his picture, we're taking him in!"

The cohort, knowing something about a yet-to-be-charged person's rights, asked for permission to do just that, but was flatly refused. Mike knew his rights. Having been allowed to change his clothes into an appropriate business suit, he was now calm, sipping coffee, standing in the middle of the yard with his grey fedora setting businesslike on his head. Unlike the agents with their turned down brim, with the exception of the crease down the middle, he wore his hat as it came out of the box.

The one agent with the camera again asked permission to photograph him; Mike refused. The photographer therefore did not take his picture, nor did he get any pictures of the kind of evidence needed to substantiate the charges. With the help of Al, all that stuff had been cleaned out the night before the raid. This could be attributed to Livia's comments and expressed concerns during Tony's visit. Her woman's intuition no doubt had some influence on her husband.

All the time the raid was in progress, Mike had very little to say. Although he was addressed as Mr. Buti, he did not acknowledge the name, nor did he volunteer any other. He would wait until he consulted with his legal counsel. When the time came, he voluntarily entered the Hudson. As the two cars pulled out of the driveway, Livia watched tearfully as her husband was being taken away by federal agents. She had been instructed to contact Al immediately upon their departure, this she did do.

Contini waved to his friend Mike, as he, too, watched the cars pull out. The mess left behind would be his job to clean up. All during the time of the raid, he had been sitting in the open doorway of the bunkhouse, leaning against

285

the frame, watching the activities in progress not more than several yards away. At one point he had to swing his body to one side to allow an agent to inspect the interior of the bunkhouse. There was little in the way of furniture. The iron post double bed situated on a carpet at the center of the room was the only significant item there. To the agent the structure appeared to be a normal bunkhouse.

The two cars having cleared the yard, Contini rose to his feet and walked back into the bunkhouse, talking aloud as if someone was there:

"Stupid idiots, just plain stupid idiots. All that good whiskey destroyed for nothing." His highly technical philosophical mind was dictating what his tongue should say:

"Don't they know better than to allow idiots like those into universities? How can society benefit by having an educated idiot? An idiot is an idiot, educated or otherwise." He was assuming the federal agents to be well-schooled.

Having retrieved his hat, as he was about to step out the door he hesitated a moment, looked back at the bunkhouse floor, and cracked a sheepish grin. Under the floor of the bunkhouse in its secret chamber, some 1,000 gallons of whiskey in 50 gallon oak barrels was going through the aging process. The barrels were up on racks on either side of the walls for the full length of the room. A real prize, had they discovered it. He stepped out the bunkhouse door, once again mumbling: "Idiots, just plain idiots."

Spotting Livia across the yard standing there wiping the tears from her face with her apron, Contini walked over and put his arms around her.

"Livia," he said, "be sure to have supper ready for Mike; he will be hungry when he gets home tonight."

"Do you think so? Will he be home tonight?" she asked sobbingly, with a ray of hope.

"Believe me, he'll be home for supper tonight."

As it was, Al, with legal counsel, arrived at the courthouse during the booking. Bail had been set at $1,000. Al peeled off $1,000 from the roll of cash he was carrying and handed it to the clerk in attendance. The lawyer stuck around to work out the details, while Al and Mike headed back home for supper.

The senior agent had pulled a first-class blunder. All he had on Mike was possession, nothing else. The law wasn't all that specific that it differentiated much between one gallon or a thousand gallons. They would play hell trying to prove that he even sold alcohol, or having manufactured it, let alone owning a still.

The chief investigator had not been informed of the intent to stage the raid. The senior agent had jumped the gun, hoping to take the glory for himself. His corkscrew mind was so saturated with Mike's Jackass that he couldn't tell a bed sheet from the American flag.

CHAPTER 44

Having driven Mike back home, Al continued up Crow Canyon heading for the stills. It was well after dark when the Buick pulled into Bellina Canyon. This night not being one of his regular pickup nights, and entering the canyon in such an extreme hurry, alerted the signalmen for all three of the still operations. The abnormal entrance started the signalmen flashing signals back and forth through the darkness. Santucci's bunch at Dutch Charley's were the first to announce the intrusion. They immediately shut the burners down and dowsed the lights. Sheep scattered every which way as men ran amongst them trying to put as much distance as possible between themselves and the still. By the time Al got through the second gate, the Jacklich gang, heeding the warning flashes from their own signalmen did likewise. Their escape route was well planned. They headed up the gully, then cut across the back of Dutch Charley's rolling sheep pastures, heading for Crow Canyon Road.

With Santucci's bunch coming up the sloping pasture pushing confused sheep ahead of them, and Jacklich's gang cutting across from Tony's place, the two groups of men, as well as the animals, were on a collision course. Just about the time they reached within detection range of each other, the Okies up on the fence line nearest Crow Canyon started flashing signals up the canyon to Mike's lookout perched atop the tall madrone tree. Seeing the lantern come on, the fleeing men froze in their tracks. They had no idea that such a signal system existed. From their position down in the secluded gullies, these signals flashing over the top of them could not be seen. They, therefore, viewed this flash of light coming from the direction they were heading as a threat. In the darkness, they introduced themselves to each other while running in the opposite direction of the flashing signal, and of course, now more confused than ever, the sheep stayed with them. Needless to say, the introduction ceremony was brief and without benefit of handshakes. Shadowy figures of men running and stumbling into panicked sheep created a bedlam of men and beasts alike. All sense of direction vanished as this whole confused mass of creatures went charging across hill and dale, crashing into fences and stampeding through patches of poison oak; Italians and Austrians alike yelling and cursing above the din of pounding hooves and bleating sheep.

The animals, not having any idea as to what this was all about, finally broke ranks. Instinct as to survival dictated they band together as a tight flock and head back down the slope to the safety of the pens. By the same token, the men as a group headed for the safety of the ridge above, only to look back and see the familiar Buick come charging up to Tony's gate. It was obvious; they had reacted to a false alarm, but nevertheless, since they were out of breath anyway, they sat it out until all signaling subsided, thus indicating an 'all clear.'

Al, having approached the third gate at Tony's place, blinked the car's headlights on and off three times, proceeded to pass through the gate, closed it behind him, and waited for the all-clear return signal. However, it was slow in coming.

The lookout up in the crow's nest, somewhat dubious, shouted excitedly down to Julio below:

"There's a lot of activity down the canyon! Can't make heads or tails of it! There must be a problem?"

And he was right—since the sudden blinking and flashing of lights in the distance took on the appearance of fireflies over a ripe grain field on a balmy, summer night. The larger lantern flashing from the fence line higher up was distinctly the Okies. That the lookout could understand.

"What's the Okie say?" asked Julio.

"An unidentified car moving at high speed has entered the canyon," came the answer from above. "Yeah, here it comes, going like a bat out of hell!" yelled the lookout excitedly, then added: "There's the headlight signal! It's coming through Tony's gate!"

"Hold up on the return signal! I'm coming up."

Julio wasn't taking any chances, he wanted to study the situation himself. Within seconds he was up in the crow's nest viewing the scene down the canyon. By this time, the various blinking and flashing lights had stopped, with the exception of the Okies' unmistakable lantern signal and the repeated headlight signal down at Tony's gate.

Al was getting impatient; he cursed as he waited for the return signal:

"Goddamn it! Come on, you bunch of Dagos, get with it—we haven't got all night!"

"It must be Al," said Julio, finally. "We're going to have to take our chances. Give him the signal, then keep an eye out for anything else unusual. You never know?"

Having received the all-clear, Al sped up the canyon. Satisfied that the car had been identified, the Okie at the fence line extinguished his lantern.

After passing through two more gates, the Buick reached Waldies' blue gate, which divided pastureland from cultivated land. To continue through this gate would lead up to the main house, ranch buildings, and barn where the main still was located. To the right, before passing through the gate, the wagon road leading to the old Peters' homestead made its way down and across the Spring Creek that flowed past Waldies' house some distance up the wooded gully to the left. Before reaching the creek, a temporary road had been cut through the wooded section leading up to the smaller still site where the lookout was posted with the signal lantern up in the madrone tree.

Al turned to the right and onto the old wagon road, then stopped to re-lieve himself and light a cigarette. A routine event that was recognized by the lookout as a last and final confirmation of Al's being the driver of the approaching car. Relieved with this final identification, Julio scampered back down out of the crow's nest, commenting as he descended:

"That's Al all right, but what's he doing here tonight? Something must be wrong, stand by."

Continuing down the wagon road, the Buick swung to the left onto the temporary road, then made its way through the wooded area to the still site where Al was greeted by Julio:

"We're surprised to see you tonight. We weren't expecting you —what brings you in?" asked Julio inquisitively.

Al made no bones about the reason for his being there:

"Shut 'er down, Julio. We're getting our ass out of here fast—like right now . . . !" he stated firmly, then walked on past the startled Julio to where another paesano was busy filling 5 gallon tin cans with warm, high-proof alcohol and announced the same thing, along with an added order:

"Run up to the barn and tell them to shut 'er down and get down here right now! And don't forget to check the bunkhouse. We're getting our ass out of here right now . . . but quick!"

Fats shut down the twin gasoline pressure burners at the main stills be-fore joining Matteoli and the two paesani that had been sleeping in the bunk-house. The four men, along with the messenger, came running down the footpath in time to hear Al answer Julio's question:

"That son-of-a-bitch raided Mike's place without warning! There were four of those federal bastards! They cleaned out the tens from under the chicken house!"

"Oh Christ!" answered Julio, "How about Mike?"

"They got him with it, but he's back home now, out on bail . . . $1,000!"

"Goddamn it!" cursed Matteoli. "Of all the times to have left those still components down there, and the high-proof—along with all that other stuff, Holy Christ . . . !"

Al interrupted. There wasn't time for long conversations. He hustled everybody into the Buick as he put Matteoli's mind at ease with a positive statement:

"That they didn't get. We got all that stuff out of there before the raid," assured Al, then added: "We could have got the tens out too, but Mike felt we'd have time later. He insisted the sheriff would let us know in plenty of time if a raid was for sure. Mike puts too goddamned much faith in that crooked bastard!" He continued to express his dislike for the bloodsuckers, as he referred to the sheriff's so-called "protection squad."

"How about the fifties under the bunkhouse?" asked Julio hopefully.

"They missed those completely," came the answer. Al then walked over to the base of the tall madrone tree, calling out to the lookout still up in the crow's nest:

"How's it look down the canyon?"

"All clear, nobody followed you up," answered the lookout, then added before the question could be asked: "No signal from the Okie, must be all clear at Crow Canyon."

"O.K., come on down, we're getting out of here . . . pronto!"

Within minutes the Buick was on its way back out the canyon with its cargo of solemn but nervous men jammed into it. Held in first gear, the car made its way out Peters' wagon road. Matteoli posed a question as they bounced along:

"What caused you and Mike to suspect a raid might come about in the first place?"

"Portuguese suspicions, coupled with woman's intuition."

Al's answer left Matteoli scratching at his chin trying to figure it all out.

Once past the blue gate, the car, now in second gear, sped back down Bellina Canyon leaving a cloud of dust behind. Al kept glancing down the canyon where the knoll obscured the old ramshackle Habberney house where the Okies lived. On the barbed wire fence running along the knoll would be where the kerosene lantern would be hanging and signaling in the event of the presence of unidentified cars at the vicinity of the canyon entrance. The fence and knoll were visible from almost anywhere along the road as it wound its way out of the canyon. The all-clear was signified by the absence of the hanging lantern at night or a stretched out coyote hide by day. If either were displayed while exiting the canyon, the exiting person would have to concern himself with the possibility of encountering prohibition agents at the canyon entrance.

In this particular case, Al had no choice but to get the paesani as well as himself away from the stills and out of the canyon as fast as possible. The risk of a raid on the still at this particular time was felt to be most eminent. If the lantern were to come on, they would have to abandon the car and hike up over the ridge and into Cull Canyon to the west. It was one hell of a hike, especially at night, because certain points along the way were quite precarious, if not outright dangerous.

The gates were opened but not closed as they hurriedly made their way down the canyon in the absence of the lantern signal; that is, all but the first gate at Crow Canyon Road itself. This gate was set at an angle since the exit road also came up to it on an angle running more or less parallel to the main road, thus putting the exiting car on the main road already heading down the desired direction. As the car, with its headlights extinguished, approached the gate, instead of stopping, Al put the accelerator to the floorboard, thus sending the Buick crashing headlong through the closed wooden gate. The car, with its cargo of wide-eyed, fearful paesani, along with Fats cursing Al for his reckless ways, careened down Crow Canyon Road at breakneck speed.

Its headlight lenses were shattered with only the dim lighting of the deep-set bulbs barely lighting the way. Al never let up or gave a backward glance, nor did he give a damn about the remains of the shattered gate left strewn across Crow Canyon Road.

Since the raid at the chicken ranch fell short of making a good, strong case against Mike, an immediate raid on the known stills was assumed to be the agents' next logical step in hopes of obtaining a witness or two and the needed solid evidence in the form of still equipment. Al was taking no chances. He couldn't be sure what or how much the agents knew or what plans they may have formulated. Regardless, he sure as hell was not about to wait around for the crooked sheriff, or his equally crooked deputies, to notify them in advance of a raid. His objective now was to get off of Crow Canyon Road as quickly as possible. Besides he enjoyed driving at race car speeds. The urgency of his mission was a good excuse for an added incentive for speeding.

As the Buick crossed the bridge at the old stagecoach stop just short of coming into view of Jensen Road above, Al switched off the car's headlights. John Baron had just stepped out his front door to relieve himself of the fair ration of boilermakers he had consumed earlier. Along with his little black and white fox terrier, the two were urinating up against the picket fence paralleling the road when the Buick charged on past him with a roar and gust of wind. Through his homebrew-saturated eyes, and in total darkness, he saw the shadowy blur shoot past him. He opened his eyes wide, hoping to get a better look at what had just gone by, but through his bushy eyebrows he couldn't see much of anything other than the blur disappear around the bend. By the time Old John reinstated his penis back into its rightful place, the car had already swung into Mike's closest driveway just up around the bend.

"Now what do you suppose that was?" John asked of his little fox terrier in a slurred voice.

The dog not only knew what it was, but he also knew who it was. He was used to this particular car with the ear-splitting (especially to a dog), high-pitched whistle roaring up and down the canyon at all hours of the night.

The ranch was engulfed in darkness, as was the Buick with its cargo of men. Everybody scrambled out of the car with the exception of Al, and Fats who chose to stick it out with his buddy the rest of the way. The car roared out the opposite driveway, again without the benefit of headlights, and so it remained until it was out of sight of the Jensen Road surveillance stakeout, if in fact it was up there. Al was now confronted with the chore of intercepting the International truck which was by now slowly working its way through the streets of East Oakland with a full load of sugar destined for Bellina Canyon. Of all times, tonight was not the night to be transferring a load of sugar onto John Soares' wagon. Al was convinced that Bellina Canyon would be swarming with federal agents before the night was out.

Considering the time of night, it was assumed the truck, with Guido's brother Lepo at the wheel, would be traveling south on either San Leandro Boulevard or on Foothill Boulevard, somewhere between Fruitvale Avenue and the city limits dividing Oakland and San Leandro. Since he was already on Foothill Boulevard heading north, Al would stick with this route first until he reached Fruitvale Avenue. Not having intercepted the truck, he then swung to the left onto Fruitvale Avenue. At a high rate of speed, he headed down across town to pick up San Leandro Boulevard where he would then turn left again heading back south. His hope was to catch up to the slow-moving truck somewhere along San Leandro Boulevard before it reached the city limits of San Leandro.

Halfway down Fruitvale Avenue, the Buick came up behind a cruising police car heading in the same direction.

"Of all the goddamned luck!" swore Al as he considered his options.

"The hell with it, take him! That Chevy is no match for this Buick, and if it's Captain Brown, he'll recognize the car and stay put!" encouraged Fats hopefully.

Al didn't give it a second thought. He floorboarded the Buick as he swung out, passing the Chevy touring sedan at an accelerated rate of speed, to the astonishment of its driver—none other than Captain Louis Eike, Badge No. 1, the state's top ranking traffic officer. In passing, the two drivers recognized each other. Eike had cited Al for speeding so many times that the two men had become buddies. Al was forever challenging Eike and Eike was forever taking up the challenge, as if they were playing a game. For the most part, if Al didn't get too overly brazen, Eike wouldn't cite him if and when he did catch him, even though he would end up chasing him all over hell's creation.

"Oh Christ!" exclaimed Al. "What the hell's Louie doing down here? We're in for it now! Hang on buddy, he'll be on our ass for sure, and we don't have time to play games!"

Without hesitation, the Chevy took up the chase. The two cars careened down Fruitvale Avenue in wild abandonment of sensible caution. The high-pitched whistle of the Buick combined with the screeching wail of the police car's siren announced their approach to East 14th Street. Al's buddies, Italians and Portuguese alike, raced to the street corners scrambling to gain a vantage point to watch this spectacle of careening cars. They well knew who the principals were.

East 14th Street, with its double sets of streetcar tracks, was a hazardous thoroughfare to cross at any speed, let alone at high speed with the added risk of ignoring stop signs. To be sure, the eager spectators would not be disappointed this night.

The whistling Buick shot across the broad busy street with the siren-wailing Chevy police car close behind, both cars sending off a loud washboard chatter of tires over rails as they zigged and zagged, slicing through cross traffic. The streetcar operators banging their heels on the bell button sent out a constant clatter of warnings that went totally unheeded. Profanity was voiced by other car drivers, pedestrians, and streetcar operators alike, but the spectators, hats waiving them on, loved it.

Once across East 14th Street, Al held his left hand straight out signaling a left turn onto San Leandro Boulevard. Because he was backing off to make the turn, he didn't want Officer Eike making the mistake of pulling alongside thinking that he was giving up the chase. The turn was negotiated amongst a screeching of tires as the two cars leaned heavily, then straightened out again once out of the turn. Accelerators pressed to the floorboards, they careened at breakneck speeds traveling south on the straight lengthy stretch of San Leandro Boulevard heading towards the San Leandro city limits several miles ahead.

On the open straightaway, the four-cylinder Chevy proved to be no match for the powerful six-cylinder Buick. A mile or so down the stretch, Officer Eike gave up the chase. He had experienced similar events with Al on many occasions before, only to be bested once on the straightaway. He therefore retreated back to Fruitvale Avenue to wait for Al to show up later in the night, hopefully with a bottle of good jackass they could sip on while rehashing the details of the evening's events.

Al caught up to the slow-moving International just as it crossed the city limits into San Leandro. Lepo expressed surprise at being pulled over:

"What are you guys doing out here?" he asked.

"You can't take the load up the canyon!" answered Al firmly as he lit up a cigarette. The light from the match reflected against his muscular neck and solemn facial features. It was obvious to Lepo that his brother-in-law was not kidding around.

"What's the matter? What happened?" asked Lepo excitedly.

Al explained the situation in brief while Fats commented his concurrence with his prediction.

"What are we going to do with this load of sugar? We sure as hell can't just leave the truck parked out on the street, can we?" asked Lepo while studying Al's thoughtful expression.

"No, we won't leave it on the street! We'll take it to Santucci's hog ranch down in Russell City!"

"Santucci's! Are you kidding? He's been down at the warehouse screaming for sugar for his own still. He was cussing Damonte for giving us this load. He thought he should have gotten it. I'm telling you, if he gets his hands on it, he'll dump it in his swill trucks and haul it off the minute we walk away from it. For Christ's sake! Al, come up with a better idea than that!" pleaded Lepo urgently.

"Who said anything about walking away from it? You're going to stay with it until I come back for you! If Santucci's there, tell him we expect a raid tonight up at Bellina Canyon!"

"You mean you're going to leave me down there all night among those pigs . . . ? By myself . . . ?"

"That's right! And make sure you park out back and let them know you're there or you're liable to get shot up and fed to the hogs!" instructed Al in a to-the-point manner. He then added: "I guess you know Santucci's men are pretty jumpy since those assholes from the D. A.'s office burned the place down last year."

"A hell of a brother-in-law you turned out to be," snorted Lepo in disgust with a wide-eyed, fearful expression.

"You could have done a hell of a lot worse! Now get going, damn it!" commanded Al.

Fats had little to say. He admired Al's spunkiness in handling matters such as this. When the chips were down, he knew his buddy wouldn't put up with any nonsense. But nevertheless, he did see fit to ask a sensible question on Lepo's behalf:

"Al, aren't those pigs dangerous? They tell me they'll at times attack and actually kill a man."

"Not these pigs. Santucci feeds them the mash waste from the fermentation tanks, which, as you know, is pretty potent stuff. His pigs are happy-go-lucky; they stagger around the pens like drunken sailors in a whorehouse."

The two men waited around until the International was well on its way. Lepo's bitching and grumbling coincided with the truck's groaning and gnashing of gears under the heavy load of sugar as it made its way to Santucci's.

Jackass Brandy

CHAPTER 45

Al had guessed it right, for it wasn't more than the better part of a half-hour after he crashed through the gate when a car full of federal agents, followed by another, came charging up to the thoroughly shattered gate at the entrance to Bellina Canyon. The agents thought they'd play it smart by coming in from the San Ramon end of Crow Canyon, but the added time consumed coming in the long way around from Dublin was enough to put them at the scene after the fact. If they intended to trap the paesani, it would have been a waste of time either way, since in no way could they approach the canyon entrance without the Okies spotting them from the knoll.

No sooner had the two federal cars started down the grade into Crow Canyon to approach the gate, the Okies up on the knoll hung the signal lantern on the barbed wire fence. However, they were wasting their time and efforts as well since there was nobody left up at the still site to receive the message. They had witnessed the Buick leaving the canyon, but thought it to be nothing other than hauling out a load of alcohol. Their instructions were to flash the warning signal whenever unidentified cars approached the canyon, and so they did. The glow of the lantern could be seen from either up or down Crow Canyon Road, as well as from up Bellina Canyon, providing you looked up.

The agents stood around viewing the shattered gate. The Hudson's big headlights illuminated the scene of the splintered boards and shattered glass strewn across the road.

"Too late! Just plain-too-goddamned-late!" cursed the chief federal agent. It was obvious, the evidence that lay before them told the whole story. "Not much point in sticking around here now. They're long gone; we might just as well head back," said the chief in a disappointed and angry tone. He was doing his best to keep from blowing his stack. The input of the senior agent, who was still smarting from the ass chewing he had received from the chief for pulling the blunder earlier that day by raiding Mike's chicken ranch ahead of schedule, didn't help matters much.

"Why not go up and raid the still anyway?" suggested the senior agent. "There could be someone still up there; if not, the equipm. . ."

Interrupting the statement, and before answering the question directly, the chief let fly a barrage of profanity and insults directed more at the senior agent than the disappointing situation at hand. The other agents retreated to the shadows, moving away from the two men, thinking it would be best not to witness the chief shooting the balls off his junior colleague. It was obvious to them that the still, and/or its related equipment, was not the only thing the chief wanted. And, of course, the senior agent knew this also, but under the circumstances, he felt something was better than nothing. Besides, they might just get lucky and find someone still up there who could be induced into fingering Mike as the head capo of the organization. This is what the chief really wanted and had it not been for the senior agent jumping the gun, they might have gotten it by raiding both the still and the ranch simultaneously, therefore booking all the paesani, including Mike, at the same time for the same offense.

The senior agent fidgeted somewhat nervously while waiting for the answer to his question, which he now wished he had not asked.

"We'll do nothing of the kind!" the chief finally answered sternly. His wide-eyed expression as he said it gave him the appearance of a mad man about to cut out a man's liver.

"Of course . . . you're right. I understand your point . . . good thinking chief," stammered the senior agent in concurrence.

He would have fared better if he hadn't said that either. The one thing he should not be doing now is brownnosing the chief. A kiss-ass or yes man was the last thing the chief needed. He despised men with this trait under any circumstances, let alone during this particular situation.

The chief walked hurriedly around to the driver's side of the Hudson, stopping long enough to instruct one of the agents leaning up against the car while waiting out the confrontation. In the reflection of the headlights, the chief's lips could be seen to tremble with nervous anger as he sternly addressed the agent:

"I'm going to ride back in the other car! You drive this one and take that frigg'n jerk with you! If he gives you a bad time, dump him! Let the idiot walk back!"

As the chief stomped away from the reflecting lights of the car, his eyes caught the Okies' signal lantern's distant glow.

"Hold it a minute! Take a look at that! Up there—see it? That's a signal if I ever saw one!" stated the chief in astonishment.

From the opposite side of the car, the senior agent looking up and seeing the glow of light, concurred with the others—it was, unmistakenly, a signal of some sort. He then stated:

"There's no house up there! It has to be a signal!" He started to squeal out a half-assed explanation as to why he might have missed that part of the bootleggers' signal system, but the chief didn't give him a chance to get past the first few words before sailing into him:

"You dumb frigg'n jerk!" was the chief's first statement, which was then followed with a barrage of profane-punctuated accusations, some related to his junior agent's disloyalty to the cause either through his incompetence or plain stupidity, and some related to his past despicable conduct in general. The chief then addressed the car driver again with an added order to his previous instructions:

"If that idiot opens his mouth again, throw the son-of-a-bitch out of the car and don't bother to slow down!"

CHAPTER 46

The gloomy, overcast morning wasn't of much help in raising the chief investigator's spirits. He wasn't accustomed to such blundering failures as what had taken place the day before. His junior colleague, the senior agent, was heavy on his mind as he sat there behind his desk pondering his next move. He was satisfied that his decision not to take the still the night before was a good one. "Let them think we don't know what's going on up in Bellina Canyon. Left alone, the bootleggers will eventually wander back and resume their activities," he thought.

His thoughts were interrupted by the voice and appearance of a young man as he partially opened the office door, sticking his head through and announcing his presence:

"I'm from the District Attorney's office—may I come in?" asked the well-groomed young man.

"Sure, come on in. What's on your mind?"

"Well, sir . . . the District Attorney asked me to inform you that other than possession, we don't have much of a case against the defendant, Buti. He wants me to explain to you why we haven't."

"Save your breath, I already know why. I'm sorry you had to waste your time coming over here."

"Hear me out, sir. The D. A. had more to say," pleaded the young man, a deputy district attorney.

"Oh, and what might that be?"

"Well, he said if you could bring in some solid evidence along with a witness or two, you know . . . maybe employees that would finger him as the head man to save their own hides . . . "

The chief investigator stopped him short and proceeded to apprise the young deputy D.A. of the preceding night's attempt to do just that. The deputy D.A. expressed disappointment in receiving the bad news. He then added a suggestion in the form of a question:

"Why not nab them when they start up again, or do you think they'll pull out of the county?"

"That was the thought on my mind when you walked through the door, and, of course, one of the reasons I chose to abort the raid last night so as not to spook them."

"I assume, then, that you have an agent following through, no doubt the same agent . . . "

Again the chief cut the deputy D.A. short, only this time he expressed anger as he declared the shortcomings of the senior agent and his despicable conduct by saying:

"He's the one that ought to be behind bars."

Realizing they were dealing with a soured agent, the deputy eagerly asked:

"How do you feel about our office prosecuting him? We can make an example of him?"

"In due time . . . yes. But for the moment, we may still need him."

"I see. Then you do have a plan of sorts?"

"Yes, but I'm afraid it won't work. These people are smart—we may run out of time."

The chief then explained his plan of staying away from Crow Canyon altogether for a while. Hopefully, the still operators, Mike's gang, would feel secure thinking the agents might not have known as much as they thought they knew and, therefore, start up again. He expressed his thoughts:

"It's a big job to move a good size distillery, what with the fermentation tanks and all the other equipment. My guess is, given enough time, they'll choose to start up again right there on the same site. But before we can move in on them, this case of simple possession of whiskey will be settled and closed. So we still don't have the big boss and . . . "

Now it was the deputy's turn to interrupt.

"Now hold it a minute! The District Attorney wants a case like this, something he can really sink his teeth in, you know . . . maybe even for political reasons."

"So, what are you driving at?" asked the chief eagerly.

This young man had something in mind, and the chief wanted to know exactly what it was.

"I'll get you the time; we'll stall the hearing."

"How are you going to do that? The attorney handling this case has a reputation of being . . . "

Again the chief was cut short.

"The D. A. knows all about Mr. Joseph P. Lacey, the defendant's attorney. He's a damned good criminal lawyer, but a shady character at heart. The D. A. wants his hide as well. Putting it bluntly, he's not clean, and remember, we're lawyers as well." stated the young man proudly. "One more thing—do you mind having a couple of our investigators ride along with you when you make the next raid?"

"Sure, why not have them along. That will be fine. I'll let you know in advance when we're ready."

The chief's spirits were now raised to incredible heights. The case against Mike would be stalled, hopefully giving him enough time to execute a successful raid on the still. Yes, things were looking up; tying the two cases together, and trying them as one would surely implicate Mike as the capo.

His first move was to summon the senior agent and alert him to the possible on-going investigation into his own conduct by the D. A.'s office, which could lead to severe disciplinary action, if not prison.

The senior agent was shaken by the chief's comments.

"Sir, I promise you it won't happen again. I will cooperate with you and others in every way I can."

"Fine, then stay the hell out of Crow Canyon until I say otherwise!"

Other than that, the chief mentioned nothing to him or anyone else about his plan. He trusted no one. Eventually he would need the senior agent since he had gained considerable knowledge as to the exact location of the still. Having studied maps of the area and talking to an old state coyote trapper that knew every auto road, wagon trail, and footpath in every one of these spur canyons that branched off Crow Canyon, did make the senior agent indispensable. When the chief was ready, he would need him to lead the raid.

The next thing he did was to pull the surveillance off Jensen Road and place it at Palomares and Eden Canyons where they intersected Dublin Canyon Road from opposite sides. The familiar Essex would soon be spotted there, and hopefully soon reported to the paesano gang. The chief had to assume that every resident within the area was a friend of Mike's, and would report anything of interest to him immediately. They all liked his Jackass and generosity, so this assumption was logical.

He then assigned the Hudson to patrolling the highway between Dublin and Martinez with orders not to slow down at San Ramon where Crow Canyon Road terminated on the Contra Costa County side of the ridge. And if it were to encounter the blue Buick, it was to purposely allow it to elude them. It was hoped that these moves would lead the paesani to believing the agents had come to the conclusion that the still was elsewhere. The senior agent, along with the original driver of the Essex, was assigned to Santa Clara County on a temporary basis. The chief wanted them away from Alameda County for a specific reason. Since it was obvious that Mike had connections high up in the local law enforcement and justice community, it was correctly assumed that information was being passed on to him. So working in collusion with the District Attorney himself, Earl Warren, the word was casually passed around that the senior agent, along with at least one other agent was about to be indicted for wrongdoing and therefore was being detained. The

302

matter of a major still being located and operated in Crow Canyon proper was scoffed at. Among other things, it was announced that the agents about to be indicted had definitely been on the wrong track all along.

Obviously Mike and his paesani were laying low, waiting things out. Attorney Lacey had assured Mike that he could settle the matter of his arrest for possession with nothing more than a fine and, of course, a substantial amount of cash funneled to the right people could even wipe the whole affair off the record. This manner of handling his clients' affairs was Lacey's stock and trade. It was also his stock and trade to always pocket a fair share (in some cases, all) of his clients' money advanced for this purpose. This personal gain was above and beyond his regular legal fee. A form of, if not outright, extortion.

As for the Jacklich gang and the Santucci bunch, once having rid themselves of their woolly companions and realizing that they in fact were not being raided after all, made their way back to their respective stills and started right up again.

Despite the approaching rainy season, the paesani decided to also start up again. Predictions were being made that the upcoming 1928-29 winter season could be expected to produce above normal rainfall. The road was bad enough the previous year without the two added operations; it could be imagined what the dirt road would be like this coming winter.

The stills were reactivated again and were now cranking out alcohol at full capacity. Not trusting anyone, the chief investigator took it upon himself to ascertain the paesani renewed their activities in and around Bellina Canyon. This was done by his regularly commandeering an old Model T Ford farm truck, then driving up and down Crow Canyon Road, in one end and out the other. He dressed himself as an unshaven farmer with an old soiled hat, bib overalls, and a corncob pipe clenched between his teeth, pre-stained and roasted along the top edge to give it a well-seasoned appearance. At times the farm truck would be hauling a few bales of hay along with a few sacks of chicken feed. At least on one occasion he was seen within sight of Bellina Canyon's entrance, stretched out under the truck with an assortment of tools scattered about as if making roadside repairs.

This man knew what he was doing. He had alcohol on his mind, not in his blood. His decisions and actions were precise, unlike the blurred uncertainties that plagued the senior agent's alcohol-damaged brain. The chief wasn't drinking brain-rotting alcohol that also causes nerve ends throughout the body to wither like spring grass sprayed with diesel oil. So far he felt he had outsmarted Mike and his paesani, and with his untouchable ally, District Attorney Earl Warren, hopefully he would bring them all to justice.

But the ever vigilant Okies at the old Habberney place knew all about farming and farmers, along with their personal habits. For one thing, a farmer, when disembarking a rattling, bouncy Model T Ford truck would have to relieve himself immediately to void his bladder. The constant bouncing and jarring was quite rough on the kidneys. For the most part, the chief didn't relieve himself at all when stopping along the road in the vicinity of the canyon entrance. What few times he did, it was not done in true farmer or rancher tradition. The dead giveaway was that the chief, when in need, would slip through the barbed wire fence and seek a secluded spot to urinate well away from view of the road. Whereas a true farmer, cattle or sheep rancher, would not bother crawling through a barbed wire fence just to urinate in such a discreet manner. He would simply step out of the truck, walk up to the handiest fence post and urinate up against the post while his ever-present dog would hoist his leg and do likewise, making sure that no portion of the post went unmarked. The two distinct sets of urine smells, human and canine, emitting from the post would let stray dogs and coyotes alike know that the area around the post, within barking or howling distance, was already established territory.

Hardly ever was the chief able to stop or park his Model T within sight of the first gate and canyon entrance without the Okies sending a signal by stretching out the coyote hide up on the barbed wire fence, thus exposing his presence. The chief was aware of the lantern signal by night, but not the coyote hide by day. There was no reason to suspect anything unusual, since the ranchers quite often stretched fresh coyote hides on line fences to ward off marauding bands of stock-stealing coyotes.

The chief investigator's vigilant surveillance consisted primarily of observing Mike's trucks and cars traveling up and down Crow Canyon Road and, whenever possible, in and out of Bellina Canyon. He was able to distinguish them from other vehicles since their description had been thoroughly spelled out to him. However, his nighttime surveillance especially should have caused him to suspect the presence of other stills besides Mike's operating in the same general area. At times there was as much traffic at night as there was by day. And of all things, highway transport trucks, not the traditional farm trucks, hauling what appeared to be loads of baled hay in and out the canyon. What was seen going by was baled hay shielding sacks of sugar that made up the majority of the load heading for the Jacklich brothers still at Tony Soares' old place. The same trucks would then be seen coming back out the canyon again with the same bales of hay, only this time, with a load of 5 gallon tin cans of alcohol stashed amidst the hay. For the most part, these trucks were escorted by a car full of tough Jacklich guards that didn't look anything like cattlemen, or for that matter, sheepmen.

Frank Jacklich's personal car was a customized, powder blue, snappy looking Studebaker touring sedan with a false bottom under both seats that extended down through the car's framework, so designed to accommodate 5 gallon tin cans of alcohol. No rancher or farmer anywhere owned such a classic automobile. It even had a fancy temperature gage mounted directly on the radiator cap. You can be sure there was no cow manure splattered on that immaculate bootlegger's car; a dead giveaway to its ownership if ever there was one.

Santucci's hog swill trucks moving in and out of Dutch Charley's sheep ranch were another dead giveaway that should have been noticed. The trucks were hauling sugar and rolled barley disguised and shielded under the swill that was picked up from restaurants, markets, and food processing plants for hog feed.

A little hog-swill tossed into the fermentation tanks, along with the sugar and barley, didn't hurt a damned thing. If anything, it helped speed up the fermentation process. Granted, the putrid smell of these swill juice-dripping trucks could hardly be assumed to be hauling anything other than what they were intended for, but at least they should have been checked out. These trucks were coming back out of the canyon loaded with 5 gallon tins of alcohol and 10 gallon barrels of jackass buried under the same swill. Besides, what the hell is a hog-swill truck doing routinely pulling in and out of a sheep ranch? Sheep are delicate eaters; they certainly do not eat hog-swill.

There was at least one other dead giveaway that should have tipped off the chief federal agent as to the magnitude of bootlegging activities within the two-mile stretch of Bellina Canyon. The parade of perfumed, mobile whores with their gaudy flowery dresses, wide-brimmed fancy hats adorned with colorful ostrich feathers waving in the wind like so many Italian military officers in full dress parade (sporting chicken-feathered head gear), constantly entering and exiting the canyon surely should have raised a question.

For God's sake! One could hardly expect the two bachelor Waldie brothers, John and Oscar, along with Mike's several little dwarf-sized paesano bachelors operating the stills, to need the services of a dozen or so professional prostitutes on such a routine basis, when only two of them could easily handle the job, or for that matter, even only one . . . in a pinch. To warrant the sexual activity that could be generated by that large a contingency of sex machines would require a platoon of young sex-starved soldiers. It should have been obvious that the canyon was teaming with young, aggressive bootlegging bachelors, loaded with money, and nowhere to spend it.

Nevertheless, the chief federal agent overlooked the possibility of anyone other than Mike to be operating out of Bellina Canyon. But he did wisely decide that he'd best move in soon on Mike's stills since the fall rains could be expected to become more intensive and therefore rendering the dirt road useless to motorized vehicular traffic.

CHAPTER 47

The stage was set. Final preparations were made to carry out the raid on Mike's Bellina Canyon still operation. This included the acquisition of a 1925 blue Buick touring sedan identical to the one Al was driving in and out of the canyon on his routine nightly pickups. The best driver that could be found within the federal agency with a knowledge of Buicks was picked to drive the car. By coincidence, the driver was physically built with features much like Al's. He was briefed in detail as to Al's style of driving, especially his approach to the canyon entrance. They knew it had to be done right so as to not set off the lantern signal up on the hillside. The agents were taking no chances; the approach to the canyon entrance had to be perfect.

The chief and the senior agent would ride up front with the driver, and the three investigators from the D. A.'s office would ride in the back seat, their presence shielded by the side curtains. Only the driver would be seen leaving and entering the car to open and close the gate. The lawmen's Buick, with its crew of six lawmen, would enter and proceed up the winding Bellina Canyon road a full two hours ahead of the Hudson, followed by a transport truck driven by the same independent trucker, Silva, that was employed to haul out Mike's confiscated distilling equipment at Niles. No one dared ask the question:

"Why prepare to haul the bootleggers and the evidence out when we don't even know for sure that we'll succeed?"

Had any one of the participants questioned the feasibility of the raid or its possible success, they would have been dropped out without much of an explanation. The chief federal agent would not tolerate pessimism.

On the night of the raid, armed with the necessary search warrants, the heavily armed lawmen took the long way around to approach Bellina Canyon. They traveled east on Dublin Canyon Road to Dublin, then north to San Ramon, where the follow-up Hudson and truck would wait, allowing the lawmen's car to approach and enter the canyon alone as was customary with Al. The Hudson was to lie in wait for and intercept Al in the event he was to show up coming in from the same direction. The truck was backed up to the loading platform of the hay and feed warehouse adjacent to the San Ramon general store on the corner, thus blocking the better part of Crow Canyon Road. The Hudson parked amongst the grove of eucalyptus trees at the sharp left bend in the road just up from the warehouse. Once slowed down to get past the truck, the upcoming sharp curve made it ideal for the heavy Hudson to dart out and broadside Al's Buick.

The Essex, with two agents, had come up Crow Canyon road from the opposite direction. It positioned itself in the driveway of the little Edenvale grade school some quarter of a mile down from the Bellina Canyon entrance. Traveling up the canyon and once past the Joseph Knowland estate, the road curved to the right then to the left swinging around the school yard with a concrete culvert abutment and gully to the right across from the school's driveway. Any car straddling the road at this point would cause an oncoming car to collide with it or hit the concrete abutment. The Essex's mission, such as the Hudson's, was also to intercept Al in the event he was to show up coming in from that direction. In this case, the Buick's familiar high-pitched whistle would announce its coming up the somewhat straight stretch in front of the Knowland estate; then the decreasing pitch would indicate its slowing down to negotiate the sharp curves. That would be the time for the Essex to dart out in the Buick's path. The senior agent had emphasized the need to collide with the car rather than engage it in a game of tag. If nothing else worthwhile, he had certainly learned to respect Al's ability as a driver. Although he was not the principle target, it was hoped that he would also get caught up in the raid.

At 10:00 p.m. sharp, without alerting the Okies, the six lawmen opened the first gate and entered Bellina Canyon. They drove through John Soares' yard without stopping. To have done so would have set off a Portuguese style confrontation the likes of which the lawmen did not care to deal with. They crossed the wooden bridge at Bellina Creek and to the left of Dutch Charley's driveway, then continued up to the second gate. This was a heavily wooded high point in the road with Bellina Creek to the right some hundred feet or so below. Dutch Charley's house and farm buildings housing Santucci's still was situated directly across the creek, although the driveway came from the opposite side of the creek. The driver went through the ritual of opening and closing the gate, then remarked as the car continued up the canyon:

"That must be one hell of a big operation up there," he said referring to Mike's still. "Christ, you can smell it from way down here," he added.

"What you're smelling is the polluted creek," answered the senior agent. "That stuff's running clean out the canyon." He was proud of the fact that it was he who had discovered the still's location. The lawmen had no idea that there was in fact not one, but three stills dumping waste into the creek.

The road now emerged out into clear pasture land, then ran somewhat downhill to the third gate at Tony Soares old 80-acre place where the Jacklich brothers still was located across the creek and up a heavily wooded draw completely obscured from view. Neither the senior agent or the chief had any idea of the existence of the Santucci and Jacklich stills so close at hand. Neither did they realize that they had actually penetrated their perimeter alarm system. As they had figured and planned, they did get past the Okies by duplicating the blue Buick and Al's driving habits, but now the real test was at hand. They now had to outsmart the lookout perched up in the madrone tree at Waldies, the better part of a mile up the canyon.

As the car moved along, its headlights illuminated Tony's gate up ahead. At this point, the senior agent, sitting between the driver and the chief, reached out to the dashboard and held the car's light switch ready to signal the instant the car stopped. The car came to a stop, the agent in a rotary motion turned the switch on and off three times in about the same sequence as described by the cowboy over at Bollinger Canyon. All eyes were fixed up towards the end of the canyon. If the signal code was correct, they could expect to see a kerosene lantern come on, hold its glow for a few seconds, then extinguish.

"There it is! Sure as hell, there it is!" exclaimed the chief with delight.

The gate was instantly opened by the driver, then closed again once the car had passed through, such as Al would have done coming in alone. The chief had thought of everything, even to the extent of what the timing and sequence of opening and closing a gate would look like in the glare of headlights from a mile or so away. He wanted everything to look perfectly normal. The lookout stayed at his post, watching and studying every move of the upcoming car. So far he was satisfied that it was Al, and he was on schedule.

In the meantime, however, Al was driving up Crow Canyon road in his usual alert manner. The Buick had just passed the Knowland estate to the left. The car maintained its speed with the accompanying high-pitched whistle until it reached the curve that swung to the right skirting the lower side of the school grounds. The Buick's headlights illuminated the row of cypress trees along the school's fence line in a sweeping arc as the car swung to the right while decelerating to accommodate the right, then left, swing that was coming up. The Essex lay in wait in the school's driveway at the end and behind the row of cypress trees, ready to dart out in front of the Buick as it would swing back to the left, putting it just ahead of the concrete abutment across the road. The driver of the Essex started the car's engine when he first heard the whistling sound through the car's open windows, then stated:

"This is it, brace yourself!" exclaimed the driver anxiously. "We'll take him head-on!"

His fellow agent, seated to his right, would no doubt take the brunt of the impact, since the Buick would be coming in from his side. He had smoked a dozen or so cigarettes during the evening while nervously waiting for the inevitable. He took one more deep drag from his cigarette, then flipped it out the car's window as the Buick's headlights swept across the row of cypress trees to his right. Through the trees, Al caught a glimpse of the cigarette glow then the shower of sparks that followed as the cigarette hit the gravel driveway. It was an unusual occurrence for this particular location at this hour of the night and timed according to his arrival. A snap decision triggered his reflexes that put the car into a screeching spin as it was coming into the left swing. His intention was to reverse his direction of travel. The Essex instantly charged out to intercept the Buick in hopes of slamming it into the concrete abutment. The car, however, came into the left turn, first skidding sideways, then as skillful maneuvers were applied, it continued around until the rear end was facing the direction of travel. While in motion, split-second action on Al's part enabled him to pick off first gear, then come down hard on the accelerator. The car was now careening backwards while its wheels were spinning in the opposite direction spewing clouds of smoke from burning rubber out from under the car's undercarriage.

To the astonishment of the two occupants, instead of the Essex slamming the Buick, it took a broadside, thus ejecting both occupants out the opposite side. Having glimpsed the shadowed form of the Essex darting out onto the roadway as he was making his maneuvers, Al figured he'd done just that. But unsure of the car's purpose for being there in the first place, he wasn't about to stop and offer assistance. Aside from the need to let up to shift gears, he kept the pressure on the accelerator, pressing it to the floorboard for the rest of the run back out Crow Canyon, while the Essex remained behind, totally disabled.

The lawmen making their way up Bellina Canyon couldn't be sure as to what parts of the road could be seen by the lookout, so they maintained the exact sequence of opening and closing of gates. When their car's headlights illuminated Waldies' blue gate, the senior agent instructed the driver to turn to the right onto Peters' wagon road. The driver made the maneuver without hesitation such as he figured Al might do, then continued slowly along without having stopped.

"O. K., now here's where I am not sure how we get to the still itself," said the senior agent. "According to the cowboy, the still should be along that creek up ahead, halfway between here and the house above."

"That looks like a recent cut over to the left," commented the driver.

"I see it, that must be the road leading to the still alright," said the senior agent pointing excitedly.

The lookout up in the madrone tree saw the Buick turn off on to the wagon road without stopping, and upon so doing, came scrambling down out of the tree and hastily retreated from the still site heading for the hills. The still had been shut down previously, so he was the only man there waiting for Al to show up to pick him up along with a dozen or so cans of alcohol. What triggered his reaction was the fact that Al had the habit of stopping at the blue gate to relieve himself before continuing down the wagon road and in so doing, lighting up a cigarette. The cowboy over at Bollinger Canyon had not put much significance in this act if, in fact, he saw it at all. He therefore neglected to mention anything about it to the senior agent.

"Well, what do you think, chief?" asked the driver.

"Take it," came the quick answer.

The car moved slowly along the narrow rough-cut road making its way through the woods.

"There it is up ahead, pull up just short of the clearing," instructed the chief urgently.

The car stopped before entering the dimly lit area of the still site. The driver stepped out first making his way casually along the car's front end with his gun at ready. The chief, also with gun drawn, was making his way along the opposite side of the car, followed by the senior agent carrying a submachine gun. The senior agent wouldn't need much of an excuse to gun down any paesano that might give any indication of knowing him for his corrupt ways. His future was on shaky ground; therefore, his cowardly instinct would be to silence anyone that could possibly testify against him, including the chief walking up ahead with his back to the submachine gun. An intentional burst from the gun catching the chief in a cross fire could never be proven to be anything but accidental under such circumstances. The findings at the deserted still site didn't please the chief one bit.

"This can't be all there is to it," he stated.

The others concurred as they eyed the well-worn path leading up to the main still. Some of the men were already heading up the path by the time the chief suggested following it up to its source. The chief's blood ran cold when he turned to address the senior agent standing there behind him holding the submachine gun leveled at his midsection with the safety catch off. The senior agent's hard look and starry wide open eyes instantly told the chief that the absence of the bootleggers had, in fact, saved his life. The thought flashed through his mind that of all the lawmen present, only he knew the extent of the senior agent's corrupt past. Not letting on his anxiety, he calmly addressed the senior agent:

"I'm going to take that path and follow the others up to the main buildings. You stay here and keep your eyes open. Let me have the sub, we may need it." With that he reached out for the gun as he stepped to one side out of its line of fire. Once the gun was in his hands, the chief breathed easier. He pressed the gun's safety latch into its safe position and, without warning, smashed the butt of the gun into the senior agent's face stunning him momentarily, thus causing him to stagger to the ground. While reaching down to lift his handgun out of its holster, he issued a stern warning:

"Don't you ever . . . point a gun at me again . . . understand?!"

As he proceeded to follow the others up the path that led to the barnyard, beads of sweat broke out on his forehead at the thought of being gunned down by one of his own men. "That son-of-a-bitch!" mumbled the chief to himself, in reference to the corrupt senior agent. "I should never have trusted that no good bastard!" Then repeated angrily: "Maybe Mike's driver did try to kill him on purpose in that tanker truck wreck. Too bad he didn't succeed," he added in an audible tone. Having caught the attention of his own driver with his last comment, the chief passed it off as a casual comment with no significance.

A close inspection of the main barn and blacksmith shop revealed nothing in the way of a still. The chief's thoughts were too occupied to concentrate on the discussion going on between the officers from the D. A.'s office as they poked around the loose hay with pitchforks. An occasional pitchfork full of hay was tossed into the mangers to satisfy the low whinnying pleading of the horses. Regaining his composure, the chief addressed the others:

"Let's walk up the road to the ranch house. No doubt the ranchers have been spooked by now as well, but nevertheless, if we're lucky, we might find something there."

Had the chief known the two Waldie brothers at all, he would have known that there was nothing in this world that could possibly spook them, especially once they were sacked out. While others snooped around the bunkhouse and small storage buildings, the chief and his driver proceeded to knock on the door of the main house, demanding a response.

The two Waldie brothers, Oscar and John, were inside the darkened house all right, but they were in no condition to respond to the knocks or spoken demands for several good reasons. Stone deaf by nature, the two Waldie brothers could not hear the knocking. Besides, they drank Mike's Jackass Brandy, or for that matter anything else that contained alcohol, in place of water. If this in itself wasn't enough to knock them out cold, the added fatigue of cutting wood all day would surely give them the coup de grace. Since there was no electricity on the ranch, they relied on kerosene lamps for light and wood for comfort heat and cooking. So they not only had the task of keeping up a good wood supply for themselves, but also to fulfill contracts with some of the bootleggers in the area who also used wood to fire some of their small stills.

To do this, the brothers had put together a huge circular wood cutting saw blade mounted on a husky belt-driven mandrel powered by a bucket-sized single piston gasoline-powered combustion engine. The engine consisted of two four-foot diameter heavy cast iron flywheels mounted on either side of the engine crankshaft. The engine's governor was the centrifugal ball type that would spin the baseball-sized cast iron weights around, therefore feeding it fuel, depending on the load. Under load, the engine caused a steady cannon-like explosion to emit from the exhaust system in a steady, continuous pounding. When not under load, the massive flywheels would keep the engine coasting in a consortium of gasps, gulps, and coughs, such as would be emitted by a drowning man. The whole of the apparatus was mounted on a sturdy wagon chassis. Its wheels had to be dropped into trenches so as to buffer the jarring action of the huge piston. From a distance, the puffs of exhaust smoke, coupled with the corresponding cannon-like explosions, gave it the appearance and sound of a war machine of sorts. Feeding logs into the huge spinning saw blade all day long, with an occasional stiff belt of Mike's jackass to wash down the sawdust, was all that was needed to put a man into a deep death-like slumber come nightfall.

Not getting a response, the chief pushed the unlocked front door open and stepped into the living room. With flashlight in hand, he peered into the first bedroom. There was Oscar, stretched out across his bed fully clothed, snoring up a storm. The calling, poking and jabbing didn't so much as cause him to miss a beat. He was out cold.

The chief then walked over to the adjacent bedroom where John also lay stretched out across the bed with his shoes off and pants dangling over the edge. Apparently he had passed out before he could slip his pants off his left leg. His socks, long johns and shirt were still in place, as was his hat drawn down tight on his head. The more the chief jabbed at him, the louder he snored. Finally the chief gave up and walked away in complete disgust as he commented:

"These guys are drunk—flat out stoned—out cold." Then added: "Christ, this place reeks of booze. They must do their laundry in the stuff!" Saturated as they were, it was a reasonable conclusion.

Soon the Hudson came driving into the ranch yard without trucker Silva following as planned. The car's driver explained to the chief that Silva was reluctant to bring up the truck until he knew for sure that it would be needed. Silva complained of the difficulty he might encounter in maneuvering the big truck on such a road, but would do so if deemed absolutely necessary.

313

He would therefore wait down at the first gate until called for. The truth of the matter was that Silva was not only hauling confiscated equipment for the D. A.'s office, but he also hired out to bootleggers whenever they, too, needed the services he provided. So a few weeks before, Mike had hired trucker Silva to haul out the main still and its component parts down to the old Habberney place where the Okies lived. The main purpose for the move was because the paesani didn't want to go through the struggle of fighting the muddy road during the approaching rainy season. So he, Silva, knew there wasn't much up there to haul out.

Trucker Silva had the best of both worlds going for him. At times he would haul a load of confiscated still components to Oakland to be stored as evidence for the District Attorney. He would then pick up a load of sugar and mash on the way back for delivery to a still operator. If the still operator had a load of alcohol ready to take out, Silva would then haul the alcohol back out with him and deliver it to its predesignated location. When the evidence at the D. A.'s warehouse was no longer needed as such, it would be worked over with sledge hammers, then turned over to Silva again for hauling to the junkyard. But Silva would first stop off at several metal shops (Duartes Metal Fabricating Shop in Hayward being one of them) that he knew were manufacturing and repairing stills for the bootleggers, and sell them salvageable parts. In addition, he would manage to accumulate high-proof alcohol by carefully draining all the equipment including smashed 5gallon tin cans that hardly ever were totally emptied. At times, with the excuse that a raided still was too hot to handle, he would wait around until the agents were all gone, then fire up the precharged still and retrieve the rest of the alcohol before hauling it out. Needless to say, Silva was making money hand over fist.

Without bothering to explain, the chief instructed the Hudson's driver to head back out the canyon, and to advise Silva that his services were no longer needed.

With the use of sledge hammers, the small still was thoroughly demolished right on the spot. After dumping the few cans of alcohol onto the ground, the lawmen pulled out of the canyon; for all practical purposes, empty-handed.

CHAPTER 48

The three inspectors from the D. A.'s office who accompanied the federal agents on the night of the Waldie ranch raid did get something out of it, even if the chief investigator did not. The three inspectors, Charles R. Blagborne, George Henningsen, and Oscar Johnsen, had said little during the entire time of the raid, nor did they give any indication of what they may have detected while poking around in the hay. They were not about to trust any of these federal agents, and that went for the chief himself. After all, some of them had transferred from the federal agency to the D. A.'s office, so they were fully aware of how the agents functioned. As Blagborne was stirring up the hay with a pitchfork in the big barn on the night of the raid, he did in fact uncover something of interest. As he was moving the hay around, whiffs of fermentation odors could be detected being released from the barn floor. It was apparent that at some time in the not too distant past a fair-sized still with its related fermentation tanks had been operating inside the big barn. No doubt the still and fermentation tanks had been moved out and immediately replaced with hay in order to get it under cover before the heavy winter rains. The hay, pressed to the damp dirt floor saturated with spilled fermentation starter yeast, created a fermentation process. The process was sending off tell-tale odors that could be distinguished above the ever-present horse manure aroma by an experienced, well-trained nose. This fact, coupled with their having noticed the road to be already somewhat muddy in the shaded areas, caused the inspectors to surmise that if, in fact, the still was a high production unit, it would best be located closer to Crow Canyon proper for easier access during wet weather. They also surmised that the small wood-burning still found cold was being abandoned for possibly the same reason, therefore only the lookout was there waiting for Al to come pick him up, along with the few cans of alcohol. No doubt had the raid been stalled another day, the lookout, along with the remaining alcohol, would have been gone as well. They discounted the possibility, suggested by their supervisor Earl Warren, that the Sheriff's men may have warned them.

Satisfied that the still had been moved to somewhere closer to, or along, Crow Canyon Road itself, the D. A.'s inspectors took it upon themselves to find it without help or, hopefully, without the knowledge or interference of the federal agents or, for that matter, the Sheriff's Department. They correctly figured that the still was located in one of the many barns strung out along Crow Canyon Road. The question was— which one housed the still?

Warren, having concurred with his inspectors, Blagborne, Henningsen and Johnsen, assigned them to the task of finding the still: "Somewhere, within Crow Canyon, that still is in operation—find it!" were his orders. And so the trio set out to do just that.

They spent the next several days cruising up and down Crow Canyon Road scanning the area for tell-tale signs of a still operation, with an occasional hike down to the creek sniffing and tasting its waters. At a point near the Edenvale School just downstream from the conjunction of Bellina and Crow Canyon Creeks, they detected distillation waste in the water, and so wondered: "Which creek is it coming from?"

"Apparently, they haven't moved out of Bellina Canyon after all, or else we couldn't help but spot them between here and the county line. Hell, there isn't that much cover along Crow Canyon Creek," stated Blagborne.

"There's one way of finding out; check the water above the confluence of the two creeks," suggested Johnsen, the driver, then added: "I think you're right; we'll drive through that rancher's (John Soares) yard and check out Bellina Creek first. If you recall, it smelled quite potent the other night."

Driving through the gate at the entrance to Bellina Canyon, the car made its way down to where the road crossed Crow Canyon Creek. While crossing over the wooden bridge, distillation waste odors wafting up from the creek below, caught their attention:

"Get a whiff of that, will you? It didn't smell like that the other night; at least not here. Get turned around!" ordered Blagborne excitedly.

In the process of getting turned around at the yard area above, they couldn't help but notice the unusual activity upstream at John's horse barn and corals. Backed up to the edge of the creek embankment, Harry Rowell's truck was winching one of John's draft horses up out of the creek. The horse, weighing some 1,500 pounds, but now dead, was destined to be hauled off to Rowell's slaughterhouse to be ground up for chicken feed. The scene drew comment from Blagborne:

"What the hell? Look at that! Hold it!" he ordered. "Let's see what's going on over there . . . "

Having parked the car, the trio cautiously approached the activity. Not being sure what to expect, the closer they got the less it seemed likely that what they were witnessing here had anything to do with what they were looking for. But still, the distillation odors were wafting up from the creek stronger than ever. Once they realized the purpose of the activity, they posed a question to Rowell's driver as he operated the power winch. Above the screeching sound of steel cable being wound tight on its spool, Blagborne asked inquisitively:

"What killed the horse?" a logical question since the animal seemed to be quite young and no sign of injury.

"I don't know. You might ask him," came the short answer, accompanied by a slight head nod directed towards John Soares as he scrambled up the embankment following the horse.

Puffing hard, John having by now reached the top and obviously frustrated, was asked a similar question only put in a different form:

"Your horse looks pretty much dead. I don't suppose you know how he died . . . do you?"

Although never having met the trio before, John surmised that they were no doubt prohibition agents of sorts. He therefore did not flat out say what he thought killed the horse, but what he did say and how he said it pretty much implied that the horse did not necessarily die of natural causes. In broken English and in short angry bursts, he barked:

"The horse is dead; not pretty much—he's dead! He drink from the creek all the time, but never die before—this the first time!"

The instant the word "drink" was mentioned, Blagborne knew what killed the horse, "fusel oil," the poisonous discharge from a still, and to kill a horse when diluted in so much water meant lots of it. Saying nothing more, eye glances between the three lawmen conveyed the message to each other; what they were looking for was in one of the several big barns upstream from Soares' horse corals. Back at the car, they talked it over:

"All right, so we now have it narrowed down," stated Blagborne. "But we must be absolutely sure of the still's location lest we spook them (the bootleggers) by raiding the wrong barn."

"I suggest we drop it for today," said Officer Henningsen thoughtfully. "They're not aware of our findings. Let's sleep on it."

In the days that followed, by applying an ingenious method of detection of patrolling the canyon at daybreak on frosty mornings, they located the one barn without a glistening frosty roof. They knew that heat generated within a barn by a gasoline-fired still would keep the roof free of frost. And so it was with the big barn at the old Habberney place where the Oklahoma family lived. Being dead sure of the still's location, they staged the raid on the fourth day of December 1928, while in full operation with Julio (alias Gelio Rossi), Fats Meehan, and Matteoli in attendance. And, of course, rancher Henry Mast, who happened to stop by for lunch and a few belts of Jackass.

At the time, the twin continuous production side-by-side stills were putting out 193-proof alcohol at their full-rated capacity, some several hundred gallons per 24-hour day. There was also approximately 10,000 to 12,000 gallons of mash under fermentation to back them up. A guard was posted in the center of a clump of second growth laurel trees, within sight of the bridge that had to be crossed to get to the locked gate. But knowing something about Italians and their habits, the raiders purposely staged the raid at a time of day when they'd catch him asleep. Being used to his afternoon siestas back in the old country, he was, in fact, sound asleep as the raiders sneaked past him. But the fact that he was not arrested along with the others raised the question of his loyalty. The answer to the question, however, was never pursued simply because he plainly disappeared.

The Oklahoma family split the scene the minute they saw the first prohibition agent climb over the locked gate. Since the destitute family didn't own anything but the clothes they wore, it was a simple matter for them to fade into the woods.

Had the prohibition agents staged the raid after dark, they could have possibly nabbed Al as well, thus sparking a little excitement. But then, unlike the senior agent, they had no vendetta going with him. As it was, rancher Henry Mast did provide the raiding party with a little excitement, an incident they cared not talk about. Following his weekly routine, Henry had stopped by the still earlier in the day to pick up his weekly quota consisting of two gallons of Jackass. The glass jugs were placed in burlap sacks which he strapped on either side of his saddle for transporting. Since riding horseback was his only means of travel, Henry then rode over the county line where he sold the Jackass to clients in the town of Danville. Having made his delivery and paid in the usual manner (twenty silver dollars), he first stopped off at San Ramon on the way back to purchase his week's supply of groceries, transported in the same manner as the glass jugs. On the way home, it so happened that he stopped off at the still for another belt or two of Jackass, along with a bite to eat, just at the time the raid was staged.

Aside from spaghetti made with a tomato sauce featuring small birds, Henry's favorite dish was quail baked in wine sauce, which is what he was munching on at the time. The paesani caught the quail by feeding them alcohol-impregnated barley, then setting horsehair snares attached to willow twigs. Once having ingested the intoxicating barley, the quail, in their tipsy condition, became easy prey.

Guns drawn, the arresting officers stepped into the big barn while announcing their arrival with sharp, commanding orders:

"Stick 'em up! You're all under arrest!"

Fats, Julio, and Matteoli responded immediately, but Henry paid little attention to the order to: "Stick 'em up!" since he was not really a member of this gang of still operators. He honestly felt the order did not apply to him.

He just kept munching on a roasted quail and sipping Jackass while listening to the mixed conversation taking place between the participants involved in the raid. Apparently, for the same reason, he was being ignored.

However the cockiest of the officers, a man of somewhat small stature, having removed his coat, vest, and necktie in preparation of knocking the bungs off the fermentation tanks, as well as smashing up things in general, kept eyeing Henry. Apparently his indifference to the whole affair irritated this one particular officer to the extent that he decided to approach Henry in a threatening manner. At the time, Henry was standing on his feet, straight and tall as was his custom, looking more like a western lawman then did the officers. He wondered just what this aggressive-looking little character approaching him had in mind. While cursing profanely, the officer reached out with his right hand with the intention of grabbing Henry by the left arm and shoving him over to the line up.

"Alright, you goddamned cowpoke! Line up with the rest of them!" he snarled as he grabbed at Henry.

He might just as well have planned to kick a Texas Ranger in the ass because the ensuing results were just about the same. Whatever gave this cocky jerk the idea that he could push a cattle rancher the likes of Henry Mast around is something to wonder. Henry, in a low threatening growl, cursed him back:

"Don't you cuss me, you little sawed-off runt," responded Henry as he tossed the roasted quail aside in preparation of taking on the officer.

"Watch your step, mister! You're dealing with lawmen here! Back off!" warned the officer.

Disregarding the statement, Henry instantly grabbed at the officer with his right hand, thus ripping his shirt clean off him. In the ensuing scuffle, the officer's shoulder holster and supporting leather strappings remained in place, but his gun, having been jostled out of its holster, landed on the dirt floor alongside and somewhat behind the officer. The astounded lawman's first reaction was to retrieve his gun, and in so doing, turned and stooped to pick it up. At this instant Henry stepped forward, grabbed the officer by the seat of his pants with his right hand, the leather shoulder strappings with his left hand, and proceeded to heave the officer into the closest fermentation tank, much like he was used to heaving 180 pound bales of hay onto a wagon. For an instant, all that could be seen floating around in the tank was the officer's grey fedora hat.

Fats, not being too keen about assaulting a police officer, scrambled up on a stack of sugar sacks in hopes of rescuing the distressed officer. He reached into the mash, grabbed the coughing, sputtering officer, and hoisted him back out of the tank while another officer confronted Henry:

"Hey, hold it! What the hell's the matter with you? You can't assault a police officer!"

"I don't take to being cussed at!"

"Now, you listen to me, mister! Damn it, knock it off!"

"No, you listen to me! Don't you try it either!"

In the face of drawn guns, Henry put up little resistance in allowing himself to be handcuffed for he really had no quarrel with any of the others. He did plead his innocence in reference to the bootlegging operation, but it was to no avail; he was taken into custody along with the others. But his close family relatives, prominent residents of Oakland, had close ties with the mayor himself, and so arranged for his release with all charges dropped. Henry's response to inquiries as to the incident was always met in his customary humble manner, a grunt accompanied by a broad grin.

The officer in the tank incident did not show up in the officers' report, and neither did they admit to it even when questioned by the judge himself at the time of the preliminary hearing. The judge, Honorable Homer R. Spencer, having been apprised of the incident, put the question directly to Officer Blagborne:

"You did not see anybody swimming around in any of those?" (referring to the fermentation tanks)

Answer: "I didn't see anybody swimming around at all."

Question: "No dog swimming around in there?"

Answer: "No sir, no dog . . . did not see anything fall into them."

Officer Blagborne was lying like hell, and the amused judge knew it.

This time the raid on Mike's still had been staged without the Sheriff's Department having received advance notice. To the frustration of Sheriff Burton Becker, the District Attorney's investigators had once again made headline news. The Sheriff was well aware of Mike's ongoing moonshine operation in Crow Canyon, as well as the extent of it. He not only lost the credit for breaking up the gang, but also his monthly annuity payments which were now suspended—indefinitely.

At the hearing, Officer Blagborne, in answer to a posed question, proudly listed the array of equipment and supplies seized:

"Oh, yes. We entered the barn then and placed the defendants under arrest, and in the barn was two 50 gallon stills in operation; there were condenser cisterns, coils, and a two-set 5 ply burners, four gasoline pressure tanks, seven 1000 gallon tanks full of mash, one 1000 gallon tank full of water ready to set, four 1000 gallon tanks with a small amount of mash, one 500 gallon tank as a reserve tank—that was placed above the still so that they could pump the mash in the tank, this 500 gallon tank, then it would operate by gravity from there to the still; one length of one-inch hose, one 10 gallon receiving keg about half full of Jackass brandy—it was a receiving keg that was under the still to catch the whiskey when it came out of the still; one 50 gallon filter barrel half full of Jackass brandy; nine 10 gallon kegs full of Jack; seven 100 pound sacks of barley; one-gallon bottle two-thirds full of caramel coloring for coloring Jackass brandy; one carton containing fifty 1 pound packages of Peereless yeast; eight 50 gallon cans of gasoline; 18 empty 5 gallon cans; one 5 gallon can half full of coal oil; about 300 empty sugar sacks; five 15 gallon gasoline drums, empty; two hydrometers; two test tubes, one two-burner coal-oil stove; three coal-oil lanterns; two single beds, one table, one table lamp— "

Much to Sheriff Becker's disgust, the news media played up the raid. He had been scooped by the D. A.'s office once again.

Once the extent of the operation unfolded, the Court, under the direction of Honorable Judge Homer R. Spence, saw fit to raise the amount of bail on the three defendants. Attorney Lacey, for the defense, argued against it, besides wanting an extension of time. But the judge didn't trust Lacey. He knew him to be a liar and an extortionist in his own right, so refused.

CHAPTER 49

The ensuing trial proved to be somewhat of a disappointment to District Attorney Earl Warren. True, he had successfully broken up the supposedly notorious paesano bootlegging gang of Crow Canyon, but the head "Capo," Mike, the one he really wanted, once again slipped through his fingers. Deputy District Attorney Harry E. Styles, the prosecuting attorney, failed to tie him into the Habberney still (otherwise known as the Nunes still) as the owner, or for that matter, anything else related to it. Therefore, his name did not appear on the record applying to either the Habberney raid or the earlier chicken ranch raid.

Apparently Mike's attorney, Joseph P. Lacey, who proved to be as much an illegal scoundrel as a brilliant legal counsel, had been able to settle the earlier raid matter separately. A substantial fine was paid, along with large sums of money, distributed through Lacey, into the pockets of influential people, which kept the affair off the records. To be sure, most of the money went into Lacey's pocket along with his exorbitant fees. He no doubt also masterminded the eventual mysterious disappearance of court documents from the files that pertained to Mike. The inducement for the latter could be attributed to the confrontation, if not all-out savage argument, that took place between Mike and Lacey, and Al's threatening interference at the time of the on-going trial of the three defendants, Julio (alias Rossi), Fats, and Matteoli, also at Mike's expense.

The name M. Buti had been injected into the court hearings, but not by any of the defendants. They refused to identify Mike as the head capo of the organization. During the time that Julio was out on bail, he was visited on several occasions by the deputy district attorney prosecuting the case. Accompanied by an interpreter, an effort was made to get Julio to crack. They wanted him to point the finger at Mike as the head capo and owner of the still, rather than himself as he so insisted. They tried their damnedest to convince Julio that it should not be he taking the rap as the owner. Pressing him, they argued:

"Why be the fall guy when it is common knowledge that Mike Buti is the still owner and capo of the entire bootlegging organization?"

But their efforts were to no avail; Julio could not be budged. He was determined to be loyal to Mike.

Although neither one supposedly was a defendant, both Mike and Al attended the trial. As the hearings progressed, it was becoming apparent to both men that attorney Lacey, for whatever reason, was allowing Mike's name to be injected in the trial proceedings. The feeling was that his own attorney, Lacey, was in fact trying to double cross him, possibly to put himself in a better standing with Earl Warren by handing Mike over to him, so to speak. Lacey was aware that the District Attorney's office was on to his shady activities, extorting money from clients. For all Mike knew, Lacey may have already made a deal with Warren.

An argument between Mike and Lacey, in Al's presence ensued. It took place during an afternoon court recess at one end of the corridor in an out of the way area of the courthouse in Oakland. It turned out to be a heated three-way discussion. At the height of the fierce confrontation, Mike fired a question at Lacey:

"Why are you allowing my name to be brought up during the hearing? I'm not on trial! I'm not a defendant in this case!"

"Mike! You're forgetting the earlier raid at the chicken ranch!" came the sharp answer from Lacey.

"What are you talking about? That matter was settled! You told me so yourself!"

"Well, not exactly," stammered Lacey. "Mike, you see . . . "

Mike cut Lacey short with an angry outburst:

"What do you mean not exactly? I paid you a lot of money because you said you could settle it! Did you settle it? Or did you put the money in your pocket as usual!?"

Mike's friend, the judge, had forewarned that Lacey was a good criminal lawyer, but also warned that pocketing clients' money rather than putting it to its intended use, was Lacey's stock and trade. He had warned Mike not to trust him because, even though he was a clever lawyer, he was an outright extortionist as well.

"You're making some strong accusations, mister! I'd be careful about that, sir!" warned Lacey.

"Is that so! Well, let me tell you something, you goddamned crook!" retaliated Mike menacingly.

Al, stepping in closer, avoided a physical confrontation. But nevertheless, the two men were now engaged in a heated argument with Lacey demanding that Mike follow his instructions to the letter, and stating that he could expect to pay thousands of dollars more to buy himself out of this one. Mike now knew what his friend the judge meant when he mentioned the word "extortion." The judge had also reminded him that as it was with the Niles trial affair, District Attorney Earl Warren could not be bought under any circumstances, and to not allow Lacey to try to badger him into believing that it could be done. Any money paid for that purpose would only end up in Lacey's pocket.

Mike firmly, and to the point, let it be known to Lacey that he was not about to become another one of his long list of victims. The truth of the matter was, he already was. Lacey, thinking he could bluff him by using his position as legal counsel for the defendants, and by now well into the trial, threatened Mike with a terse statement:

"You'll do what I say! And you'll meet my demands! Or, I assure you, you will go to San Quentin!"

Mike was not to be pushed around or threatened. Controlling the rage within him, he responded accordingly, and to the point:

"No, Mr. Lacey! You will do what I tell you! Or you will go to San Quentin! And I am telling you to see to it that my name stays off the record! Do you understand . . . ?"

The two men were facing each other in a menacing manner with fierce looks in their eyes when Al distracted their attention by injecting his own statement. In a calm, but seriously threatening manner, he said to Lacey:

"Do what he says! How you do it, I don't care! Just do it! Or you may never leave this place alive! And if you do, you won't get very far; I'll catch up to you! Do you understand what I'm saying?? Mr. Lacey!!"

With a mouth-open, fearful expression of amazement, Lacey switched his attention from Mike to Al. He was well aware of his reputation in the use of motor vehicles, trucks or autos, to settle his differences with adversaries. Saying nothing in response, his look of cockiness gave way to an expression of nervous fear. He suddenly realized that in dealing with Mike, he would also have his henchman, Al, to content with. This he didn't like, so he'd best readjust his attitude.

Lacey had already instructed Matteoli to bring his wife and young boys into the courtroom. Now, he also instructed Fats Meehan to bring in his robust wife, along with her infant son, and for her to nurse the baby intentionally during the trial. She did this by hanging out her enormous breast in plain view of all present. The fat little baby slurped and nursed contentedly each day while the court was in session. The Honorable Homer R. Spence, the presiding judge, didn't mind it at all. However, Harry E. Styles, the presiding deputy district attorney handling the case opposing Lacey, did, but he couldn't do much about it. Lacey was taking advantage of the judge's good nature and sometimes sympathetic attitude towards the defendants, especially Matteoli and Meehan. As for Julio, alias Gelio Rossi, the judge knew damned well that he was Mike's employee, and not the head "Capo."

But since there was no evidence produced other than a 5 gallon barrel of Mike's finest well-aged, smooth sipping Jackass Brandy sitting on the evidence table, that had to be without question attributed to Mike's expertise in this field, there was nothing to tie him into the case.

Lacey argued that even at this point, the prosecutor had not produced anything other than an oak barrel as evidence that could, in fact, be used for almost anything other than an alcoholic beverage.

The judge interrupted the sparring that was going on between legal counsel, and asked a simple question:

"Is there . . . Jackass in that barrel? Has anyone . . . opened it to be sure?"

The answer was "No" to both questions.

"Well then, let's get it open and see what's in it," instructed the judge.

So the bung was tapped off the barrel and several coffee cups were brought into the courtroom. The judge came around the bench and approached the evidence table where the now open barrel sat. The contents were then poured from the barrel into the cups. As serious as this matter was, Mike and Al, seated to the rear of the courtroom, couldn't help but grin as the cups were passed around, beginning with the judge. The judge took a fair sip of the barrel's contents, hesitated while peering into the cup with a pleased expression, then commented to the prosecutor:

"Jesus, this is good stuff. Damned, it's the best Jackass I've ever tasted . . . unbelievable . . . here, try it."

The prosecutor also took a fair sip and concurred with the judge. Apparently these men were accustomed to drinking whiskey and could very well distinguish the difference between good whiskey and bad whiskey. The final comment by the judge before returning to the bench was:

"Boy, this Jackass is really good. At least they're not making poison like some of the others. This stuff sure as hell won't kill anybody."

The judge was no doubt referring to the many reports of poison liquor that were beginning to surface, especially the one report that had made headline news in just about all the newspapers across the country. In that incident, which occurred in New York City, 17 people were killed and 70 people hospitalized from drinking bathtub gin.

The judge slammed his gavel down on the bench and instructed the trial to proceed back on the record without the chatter and chuckles that had by now escalated to laughter.

Another point of interest was that defendant Meehan, a non-Italian, but somewhat versed in the Italian language, was allowed to act as interpreter for Julio and Matteoli throughout the entire trial. This would be like asking a mother to evaluate her own son. Since Julio and Matteoli would only speak in their native Italian language, and no one other than the spectators of Italian extraction could understand what the conversation was about, the Court really didn't know for sure if Meehan was actually translating accurately or not. But regardless, the questioning continued.

Meehan, using his wits, and if need be the excuse that he was not really all that well versed on the Italian language, was able to maintain through interpretation that Matteoli had just met Julio (alias Rossi) a few months before the raid. Therefore, he passed Matteoli off as a stranger to Julio, when in fact Julio and Matteoli were first cousins raised in the same small village on the outskirts of the City of Buti, Italy. They had also married two sisters and were therefore brothers-in-law as well. Misinterpretation was par for the course throughout the entire trial.

The judge had to be somewhat sympathetic in order to allow the trial to be conducted under such circumstances. But then, as it was in most of these bootlegging trials, the courts relied heavily on the testimony of the arresting officers rather than the immigrant principals. Nevertheless the three defendants were found guilty of violating Chapter 277 of the Statutes of 1927. The verdict was handed down on January 8, 1929.

Although his beloved paesani, along with Fats, had been convicted, Mike felt that attorney Lacey had done the best he could and, under the circumstances, was feeling lucky not to have been implicated himself. However, there were no congratulatory handshakes between Lacey, Mike or Al. Had Lacey reached out to shake Al's hand, he would no doubt have had it broken off at the elbow.

Satisfied that Matteoli and Meehan were only employees with no ownership in the still, and having already served some time in the county jail, both defendants were released on probation with fines imposed, which were paid on the spot. They received warnings to stay away from the bootlegging industry in the quest for jobs. Meehan was again called upon to interpret for the Court. From the Court:

(The defendant Meehan interpreting to the defendant Matteoli)

THE DEFENDANT MEEHAN. Yes. He says that he done wrong by going to work up there, your Honor, and he understands the penalty of it, from one to five years in San Quentin, and a thousand-dollar fine.

THE COURT. You ask him if he is given probation with a fine of $500.00, or a County Jail sentence of 100 days, and placed upon probation in addition, whether he thinks he can keep away from stills and obey the law in all respects.

THE DEFENDANT MEEHAN. He says, "No, your Honor, I won't go to work in those places any more."

COURT. And he will obey the law, will he?

THE DEFENDANT MEEHAN. (After interpreting) Yes, Your Honor.

THE COURT. I want you to know, Meehan, and I want you to tell Matteoli, that in the event there is any subsequent violation of the law, that neither in this court nor any other court will you be granted leniency in the way of probation. You understand that, do you Meehan? You tell that to Matteoli also.

THE DEFENDANT MEEHAN. (Interpreting to Matteoli) Yes, your

Honor, he said he understands that.

THE COURT. Both cases will be handled in the same manner, gentlemen; and, if there is no objection, the Conditions of Probation will apply in each case and will be read but once and imposed rather than reading them in the case of each defendant. No objection to that, Mr. Lacey?

MR. LACEY. None, your Honor.

Julio, who stuck with his alias, Gelio Rossi, and having been convicted as the still owner, was sentenced to serve three years in San Quentin, in addition to the fines that Mike also paid. Earl Warren knew very well that Julio was not the owner of the still; however, upon conclusion of the trial and sentencing, he had no choice but to submit his statement (dated March 4, 1929) accordingly; in part:

The above named defendant was convicted of the crime of a felony, to-wit, operating a still, and was thereafter on the 8th day of February, 1929, sentenced to San Quentin Prison for the period prescribed by law by Honorable Homer R. Spence, Judge of the above entitled court . . . .

Soon after being incarcerated, Julio's pleasant and likeable attitude earned him a trustee rating and was therefore put to work on the prison grounds as a gardener. It was a job he enjoyed. He was not the least bit depressed with his prison stay.

As for Mike, since in no way could he be tied to the still at the Habberney place, all reference to his possible involvement was struck from the records. This, of course, didn't please Earl Warren one bit. He let his feelings be known. Now more than ever before, Mike would have to watch his step. Any attempt to set up a major still in and around Bellina Canyon was out of the question, at least for the moment. Mike felt certain that sooner or later, Earl Warren's men would catch up to Jacklich and Santucci as well, since the flow of alcohol was still pouring out of the Bellina-Crow Canyon area.

CHAPTER 50

As predicted, the winter of '28-29 turned out to be extremely wet, thus making the road into Bellina Canyon practically impassable. While Mike, now shut down completely, was struggling with the ongoing trial of Julio, Matteoli, and Meehan, that could also implicate himself, the Jacklich brothers and their gang of Austrians at Tony's were struggling with the horrendous task of keeping their still operating, due to the difficulty of transporting supplies through axle-deep mud.

Their use of motorized vehicles came to an end when one of the brothers was bringing in a load of supplies over the muddy rutted road. Despite the use of chains, the Model T Ford truck slid off the slippery road, down an embankment, and up against a barbed wire fence in a tipped over position. The vehicle and its cargo had to be retrieved by using a team of Soares' draft horses. With the exception of Jacklich being sober, and Terzo being tipsy, the situation was not much different than the rescue of Terzo and his Model T Ford the winter before.

In his attempt to crawl out from under the truck, Jacklich slipped and slid down the steep embankment, ending up in the swollen creek below. Santucci's pig men, at Dutch Charley's directly across from the incident, having heard the commotion, fished the cursing, sputtering Austrian out of the muddy waters.

From that day on, the task of moving the Jacklichs' supplies in, and alcohol out, of the canyon fell to the Soares brothers with their horse-drawn freight wagons. But the constant tramping of teams of horses pulling heavily loaded freight wagons soon churned the road into a complete mass of mud. The section of road leading from Tony's old house and down across the creek to the still site located up in the gully especially lost its identity altogether. The creek itself had become a muddy, impassable, bottomless swampy bog. The use of wagons had to finally be abandoned completely. But the Austrians were determined.

For lack of available jackasses like those used at their Jackson still operation in Amador County, saddle horses, used as pack animals, were now being employed to transport sacks of sugar in, and 5 gallon tins of alcohol back out. This means of drayage continued until the accidental death of one of the overloaded horses with three cans of alcohol strapped on either side of the saddle. In trying to skirt the bog, and while struggling with the heavy load, the horse, knee-deep in mud, panicked, and in its thrashing frenzy, broke its neck. However, regardless of the hardship, the Austrians did keep the operation going by hand, carrying supplies and alcohol over stretched out planks, makeshift bridges, and lengthy alternate routes.

As for Santucci's bunch, the going was easier since the road into Dutch Charley's was somewhat level with no creek to cross. Whenever the rain would stop for a while, the swill trucks could move in and out of the still site without too much difficulty. Besides, their field of expertise, that is, the hog raising business, certainly qualified them for dealing with mud. Handling pigs in sloppy pens, with the exception of the squeal, was not much different than handling slippery, mud-splattered cans of alcohol.

So, putting Mike out of business had not really slowed down the flow of alcohol out of the Bellina-Crow Canyon area by much. Surveillance would have indicated that there was much activity still going on in and around Bellina Canyon that was not related to ranching. Truck loads of hay and stock feed (disguised alcohol, etc.) were forever present, while cows were grazed belly deep in spring grass, and sheep foraged on grass-carpeted hill-sides. The hills were green and lush, so why the need to continue hauling stock feed in and out of the canyon? A question never addressed, at least not for the moment.

Mike studied the situation carefully before deciding to start up again. The high costs of the recent trial, coupled with the large sums of cash his attorney, Lacey, had extorted from him, to say nothing of the money paid in the form of bribery to Fred C. Smith for Sheriff Becker's phony Becker organization fund, pretty well cleaned him out. And to start up again would certainly bring extortioner Smith back on the scene.

But Smith, finding himself faced with trying to collect from tough still operators such as the Jacklich brothers, who by now were big enough to push their own weight around, as were others that appeared on the scene touting submachine guns, got a little edgy. He didn't relish the idea of reaching out to grab a handful of bills from the hands of a person fondling a submachine gun. Besides, it became apparent that Warren was onto him. So, he headed for parts unknown, leaving behind his automobile business, and whatever else that could not be stuffed into a suitcase. District Attorney Warren was by now not only wise to and searching for Smith, but he was also onto Sheriff Becker, his deputies, and others. When instructed, Sheriff Becker refused, or at least purposely failed, to bring Smith in on a warrant, insisting that he did not know Smith's whereabouts, when in fact he was sending him money to satisfy his blackmail demands. The extortioner (Becker) had now become the extortionee. Sheriff Becker even went so far as to send Smith money through another one of his shady friends by the name of P. D. Gunness, so that Smith could make his escape from Los Angeles to Mexico and, hopefully, never return.

Having been apprised of the turmoil within the law enforcement agencies, and no longer having Smith to deal with, Mike took advantage of the situation. He immediately contacted trucker Silva and let it be known that he was in the market for a continuous still, along with its related equipment. Trucker Silva responded immediately by delivering him such a still. It so happened that the still delivered was one of Mike's own stills that was confiscated at the old Habberney place. It had been turned over to Silva for disposal, but instead, he salvaged it. Under the cover of darkness, the still was unloaded and paid for. Mike was pleased and content, that is until daylight disclosed the fact that it was his own still. The thought of having paid for it twice obviously didn't set too well with him. Nevertheless, he hauled it up to Waldies at the extreme end of Bellina Canyon and started moonshining again along with Jacklich and Santucci; however, on a much smaller scale than before. Since, for the most part, his gang of paesani were scattered, each going his own way, Al included, Mike was now operating as a small independent one-man operation, inconspicuously, in the shadows of the big boys, Jacklich and Santucci.

CHAPTER 51

Is was no mystery to the District Attorney as to why, after putting so many stills, large and small, out of business, the supply of liquor in the county was in fact on the increase rather than on the decline. He correctly concluded that Sheriff Becker was working in cahoots with big-time operators that were hauling in truckloads of alcohol, along with all sorts of related finished liquor products, from outside the county. Amongst them were the Jacklich brothers, who by now had major stills operating in about every county within overnight delivery of Alameda County. At least one prominent attorney from San Jose, a certain Louis King (as reported in newspapers), was also suspected of moving truckloads of alcohol into the county, under Sheriff Becker's protection.

These findings by Warren no doubt caused the need to shift some of his inspectors from the still operators to the task of building up a case against Sheriff Becker and his unholy associates, of which there were many. The investigation was to also include the gambling industry heavily concentrated in and around the now wide open district of Emeryville and San Pablo. Chinese lottery, slot machines, card rooms, and flamboyant prostitution was running rampant, with prostitution even extending to the streets. In the business district after hours any shadowed recessed doorway could very well be occupied by a long-legged whore carrying out her duties under the protection of a cop standing around up the street slapping his billy club in his hand to the rhythm of the action in the doorway.

Sheriff Becker and his deputies were now too occupied to fool around trying to outdo the District Attorney's squad of investigators. And since the investigators were now preoccupied with the gambling industry as well as bootleggers, it was thought, or at least assumed, that there was only token effort being put into the investigation of the corrupt law enforcement agencies such as the Sheriff's Department. But such was not the case. As yet, the newspapers had not been apprised of the D.A.'s ongoing investigation of the Sheriff's Department. So far reports were concentrating only on the activities surrounding the apprehension of bootleggers and still operators. Newspaper accounts of local alcohol and gambling related incidents was as much of interest to Earl Warren who played a major part in creating such news, as it was with the general public.

Front page news emitting from the Midwest and East Coast was also of interest and disturbing. Wholesale machine gun killings such as the Saint Valentine's Day Massacre in Chicago, followed by the disturbing news report from Washington shortly after, making inference to wholesale killings, was indeed disturbing. Many persons, civilians and federal agents alike, were becoming casualties in unbelievably large numbers over short periods of time. Local newspapers, as well as eastern papers, were hitting the streets with headline news displaying the words "Gang War" in large bold print, followed by accounts of gangland style slayings.

Killings were becoming commonplace, especially in incidents of hijackings. Terms such as "machine-gunned to death," and "riddled by bullets," were also being plastered all over the front page. To some extent even news of violence within families was also starting to crop up, all because of the excitement the criminal element was generating.

Alcohol-related casualties were by now becoming common-place amongst the civilian population even though many had nothing to do with its manufacture, or the enforcement of the laws pertaining to it. Drunken drivers were taking their toll of deaths on the nation's highways, narcotics were being used with increased frequency, and alcohol-saturated parties flourished throughout the county.

To meet the ever-increasing demand for alcohol, amateur backyard distillers, with no knowledge of chemistry, were putting together makeshift alcohol rectifiers in their endeavor to purify poisonous denatured industrial-grade alcohol, converting it from unfit to fit for human consumption grade. For the most part, few, if any, of these amateur entrepreneurs ever turned out a totally safe product. Other poisonous elements such as lead and zinc were used in abundance in the manufacturing of the stills, storage vats, and other related equipment that made up the various stages of these alcohol rectifying plants. Zinc and cadmium-galvanized metals used along with lead solder, including cyanide used in the metal plating process, when subjected to extreme heat and scorching, could create poisonous elements which had no place to go but into the alcohol.

Even without these added poisons, provisions in the distilling equipment to remove deadly fusel oil (alcohol by-product) from even normally good alcohol were seldom done. Many of these amateurs never even heard of it. Heavily laden with this poisonous fusel oil, the prolonged ingestion of this poorly rectified alcohol could cause death, and in many cases did. Or if not death, brain damage, bringing about sporadic insane conduct, impaired vision and total blindness.

This homemade product was often referred to as "bathtub gin," so called because it was stored in bulk in the bathtub so that in the event of a raid, the drain plug could be pulled and quickly dispersed down the drain. It was also stored in open containers that could be quickly poured into the toilet and thus flushed down the sewer.

Under Sheriff Becker's so-called protection plan, these amateur rectifying plants (stills) were allowed to keep right on functioning while turning out cheap but tainted alcohol.

No better example of the devastation wrought upon a community flooded with bad alcohol was the incident of the so-called "B Street Shootout" that took place in the city of Hayward, on the evening of September 16, 1929, when a certain citizen by the name of Vincent Cataldo apparently went berserk. The fire chief and two police officers responded to a concerned neighbor's call of an on-going severe family dispute within the Cataldo residence, which culminated with him firing a deer rifle in an upward direction, causing his wife to flee the premises. Within minutes of arrival, the officers engaged him in a discussion that escalated into a shooting match, leaving one officer mortally wounded and the other seriously injured.

Lack of understanding in dealing with such a mentally deranged person contributed to the two officers' misfortune. Even after Cataldo's capture, a real in-depth study into the true cause that may have distorted the man's sense of reasoning, and then triggered the crazed violent reaction within him, was not pursued diligently. Although never proven, simply because it was never pursued, bad alcohol was felt by many to be the contributing factor in triggering the man's erratic conduct.

During hearings that followed the incident, the question of insanity and drunkenness did surface, but not the question of mental illness, or brain damage, possibly brought about by the prolonged ingestion of poisonous alcohol. Everything possible was done to suppress this argument, primarily because of the nature of the uncalled for escalation of the incident that could prove embarrassing to the law enforcement agencies involved in this horrendous shootout.

Overreaction on the part of law officers, and to some extent arms-bearing citizens with the blessings of lawmen, that joined in on the shooting, should have been scrutinized rather than suppressed such as it was. There was no question that the sense of reasoning of the some 50 or so law officers that responded to the incident was affected by the "chase 'em down, shoot 'em up" mood of the times. They, too, suffered from emotional problems that to some extent altered their sense of reasoning. Once the shooting subsided, and Cataldo was finally taken into custody, at least some of the spectators that were not influenced by the times questioned the methods and reasoning of the lawmen, as well as the part played by a civilian shooter by the name of William Stebbins.

Realizing the mishandling of the whole affair, the powers that be, circulated conflicting and misleading statements in an attempt to justify everyone's conduct except the conduct of the suspect, Cataldo. He was portrayed as a "killer," as if it was a habit with him when, in fact, to the people who knew him well, he was a nice person.

The District Attorney's office, under the direction of Earl Warren, also influenced by the times, as was the Court, now had something really big and newsworthy to work on. The killing of a highly respected and popular police officer, George E. Vierria, had to be proven as a vindictive act by his killer regardless of the circumstances. The justice system drooled over their prize catch, an Italian immigrant, a Sicilian no less, caught red-handed in the act of having committed an unspeakable felonious killing.

Hearsay statements, regardless of which way they tended to lean, were used against the defendant. Those statements that depicted him as a reasonable, rational person, conducting his business in a normal manner, were used to prove his sanity. Those statements that depicted him as quarrelsome, quick-tempered, or displaying violent conduct, were used to prove the man's capability of killing. One can be sure that the justice system was to some extent being influenced by the fact that the defendant, Cataldo, came from the ethnic group called, "The Sicilians." It was common knowledge that many Sicilian family organizations had dominated the alcohol, narcotics, prostitution, gambling, or other equally illegal businesses. Mafia-controlled alliances were formed with some connections extending to families and organizations centered in old Sicily itself. They were so deeply entrenched in the Midwest and East Coast especially, that law enforcement agencies were incapable of stopping their rapidly expanding and escalating illegal activities. These activities also included outright murder.

But all Sicilians were not mafiosi. The word "mafia" was by no means a household word. The Italian population knew its true meaning, and therefore were very careful about how they used it, especially when insinuating that a fellow Italian was mafioso, or having mafia connections. The Italian bootleggers especially felt that Cataldo was being tried as a mafioso, which they were satisfied he was not. But the whole affair, right from the time the lawmen swooped in for the kill, had the earmarkings of an outright shooting war between organized crime and the law. Disposing of this one Sicilian was apparently being felt by the justice system as a crippling blow to the notorious mafia as a whole. The fact is that Cataldo was not even a bootlegger. True, he associated with and was in daily contact with alcohol distillers, but only from the standpoint of a chicken dealer. Since many of the chicken ranches were fronts for the makeshift stills, he was obviously knowledgeable about their bootlegging activities, as well as Sheriff Becker's extortion racket, but kept his mouth shut. It was never proven that he was anything more than a respected poultry dealer and buyer. However, he did have the misfortune of drinking too much of this cheap, tainted alcohol produced by inexperienced distillers operating out of chicken ranches. This fact most likely damaged his brain. He was also cursed or blessed, whichever way one cares to look at it, with the old Sicilian trait of maintaining no-nonsense family traditions. Total obedience by family members at all times was expected, and interference in family affairs by intruders was not permitted, not even by authoritative agencies.

The extensive investigation into Cataldo's past did not uncover any connection at any time to the mafia or to any other criminal activity. All that could be found was that one of his sons had stolen some chickens at one time or other and, therefore, was convicted of burglary. "Big deal!" While crooked law enforcement agencies, along with greedy politicians, were deeply engaged in extortion, conspiracy, and God only knows what else, the D. A.'s office made an issue about some family member stealing a few chickens. The chicken stealing matter by a family member should never have been allowed to surface. It was Cataldo senior that was on trial, not his eldest son. But apparently the prosecutor was seeking the sympathy of the many non-alcohol-related chicken producers in the area that were constantly losing chickens to chicken thieves. There were also many law-abiding citizens that didn't necessarily agree with the justice system's manner of handling the apprehension of Cataldo, so public opinion had to be swayed.

The news media's main source of information came primarily from authoritative persons who slanted the facts in their favor. However, there were many discrepancies, as seen by eyewitnesses, versus what was reported by authorities. To quote one newspaper article:

CRAZED POULTRY BUYER KILLS ONE OFFICER, WOUNDS ANOTHER, HOLDS POSSE AT BAY FOUR HOURS
Vincent Cataldo in County Jail After Night of Battling in B Street Home; Constable LaCunha Recovering from Wounds in Hospital; Mob Packs Streets Around Scene as Officers Assail Stronghold with Guns, Bombs and Streams of Water, Compelling Surrender of Slayer.

George E. Vierria, popular Hayward police officer, is dead, A. J. LaCunha, constable, lies in Hayward Central hospital with two bullet wounds, and Vincent Cataldo, aged about 70, poultry buyer of 1261 B street, is in the county jail and probably will be charged with the murder of Policeman Vierria, as the result of a gun battle which raged for four hours about the Cataldo home Monday night.

Cataldo surrendered to a posse of police of Hayward, Oakland and Niles shortly after midnight, his face and breast streaming with blood from numerous small wounds inflicted by a load of birdshot from a shotgun in the hands of Manuel Bernardo, deputy constable of Niles. During the four hours in which police sought to capture the apparently drink-crazed Cataldo, the Cataldo house was raked by fire from machine guns, shotguns, rifles and revolvers in the hands of the officers. A few houses nearby were struck by stray bullets and other projectiles whizzed over more distant portions of the city.

A huge crowd of men, women and children collected and filled the street in front of the house, despite the gunfire, running to shelter at an occasional alarm of "He's loose!". Some took shelter behind houses and trees. Searchlights played on the Cataldo home, in which the slayer of Policeman Vierria defied arrest. Excitement reigned supreme.

Near the end the officers tossed tear bombs into every room of the house and the members of the Hayward fire department, led by Fire Chief Manuel G. Riggs, turned water from two high-power hoses into the building, driving the slayer out into the yard to surrender.

The affair started about 8:30 o'clock when Cataldo, arriving home late, started firing a rifle, apparently in the course of a quarrel with his wife. He pursued her into the yard in rear of the house, firing six or seven shots into the air. Alarmed neighbors sent in a call to the firehouse.

Policeman Vierria, Constable LaCunha and Chief Riggs jumped into an automobile and quickly arrived in front of the building, which contained a storeroom on the first floor and the Cataldo living quarters on the second floor. All three got out of the car, Chief Riggs going to the house next door to talk to Mrs. E. N. Gay, who resides there.

Meanwhile Cataldo himself opened the window above the two officers, threatening to shoot if they interfered.

He menaced them with his gun as he spoke, and the officers returned to their car. One of them a few minutes later turned the searchlight of the car on the window where Cataldo was stationed, and the latter promptly opened fire.

His first shots struck Officer Vierria, one piercing the chest over the heart, and another breaking his right arm. Constable LaCunha immediately returned the fire but dropped with a bullet in the right shoulder and heart, and another breaking his right arm. Constable LaCunha immediately returned the fire but dropped with a bullet in the right shoulder and another in the left leg just below the hip.

Chief Riggs quickly sent in a general alarm to the fire station, whence it was relayed to the office of Sheriff Burton F. Becker and the Oakland police headquarters. About 50 officers from all parts of the state, in Oakland attending the annual convention of the California Sheriffs' and Peace Officers' association, answered the alarm.

Cataldo was known to be a drinker, but he wasn't staggering drunk when he was triggered into maniacal conduct, because if he was, he could not have sustained such deadly, accurate fire against his adversaries. It would seem that he was suffering from some sort of mental disorder. Both the question of drunkenness and insanity did arise, but not the question of mental illness, alcohol-related or otherwise. Brain damage from the ingestion of tainted alcohol that could cause sporadic insanity apparently was not that well understood.

Two medical experts called by the defense expressed the opinion that the defendant was insane at the time of the shooting incident, but apparently could not give the exact reason why. On the other hand, three medical experts called by the prosecution expressed the opinion that the defendant was sane at the time, no doubt basing their findings on hearsay more than anything else. Hearsay that was passed on to them by authorities with their slanted biased opinions.

Regardless, in each case the experts leaned all one way, either totally sane, or totally insane, nothing in between. Apparently the two experts for the defense were not in any way associated with the state insane asylum at Agnew, whereas the three medical experts for the prosecution were. They were so accustomed to dealing with totally insane and outright crazy people that anything short of having a totally blasted brain appeared normal to them. Since this involved the death of a popular and respected peace officer, they no doubt felt obligated to serve the justice system by giving it what it wanted. Besides, in this case, the system, to some extent, was their employer.

What was needed here was to have Cataldo examined and evaluated by an Italian medical expert educated in an Italian school of medicine. No doubt the first thing the medical expert would have done is to test Cataldo for lead poisoning, or some other kind of brain damaging poison. It was common knowledge amongst Italian medical doctors that lead poisoning contributed heavily to the sometimes erratic behavior and conduct of Caesar's court, considering they made a practice of pitting gladiators against each other in the midst of ferocious beasts. Then, to square things with the Al-

Since the jury was totally ignorant of such matters and alcohol-related madness was not an issue, it was convenient for them to go along with the court-appointed medical experts from Agnew. Because it was expected of them to do so.

So much incriminating hearsay was allowed to be injected into the hearings that to strike it from the record once it was heard became futile. The jury heard it, registered it in their minds, and therefore was influenced by it.

The fact that Cataldo had a quarrelsome disposition and quick temper doesn't necessarily make him a killer. Many people display these traits, especially when pushed around or taken advantage of. When convenient, the prosecutor portrayed the man as a savage, quarrelsome, madman killer, but then shifted to portraying him as a normally rational man to offset the defense's argument of insanity coupled with drunkenness.

The prosecution, in its attempt to portray Cataldo as totally sane, no doubt assumed that in Sicily, it was common practice for a Sicilian husband to chase his wife around the house while firing bullets from a high-powered rifle through the ceiling. This kind of conduct could hardly be construed as a love ritual, even for a Sicilian, as romantic as they are. Other than fellow Italians, none of the authorities at whatever level, or for that matter the jury itself, understood Sicilian tradition.

Cataldo, in a normal state of mind, would not have shot at the police car or the officers, or for that matter, through the ceiling of his house. It was obvious that something snapped within him right from the time he first picked up the rifle. For whatever reason, his mind was shattered and stayed that way throughout the entire ordeal, including the trial that followed.

His conduct was too apparent to be totally ignored. He did have a verbal confrontation with the police officers and did fire at or in the direction of the police car, but did he truly, rationally, premeditatedly intend to kill them, or just run them off? Cataldo had not armed himself for the sole purpose of shooting the officers. He was already displaying the gun while firing shots through the ceiling long before the officers arrived. Neither was he intentionally trying to attract them to the scene so that he could shoot them. If that were the case, he would have shot them immediately upon arrival instead of trying to send them away. He even referred to them as his friends. Under these circumstances alone, how could anyone arrive at the conclusion of premeditation?

One report stated that the officers used a flashlight to light up the open window Cataldo was standing at while the verbal discussion was in progress. What the report did not say was that the officers then turned on the patrol car's spotlight, directing the powerful beam through the front window of this old Victorian house, thus fully illuminating Cataldo standing at the window. To do this, the officer had to be standing alongside, if not in, the car, in order to manipulate the spotlight. This meant that in no way could the officers have been illuminated in the total darkness since they had to be behind the spotlight's blinding beam. Cataldo was without question instantly blinded when the light flashed in his face. In his state of mind, half-crazed as he was, he undoubtedly interpreted this act as a threat upon himself, and therefore opened fire through the window.

The question is, at what? The car or the police officers? With the light beam blinding him and with them standing behind the source of light, he could hardly see the officers, if at all. A normal reaction in a situation like this would be to shoot out the light, especially if he had been fired upon first—something that was never proven, one way or another. This could have been what he was intending to do, but in so doing, the act brought about return fire, if in fact he did fire the first shot. Once the shooting started, it continued until the return fire subsided; a sure sign that the threat had been put to rest.

Firing upon a police car, police officers, or for that matter, anyone else, was wrong. Had Cataldo been in a normal, rational frame of mind, he would have opted to retreat back away from the window, but then had he been normal and sane, he would not have fired his rifle throughout the house and yard in the first place.

Questions lingered on people's minds: "Was flashing the spotlight in Cataldo's face an intentional act of provocation on the officer's part? Did they do this with the intent to shoot him? Did Cataldo beat the officers to the draw? Did he outgun them?" Sane or insane, drunk or sober, one must understand Sicilian tradition. A Sicilian is not about to walk away from a fight that is brought to his doorstep.

Upon arrival of the Hayward police chief, Cataldo was ordered to surrender immediately and remove himself from the premises in the chief's custody. The chief's demand was proper and Cataldo should have complied, but again, one must understand Sicilian traits and traditions. In his frame of mind especially, he was to hold his ground. This was his home, his sanctuary. Within the confines of his domain, he was sole master. Intruders interfering in his private family affairs, lawmen or otherwise, were not welcomed under any circumstances.

Being in such an unstable, unreasoning state of mind and since there was no one but himself left in the house, his plea to be left alone should have been granted. The area should have been cleared of all personnel with the exception of posting guards out of line of fire to give the man time to think things out. Many civilians on the scene felt that to be the proper thing to do, but the mood of the times was to shoot first and ask questions after.

So the chief put in an urgent call to Sheriff Burton Becker who happened to be hosting some 50 or so lawmen attending a peace officers convention in Oakland. He and his fellow lawmen responded to the last man. They rallied to the frantic call to arms. They were not about to miss out on this one opportunity of a lifetime—gun down a supposedly notorious gunman, a cop killer at that.

What the chief should have done even before the shooting started was to enlist the services of the local priest rather than an army of gunslingers. Sicilians are religious people and where they may not heed the demands of a mortal being, they do seek guidance from and do heed their immortal God.

What harm could have come by having a priest, God's representative, with rosary in hand approach Cataldo while repeating a fair ration of the Lord's Prayer and Hail Marys? In the course of making his way up the front steps of the old Victorian house, the priest would no doubt have been inter-mittently thrusting and shaking his aspergillum ahead of himself, sprinkling holy water in the act of blessing the whole affair. An appropriate ritual since the congregation of attending lawmen were hell-bent on culminating the af-fair in Cataldo's funeral. A little spillover of blessings may have also pen-etrated through the hard shell of the lawmen so eagerly intent on drawing blood rather than exercising reasonable understanding.

Cataldo would not have shot at a priest any more than did he shoot at the four firemen, Fire Chief Riggs, Mendonca, Brieto, Silver, or Dr. Whetstone, who, accompanied by the firemen, went to the two wounded officers' aid. They did not pose a threat to him such as the two officers had, so he had no reason to shoot at them. Another indication that his intent was not to kill for the sake of killing.

Being surrounded by what appeared to be a lynch mob, some 50 armed lawmen, backed by a mass of civilians, some armed as well, was not condu-cive to a peaceful surrender. If it was Cataldo's desire to just plain shoot people without just cause, he could have had a field day. Like a tight bunch of quail, he could have flock-shot the whole lot of them.

The army of lawmen had the firepower at their disposal and were eager to use it. They expressed little patience nor did they exercise understanding and sympathy for the mentally deranged Cataldo. They opened fire with everything they had, sending bullets of every caliber imaginable whizzing through the upper floor of the old Victorian house. Bullets penetrated the house from every angle and direction. Those men firing on opposite sides of the house were endangering the lives of each other as high-powered rifle bullets, having passed clear through the wooden house, whizzed and whined in a ricochet pattern over each other's heads, and into and over the tops of adjoining houses.

The whole affair had become a free-for-all fun thing with gun-wielding civilians joining in on the shootout. The house in general was the target rather than the person in it. If asked, it would have been doubtful if anyone of these idiots on the firing line could have intelligently answered the simple question: "Why are you shooting at that old house?" The logical answer would have no doubt been: "Why not? Everybody else is shooting at it."

During the concentrated fire, a contingency of submachine gun experts gained access to the lower ground level portion of the two-story house. Luckily for them, they weren't shot in the back by their own colleagues. Since no one could be sure as to whether or not blood had yet been drawn, and blood is what everyone wanted to see, this possibility was not as remote as one might think.

Once having gained this vantage point, the submachine gunners worked in pairs punching holes up through the upper floor in a zigzag pattern. They moved back and forth from one side to the other while holding their chattering submachine guns in front of them in a vertical firing position. The maneuver sent a steady stream of bullets coming up through the floor forcing Cataldo to dance the Tarantella to dodge the upcoming bullets, as well as the horizontal pattern of lead that was chewing up the walls around him. Through shattered windows, Cataldo could at times be seen skipping and dancing in his efforts to stay out of the submachine gun's zigzag pattern of deadly fire.

However, even in his half-crazed state of mind, he was able to reason that the lead slugs working their way towards him would not penetrate the cast iron bathtub. So that is where he took refuge. He lay in the bathtub, at times praying, while the concentration of submachine gun fire was all but reducing the house to splinters.

Finally, while kneeling in the bathtub, he was shot in the head by a non-fatal charge of birdshot from a 12-gauge shotgun. The person to draw first blood was a shotgun-wielding, suede-shoed automobile salesman by the name of William Stebbins. He was a civilian that should never have been allowed near the place with or without his shotgun. The shotgun shooting by a civilian was so bizarre that a coverup was attempted by first declaring the suspect Cataldo was shot by Deputy Constable Manuel J. Bernardo. But too many people knew otherwise, so the story was then changed to shooter Stebbins standing alongside Deputy Bernardo when the shot was fired, making it appear that Stebbins had Bernardo's blessings in the matter. That version raised another question: "Why, if the two men were standing side by

342

side, did the deputy allow or instruct the civilian to do the shooting? Why not he, the deputy, do the shooting since he had the authority to do so, whereas the civilian did not?" Besides, from ground level, neither one could possibly see into the bathroom on the upper floor of the house.

The truth of the matter was, Deputy Bernardo was not standing alongside or near civilian Stebbins when the crucial shot was fired. Stebbins had correctly concluded that Cataldo was avoiding being hit by having taken refuge in the cast iron tub. He shared his findings or thoughts with no one, but instead, at the risk of being shot dead by Cataldo, made his way into a neighboring back yard, climbed up a tree overlooking the upstairs bathroom window, and seeing Cataldo kneeling in the bathtub, fired his shotgun, hitting the kneeling man in the head with a charge of birdshot. The shooter's intent was to kill the praying man outright. Not only did Stebbins have no authority to commit the act of shooting, but neither could he be sure that the man he had shot was indeed a person having committed a crime. What Stebbins' shooting act boiled down to was, Cataldo had been judged, convicted, sentenced, and nearly executed by a suede-shoed automobile salesman, all in the space of minutes. At best, an embarrassing disgrace to have allowed a civilian to shoot a man while in the act of praying. However, the whitewash attempt didn't stick; eventually William Stebbins told it as it was.

Amongst the bootleggers, speculation had it that Sheriff Burton Becker may have had something to do with auto man Stebbins appearing on the scene with a shotgun, intent on killing Cataldo in order to shut him up.

It was a well-known fact amongst the bootleggers that certain automobile dealers were deeply involved in the Sheriff's extortion racket. Although the shotgun blast failed to kill Cataldo, it most certainly got the message across, because once in custody he chose not to say or offer anything that might implicate anyone with the alcohol rectifying industry, not even to aid in his own defense. Rather, his courtroom appearances were punctuated with insane maniacal outbursts even to the extent of nearly severing his own defense counsel's thumb in a savage animal-like biting rage.

Nevertheless, a verdict of premeditated first degree murder was handed down, based on much slanted hearsay evidence depicting him as a bad man, when in fact those that knew him well felt him to be a nice man.

The justice system's attempt to brand Cataldo as a Sicilian mafioso or to uncover some past criminal activity failed. So the next best thing was to have the record specifically show where he came from:

Defendant was born June 13th, 1868, at Palermo, Sicily. He came to the United States in May, 1889 through New York. He married a woman who was a native of the state of California.

The District Attorney's and the judge's statement made it a point to clearly state that Cataldo was a native of Sicily, portraying him as a Sicilian from Sicily, which was true, but with no mention of his being an Italian from Italy. A man from a place rather than a country.

Having been found guilty of murder in the first degree, a harsh sentence was handed down based as much on what he might do in the future as opposed to the actual crime committed:

At the time that sentence was pronounced by Judge Spence, the Judge declared, as will be noted in the proceedings on sentence, that in his opinion by reason of the character of the defendant and the nature of the crime the defendant should not be granted parole. The District Attorney concurs in this recommendation to the Board of Prison Directors believing that the defendant is the type of person who, if allowed to regain his freedom would unquestionably murder other persons with whom he might come in conflict. The defendant's attitude over a period of years as proven at the time of the trial was one of defiance of law and order and to authority in general.

The sentence: life imprisonment without the possibility of parole.

CHAPTER 52

District Attorney Earl Warren finally concluded that in order to remove the criminal element from the county of Alameda, he must also remove the criminal element from the law enforcement agencies within the county. The Sheriff's Department, being the most blatant of the offenders, became the main target of the D. A.'s special investigators. By the end of 1929, enough information had been gathered and evidence put together to present a stunning report to the Grand Jury. In turn, the Grand Jury's report signified the scope and extent of the graft machine having been organized and run by one Burton F. Becker, Sheriff of Alameda County. The names that cropped up as fellow conspirators in some way connected with the fraud machine and/or Becker's activities were quite impressive. To name a few: Four of his deputies—Shurtleff, Davis, Collier, and Parker; at least two prominent attorneys—Ormsby and King; civilians and businessmen—Smith, Norman, Garbutt, Gunness, Vierra, Ramsey, Lamberson, and Batch; plus a few other shady characters of lesser importance.

The Gardellas, prominent Livermore bootleggers, although victims more than fellow conspirators, also got caught up in the D.A.'s dragnet. True, they did solicit and act as a go-between in the Sheriff's extortion racket, but did not share in any of the bounty. In fact, since they were ordered to do so, "or else," it could be said that they, in effect, were acting on behalf of the law—following orders, so to speak. Besides, bribes are bribes, whether in the form of special services being offered, as with the Gardellas, or as with the bootleg and gambling industry that was paying in the form of cash. So why come down hard on the Gardellas, and not the rest of the bribe payers? Somewhere along the line, Frank did get dropped, but not Jack. He had to stand trial along with the real crooks, the Sheriff and his deputies who forced him into the extortion racket. They wielded so much power that Judge E. W. Eng, who would not let any of the accused off the hook, mysteriously disappeared after denying a direct verdict for acquittal, which could mean that judges were not immune to harassment and/or threat either.

In total, 56 witnesses, including many of the accused, were examined by the Grand Jury before rendering a final 13-count indictment consisting of 25 pages, against Sheriff Burton F. Becker alone. The indictment was handed down February 28, 1930, asking for removal of Sheriff Becker from office.

In addition to the Grand Jury's indictment, Earl Warren, over his signature, issued a two-count indictment of his own, consisting of 10 pages and citing nine overt acts. In effect, it was a condensed version of the Grand Jury's indictment, with the exception that the Grand Jury did cite a letter of authorization having been given to Fred C. Smith, the one known automobile dealer, by Sheriff Becker establishing Smith as a confidential operator operating directly under the Sheriff's direction.

In Earl Warren's condensed version, he also included Attorney Cromwell L. Ormsby's and Deputy John L. Davis's activities as conspirators with about the same qualifications as Smith. Of at least some 15 or so upper-echelon conspirators that made up the fraudulent ring associated with Becker, with the exception of Gardella, who was not really one of them, none were Italians. Earl Warren had taken a flock shot, so to speak, and nailed the whole lot of them, all birds of a feather. The final result, for the most part, resulted in the Sheriff and his conspirators being convicted of extortion-related conspiracy and bribe charges, thus ending up in San Quentin to serve out their jail terms.

The seven-page statement by the District Attorney dated September 26, 1930, as it pertained to the defendant Deputy A. R. Shurtleff, with the exception of Shurtleff receiving a bribe in the form of an automobile, was worded pretty much the same as it was with the other deputy defendants.

The Sheriff of Alameda County, Burton F. Becker, finally got the news media recognition he had been striving for. Needless to say, it was not to his liking. By the time he passed through the steel gates of San Quentin to serve his sentence, Cataldo, the man Sheriff Becker purportedly (believed by the bootlegging community) tried to have killed in the Hayward shootout incident by his co-conspirator, the shotgun-wielding car salesman Stebbins, was already seasoned to the rigors of prison life. Becker would soon learn to respect Sicilian tradition.

Of the various lengthy indictments handed down by both the District Attorney and Grand Jury prior to the trials of the conspirators, and the statements of the District Attorney and the judges at the conclusion of the trials, the one statement dated September 26, 1930, as it pertains to Deputy Shurtleff, brings the whole of the conspiracy into focus as to who did what and more or less when, with the exception, for whatever reason, of the name of the still owner (Mike) in Bellina Canyon who paid Smith the $500 (and then some). To wit:

Statement of District Attorney and Judge

The defendant, A.R. Shurtleff, was charged along with John J. Collier,

John L. Davis and Jack Gardella, in an indictment containing four counts. The first count charged a violation of Subdivision 1 of Section 182 of the Penal Code, to-wit, conspiracy to violate Section 68 of the Penal Code, that is, conspiracy to ask and receive bribes. The second, third and fourth counts charged the defendants with receiving bribes from certain alleged bootleggers.

The defendant, A.R. Shurtleff, along with defendants John J. Collier, John L. Davis and Jack Gardella, was convicted by verdict of jury on the first count and acquitted on the second and fourth counts. The third count was dismissed on motion of the District Attorney.

The defendant, A.R. Shurtleff, along with defendants John J. Collier, John L. Davis and Jack Gardella, was sentenced on June 12, 1930, by Judge Lincoln S. Church, under the first count of the indictment, to the State Prison at San Quentin, as prescribed by law.

The facts of the case are substantially as follows:

The defendant, A.R. Shurtleff, was made chief criminal deputy by Burton F. Becker when the latter became Sheriff of Alameda County in January, 1927. Previous to that time the defendant Shurtleff had been a Federal prohibition agent or officer. As chief criminal deputy, Shurtleff was in charge of the investigation and raiding of bootlegging and gambling places and of law enforcement generally. Directly under him, in the same department or squad, and subordinate to him, were the defendants Collier and Davis. John L. Collier was a hold-over from the regime of Sheriff Barnett, and had been a deputy sheriff in the Sheriff's office of Alameda County for about twenty years. Mr. Collier was assigned to work with and travel around the county with Davis. The defendant Davis had been desk sergeant under Becker in the Piedmont Police Department when Becker was chief of that department. When Becker took office as Sheriff of Alameda County, he took the defendant Davis with him.

Among others to whom Becker gave important positions in the Sheriff's office at that time was one William H. Parker, who, like Becker, Shurtleff, Collier, Davis and other of their intimate associates, is not an inmate of San Quentin Prison.

About a month or six weeks after Becker's inauguration as Sheriff, the defendants Davis and Collier called upon one Fred. C. Smith at the latter's automobile agency in San Leandro. Smith was very close to Becker and was one of his collectors of bribe money. On this occasion Davis, in the presence of Collier, broached a proposition of collecting bribes for bootleggers in return for protection from the Sheriff's office. Smith agreed to the proposition and was taken by Davis and Collier to Livermore where Davis, in the presence of Collier, introduced Smith to Jack Gardella and Frank Gardella, stating at that time that Smith was the closest man in the county to the Sheriff and the one with whom to do business.

Jack Gardella and Smith discussed bootlegging conditions and an agreement was reached whereby the Gardellas were to pay $75.00 a month for protection. After Collier had left the room Davis suggested that if Jack Gardella had any other bootlegger friends around Livermore he could extend them the same proposition. Jack Gardella said he would talk to them. The $75.00 was divided between Smith, Davis and Collier, each receiving $25.00.

Subsequent to this occasion, Smith called upon Jack Gardella and the latter handed him two envelopes containing bribe money from two other bootleggers in Livermore. One envelope contained $25.00 and the other $50.00. Jack Gardella introduced Smith to another bootlegger named Croce in Livermore, and the latter agreed to pay, and did, Smith $50.00 and $75.00 a month for protection from the Sheriff's office. Croce introduced Smith to a bootlegger at the Livermore Hotel who agreed to pay, and did pay, Smith either $25.00 or $35.00 a month for protection. Other bootlegging places, among them Schenone's, Ma Fiscus', Sweeney's Restaurant, and Santa Rita Inn, received protection from the Sheriff and paid a certain amount each month to Smith for this protection. The bribe money thus received by Smith was divided as follows: 25% to Davis, 25% to Collier, 25% to Smith and 25% to the Becker organization fund. The collection of these bribes by Smith and the division thereof with Davis and Collier, went on for several months, to-wit, from February, 1927, to August, 1927, at which time Smith left Alameda County.

The defendant Shurtleff participated in the conspiracy in the following manner: Defendant Davis told Smith that Shurtleff would have to be cut in on the graft money, and suggested that it be done by Shurtleff purchasing an automobile from Smith and by having Smith take the monthly payments on the automobile out of the graft money collected. Pursuant to this proposition Shurtleff did buy a car from Smith and the latter took the monthly payments on the car out of graft money which he collected. Cancelled checks signed by Mr. and Mrs. Smith, payable to the Commonwealth Acceptance Corporation, a finance company, and other records of this finance company, together with the testimony of one of its executive officers, corroborate the testimony of Mr. and Mrs. Smith, and showed that Mr. Smith did make the payments on the Shurtleff car which was purchased shortly after the beginning of the conspiracy. It was proved also by documentary as well as oral evidence that, contrary to the strict rule of the finance company, the duplicate contract and notices of payments due were sent to Smith, the seller, instead of to Shurtleff, the buyer.

Jack Gardella, after collecting one payment of $50.00 from Duarte, a bootlegger, continued to collect $25.00 a month from another bootlegger in Livermore, all of which he turned over to Smith, and in turn divided it with Collier and Davis. Jack Gardella continued to pay $75.00 a month to Smith, and there was evidence to the effect that he continued to pay bribes to the Sheriff's office for protection of his bootlegging business after Smith had left Alameda County.

Smith collected $500.00 for the protection of a still in Bellina Canyon, which money was likewise divided 25% to Davis, 25% to Collier, 25% to Smith and 25% to the Becker organization fund.

A Mr. Cromwell L. Ormsby, attorney at law, and one of Becker's graft collectors, collected $3,000.00 a month from Manuel Pisani in return for protection from the Sheriff's office for a still owned and operated by Pisani, John Tognotti and Oreste Santucci on the Santucci Ranch near Russell City in Alameda County. Pisani and Santucci testified that the defendant Davis was present in Ormsby's office and a part to the conversation when this protection was promised, on which occasion David assured them of the protection from the Sheriff's office. Pisani testified that on one occasion, when he called at Ormsby's office to confer with Ormsby about the protection, he saw and talked to the defendant Collier.

Mr. Ernest Q. Norman testified that he was associated in business in 1927 with a Mr. Jack Garbutt, who is now in San Quentin; that he was present at a conversation between Garbutt and Davis, in which Davis stated, among other things, that the lotteries were running in the County; that they were anxious to get started in the city; that Davis stated he wanted them, Garbutt and Norman, to meet Ormsby, who was the attorney for the Chinese lotteries, so that they could help Ormsby in getting protection for the lotteries in the City of Oakland. Norman testified that subsequent thereto, in July, 1927, Davis and Collier took Garbutt and himself to Ormsby's office and introduced them to Ormsby for the purpose of discussing and arranging said protection.

Norman testified that on various occasions he and Garbutt discussed bootleg protection with Davis; that Davis proposed a plan whereby all the alcohol could be handled through one source and whereby the Sheriff's office would give this source protection and would knock over all the bootleggers who did not buy through this source; also that the smaller bootleggers who bought from the one source were to pay protection money to the head of the alcohol ring, who in turn would pay it to Garbutt; the latter, after taking ten per cent for his efforts, was to turn over the money so collected to Davis.

A short time later Mr. Davis introduced one Pi Vierra to Garbutt and to Norman as the man who was to be the head of the alcohol ring, and for the purpose of having Vierra, Garbutt and Norman work out the details and put the plan into operation. Vierra accepted the proposition and paid Garbutt $1,000.00 at the outset for the privilege and the distinction of being the head of the ring. This money was to be paid to Davis.

Norman also testified to a conversation with Davis regarding protection being extended and arranged for slot machines belonging to the Mills Novelty Company; that Davis said the Mills Novelty Company was running slot machines in the county and wanted to get into the City of Oakland, and that they were willing to pay for the privilege; that Davis said they ought to pay $10,000.00 cash down for the privilege, plus ten per cent of the earnings of the machines. A few days later a Mr. Ramsey, of the Mills Novelty Company, paid Garbutt $5,000.00 as one-half of the initial $10,000.00 payment for the privilege of operating slot machines with protection in the City of Oakland.

In November, 1927, Davis arranged for Garbutt and Norman to meet a bootlegger in Emeryville named Botch for the purpose of having Botch obtain alcohol from a still in Santa Clara County and run it into Alameda County. The plan, according to a conversation between Davis, Garbutt and Norman, was for Garbutt and Norman to put Botch in touch with the operator of the still and for the Sheriff's office to give protection on the transportation in Alameda County. Garbutt and Norman met Botch pursuant to an appointment made by Davis, discussed the proposition with them and directed the beginning of this phase of the conspiracy.

Part of the plan as expressed by certain members of the conspiracy to bootleggers and still operators from whom they were collecting or trying to collect bribe money, was to knock over all the small bootleggers and still operators who would not or could not pay, leaving only a few big stills operating in the county, thus concentrating the source of supply and enabling those who were paying to charge and receive higher prices for their liquor.

There was abundant proof and ample corroboration of the charges contained in the indictment. Undoubtedly Burton F. Becker, shortly after taking office as Sheriff in January, 1927, inaugurated a vicious system of graft, country-wide in scope, having for its object the collection of bribe money from bootlegging and gambling interests in return for protection.

It should be said on behalf of the defendants Collier, Davis, and Shurtleff, that they were merely aiding Becker to put into effect and carry on this system of extortion.

With reference to defendant Jack Gardella, it should be said that he likewise became a victim of the system and a cog in the machine in order to keep from being put out of the bootlegging business. The only difference between him and the other bootleggers who were paying protection was that in the beginning he aided in the conspiracy by collecting from two bootleggers on a few occasions and by introducing Smith to Croce and Duarte. Jack Gardella did not share in any of the bribe money received by Smith or other members of the conspiracy.

Burton F. Becker and Cromwell L. Ormsby were both tried and convicted for their part in this country-wide conspiracy, and particularly with reference to the receipt of bribes from Chinese lottery operators. The defendants Davis and Cromwell L. Ormsby were charged in an indictment in connection with bribes received and protection promised to Manuel Pisani, John Tognotti and Oreste Santucci. These latter charges, however, were dismissed because of the fact that both Davis and Ormsby had already been convicted in other cases.

For statistical facts with reference to defendant A.R. Shurtleff see copy of probation officer's report hereto attached.

Respectfully submitted,

EARL WARREN
District Attorney,

by J.F. Coakley, Assistant

DATED: September 26, 1930,

I hereby approve the foregoing statement and adopt the same as the statement of the Judge.

/s/ Lincoln S. Church
Judge of the Superior Court

Jack Gardella, being tried along with the three deputies, Shurtleff, Collier and Davis, didn't stand much of a chance of getting an acquittal. Of the four counts in the indictment, he was convicted of the one count that did send him to prison along with the deputies. However, counsel for the defense, L. A. Sullivan, was convinced that at least Gardella was getting a raw deal, and therefore appealed. A new trial was granted, but again, it pertained to all four defendants; a tough situation to get one defendant split out of the group.

However, District Attorney Earl Warren, in all fairness, motioned to dismiss Jack Gardella on the grounds of insufficient evidence. So in furtherance of justice, Jack Gardella was discharged, but not the others. Their convictions were affirmed. They went back to prison.

CHAPTER 53

By the early thirties, putting bootleggers out of business and into jail had lost much of its popularity. This was especially true since by now many bootleggers like Mike whose lucrative enterprise had been reduced down to nothing more than a home occupation were struggling to keep a family fed through the tough economic times that prevailed. The nation as a whole was experiencing a severe depression.

The citizens of Alameda County expressed greater pleasure in seeing the likes of Becker and his gang of crooks put behind bars than they did bootleggers. Also, the public relished the idea of Warren hitting hard against his own lawyer colleagues that chose to flaunt the law as it pertained to them. Apprehending and convicting criminals of prestige, as in his own profession, is what the public wanted to see, especially a crooked criminal lawyer who preyed on poor hapless immigrants, fleecing them out of their meager possessions or the few hard-earned dollars they managed to set aside in a fruit jar. Now this was the kind of news Warren's constituents wanted to hear.

Earl Warren didn't have to look far or wait long to come across such a scoundrel. None other than Mike's own attorney, Joseph P. Lacey, was now his target. He had been under investigation all along, and no sooner was the Becker case resolved, then Lacey, on September 17, 1930, was indicted by the Grand Jury on a score of counts equal in number to Becker's.

The first trial started on November 3, 1930, with a second trial commencing on January 19, 1931. By now numerous subpoenas were issued bringing forward an unbelievable parade of witnesses that defendant Lacey had victimized over the years. Once the door was opened, his many victims stepped forward to testify; that is, all but Mike. Although it had cost him a staggering sum of money, much of it ending up in Lacey's pocket, he was not about to step out into the limelight again. Besides, once Al had adjusted attorney Lacey's attitude, dago style, Mr. Lacey had in fact done a fair job of defending Meehan and Matteoli who got off on immediate probation, and Julio who was to serve only one year of his sentence in San Quentin, and was now out serving a one-year probation period.

As with the Becker case, Mike was now following the Lacey case through the news media. Up at the Waldie ranch at the extreme end of Bellina Canyon, he sat back in an old beat-up discarded sofa chair, puffing away at the

353

endless task of keeping his Toscanello cigar going, and read the many newspaper reports as the trial progressed. As he read the news, he would give an occasional glance towards the still as it percolated along, sending alcohol vapors up through the cap and into the cooling coil, then back down again in the form of condensed "alcohol." He was not only grinning at the constant dripping sound of the alcohol as it slowly filled the container below, but was also grinning over the news he was hearing of the achievements of Earl Warren in prosecuting Lacey. Both were music to his ears.

Assistant District Attorney J. F. Coakley, by now well seasoned, did a superb job of prosecuting attorney Lacey. The justice of the superior court, the Honorable Stanley Murray, showed no mercy or leniency in dealing with defendant Lacey. Judge Murray listened to his final and last comments in reference to his, Lacey's own, conduct, then cut him short with a sharp, to-the-point assessment of his disgraceful conduct, along with a firm reprimand that abruptly ended the whole matter. Considering the array of common, ordinary citizens who had been bilked, the judge had no qualms about imposing a stiff sentence upon a person of his own profession.

District Attorney Earl Warren then issued an elaborate statement, citing the various offenses committed by Lacey that were undoubtedly premeditated and prearranged as if practicing law itself was a sideline to the main business of extortion.

Excerpts of Statement of District Attorney and Judge

The evidence introduced at the first and second trials was substantially as follows:

With reference to the charge in indictment number 11610, the evidence showed that Manuel Perry and his wife, Mary Perry, went to the defendant, who was a practicing attorney in the City of Oakland, when they were sued in a civil action upon an old grocery bill in the amount of Sixty-six Dollars in which action their Ford automobile had been attached. They were referred to Mr. Lacey by a Philip Wagner who had become acquainted with them endeavoring to sell them a lot. Mr. Lacey upon being consulted by them represented to them that he had to have One Hundred Dollars for the purpose of putting up a bond to release their automobile from attachment; that in a short time they would get this One Hundred Dollars back. In the course of his conferences with the Perrys the defendant discovered that in August, 1923, Manuel Perry had been arrested for violation of the Prohibition Law and had been charged in the Federal Court in San Francisco; that he had failed to appear in the Federal Court in answer to this charge and that he and his wife had fled to Massachusetts where they remained two and a half years; that the Perrys had returned to California after an absence of two and a half years and had never been bothered in any way whatsoever with reference to the old liquor charge. When the defendant found out about this old liquor charge he represented to the Perrys that it was absolutely necessary for them to pay Four Hundred Fifty Dollars immediately to the Judge in San Francisco and the policemen who arrested Perry in 1923, and that by the payment of this money he, Lacey, could get the old liquor case dismissed. He also told them and impressed upon them emphatically that unless this money was paid immediately Mr. Perry would have to go to jail. Both Manuel Perry and his wife were working for small wages and having no money of their own they, under the persuasion and suggestion of the defendant, borrowed Four Hundred Fifty Dollars from a brother-in-law named Alfred Souza who mortgaged his home in order to raise the money. The defendant knew that Souza had to mortgage his home in order to raise the money because in his efforts to obtain the money he had gotten Souza into his office on two occasions along with the Perrys and persuaded him to raise the money by putting a mortgage on his home. Souza, like the Perrys, was a poor man with a family working for small wages. Both Souza and the Perrys lived in a very poor part of West Oakland. June 12, 1930, the Perrys paid Four Hundred Dollars of the Four Hundred Fifty Dollars which they borrowed from Souza to Lacey for the specific purpose of having him use this money as he represented he was going to use it, in paying off the Judge and officers in connection with the old liquor case in San Francisco and in thus getting the case dismissed. A week after having obtained the Four Hundred Dollars the defendant demanded more money from the Perrys, representing that he had to have it to pay the officials more than he had first specified in order to get the case fixed and dismissed and on this second occasion he received One Hundred Dollars from the Perrys in connection with and for the purpose of fixing the old liquor case. Two weeks later on July 2, 1930, he represented that he had to have more money in order to re-imburse and settle with the bondsmen who were on the bail bond which was put up in August, 1923 after Perry's arrest on the old liquor case and for this purpose he obtained Two Hundred Dollars. Each time after he obtained moneys in this fashion from the Perrys defendant would tell them to go home and forget about the case and not to worry because the men were waiting in San Francisco for the money and as soon as the money was paid it would be all right and the case would be all over. Approximately three months passed after payment of the last Two Hundred Dollars by the Perrys to the defendant and on September 3 the Perrys' Ford automobile was again attached by the plaintiff who had sued them on the Sixty-six Dollar grocery bill. Mrs. Perry went to see defendant about this and demanded an explanation in view of the fact that defendant had told both she and her husband that the suit on this old grocery bill was finished. The defendant then had the temerity to urge her to pay the grocery bill again, although in the first place when they first consulted him about it he had contended that it was outlawed and should not be paid. The next day Manuel Perry related his experiences with the defendant to his employer, Captain Stendahl. Captain Stendahl went with the Perrys to defendant's office and accused him in no uncertain terms of having defrauded the Perrys and demanded to know from the defendant why he, the defendant, had obtained over Eight Hundred Dollars from these people in connection with an old grocery bill of a small amount and an old liquor case, both of which cases were outlawed. The defendant tried to evade the questions of Captain Stendahl and as was typical of him when discovered in any of his countless perpetrations of frauds on clients, he, the defendant, tried to stall for time by promising to pay the money back. He promised to pay the money back, however, only after Captain Stendahl had threatened to have his own attorney investigate the matter and after he had threatened to report it to the Bar Association. Because of certain false statements and false representations made by defendant in his efforts to stall for time and because of his failure to pay back all of the money which he had obtained from the Perrys Captain Stendahl took Mr. Perry to the District Attorney's office on September 8, 1930.

Investigation which was begun by the District Attorney's office disclosed that judgment in the civil action on the old grocery bill had been obtained against the Perrys by default because of the failure of the defendant to appear in defense to the action on the date that said action was set for trial. The investigation of the District Attorney's office also disclosed that the old liquor case against Manuel Perry in the Federal Court had been dismissed in 1925 and that no money had ever been paid by the bondsmen on the bail bond which was put up in that case. Also that both the bondsmen had died in 1926. After defendant discovered that the Perrys had appealed to the District Attorney's office he urged them to stay away from said office.

After the Perrys had been subpoenaed to testify before the Grand Jury and the day before the Grand Jury hearing of the matter, the defendant, Lacey, appeared at the factory where Mrs. Perry worked and attempted to persuade her to give false testimony before the Grand Jury in order to shield him, the defendant. After he was indicted he attempted on more than one occasion to have the Perrys change the testimony which they had given before the Grand Jury and on November 4, 1930, after the trial of the case had started in the

Superior Court and after the jury had been impaneled he paid the Perrys Three Hundred Dollars and at the time he did so he asked them to give certain false testimony in order to protect himself.

The evidence showed also that the defendant had a rather well defined scheme of defrauding clients in a criminal manner and that particularly where he was dealing with clients who were foreigners, who were illiterate and unfamiliar with legal processes.

The list of victims was quite impressive. To name a few: Mitt Singh—$15,000; Frank Lee—$80.00; Mrs. Laird—$1,500; Frank Lew and Chew Lew—$1,000; Mrs. Gantadine—$500; George Burum—$250; Mrs. Gregoria—$250; three Japanese from Sebastopol named Okano, Shimazu and Kai—$300; John Paulo—$960; Peter Matulovich—$400; Mrs. Desmond and a Mrs. Weir—$275; Mrs. Montero—$200.

Mike, like so many other bootleggers who preferred to stay out of the limelight, was also bilked of thousands of dollars. The scope of extortion committed by Lacey against his very own clients was, to say the least, astounding.

When the dust finally settled in the case, defendant Lacey was found guilty as charged and sentenced on February 16, 1931, to two five-year prison terms to be served consecutively in San Quentin.

The news media had a field day in keeping up to the trial as it proceeded, thus giving Earl Warren the favorable recognition he respectfully deserved.

CHAPTER 54
THE CONCLUSION

District Attorney Earl Warren's perseverance in the quest to seek and prosecute those that chose to exploit the Prohibition Era, soon put the damper on flamboyant alcohol-related activities within the county. With the hand-writing on the wall, Mike let it be known that he had no intention of bucking the tide. As far as he was concerned, Prohibition was doomed, as was the big-time bootlegging era. However, out of necessity to support a family, he would stay with his one-man operation. His fellow countrymen, the paesani, by now had split up, each going his separate way.

Mike's nephew, Primo, eventually retired to a grape ranch at Healdsburg, but still kept close ties to his buddy, Pucci. Although they chose to stay out of the alcohol business, Pucci never did lose his zest for hijacking, nor Primo his admiration for his buddy. What Primo saw in the grape vines, Pucci saw in the big ranch barn: real potential. So he immediately set out to fill it, not with grapes, but instead with merchandise hijacked out of San Francisco warehouses. By the time Primo harvested his first crop of grapes, Pucci had the barn full to the rafters with an unimaginable assortment of hijacked goods beyond description. The worth of the barn's contents was far in excess of the worth of the grape crop.

Al Giovanetti soon returned to his auto mechanic trade, then into the trucking business, but not until he had been propositioned by a prominent, popular, high-class movie star of that era by the French name of: "Belle Malliat." Al had become well acquainted with her since she was a regular customer and connoisseur of Mike's Jackass Brandy. Her lavish, swinging parties among the elite demanded the very best. In announcing that the de-liveries to her Piedmont mansion would soon cease because of his disassoci-ating himself from the bootlegging business, the movie star promptly of-fered Al a job. She had a crush on him, no doubt partly because of his adventurous and sometimes reckless ways, his expressed sex appeal, and maybe more so because she was just plain sexually horny. In her sex-ravaged mind, Al displayed the libertine qualities of a Lothario, and she did on many occasions exploit them.

She now made a pitch to get him in the sack, full time. She had it all figured out. He would chauffeur her limousine and stay overnight in her guest cottage whenever the need for his services demanded it, which would extend beyond just chauffeuring. Besides, having a full-time chauffeur was a status symbol and to her, position was everything in life. However, her favorite position was to be stretched out on her back across the sweeping front fender of her limousine while being pounded by a stud and staring up at the moon with stars in her eyes.

Al was all for the idea, but his wife wouldn't hear of it. She knew enough about this woman's lifestyle to know that the services she was seeking, were those of a stud, rather than a chauffeur. Needless to say, he went back to crawling under automobiles and not bed sheets.

Guido Bronzini, having returned from Italy with his new bride, eventually teamed up with his brother Lepo, along with two other paesani, and opened up a fruit and vegetable stand in east Oakland which came to be known as the "Banana Depot." In time, they became one of the most prominent retailers of bananas in the East Bay.

Raymond "Fats" Meehan, thanks to his buddy Al's connections, went to work at the Chevrolet plant in east Oakland assembling new automobiles.

Matteoli stayed in the area with his family to serve out his probation period while working at whatever legitimate jobs were available to him. He then moved his family back to Sonoma County to take on the job of field superintendent for the Italian Swiss Colony winery. He never for a moment lost his zest for engaging others in philosophical combat.

As for Julio, Mike had kept his word, and with enough money and influence peddling, he was able to cut Julio's jail time considerably. He served one year of his three-year San Quentin sentence before being paroled to serve a one-year probation period. Upon serving his probation, he departed for his beloved Italy with a stash of one hundred dollar bills sewed into the lining of his top coat. The coat's lining was carefully removed, the bills placed in a quilted pattern, then sewn back to support the bills evenly. The coat, now heavily laden with money, stayed on his back until the time he reached his home in Italy.

Terzo stayed with the Jackass peddling business right up to the repeal of Prohibition. His daughter, Zira, nicknamed 'Boots,' short for bootlegger, as smart and aggressive as her father, became his constant companion and contributed heavily to the successful administration of her father's lucrative bootlegging business. The district attorney never even came close to catching up to this father and daughter team. They were just plain too smart and clever.

Warren's men were no match for either one of them. Prohibition repealed, Terzo wasted no time in setting up a legitimate retail liquor business and investing his money wisely.

Quinto, one of Mike's paesani, having ridiculed him for not jumping on the bandwagon and marching to the tune of the pied pipers of Wall Street, found himself caught up in the great stock market crash of October 24, 1929, when some $14 billion worth of stock equities went down the tube, so to speak. He, along with many other Italians, refused to heed Mr. A. P. Giannini's warnings. Most lost everything they had, including their homes that were mortgaged to the hilt to buy stock on margin, following their stockbroker's ill advice. Quinto, instead of now bragging about his stock holdings, was begging Mike for advice. The stock market crash not only shattered his pocketbook, but his brains as well. The psychological trauma of the whole affair would cause him to bang his head into whatever structure happened to be handy in a supposed attempt to do away with himself. This conduct, of course, caused him to scatter his brains even more than they already were. Finally, Mike became annoyed with Quinto's bizarre conduct, so one day he loaded the shotgun and handed it to him and said: "If killing yourself is what you want to do, then do it right." Quinto, sensing a seriousness to the offer, backed off. At least for the moment, Mike's gesture had snapped him back to his senses. Needless to say, it was a risky way to cure a mentally ill person by handing him a gun.

Contini chose to stick around the chicken ranch for a while since he had no particular ambitions or place to go anyway. Besides, his mission was yet to be completed. He had embarked on a program of teaching the pigs some manners. To a point, he did succeed. He was able to get them to respond when called by their individual names, addressed in Italian, of course. On command they would behave much like pet dogs with the exception of their feeding habits. Contini was forever trying to instill in their minds that success was not measured by how much fat they packed around, but rather in sharing and helping those needier than one's self. But as it is, and no doubt will forever be with pigs, as it is with men, they would insist on plunging their feet into the trough pushing and shoving to gain superiority. The fattest ones pushing the leaner ones aside and forcing them to subsist on meager scraps while they, the fat ones, overindulged, gorging themselves beyond their needs.

Pioli, such as it was with Natale, was forgiven, thus their friendships renewed. The same applied to all others who may have had a falling out, for whatever reason.

While the trials were in progress and during their prison stay, those arrested and incarcerated continued to draw full pay. Financial assistance to their families was continued until such time as the men were situated in paying jobs. All legal costs and fines were also borne by Mike. These costs, along with Guido's medical and hospital bills and the thousands of dollars paid out to extortionists like Becker and Lacey, just about wiped him out financially. This was not a pleasant situation to be in, considering the nation as a whole had by now slipped into a devastating depression.

President Herbert Hoover could only offer a token measure of hope with his slogan: "Prosperity is just around the corner." A more appropriate slogan might have been: "Prostitution is just around the corner," because that is what many women, married and unmarried alike, had to resort to for subsistence. The only corners worth noting were the ones that led you to the door of a failing bank or the one you rounded to pick up the tail-end of a two-block long soup line.

In the absence of innovative ideas that could bring about economic change, the nation's population was now putting its faith in the democratic nominee for president, Franklin D. Roosevelt. And if elected, he promised to abolish Prohibition immediately. He successfully carried the election in November 1932. Before he even took up the reins of office, the enforcement of Prohibition laws started to slack off. The Governor of California, James Rolph, Jr., was one of the first to announce on November 14, 1932, a matter of days after the election, that he would immediately pardon the 1000 or so offenders still in jail for having been convicted of Prohibition-related offenses.

However, the pardon did not apply to Attorneys Lacy and Ormsby, Sheriff Becker and his deputies, Shurtleff, Collier and Davis, because they were convicted of "extortion," a non-Prohibition offense. They had to serve out their prison terms.

There was no longer much point in District Attorney Earl Warren pursuing bootleggers and still operators since the bootlegging era would soon drift into obscurity. But, he was not to be idled. The district attorney's office immediately embarked on an investigation of the Oakland police department, which according to Warren's quoted news statement, some 150 or so police officers' conduct was questionable, as it related to bootlegging, gambling, and speakeasies with their related in-house prostitution. And of course Captain Brown also got himself caught up in the sweep. Warren was determined to bring back respect for law and order, even if it meant jailing the entire Oakland police department.

Finally Congress moved in an attempt to remove the criminal element from the liquor business once and for all time by submitting the Twenty-First Amendment in 1933, which provided for the repeal of Prohibition. It was ratified within a few months by the necessary 36 states and adopted on December 5, 1933. The Prohibition Era was over, and so ended this saga that one might refer to as: "The Good Old Days."

EPILOGUE

My father Mike's real expertise was in the field of distilling, making good alcohol and converting it into fine whiskey or Jackass Brandy, as it was for the most part referred to. His continuing with a small one-man distilling operation during the depression years was strictly out of necessity to support his family more than to satisfy an ego of making it big.

As I recall, one time the still itself was brought into the basement of our Crow Canyon home for needed repairs. The main unit stood about 5 to 6 feet high and was approximately 4 or 5 feet in diameter. The coppersmith was working on it there in the basement while his car, a Dodge brothers touring sedan, was parked in the back yard a few feet from the basement door. The hot summer sun was beating down on the car's two spare tires mounted on either side of the hood in fender tire wells. They were held in place with leather straps, but no covers. The intense midday heat caused one of the tires to explode in a shotgun-like blast. Out of fear, my first reaction was to look to my father for protection, which was futile since he was not in a position to comfort me. Instinct then caused me to dive under the closest shelter available, which was the row of wine barrels supported by slightly elevated wooden rails. From my secluded position I could hear the whispered discussion going on between my father and the coppersmith.

The coppersmith volunteered to investigate the cause of the unusual disturbance. It was felt that if anything, it would be hijackers rather than Prohibition agents that would pull such a stunt without provocation. Nevertheless, my father's instructions were: "If it's the still they want, don't argue, they can have it." It was apparent that my father had just about had enough of the bootlegging business, even in a small way.

From the backyard the coppersmith called out laughingly to my father to come on out, everything was all right. His investigation had revealed the cause of the explosion as being his car's ruptured spare tire. Certainly, a relief for all concerned.

Prohibition ended in 1933 and so did my father's career as a distiller. He was now back in agriculture doing the next best thing he understood. A blessing as far as my mother, Livia, was concerned. She had done the best she could to cope with the trauma of facing up to the rigors of trying to raise a family amidst a gang of bootleggers and crooked lawmen. Much like a mother hen might do to shield her brood of chicks from the fangs of a bloodthirsty weasel, she feigned aggressive defense against incredible odds. Her arms were my sanctuary; being the youngest of the family gave me priority. Shutting down the still, however, meant cutting off the flow of money, thus obliterating the household budget, another setback for her. But rather than sit back wringing her hands in despair, and determined to maintain a decent quality of life for her family, she went back to work in the garment sweatshops. Her many years of being exposed to crooked lawmen and tough bootleggers, conditioned her for dealing with evil-minded supervisors who relished sexually harassing their women employees. She stood up to them in a defiant manner. However, her nightmares and nightmare screaming never did subside. It stayed with her the rest of her life.

The vineyard produced more than enough wine for family consumption. The excess wine produced was sold to select persons at $1 per gallon, a much-needed revenue. Although illegal to sell the excess, it was not considered a big deal by the D. A.'s office. It is true that District Attorney Earl Warren was tough in most respects when it came to law and order, but it is also true that he was understanding as well. My father grew to respect Earl Warren's fine qualities and therefore voted for him whenever he ran for public office.

What came as a surprise one summer day was the arrival of a black sedan which pulled into the back yard disgorging two cocky federal Treasury agents. These agents were now referred to as T-Men since they worked for the Treasury Department for the purpose of seeing to it that federal taxes were paid on the production of alcohol products. My father and I were the only ones at home that particular day, having lunch in the basement kitchen at the time. He rose from his chair, walked to the screen door, and was about to step outside when he recognized the same crooked, doublecrossing senior federal agent from the past. The agent now introduced himself as a Treasury agent. My father instantly retreated back into the basement, pulling the screen door closed as he did so.

I was gripped with fear as the two men engaged in a bitter argument. The agent was accusing my father of being afoul of the law by not paying the federal tax on his wine-making activity. He therefore was making demands much the same as he had done some years before, soliciting payoff, or else.

As the confrontation escalated, the Treasury agent was holding the screen door open, but hesitating to step across the threshold. The second agent was directly behind him ready to follow him into the basement. Apparently my father knew his rights well enough, rights that did not permit the agents to enter the house without a search warrant. The shouting match reached its door open, but hesitating to step across the threshold. The second agent was directly behind him ready to follow him into the basement. Apparently my father knew his rights well enough, rights that did not permit the agents to enter the house without a search warrant. The shouting match reached its climax when my father instructed me to fetch the 12 gauge, five-shot Browning automatic shotgun, which was leaning in the corner a few steps from where we were standing. The family's hunting guns were seldom unloaded except for the shell in the barrel chamber itself. I retrieved the gun as ordered. Whether or not the agent could clearly see what I was doing, I couldn't be sure, since he was standing with his back to the sunlit yard and I was in the shadowed basement behind my father. The gun was almost as long as I was tall, but I did know how to handle it. I had shot it before.

My father stepped to one side, put his hand on the gun and to my astonishment said:

"See that man standing there? If he tries to enter the basement, you shoot him." The statement was made in Italian, but having dealt with so many Italians in his career, the agent understood what was said.

Orders were orders. I raised the shotgun to firing position and at the same time pulled the chamber bolt back hard and let it go. The bolt's mechanism received the shell from the magazine, then slammed it home in the gun's firing chamber with a loud slamming metal-to-metal clatter resembling the slamming shut of a cannon breech.

In the meantime, my father had hurriedly made his way to the upstairs stairwell, his footsteps fading away as he ascended the stairs to the upper floor. I was left standing there in the middle of the room with tear-swollen eyes, trembling as I held the loaded shotgun leveled at the figure in the doorway. My trigger finger was keeping pressure on the gun's trigger just as it would be while waiting for a quail to spring into flight. There was no question that I was expressing fear, but so was the Treasury agent as he stood momentarily frozen while staring into the business end of the shotgun barrel with a hole the size of a buffalo nickle.

The agent studied the situation carefully. Without uttering a word either to me or his cohort standing behind him looking over his shoulder, the agent took a slow, careful step backwards as he gently allowed the screen door to close. Much to my relief, the two Treasury men walked to their car, entered it, and drove out of the yard for the last time.

My father and I never discussed this incident and as far as I know, he had never mentioned it to anyone else, at least not the part I was asked to play. It was not until after his death at the ripe-old age of 86 years, when I decided to write this book, did I ever mention or talk about the incident.

Regardless of the tough times spawned by the depression era, tranquility and happiness had prevailed over the fear and unpleasant anxieties of the Prohibition era. Of course, reminders of the latter would on occasion crop up. Contini, such as many of the other paesani drifting around during the depression era, would at times visit us there at Crow Canyon, stay a few weeks or so, then move on again. On one such occasion, he was to engage my father in a philosophical evaluation of my father's financial downfall. I was present that summer day when the discussion took place in the basement kitchen. It went like this:

"Mike, a man of your character and ambitions, and having once achieved a prominent financial position such as you had, you certainly should have found yourself in a much better situation than this."

The statement was made in reference to my father's financial downfall, and it was said in all sincerity. My father gave considerable thought before answering:

"Contini, how can you criticize me? Look at yourself; am I not much better off than you?"

"Yes, that is true, but my ambitions have never been any different. I always manage to eat and to have clothes on my back, and I'm satisfied. A measure of success in itself," answered Contini.

My father realized that he was being pushed into a corner where he would have to admit to failure, by having lost his shirt, so to speak; a measure of being a failure by some people's standards, but not my father's. He had his self-respect, self-confidence, and having held his family together, to him, this was a measure of success in itself, so he responded to Contini's insinuation appropriately:

"Contini," said my father, "You are a learned man, surely you are familiar with Jesus Christ. Do you consider him to have been a success?"

"That is a foolish question to ask," answered Contini with indignation. "Of course I consider him a success; only a fool would think otherwise. Why do you ask a question like that? I would think that you, of all people, would know better," retorted Contini.

My father responded: "Christ died on the cross stripped of all his belongings, including the shirt on his back. Tell me, Contini, is that not true?"

Contini's jaw dropped, his owlish eyes staring unblinking at my father, Mike, standing there before him with a look of self-confidence and determination. The thought had never occurred to him, that one can be a success even when stripped of the shirt on his back.

— END —

A Footnote by the Author:

To escape the wrath of the District Attorney of Alameda County, Earl Warren, many still operators took refuge in the foothills of the Sierra Nevada mountain range where the law enforcement climate was more to their liking. The remote locations of the mining claims scattered throughout the region proved to be ideal, not only from the standpoint of the law, but also to better repel hijackings by tough, gun-wielding professional hijackers the likes of Al Capone's men sent out west from Chicago for that express purpose.

The miners welcomed these alliances with the bootleggers since it was more of a money-making proposition than digging for gold, which by the Twenties had pretty much petered out. And of course, the abundant supply of whiskey provided, so savored by the miners, was an added inducement. Their experience in handling pack trains of ornery, but surefooted, jackasses needed to haul sacked sugar to the stills and tin cans of alcohol back out along the precarious, rocky trails leading into these remote still sites, was a definite plus for the bootleggers. Handling these animals was no easy matter, not even for their masters. They were so independent in their thinking that they'd balk at the least indication of being approached in an authoritative manner. Therefore, in addressing them, the handlers would garnish their statement with a lambasting of profanity coupled with their individual names. The jackasses, giving no indication of their displeasure to the derogatory remarks, waited until the handler was in range when, with a sideswiping kick, they would even the score. Uncanny as it may seem, these ornery critters could sense trouble well in advance, and in acting accordingly, the pre-warning thwarted many a hijack.

The community of Jackass Hill, located on the outskirts of Angels Camp in Calaveras County, where the legendary Samuel Clemens— pen name Mark Twain—made his mark was one such area where the aforementioned alliances were made.

The illustration on the following page by Dug Waggoner, coupled with my accompanying poem, gives the reader an insight as to how jackasses reacted to the threat of an attempted hijack.

Jackass Brandy

The Legends of Jackass Hill ©

From the still site they charged in a wild stampede,
These frenzied jackasses that made up the team.

Not about to be shot through ears or tail,
Loaded with tin cans of alcohol, they hit the trail.

Knowing damned well what they were doing was wrong,
They shed the tin cans as they galloped along.

Like a runaway train's wheels clacking to rails,
Stones under hooves clattered as they were flailed.

Wide-eyed and frothing, they careened around the bend,
To these notorious hijackings, they'd put an end.

They cared not a farthing of hijackers blocking their path,
It added more, not less, to these mad critters' wrath.

The Devil himself had taken charge that day,
Having no desire whatever to hold them at bay.

Urged on by jabs in the ass from Satan's fork,
Like a curse out of hell, they'd popped their cork.

Down the hill they galloped giving no heed,
To the sinners they trampled that have no creed.

And so to Jackass Hill's legends penned by Mark Twain,
Comes yet another to add to the hill's fame.